A RECKONING FOR THE YOUNG PISTOLERO

Young Pistolero Series Book 5
by
Robert J. Alvarado

OTHER WORKS

Robert J. Alvarado
www.youngpistolero.com

Non Fiction

Elfego Baca Destined to Survive
2013 Sunstone Press, Santa Fe, NM, First Printing
2016 Sierra Press, Albuquerque, NM, Second Printing

Fiction
Award Winning Young Pistolero Series

The saga follows Rafael Ortega de Estrada, a seventeen-year-old Mexican peón on the run, riding a stolen Appaloosa stallion. After shooting the haciendero who raped his younger sister, Rafael heads north and enters the United States in 1866 and finds life on the other side of the border holds new dangers along with the promise of a new life.

This gritty tale is set in the American Southwest as Americans and Mexicans struggle after the Mexican-American War. In this tumultuous era in the late 1800s, Rafael (Rafe) grows into a man who respects both his heritage and embraces life in his new country.

Young Pistolero (Book 1) 2013 Sierra Press
2018 Finalist for Drama TV Series category, by the Latino Books into Movies Awards sponsored by Latino Literacy Now.
#1 Fiction Book for 2015; by The Latino Author, by Corina Martinez Chaudhry

Star of the Young Pistolero (Book 2) 2014 Sierra Press

Death Stalks the Young Pistolero (Book 3) 2015 Sierra Press #1 Fiction Book for 2016; by The Latino Author
Legacy for the Young Pistolero (Book 4) 2017 Sierra Press #3 Fiction Book for 2017; by The Latino Author
A Reckoning for the Young Pistolero (Book 5) 2018 Sierra Press
Dangerous Venture (Book 6) 2019 Sierra Press
Justified Vengeance (Book 7) 2019 Sierra Press
The Black Phantom (Book 8) 2020 Sierra Press
Lost Treasure (Book 9) 2024 Sierra Press

Other Fiction
The Jalapeño Republic 2020 Sierra Press
2021 International Latino Book Award Medalist. Insights from the ILBA judges, "It was an interesting book, quite different from most futuristic novels I have read."

Jake Flores Mystery
Just Vanished –2020 Sierra Press
2021 International Latino Book Award Medalist. Insights from the ILBA judges, "From the moment you start reading it, you imagine an action TV series that keeps you involved."

Zia Westerns
Set in the New Mexico and Arizona territories of the Southwest, these westerns draw from the Southwest's unique flavor. Originally part of New Spain and then Mexico, the Spanish settlers and native Indians forged an informal peace until the years after the Mexican-American War brought them into the Wild West. These stories are set during this chaotic time and attempt to paint a realistic picture of the meaning of the Zia symbol.

The Spanish Sword 2020 Sierra Press
2021 International Latino Book Award Medalist. Insights from the ILBA judges, "This book is carefully crafted and felt thoroughly researched."

Valentina 2022 Sierra Press

Spanish Language Books

Este libro constituye la traducción de una obra de ficción realizada por su propio autor. La serie original, galardonada y titulada Young Pistolero, fue escrita en inglés estadounidense y posteriormente vertida al español mexicano por el autor con el apoyo de la herramienta de inteligencia artificial ChatGPT. Cualquier error o imprecisión que pudiera encontrarse en la traducción es fortuito y responde únicamente al uso de dicha herramienta.

Publicación en español de Sierra Press:

Joven Pistolero (Libro 1)
Estrella del Joven Pistolero (Libro 2)
Muerte Acecha al Joven Pistolero (Libro 3)
Legado para el Joven Pistolero (Libro 4)
Ajuste de Cuentas para el Joven Pistolero (Libro 5)
Aventura Peligrosa (Libro 6)
Venganza Justificada (Libro 7)
El Fantasma Negro (Libro 8)
Tesoro Perdido (Libro 9)

PRAISES AND AWARDS

Young Pistolero, Young Pistolero Series
2018 Finalist for Drama TV Series category.
The Latino Books into Movies Awards are conducted by Latino
Literacy Now, a 501c3 nonprofit co-founded by Edward James Olmos
and Kirk Whisler. The judges for these awards are screenwriters,
directors, producers, and others from the entertainment industry. They
have deemed these books worthy of consideration for future television
and movie production.

Young Pistolero, Young Pistolero Series
#1 Fiction Book for 2015; by The Latino Author
Death Stalks the Young Pistolero, Young Pistolero Series
#1 Fiction Book for 2016; by The Latino Author
Legacy for the Young Pistolero, Young Pistolero Series
#3 Fiction Book for 2017; by The Latino Author

Young Pistolero Series is a great fiction story that
incorporates both history and a great story plot of a young man
whose life spirals after avenging the rape of his younger sister. It
has all the muster of a good western including gun fights,
murder, and survival. The author does a fantastic job of
incorporating the history of the United States and Mexico during
a time when the Wild West was in full swing and struggles
occurred on both sides of the border. The descriptions of history
add much to the story and make the life of Rafael, the
protagonist, really interesting.

Mr. Alvarado weaves a plausible plot and his setting
descriptions and actions are right on. His graphic scenarios of
land and territories make you feel as if you are right there
alongside the rider as he heads through some rough terrain. His
characters were exactly what you might expect of people living in
the 'rough' west trying to survive the elements and mayhem of
that time.

The writer incorporates Spanish words, which allows the
reader to identify with the characters; however, he brilliantly
illustrates the meaning after each and every word so non-Spanish
speaking readers don't miss a beat. The book is filled with so
much action that you can't put the book down. It has all the
earmarks of a great western series. If you are looking for a good

book to read, then this is one to put on your list this year. An excellent read! – Corina Martinez Chaudhry

I know this series will earn many more awards. A wonderful contribution to Southwest Hispano history and culture. - **Rudolfo Anaya, acclaimed novelist, poet, playwright, professor emeritus, 2015 National Humanities Medal Award recipient**

I just completed reading *A Reckoning For The Young Pistolero*. Great book. I've read the entire series and I'm looking forward to the next book. Mr. Alvarado is very skilled at utilizing historical knowledge as well his own personal experiences to keep you captivated from beginning to end. Being from New Mexico, I can personally relate to the language and setting so appropriately used in the book. I highly recommend the entire series. You won't be disappointed. - **Sammy Soto, retired high school educator/administrator Albuquerque, NM**

I am impressed by the historical detail and fast-moving plots. I also like the way he incorporates two very different young men and follows their lives. The author does a good job of developing these contrasting characters so that readers can walk in their boots and see how fate has shaped them. My father was a screenwriter for television when I was growing up in California and he wrote many westerns, including Wagon Train and Gunsmoke. Alvarado's novel could be the basis for one of those television westerns because of its engrossing plot and its clear depiction of heroes and villains. - **Dr. Jennie Nelson, PhD in Rhetoric and Writing, Carnegie Mellon University, post-graduate professor of writing, University of Idaho**

Mr. Alvarado vividly illustrates many rugged times after the Civil and Mexican American Wars through the eyes of a 17 year old peon who comes to the U.S. and adapts and grows into a hero. The Young Pistolero is a great new historical western series!
– by Richard Golenda, post Secondary and College History Teacher post Chairman of the Pueblo Economic Development Corporation.

A RECKONING FOR THE YOUNG PISTOLERO

A glossary of *italicized* Spanish words is provided at the end of this book, with the exception of words which are equivalent in both languages, such as *importante* = important, *Mamá* = Mama, or words of Latin origin found in the English dictionary. Other words, phrases, and sentences written in Spanish are immediately explained within the text itself.

Printed in the United State of America
ISBN-13: 978-0991477753

Published by Sierra Press
Phoenix, Arizona
First Printing, March 2018

Cover Art and Design by John Flinn
Graphic Art by Lina Luna

Dedication

This book is dedicated to Maxine Louise Golenda. In the wake of unthinkable odds, you face each challenge with grace and beauty. It has been our pleasure and blessing to get to know you. Keep fighting Max.

ACKNOWLEDGEMENT

First and always, I owe more than thanks to my wife for her unending hours of critique, review, and clarity. She always keeps me honest in my writing and helps me find and keep each character's vision.

My thanks to Gus Swanson for inspiring the character of Desperate Billy and to all my friends who have supported my writing and encouraged me.

My special thanks to Rich Golenda for believing in the saga of the Young Pistolero Series, thank you. I am proud to call you my friend.

I would like to acknowledge the wealth of historical information which is weaved into this work to depict the places and events of this saga's time period. As a work of historical fiction, where real-life historical figures or actual locations are used, the situations, incidents, or dialogues concerning those persons or places are entirely fictional and are not intended to depict actual events or to change the entirely fictional nature of the work.

DISCLAIMER

In an effort to accurately describe the social fabric of New Mexico during the timeframe of this book, readers should consider the author's transitions from the use of the terms, Spaniards and Mexicans. After the discovery of South America in 1492, New Spain, considered to encompass Mexico and much of central America, was under the control of Spanish Kings and Queens.

Over the next several hundred years, Spaniards emigrated north into what is now the American Southwest. Legions of settlers traveled to spread the Catholic religion and to seek fortunes in gold and silver. For their efforts, the Spanish royalty bestowed land and titles to the adventurous settlers. In New Mexico, Spaniards founded Santa Fe as the capital of the Kingdom of New Mexico in 1610. Industrious, the Spanish settlers created a robust economy and raised their families for generations. Rather isolated, New Mexico remained an extension of New Spain until the Mexican Revolution began in 1820.

After the Mexican Revolution ended in 1821, the country now known as Mexico emerged from under Spanish control. After the Mexican-American War ended in 1848, the border between Mexico and the American Southwest was in dispute. Finally, the Treaty of Guadalupe Hildalgo created the border as we know it today. In the treaty, Articles VIII and IX ensured the safety of existing property rights of Spaniard/Mexican citizens living in the Southwestern territories. Despite the treaty's assurances to the contrary, land grants owned in New Mexico were often not honored by the United States because of interpretations of the treaty and U.S. legal decisions. Fraud and greed by powerful American lawyers and politicians stripped many descendants of original land grant owners of their land.

Because this book is set after the Treaty of Guadalupe Hildalgo, the terms Spaniards and Mexicans are often intertwined. Even today, the descendants of the original Spanish settlers maintain their heritage as Spaniards. However, Americans who began settling in New Mexico at that time used the term Mexicans for the local population living in the territories.

In today's world, the term Hispanic is often used to describe a diverse population of Spanish-speaking peoples. However, this book attempts to be true to the fundamental use of the terms, Spaniards and Mexicans, as it might have been used by the different characters in the story. In no way does it intend to disparage the people described by the usage of the terms.

CHAPTER 1

Rumbling thunder rolled along the valley from the ocean toward the east into the San Fernando Valley threatening to pour a good December rain on Rancho Simi. Rafael Reyes de Estrada and Ana Teresa de Soto were sitting under an aged oak tree spending time alone together. They heard the thunder, but subconsciously ignored it. All they cared about was being alone. It was a ritual now, where after lunch they saddled their horses and rode to this remote spot, secluded by the shade of the old oak tree. It was a quiet spot and their horses grazed on green grass nearby. Today the thunder threatened they might get wet, but it did not sway them to leave.

"We can't wait for permission from my father," Ana Teresa said. "It will take too long for a letter to get to Spain and for my father to answer back to us here in California," she continued the conversation about their dilemma.

"I agree my love, but I worry your family will shun you and our children. I do not want that to happen. Believe me, family is very important and we must respect them. Your father will be insulted if he is not allowed to give us his blessing," Rafael told her.

"Of course you are right, but remember what happened to us in Santa Fe. My father is stuck in the old ways, just like my uncle Pedro. He will never give us permission and most likely he'll have you run out of this valley because you are *mestizo*. Then what?" She pulled away from him. There seemed no solution. They were in love and had every right to marry. It was a legal right, not a right according to Spanish traditions.

Rafael had been in the valley of Rancho Simi, near the California coast north of Los Angeles for almost two weeks. After escaping from the hellhole of the opium fields in Jalisco, Mexico, Rafael miraculously found her living with a cousin. Her parents were in Spain trying to obtain proof of their rightful land grant for their ranch here in this fertile valley.

Ana Teresa was a pure-blooded Spanish woman born in California and Rafael was considered a *mestizo* from Mexico, a man of mixed bloodlines, both Spanish and Mexican Indian. Old Spanish traditions forbade this type of marriage, regardless of the fact Rafael was a successful American businessman and Ana Teresa penniless.

Over the past week, he viewed several available parcels of land in the Simi Valley area. The land here in California was expensive, more than three times what he paid for his land in Santa Fe, New Mexico. However, the land was lush and his horses could graze on the hillsides year round. Though it was December, the weather was mild and temperate and the grass on the hillsides was still green. Ana Teresa told him it never snowed in Rancho Simi. It would be a good place for a horse breeding business to flourish.

Unfortunately, Rafael's family and his business in Santa Fe nagged at him. He could not abandon his mother and his sister María's children. In a recent telegram, his adopted father George Summers wrote the builder had reframed the ranchhouse and would continue working until the colder winter weather stopped progress. The original home he was building for his mother and Ana Teresa had been burned to the ground last spring by Diego de la Torre's friends as an act of revenge.

George's telegram also alluded to continuing anger toward him over Diego's death. Apparently, the sheriff wanted to have a formal trial to finally put the matter to rest. Rafael knew he was innocent and had many witnesses to that fact. However, the Spanish aristocrats of Santa Fe still had clout and he worried they could pay off or intimidate a judge or jury. Diego's friends were another matter. He felt confident he could best them in any fair fight. It was the part about fair, which troubled him. Diego's friends traveled together and would most likely catch him alone, as they did last year surrounding him with their swords at the abandoned *hacienda*. It would make living in Santa Fe perilous for both he and Ana Teresa.

He pondered what Ana Teresa told him about her father. If her father refused him just because of his heritage, Rafael feared how he would react. If her father was anything like his brother, *don* Pedro in Santa Fe, things would get ugly. The last thing he wanted was to come between Ana Teresa and her family. He wanted to avoid trouble or confront it before they got married, but in his heart he knew she was right. Her father would never accept him.

A loud clap of thunder shook the earth around them as big fat drops began hitting the ground. He pulled her close under the protective canopy of the oak tree. There was no course of action for them not fraught with some peril, which both angered him and pushed him to action. It would be Christmas soon and he wanted to share the holiday with his family in Santa Fe, and he wanted to take Ana Teresa with him as his wife.

"Ana Teresa, I love you and I will not leave here without you. You are probably right to believe your father will never accept me. All I can promise you is my love forever. Let's go to the padre and ask him to marry us today," he suggested having decided on a course of action.

"No, he will summon my cousin, Francisco, and he will put a stop to it," she warned him.

"Then let's go to Los Angeles and be married there. We will find a church and they will not know of your family. Then we can take the stage to Santa Fe to spend Christmas with my family. After that, well, after that we'll make plans for our future," he said holding her hands in his.

She threw her arms around him and kissed him as her response. Yes she would go with him. It was what she wanted with all her heart.

"Everything I own is in my saddlebags or in Santa Fe. What things do you have at your cousin's house?" he asked.

"Nothing worth much. All my clothes are old and well worn. I have no money and have been living off my cousin's kindness," she answered as tears trickled down her cheeks. As the rain poured around them, they plotted their escape. Ana Teresa thought her cousin, Francisco, might try to stop her from leaving. Though he had no real authority, he might feel compelled to take action.

"We must just go and not look back," she told him.

"If you do not at least tell Francisco we are leaving, he will call the sheriff when you do not return tonight," Rafael responded.

They waited until the rain subsided, cuddling near the trunk of the oak tree until the first hint of sunlight peeked through the clouds. He helped her up on her horse and mounted the Appaloosa he called Rayo. They decided Ana Teresa would leave a letter at the mercantile in Rancho Simi. It would be delivered to her cousin later in the afternoon. The letter would explain her disappearance.

They rode from the secluded spot toward the main part of Simi. Making the quick stop at the mercantile, they then headed east out of the valley of Rancho Simi toward Los Angeles. It was nearly seven o'clock Monday night when they reached the Pico House in mid-town Los Angeles. Rafael led them to the stables where he gave the liveryman two dollars to feed and brush both horses well. At the desk of the hotel, he paid for two rooms.

"First thing tomorrow, we'll go to the Farmers and Merchants Bank to retrieve the funds George wired for me. Then we'll go and buy clothes for you and a new suit for me. After that, we'll find a padre who will marry us. Good night my love," he told her taking her in his arms.

Ana Teresa clung to him not wanting to let go. She knew what they were planning would be frowned on by her family and by Spanish aristocrats both here and in Santa Fe. It had been the world she grew up in, but not the world she believed in.

The following morning was cool and sunny. All remnants of yesterday's storm were gone. They rode to the bank and Rafael retrieved the funds from the teller. He asked the teller where to find a dress shop nearby. Ana Teresa chose a simple cream dress for the wedding, three other dresses, sleeping gowns, undergarments, and a winter coat as traveling attire for their trip to Santa Fe.

"We'll go talk to the padre while the dresses are being altered," he said as they left the dress shop. Towing their horses, they walked across the plaza to a small Catholic church where they found an elderly priest tending a nativity scene to the side of the front steps. The wood carved statue of one of the three kings had fallen over and he was trying to anchor it with some large rocks. It was the fourteenth of December and only ten days before Christmas. Rafael stepped up and helped the padre with his task.

"Padre, my name is Rafael and this is Ana Teresa. Is it possible you can marry us today?" Rafael asked after the statue was stable.

The padre got slowly up off his knees and adjusted his eyeglasses taking a closer look. The young couple standing in front of him was definitely old enough to get married. The woman was obviously Spanish, with long brown hair and her eyes shone a soft golden brown. The young man was darker of skin with a handsome face framing white teeth. His Mexican-Indian heritage was apparent, though he was over six feet tall and broad shouldered.

"You say you want to get married today?" he asked in a raspy voice and Rafael noticed his hands trembled slightly. "You are not from my parish. Where is your family?"

"Padre, we have no family near here. Ana Teresa's family is in Spain and my family is in Santa Fe, New Mexico. I will tell you her family would not allow us to marry because I am a *mestizo,* but we do not believe in those old traditions. They do not fit into the ways of the United States. We will marry, even if we do it with a civil judge, but we would rather be married here by you padre, in the sight of God," Rafael told him as he took Ana Teresa's hand in his.

"And how do you feel, my daughter?" he asked Ana Teresa after he slowly turned and adjusted his eyeglasses again.

"Padre, I love Rafael. Nothing will stop me from marrying him," she replied.

"Very well my children come back after evening Mass and I will hear your confessions before I marry you. Do you have any witnesses?"

"No padre we are alone here," Ana Teresa answered.

"Not to worry, I will have one of the brothers witness for you," he said and shuffled off into the church.

They looked at each other and smiled. "Let's go back to the hotel and have some lunch," Rafael said. They walked back to where they left the horses tied near the front of the church. He helped her mount her horse and they rode across the plaza toward the hotel. Two cowboys lounged near the hotel, but Rafael only gave them a brief glance. Jumping off Rayo, he was tying him to the rail on the left side of the wide steps in front of the hotel.

"Hey thar Mex, whard ja steal that Paloose," a gruff voice stopped him.

"Who wants to know?" Rafael asked instinctively keeping his left hand on Rayo's reins. He backed away from Rayo and pulled his coat away from his guns. He had heard the same question and tone of voice when the Reynolds' boys confronted him like this in El Paso and it would not happen again.

"The Citizens Security Patrol wants to know. Ain't rat a Mex like yew cud own a hoss like that," one of the two men answered. Rafael's instincts heightened seeing the two cowboys glaring at him. They stepped along the sidewalk nearer him. Both men wore western hats and boots with leather vests over checkered flannel shirts. The one who spoke wore a dusty black Stetson.

The speaker and the other man stood just off the sidewalk. Rafael knew he could take both of them before they could thumb the hammers on their holstered pistols. Another man stood nearby, dressed in a black business suit and no hat. Rafael was not sure if the man was part of this group or just an interested bystander.

"This is my horse mister," he responded not taking his eyes off them. "I'm here in Los Angeles from Santa Fe where I breed blooded horses." He took another step away from Rayo keeping his view of the two men clear.

"Doncha yew lie ta me Mex. I know yew stole it. Now, step away from that hoss," the bold one wearing the black Stetson raised his voice at Rafael.

"Mister, I want no trouble with you. I said this is my horse and I plan to keep it," he replied.

"The Appaloosa is his horse. You need to let it go," Ana Teresa interrupted.

"Yew stay outta this sen'o'rita," the other man sneered at her. "What yew doing with this Mex anyaways?"

"Im'a takin that hoss. Yew keep yer hands away from them guns," the man wearing the black Stetson warned.

By now a crowd gathered near the confrontation along the sidewalk. People were whispering to each other and women grabbed their children, holding them close. A few hurried away down the street. Rafael sized up his competition and had no concerns except was still not sure about the third man. He was standing at the front of the crowd and was wearing a gun, though not dressed as the cowboys.

"If you come for this horse you better come shooting," Rafael warned him right back.

"Why yew uppity Mex. Who the hell yew think yew are," Black Stetson growled as he went for his gun.

Rafael pulled both of his GSW double-action revolvers out and shot Black Stetson in the right shoulder before the man's pistol cleared the holster. He held the two pistols on the other cowboy and the third man before they could react, but did not shoot. Ana Teresa's horse gave a small buck from the report of Rafael's pistol, before she got it under control.

"I'm warning you, don't go for your guns. I could have killed him and I have no problem killing you. Now you better take your friend to a doctor before he bleeds to death," Rafael told the other cowboy.

The wounded cowboy was standing holding his arm and groaning. "Yew fuckin Mex. Yew gonna pay fer this. Yew gonna pay," Black Stetson cried out.

"This is your own fault. I told you this is my horse and I will fight to keep it. Now take him to the doctor,"

Rafael retorted.

The third man stepped toward the wounded man. "You'll be hearing from the Citizens Security Patrol," the man in the business suit said. He and the cowboy shouldered the injured man and helped him to the sidewalk. Rafael knew these men were part of the local vigilantes who targeted Mexicans.

He walked over to Ana Teresa and put his hand on her thigh. "Do you still want to marry me?"

CHAPTER 2

With a smug look, Ana Teresa sat tall and proud in the saddle watching the vigilantes cart off the wounded cowboy. She mulled their encounter grumbling internally at the sheer audacity of the men who affronted them. How dare they accuse Rafael of horse thievery? Of course she still wanted to marry him, even more now than before. Ana Teresa was born into the Spanish aristocrat de Soto family of Rancho Simi, but was now penniless. Her father's vast lands taken by American lawyers, thieves just like these men. Nothing about her life had been fair since then, except for God sending Rafael to her. With him by her side, she could face anything life could throw at her.

Rafael helped Ana Teresa from the saddle. "Go inside and go up to your room and lock the door. I'll be up shortly. Don't let anyone in." She so wanted to throw her arms around him right there in the street, though seeing the worried look in his eyes she followed his instructions and climbed the hotel steps.

He watched until she disappeared safely inside. Jumping up on the Appaloosa and pulling the mare, he rode through the side alley to the back of the hotel watching the hotel windows and looking for any odd movement in the shadows. He pulled his coat back away from his holster so the double-action pistols were ready for any lurking danger. Though he saw nothing amiss, his instincts felt the burn of eyes watching him.

His friend and shipmate on the California Gold, Randolph Schelstrate, had warned him about lawlessness in Los Angeles especially around the docks and Rafael remembered his words, "That horse of yours would be enviable. Take care not to leave it, even in a livery." Randolph warned him to be especially careful near the docks where men were shanghai'd regularly. Here in central Los Angeles he had felt safe, at least until now.

As he entered the hotel's livery, Rafael pondered how

to secure his horse. Rayo's breeding and distinctive markings made the big Appaloosa desirable and apparently Mexicans were deemed unfit to own such a horse. A rue smile spread across his tan face. The vigilantes were not the first to covet his horse and not the first to feel the sting of his GSW pistols.

Ducking under the beam of the livery's doorway atop Rayo, he saw a man in one of the stalls brushing a black mare. Three other horses stood quietly in their stalls. An aroma of fresh hay greeted his nose. The liveryman man looked up at him as he rode in.

"How are these horses protected here in the stalls?" Rafael asked as he jumped off Rayo's saddle. Hearing the question, the man turned and looked at him. This livery worker was older, not the young man who Rafael saw earlier. His bib overalls were flecked with straw and his hat pulled back on his head showed a weathered face with a droopy graying mustache. A two-holster gunbelt hung low on his hips. The holsters tied around his legs in a style used by a gunman, not a livery worker.

"Well now, I tell you son, I've been working here for nigh on ten years and they pay me well to tend to these animals. Ain't lost one yet. See these guns, everybody knows I can use them, so they stay away from here," the man proudly said as he took time out from rubbing the mare.

"What about the so-called Citizens Security Patrol? I just shot one trying to take this Appaloosa and was warned they will be coming after me."

"Was that you who fired the shot? I heard it from back of the stalls, but thought perhaps it was just a pistol going off accidently. It happens sometimes. Them vigilantes travel in packs. How'd it be you only shot one and you be still standing?" he asked.

Two guns were holstered around the young Mexican's slim waist. The man judged him to be in his mid-twenties, lean with a handsome bronze face and white teeth and well dressed in a business suit. His white shirt was clean and the collar starched with a narrow black tie. His black boots were dusty, but the man could tell they had many coats of polish.

"Yes sir. There were three of them and they accused me of stealing my own horse. One of them got brave enough to go for his gun and I shot him in the shoulder. I could have killed him, but didn't," Rafael told him.

"Saw this horse here a couple weeks ago. No mistaking his marks. I asked the desk clerk and he told me a young Mexicano owned him. How did you get such a fine horse?" His question hinted of interest rather than an accusation.

The truth was something Rafael did not want to say. Rayo was a blooded horse born in the barns at *don* Bernardo Reyes' *hacienda* in Torreón, Mexico, the large estate where he was born a peasant. The Appaloosa was of the finest Mexican bloodlines and was the foundation of his horse breeding business in Santa Fe, New Mexico. Rafael had stolen Rayo when he was seventeen after he shot *don* Bernardo for raping his sister. It seemed a lifetime ago and a world apart from here.

"I am a horse breeder from New Mexico. I have many fine horses," he replied keeping his explanation simple.

The older man walked over to Rayo and stroked his flanks. Lean taut muscles rippled under his touch. The horse stood at least sixteen hands tall, taller than most. Brown splotches splayed over its white rump and down the hind legs were distinctive of the Appaloosa breed. The liveryman had been around horses his entire life giving him an innate sense toward these animals. Rayo's head was held high, ears perked to their conversation. This horse was not only blooded, he was smart and well trained by his master.

"If this horse is an example of your breeding stables, I commend you son, though I am not surprised the vigilantes made you a target."

"Why? I have done nothing wrong. I have every right to own fine horses. Is not California a state of the United States? Where is your law here?" While New Mexico was only a territory of the United States in 1872, California had been admitted into the Union many years ago. Rafael learned the facts during his education in Santa Fe.

"Well, it's like this. Them Spanish *dons* controlled California when I was a young man. They didn't like Americans much. They owned all the land and didn't want to give it up," the man stated.

"Yes, they owned land grants given by the King of Spain," Rafael retorted.

"Well now, most newcomers don't give a rat's ass about no King. The Americans got mad and made the *dons* sell their land."

Rafael knew it was a lie. Newcomers came to the southwest territories and took the land, often at gunpoint or worse. Ana Teresa and his friend Carlos Zuniga were just two examples of the lawless transition of vast portions of land here in California and at home in New Mexico. Though he wanted to correct the liveryman's viewpoint, he held his tongue.

"That still does not give those vigilantes the right to harass people for no reason."

"California has many newcomers. They come from all over and at first those vigilantes did some good by catching thieves and murderers, but now they are just out of control. They turned against Mexicans and Indians and they've hanged many innocent men. The governor has tried to put a stop to them, but there are some groups wanting to hold on to their power by terrorizing anyone with brown skin. You need to be very careful, specially cause you winged one of them. They won't take kindly to that."

"I can protect myself. I'm more worried about my horse."

"If they come around here, they know I don't put up with no nonsense and will shoot to kill. Your horse is safe here son, don't you worry," the man assured him. "Name of Pete, Pete Walker," the man introduced himself and stuck out his hand.

Rafael took it. "Rafael Reyes de Estrada. You can call me Rafe."

CHAPTER 3

Pacing within the hotel room, Ana Teresa fumed at the injustice. How dare those men disrespect her and attempt to steal Rayo from Rafael only because he was Mexicano. This was not the California she knew or wanted to know. Her memory of California was of cool ocean breezes, blue skies, green rolling hills, and people who cared for each other. When she was young, she rode horses with abandon across the hills, nary a care in the world.

She was the daughter of a prominent Spanish family in Rancho Simi. Her father, *don* Bartolo de Soto, inherited the Spanish land grant to their *rancho* which was handed down for generations before him. Their ranch sat in the base of a valley where the subtle winds from the Pacific Ocean blew across the green rolling hills.

Like their neighbors in the Rancho Simi valley, their estate covered thousands of acres where cattle and horses roamed freely. Tenant farmers grew grains, corn, vegetables, and grapes. Cascading flowers in reds, yellows, and purple hung from iron railings of their traditional Spanish-style home all throughout the year due to the mild California climate. Orange and lemon trees hung heavy with fruit in the courtyard. Routinely her parents held lavish parties in that courtyard where musicians played music and wine flowed freely.

While her mother spent most of her time fussing over dresses, parties, and furnishings in the house, Ana Teresa's childhood nanny tended her when she was sick, brushed her hair for hours, and held her when she was sad. Ana Teresa grew up playing with her nanny's daughter, Rosa. They were more like sisters. A *mestizo,* her nanny received harsh words and it was not beyond her mother to strike her. "You must keep them in their place," her mother or father would say. Ana Teresa heard similar words and ideals spoken most of her life.

At fifteen, a *quinceañera* in her honor formally

presented her to society. A debutante of distinction, her time at the special coming-out party was coveted by many young suitors. Young Spanish gentlemen, *caballeros,* came calling and seeking her favor knowing her hand carried a large dowry. She was raised to be the adored wife of a Spanish *caballero,* a *doña* of a prominent gentleman. Her life would be as a woman whose desires and whims were attended by a houseful of servants. Hers was to be a life of privilege and excess.

Then one day it all evaporated. American lawyers demanded proof of their land grant. The lands of her father had been de Soto lands for hundreds of years. Rights assigned from a King of Spain through emissaries and royal decrees. Like a bad dream, she was sent to her uncle in Santa Fe, penniless and alone, while her parents fled to Spain.

The graceful two-story stucco home with the fine European rugs and tapestries was gone. Her wardrobe of fine Parisian and Spanish dresses gone, along with her trunks of silver candlesticks and tea servers and her trousseau for her upcoming marriage to *don* Ramon de Salinas' son Domingo. He was dashing and handsome, considered one of the best catches in Rancho Simi. Theirs would be a marriage of power brokering, though Ana Teresa thought they were in love.

After her father lost their land Domingo no longer wanted her, breaking their engagement. It was then Ana Teresa realized the marriage was only for her dowry. With no money to offer for her hand, Domingo left her for another girl whose father owned a large vineyard.

She used to curse Domingo for his despicable ways, calling him a *desgraciado.* Then she met Rafael and her viewpoint changed completely. Rafael's heart was pure and his soul the same. He was truly a man of honor. He made her feel complete, his love steadfast. He wanted her and only her, no dowry or status mattered. He was a self-made man, a man born a *peón,* a Mexican peasant, but now an educated businessman. He was a man not afraid of hard work and started a horse breeding business in Santa Fe.

She knew it bothered him that they did not have her father's blessing, but her father would never approve. No matter what, her father would never approve of her marrying a *mestizo*. Like her uncle Pedro in Santa Fe, who thought Diego de la Torre was a fine gentleman, her father believed only in the sanctity of the blood line and cared little for love or honor.

Her father and the local *dons* were stuck in the past, trying to hold onto their opulent lifestyle. If not for losing her dowry, she would have ended up as Domingo's pampered wife. Now though it was not quite two years ago, it seemed a lifetime. She had grown up from that privileged young girl into a woman who saw the truth in this new world.

In many ways she did not blame the Americanos who riled against the power of the Spaniards. They fought for their freedom against the tyranny of the King of England. They fought to be free and to create their own destiny. The land owned by the Spanish *dons* was generally given by favor of a Spanish King. It was not fought for and won. The *dons* of the 1870s were mostly paunchy old men who managed the lands on the backs of others.

Her father, like all the other *caballeros,* treated his *mestizo* servants and tenants with disrespect. Ana Teresa now saw the world through different eyes. Money and power were not the true measure of a man and it did not matter if his skin was slightly darker tan from a mixed heritage. The measure of a man or woman was in their heart. Rafael was such a man.

She knew her father would never understand nor give his blessing to their marriage, but she no longer cared. Rafael loved her for herself and nothing more. He would protect her to the death. She would go with him and live forever loving him in return. Though she loved the green rolling hills of California, tonight they appeared to be brown and ugly.

A tapping on her door broke into her thoughts. "Open the door," she heard Rafe's voice. Pulling at the large door, she fell into his arms.

"I'm sorry you had to see what happened outside," he said taking Ana Teresa by her hand after she finished clinging to him. "I will not let anyone hurt you. Please do not be afraid, my love."

"I'm not afraid. I'm never afraid when I'm with you."

Her words made him proud, though he still internally worried she was not fully ready to understand his sometimes precarious position in life. "Let's order lunch," he said trying to lighten the mood. "It is our wedding day and you should be smiling and happy, not fearful."

Rafe rang the bell. Shortly, a young man knocked on the door and Rafe ordered them a lunch and asked to have Ana Teresa's purchases sent from the dress shop. They had several hours to wait before they needed to go back to the church.

Waiting for lunch, Rafe repeated to her what Pete told him in the livery. "The vigilantes are out of control, harassing innocent Mexicans all over town. The governor is trying to stop them, but not having much luck."

"Those men are evil. It reminds me of the lawyers and government officials who came to our house armed with rifles and ordered my father off our ranch," Ana Teresa said. "There was nothing we could do but leave. They threatened to shoot us if we didn't leave, so we got in our carriage and went to my cousin Francisco's home."

"The same thing happened to Carlos' family in New Mexico. The government agents killed his father and it set his brother Benicío into a life as an outlaw. Benicío cared for only two things, killing and robbing, as revenge for losing his birthright."

"You told me how Benicío killed Chiwiwi." Rafe had explained the events of that fateful day and about his love for Chiwiwi. Ana Teresa only admitted to herself she was a bit jealous. Chiwiwi was Rafe's first love and now she was dead. She knew he had loved Chiwiwi, but Ana Teresa also knew his love for her was pure.

"What about us? Could we lose what you have in Santa Fe? Would it be better for us to live on your *hacienda* in Mexico?" she asked.

Rafe could see the worry in her golden brown eyes and it tore at his heart to see his beloved feeling insecure. He expected her to have misgivings. He was not a man of privilege or status. He was a *mestizo,* born of mixed Spanish and Mexican Indian blood, raised a peasant. Their life in the American Southwest would be hard fought, but probably even worse in Mexico.

"Don't worry, I bought the land and am paying for the house being built on it. It's all legal, so no one can take it away from us. The only problem I have in Santa Fe is with Diego de la Torre's friends, but I can handle them," he assured her.

It nagged at him that he had not told her about the sheriff wanting to arrest him for Diego's murder as soon as he returned to Santa Fe. It was not fair, though he had absolute belief in the truth. The truth was Diego came after him for the fight and Diego's horse fell on him killing the young *caballero.* It was not murder, though Rafe wished he could change the past. He did not want Diego to die. He only wanted to protect Ana Teresa.

George wired him how the Spaniards of Santa Fe continued to fret and fume about Diego's death. In many ways they were like the Citizens Security Patrol, taking the law into their own hands. The vigilantes saw only the color of his skin, while the Santa Fe aristocrats used his lower birth class to disregard his guilt or innocence.

Though Rafe found California's mild weather delightful and toyed with the idea of moving his horse breeding business here to the lush green hills, he now thought it unwise. Trouble lurked here and Rafe doubted Ana Teresa's cousin would embrace their decision. Now, all he wanted was to marry Ana Teresa, get on the stage heading east, and get to Santa Fe before Christmas. Once home, he would clear his name so they could live in peace.

CHAPTER 4

Cool, almost cold December air filled Rafe's room on the second floor of the Pico House Hotel. He opened the window to clear the stuffiness of the room, but it was his nerves surrounding him in worry. The clock on the wall showed four thirty and already the long shafts of sunlight warned of winter's early sunset. Ana Teresa was in the next room getting ready.

He told her to be ready so they could get to the chapel in time for the padre to hear their confessions before Mass. Tonight after they were officially married, he would make sweet and passionate love to her and consummate their wedding vows. He would give her a million kisses and surround her with his love, now and forever. At least he hoped he could live up to that promise.

The past year had been a whirlwind of adventure, secrets, deceit, dismal escapades, and Diego's death. A year ago he was Rafael Ortega de Estrada and now was Rafael Reyes de Estrada. He took his rightful name after learning the truth about how his real father, *don* Bernardo Reyes, raped his mother. He inherited the Reyes *hacienda* in Torreón, his lowly birthplace. It was his legacy, but his heart was in Santa Fe, New Mexico. He wanted to breed horses and live there with his family.

The encounter with the Citizens Security Patrol was only too familiar. They were not the first, nor probably the last, to believe he was not fit to take his rightful place in society. Unfortunately, Rayo his prize Appaloosa only embodied that belief. After all the trouble he faced in Santa Fe with the city's Spanish aristocrats, he left to claim his inheritance in Mexico. Rejected of what she thought rightfully hers, *doña* Carmela Reyes stole Rayo in Mexico City. It almost cost Rafe his life. If not for the kindness of Longwei, Rafe would still be imprisoned on the agave plantation or worse, dead.

In both Mexico and Santa Fe, he was deemed unfit

due to his birth bloodline. He was not a pure-blooded Spaniard, instead considered a mixed-blood *mestizo*. Here in California he was Mexicano. Apparently they did not differentiate or care so much about the bloodline. Anyone with brown skin or speaking Spanish was a target, possibly even Ana Teresa.

He loved Ana Teresa with a passion, even more than his first love Chiwiwi. What kind of a life was he going to give her? Was he destined to always have to fight for his life at the tip of a sword or the bark of a gun? Would they and their children ever live in peace? If anything ever happened to her because of him, he could not bear it.

"Aaahhh," he grumbled to himself remembering the pain of losing Chiwiwi. Perhaps he was cursed in this life. For long minutes, Rafe stared out the hotel window lost in his thoughts.

A door slamming in the hallway broke him from his reflections. Deep inside he decided he would tell Ana Teresa to leave him, to go and forget him. Their resolution to marry without her father's permission was rash. She would regret it someday.

As the clock reached four forty-five, he opened the door. Knocking quietly on the next-door room, he took a deep breath. She opened the door looking radiant in a cream dress and a brown coat collared in fur. Her golden eyes took him in.

"I'm ready my love. I'm ready for our new life together," she said to him reaching out her gloved hand to touch his cheek.

This was the woman he wanted more than anything in the world. She was his match in every way. She loved him and he loved her. This was the United States of America and their children would be Americans, not Spaniards, not *mestizos,* but Americans. Holding open his arms, she fell into them and they stood for a long moment in a tight *abrazo*. Whatever resolve he had to push her away from him and his uncertain life, evaporated.

"You are beautiful," Rafe complimented her. "I am the luckiest man in the world."

"I'm the lucky one to have you," she replied with a visible blush.

One more time he asked her about her feelings. "Are you sure my dear? Are you sure this is what you want to do?"

"I am more than sure *señor*, because I love you with all my heart. You will not get away from me that easy after tonight. You will belong to only me for the rest of your life!" she exclaimed and gave him a wicked grin he would never forget.

"I'll go to the livery and get the buggy. I'll pick you up in front of the lobby," he told her.

"I can go with you," she retorted.

"No, you are a proper lady and should not taint your beautiful wedding dress with the smell of horses. Pete will have the buggy ready for me." Rafe kissed her on her cheek and headed down the hallway.

He bounded down the stairs and through the quiet lobby heading to the livery in the back of the hotel. As he walked through the alleyway on the side of the hotel, his mind flicked to his encounter with the vigilantes earlier in the afternoon.

Ana Teresa checked her image in the oval mirror above the dresser. She was dressed in a simple cream dress with matching gloves. Her brown hair cascaded over her shoulders. It was not the image she imagined for her wedding day when she was a little girl. In those images, she would be dressed in an ornate dress with a tall, jewel-studded *peineta* holding a long lace veil covering her head. A smile curled on her lips, satisfied with her new life.

Closing the door, she walked down the hallway and carefully descended the highly polished wooden steps to the lobby. Ornately framed paintings lined the wall. The paintings were of churches, not people. She recognized them as California missions, which doubled as traveling respites along the California coast as well as Catholic monasteries. She walked across the lobby to the front doors of the hotel to wait for the buggy.

As Rafe walked into the livery, Pete was checking the

buggy reins.

"Hello Pete. Is the rig ready?"

Suddenly a shot ricocheted off the doorway frame.

"Get down!" Pete yelled at him. "They were here once before, but I scared them off. I told you they would not mess with me. I think they were checking you were still here."

"They must have been watching the front of the hotel," Rafe replied. "How many do you think are out there?"

"At least two, maybe three."

Instinctively Rafe felt for his pistols. They were upstairs in his room. He left his holster hanging on the post of the bed when he dressed for Mass.

A shadow ducked near the doorway and Rafe knew he and Pete were trapped in the livery. Crouching his way toward Rayo's stall, he spotted his saddle hanging on the wall. His rifle was in the scabbard.

"We know he's in there Pete. We don't got no issue with yew, just the Mex. He shot Sam Duncan and he needs to pay for that," a voice yelled out.

"You can try to come in here and get him, but you'll have to come through me," Pete yelled back.

Rafe reached the saddle and pulled out his double-action rifle, just as another shot hit the wall near Rayo. Pete returned the shot from Rafe's left.

Rising slightly, Rafe aimed and placed a rifle shot toward the door. The sound reverberated in the small livery.

Return shots rang out immediately. From his position, Rafe saw gun barrel flashes from three locations. He took Pete's position in a stall into consideration.

Taking careful aim, Rafe placed shots just above where he saw the gun barrel flashes. They were rapid shots from his double-action rifle and Pete took his lead and returned several shots as well. Rafe hoped their firepower would confuse the shooters.

He saw movement in front of the doorway and Rafe placed a couple of rapid shots in that direction, aiming high. No shots were returned.

"Thought yew said it was just the two of em." Rafe heard a voice grumble.

"Only saw him and Pete in there," another voice said.

While the two vigilantes argued, Rafe reloaded the spent shots in his rifle. A bullet whizzed just above his head and splintered the corner of a wall. Rafe squatted and returned six rapid-fire shots. One of the shooters screamed.

"Damn Doug, I've been hit. We need more men," a voice shouted. Rafe and Pete heard the men scrambling away and in the dim gaslight he saw two men helping a third man as they ran away from the front of the stables.

"Pete!" Rafe called out. "You okay?"

"Yep," Pete stood up and walked back to where Rafe stood near Rayo. "What kind of a rifle you got there? Never saw the likes of it."

Rafe handed the rifle to Pete. "A double-action. You don't have to cock it to fire. I make them in Santa Fe."

"Thought you bred horses?"

"I also make guns in my father's foundry in Santa Fe. He invented them."

"Sure did scare those varmints, but they'll be back and soon. You and your missus need to get outta here."

"They warned me they would come after me, but I thought . . . " Rafe's voice trailed off. He and Ana Teresa were supposed to get married after Mass. His mind spun with indecision.

"If I were you son, I'd hightail it out of here now. It won't take them long to round up more men."

"Pete, get our horses saddled. Is there a back way into the hotel?"

Pete walked over to a small door on the far back wall. "This will put you behind the counter in the lobby. I'll get your horses ready. You better be quick about it."

Rafe emerged from the door behind the desk scaring the desk clerk.

"I heard shots," he said seeing Rafe.

"Vigilantes."

Rafe could see Ana Teresa peering to the street at the

front door. He strode to her and turned her around. "Rafael." She fell into his arms. She heard the shots and looked worried.

"Come, we must go," Rafe said. As they walked across the lobby, the desk clerk stopped them.

"When I sent my porter to get your lunch from the cafe, the news is all over the town. You shot Sam Duncan and they have sworn their revenge. They know you are supposed to be at the church after Mass and they will be waiting. They will have many guns, but I fear they will prefer to take you alive and hang you in a public display." He bowed slightly toward Ana Teresa seeing the young woman's expression. She looked stricken. "I'm sorry to speak so frankly in front of you ma'am."

Ana Teresa gasped, clutching at Rafe's arm tighter. The vigilantes had accosted Rafe for no reason, trying to steal Rayo. Rafe showed restraint in return and only wounded the man.

"Where is the sheriff? Have you called him?" Rafe asked. "Surely the law here in Los Angeles can stop those murderous louts."

"I'm afraid our illustrious sheriff sides with the vigilantes. They have made his job easier. Besides, Sheriff Kemper is from Oklahoma and disregards Mexicanos as much as the rest of the vigilantes. Your only chance is to leave Los Angeles quickly."

"And you? Why are you helping us? You are not Spanish," Rafe responded to the sandy-haired, freckled desk clerk.

"I grew up in Los Angeles. My family has been here for many years. The Spaniards were good to my grandfather and shared land and food when necessary. Los Angeles used to be place where the people were like the calm ocean breezes. Now it is full of hate between people. There is good and bad on both sides, but I do not condone the vigilantes," the clerk responded.

"I deeply regret questioning your motives," Rafe responded feeling ashamed of his quick distrust of the man.

In the past Rafe might have wanted to fight, wanted

to defend himself and let his GSW pistols put such scoundrels in their place. Now Rafe's only concern was for Ana Teresa. Though he cared for his own life, it was nothing compared to hers.

"Pete is readying our horses in the livery. We must go pack."

Quickly climbing the stairs, Rafe left his door open until she returned with her small suitcase. Picking up his satchel and her bag, they walked down the stairs again.

"Follow me," the clerk said. Walking quickly behind the front desk, the clerk led them to the door that exited into the livery. Rafe stuck out his hand and the clerk shook it. "God's speed," the clerk said as he closed the door behind them.

"Psssst," Pete whispered at them as the door to the livery opened. "Keep low."

Rafe saw Ana Teresa's horse standing quietly, ready to go. Rayo was standing nearby, his distinctive rump covered in mud to hide the white splotches. A brown blanket covered the saddle and more of Rayo's markings.

Pete picked up Rafe's satchel and Ana Teresa's suitcase and tied them to the saddles.

"Now you listen good. They'll be looking for two people on horseback, specially that Appaloosa."

"Where can we go?" Rafe asked.

"From what I hear all the passes from Flagstaff, Arizona to the New Mexico border and beyond are closed because of snow. If I were you, I'd head east to El Monte. It's about ten miles. You'll find an inn there and will be safe. The vigilantes don't patrol that far out of the city. From El Monte go south to Warner's Ranch. There you can take a stage east to Fort Yuma and then on to Tucson," Pete advised.

"Can't thank you enough, Pete." Rafe held out his hand.

"Just get going. I'll deal with them varmints when they come back here looking for you."

They shook hands again and Rafe handed him several gold coins from his vest pocket. He had thirteen gold coins in his vest originally intended for the wedding ritual. "I owe you Pete."

Rafe paused and pulled another gold coin from his vest. "See the desk clerk gets this. It will cover our rooms and thank him for me."

"Sure will," Pete said. "You best be going."

Rafe jumped onto Rayo's back. The horse fidgeted and Rafe knew he wanted to bolt. "Shhh, easy boy. We have to take it slow." Gently stroking Rayo's flank, Rafe calmed him. He clicked his tongue and the horse trotted slowly from the livery. Ana Teresa followed on the mare. The nighttime swallowed them up as they left the lighted livery.

Rafe knew the Pico House was near the center of the town of Los Angeles. The three-story hotel was smaller than some of the larger government and office buildings lining the main street. The alleyway from the livery put them onto a side street. Looking right and left, no one was in sight. He turned left toward the main road.

When they reached the main road, a few wagons moved slowly and horses lined the hitching posts. Gaslights lit the sidewalk and shone out to the street. A couple of mother's with young children walked casually along the sidewalk. Two men were avidly engaged in conversation. Three cowboys stood near their horses.

Rafe decided to keep a steady pace so as not to attract attention. Rayo's rump was covered in mud and a brown blanket hid his Apploosan markings. Rafe prayed it was enough to disguise the horse.

Continuing to ride east, the large buildings ended and the street was lined with elegant large homes. These were not Spanish homes. The wood or brick houses were set back from the street. Wrought iron fences or neatly trimmed hedges surrounded the yards of green grass in front of the houses. Most houses had two-story white pillars rising from the front porch to the roofline. Lights blazed from the houses' windows, but they saw little activity around the large homes. Only one had a carriage parked in the front driveway.

Rafe kept Rayo striding at an even pace. He could hear Ana Teresa's mare behind him. As the large houses ended and the road led off into the dark night, Rafe kicked Rayo to a gallop.

CHAPTER 5

As they rode quickly east from Los Angeles and further from the mild ocean breezes, the temperature dropped quickly. Ana Teresa was shivering as she urged her horse to keep up with Rafe. Only a slight moon lit the sky and otherwise the dark night felt as if it was swallowing them up.

The road was lonely and occasionally animal noises scared her. She prayed to Saint Christopher to give them strength and protection. She and Rafe had not spoken since they left the livery. She knew every ounce of his being was intent on getting them to safety.

Finally a dim light shone up ahead. She whipped her horse a bit faster toward the light, riding up beside Rafe on Rayo. Out of the darkness, a small group of buildings sat eerily in the moonlight, but their sight filled Ana Teresa with joy.

Arriving at the small inn, Rafe jumped off Rayo and spoke to the sable boy. He then turned and took the reins from Ana Teresa's shaking hands and helped her down.

"I will take good care of your horses, *señor y señora,*" the boy said.

Ana Teresa almost corrected him to their marital status, then thought better of it. Traveling as someone's wife was more acceptable than a young girl traveling alone with a man. They walked the short distance to the stage stop's building. Pushing in the door, warmth and the smell of roasting pork greeted them.

"*Ah señor y señora, bienvenidos,*" the proprietor welcomed them. "Come sit by the fire and warm yourselves."

"*Gracias,*" she responded. "We did not realize how much colder it would be here than in Los Angeles."

The proprietor thought it very odd. The woman looked Spanish, dressed in a fancy cream-colored dress and a brown coat with a fur collar. She was obviously of some means, but not dressed for traveling. The man was also dressed in a tailored suit and narrow black tie. They looked dressed as if they were going to Mass and not riding in the dark, except the man had a two-gun belt wrapped around his slim waist. The door opened and the stable boy carried their suitcases into the room and set them by the door.

"In winter the desert gets cold at night. Are you hungry?" the proprietor asked them.

"Yes, that would be much appreciated," Ana Teresa responded.

"I have stew or tamales?" he asked speaking to her.

"Some stew would be nice and strong coffee, if you can," she responded.

About an hour later, she sat looking at her empty bowl of stew. Rafe seemed more wary of their surroundings and they talked little.

"We are closing for the night. Your bags have been taken to the last room on the right."

"*Gracias,*" Ana Teresa replied.

"I'm going to check on the horses. You go ahead and I will join you," Rafe told her.

She walked to the small room down the hallway. Pushing open the door, she raised the candle to peer inside the room. A musty smell hit her nose. This was not the Pico House with its elegant velvet wallpaper and overstuffed chairs. A simple small bed and a wooden chair were the only pieces of furniture in the room. The bed hardly looked big enough for one, let alone two.

Her suitcase sat on the bed, Rafe's satchel on the floor. Hanging her coat over the chair, the room was colder than the one in the front with the big fireplace. Carefully she stripped her dress and draped it over her coat. Opening her suitcase, her belongings were a jumble.

She had purchased a lacy nightdress for tonight. She dreamed of wearing it at the Pico House after they returned from the church as man and wife. She imagined Rafael would devour her with his eyes and then tenderly pull the straps from her shoulders. He would not be rough, but gentle making sure she was happy with his touches.

Her mind flicked to her encounter with Diego de la Torre near the stream the day she went riding. Diego grabbed at her dress and tore it off her arm. He then growled at her calling her a *puta*, a whore, gripping her arm so tightly it left a bruise for over a week.

Diego thought himself privileged, son of a prominent *don* in Santa Fe. He was not much different than Domingo, her ex-fiancé. Raised to believe he was superior to anyone not perceived of his status and class, Diego was an insolent rogue. She remembered the day Diego mistreated her was the day she realized her love for Rafael.

A chill sent a shiver up her spine. She pulled the sheer nightdress aside and chose the warmer one, slipping it over her head before crawling under the blankets.

The bed was freezing and Ana Teresa tucked the three heavy quilts around her. Her body would not stop shivering, though she tried hard not to move around to the colder parts of the bed. She closed her eyes just for a moment, nervously waiting for Rafe to join her. Exhaustion from the day's events quickly took her to the hills near her home in Rancho Simi. In the dream, they were sitting under the huge oak tree.

Suddenly his arms surrounded her and held her tight. The warmth of his arms wrapped her in comfort and she felt his breath on her face.

"Rafael, Rafael, hold me," she clung to him as if she would never let him go. Her mouth found his and they clung in their embrace. He placed kisses on her cheeks and neck. This time the shivers coursing through her body were not from the cold. She pulled at his shirt. She wanted to feel him, feel him close to her. Pulling off his shirt, she ran her hands over his chest. She had never seen him without a shirt. Though the room was dark, she felt his chest rippled with muscles.

Rafe strained with desire. Lost in her kisses he knew if he wanted to, he could have her now. "My love, we are not married in the sight of God," he said pulling up and away a bit.

"This is our wedding night, regardless whether the priest blessed us or not. God understands." Her words shocked him. He wanted to believe she would not feel unclean in the morning.

"No. It is not right. We need at least a priest's blessing to start our life together."

He pulled her into his arms, tucking her head into the crook of his armpit. "We will travel as husband and wife, but we will not consummate our marriage until we are blessed."

"I don't care. God is everywhere, even here," she told him.

His want and need for her nearly melted his resolve. "No, not without a priest's blessing. Now go to sleep. We are safe and together. That is enough for now."

CHAPTER 6

When Rafe woke in the morning, Ana Teresa's arm circled his chest and her breath tingled his neck. Her long brown hair cascaded over his shoulder and out across the pillow. God he loved her. He knew if he had taken her last night, she would have given herself freely to their love.

Trying not to disturb her, he lay staring at the ceiling pondering their plans. Pete had told them to get to Warner's Ranch and to take a stage east from there. Though he hoped they could make Santa Fe for Christmas, the calculation of days was starting to make that doubtful.

A whistling rattled the small window above him and cold air drifted over his head. It was mid December and Pete said a heavy snowfall had closed the passes to Santa Fe. Los Angeles had been temperate and mild, but the wind and cold air here in El Monte made him contemplate whether they could travel on horseback and coach. It would only get colder as they traveled east.

Ana Teresa shifted slightly in his arms. Closing his eyes, Rafe tried to relax. She was in his charge and her life and safety his entire responsibility. So far, he had put her in danger from the Citizens Security Patrol and stolen her unmarried in the night. Not a very good start.

From the main room a pan clanged on the metal stove and Rafe heard a voice curse. It wakened Ana Teresa. She opened her eyes and looked at him dreamily.

"Good morning my love," she whispered and snuggled him. She ran her hand over his bare chest and down toward his belly. Her touch awakened his desire and he was instantly aroused. He groaned aloud with pleasure.

"You are not making this any easier, my dear," he teased her taking her wandering hand and holding it in his.

"Can I help it if I find my husband attractive? Do you think only men have such feelings?"

"I am not yet your husband and yes I know women have feelings. I am glad you want me as much as I you, but we must wait to be married. It will only be a few days."

As he wound from her embrace and swung his legs over the bed, his back was to her. She gasped seeing white crisscrossed scars lining his brown skin. Though they were not raw, she could tell the scars were relatively recent.

"Rafael, what happened to you? Who did this to you?" She reached out a hand and tenderly traced one of the scars.

He had almost forgotten about his beatings on the agave plantation in Mexico. It was the guard's whip, which cut his back repeatedly for some small infraction of effort.

"It is nothing. They are healed now," he responded.

"Nothing? Your back is laced in scars."

He had promised Longwei never to tell anyone about the agave and opium plantation in Jalisco. It was Longwei's condition of his release. "It happened when I was in Mexico and nothing can be done. Come we need to get some breakfast and get moving," he said.

Dressing, Rafe walked into the front room startling a woman in the kitchen. *"Disculpe,"* he excused himself, "My wife wondered if she could get a pan of warm water and a towel?"

"Of course, *señor. Querido,* bring water," she called out to her husband.

The man who served them supper last night came from the back with a pail of water.

"Buenos días señor," the proprietor greeted Rafe.

"Buenos días," Rafe returned the morning greeting.

As the woman heated the water on the iron stove, Rafe took the opportunity to ask some questions.

"Can you tell me how we can get to Warner's Ranch? We need to catch the stage east," Rafe asked.

"Ah sí. You could ride south to Warner's Ranch, but it is a very long way. It is closer to go east to Chino Hills. The Butterfield Stage used to stop here, but now Wells Fargo uses a different route. You can catch the stage to Warner's Ranch at the Chino stop," the man explained.

"Gracias. We will leave after breakfast."

After a breakfast of bacon, eggs, and biscuits, Rafe

and Ana Teresa rode southeast to Chino Hills. The proprietor told them to follow the main trail for several hours until they reached a road heading south. He said it would be well marked.

The stable boy had washed and brushed the mud from Rayo's rump. Rafe wrapped Ana Teresa in the extra blanket to ward off the biting wind. Thankfully the wind was at their back as they headed east on the road out of El Monte.

Conversation was difficult, though Rafe yelled to Ana Teresa several times to make sure she was all right. She nodded in return afraid to open her mouth for fear of inhaling the dust. Finally they reached the crossroads and a sign to Chino Hills. The number fourteen was carved into the sign.

"Fourteen miles," Rafe told her. Ana Teresa thought it seemed an easy ride, but the wind had increased.

As they made the turn south to Chino Hills, the wind blew from the west buffering them directly. Sand stung her eyes and face. Rafe took a position on her right, trying to give her any shield he could from the wind.

After what seemed like many hours, they finally reached the Chino Stage Stop. A stage stood in the courtyard and Rafe called to the driver, "Are you going south?"

"No, I'm headed north to San Francisco. The southbound stage will not be here until tomorrow."

Rafe and Ana Teresa rode their horses to the small barn. He helped her to dismount and untied their baggage. Dirt streaked her face in tiny lines down her cheeks.

"You've been crying my love." Rafe tried to rub at her cheek.

"No. The wind was making my eyes water and I think my clothes are filled with sand," she replied.

The last several days were fraught with peril and hardships, but Ana Teresa had not complained. Rafe was amazed at her resolve. "It seems trouble finds us now no matter where we are," Rafe apologized to her and kissed her dirty cheek.

"We are here and we are safe. Nothing else matters except that we are together," she replied.

The Chino Hills Stage Stop was delightfully warm and more comfortable than El Monte. The large dining area had a roaring fire snapping and crackling.

"Hello," a man called to them. "Saw you ride in. Northbound stage is set to leave in about a half an hour."

"We're going east to El Paso."

"Oh, then you be needing beds for the night. You're lucky we got two open. Had a coach breakdown and it stranded some people here. The next easterly gets in about ten tomorrow morning."

The man's talk was easy and friendly. He ushered them to a table and a woman came with coffee and biscuits.

"I'll be putting supper on in about an hour," she told them.

"Might I clean up? I'm afraid I'm full of dust." As Ana Teresa spoke, she looked up at the woman who noticed her dirt streaked face.

"Lordy be gal! You come with me," the woman exclaimed and Ana Teresa followed her out of the dining area.

While Ana Teresa bathed, Rafe spoke at length with the stage stop owner. He talked Rafe's ear off about the stage lines, the business war between the Butterfield Stage and Wells Fargo. He thought Wells Fargo had better coaches and ran a tighter schedule. Only problem as he saw it was they also carried payrolls and sometimes gold. The Wells Fargo coaches were often the target of bandits.

"Not likely in this weather," he said. "Even bandits hate to ride in these winds."

Before Ana Teresa returned, several people drifted out of the back area to the dining room. They were all Anglos. One couple was definitely more elderly. Shortly before supper was served, Ana Teresa returned to the dining room looking clean and relaxed. Dinner was hearty chunks of beef in a rich sauce, carrots simmered in butter, and more biscuits. The proprietor offer them wine.

Ana Teresa took one sip of the wine and made a face.

"I don't think this is wine," she whispered. Her father had grown grapes and made wine. Her father's wine was sweet and tangy. This wine tasted more like vinegar.

After their meal, the woman poured coffee and served a small piece of apple pie. Several people sat for dinner. Rafe assumed they would all be on the eastbound stage in the morning, making it a full stage. As night fell and the supper dishes cleared, the people began to filter to the back.

The Chino Hills bedrooms had four small beds in each room. In their room, an elderly couple by the names of Hiram and Elvira Hoff claimed the other two beds. They were also going to Warner's Ranch in the morning. Hiram coughed frequently during the night and neither Rafe nor Ana Teresa got much sleep.

In the morning, the coach going to Warner's Ranch was packed full with people and luggage. The wind from yesterday continued, though Rafe thought it had diminished a bit. They stopped for several hours with wheel trouble and Rafe helped the driver fix it. After an otherwise uneventful ride, their coach arrived at Warner's Ranch the following evening.

Wearily Rafe checked in and a waiter served a good meal of fried chicken and a hearty soup. Rafe thought Ana Teresa looked tired and they were nowhere near El Paso.

"You look tired. You can get a good night's sleep tonight," he told her.

"I'm fine Rafael. It's really the swaying and bumping of the coach which is so tiresome."

Pete had told them Warner's Ranch was a good-sized stage stop. However, Rafe was not prepared for the sleeping accommodations. It was an open bay room with many single beds placed close to each other. They were separated by only a small space between them, just enough to allow a person to walk. No one had any privacy. Their bags were set on two beds near the back of the room.

"Outhouse is out that door," a big man said pointing to the door out the back of the room. "See that candle there?" He pointed to a lit candle sitting on a shelf. "If the candle's not there, then someone's a using it," the man explained the bathroom rules of the house.

Ana Teresa fell asleep immediately, but it took Rafe a short while before sleep overtook him. A man snored quite loudly from another bed. His mind wandered with both ideas and fear. He worried even this far away from Los Angeles the vigilantes might find him, but more importantly he worried about Ana Teresa. They were supposed to be married and it was important they return to Santa Fe as husband and wife. He felt it the only way to protect Ana Teresa from any repercussions by the Santa Fe Spanish aristocrats and her uncle Pedro. By the time he fell asleep, he had formulated a plan.

The passengers were awakened an hour before the stage was ready to depart the station. Ana Teresa waited her turn for the outhouse while most of the men used a tree in the back. Rafe shook the dust from his traveling clothes then went to the dining area for breakfast.

While Ana Teresa waited for bathroom privileges, Rafe sent two telegraph messages. One to Santa Fe, telling George Summers they were headed to Fort Yuma and then El Paso because of weather. The other message was to his uncle Jose in El Paso telling him they were coming. He also asked his uncle to wire María and Rodolfo asking them to come to El Paso as soon as possible. Rafe wanted to make sure all the required paperwork was filed in Mexico and most of all wanted to see his sister. He hoped the timing would allow them to share in his happiness with Ana Teresa.

As they sat eating breakfast, Rafe told her of his plans.

"The way I see it, it will take about eleven or twelve days to reach El Paso. I have family there and know the padre at the mission. I promise you, as soon as we get there we will be married, and then we'll stay at the Hotel Stratton and not come out until we have our fill of each other," Rafe told her holding her hand in his.

"We won't make Santa Fe for Christmas then, not even El Paso. I'm sorry my love. I know you wanted to get home," Ana Teresa said to him tightening her grip on his hand.

"It will give us something to tell our grandchildren, how we spent our first Christmas on a stagecoach," he replied with a grin. "Also, I'm planning on selling your mare. I have many better horses in Santa Fe. Do you agree?"

"Whatever you think. She is my cousin's mare. Perhaps we should wire him the money when we get to Santa Fe," she responded and Rafe agreed.

After the breakfast of bacon and eggs, Rafe paid for their stage fare through to El Paso and sold the mare. The driver called the passengers outside and their luggage and other belongings were loaded in the boot and on top of the stagecoach. Rafe tethered Rayo to the rear of the coach and got in sitting next to Ana Teresa. She slipped her arm through his.

CHAPTER 7

The passengers sat facing each other. Rafe and Ana Teresa rode backwards. Across from them, an elderly couple and another man assessed them. He nodded a greeting. Seeing the guns wrapped around Rafe's hips, the elderly woman clutched her husband's hand tighter. Rafe smiled in return, but the woman's eyes remained guarded.

Thankfully, there was more legroom than the coach from Chino Hills and there were several open seats. The seats and seatbacks were comfortable having enough padding to absorb the smaller bumps. As the horses reached their pace, the lurching of the carriage took on a rhythm as they rode.

Ana Teresa leaned her head on Rafe's shoulder and rested. He leaned his head back and closed his eyes, but did not sleep. He heard the passengers talk quietly, though no one spoke to them. He was glad, as he had not slept well and Ana Teresa was resting on his shoulder. He must have fallen asleep for a short time before the coach swayed and jerked him awake.

"What was that?" Rafe spoke to the man across from him.

"Ah, you speak English? We were not sure. Name's Rudy Cannon. I'm headed home to Tucson." The man sitting across and next to the elderly couple stuck out his hand. Rafe took it. The man wore a gray three-piece suit and a derby hat. Rafe took him to be around forty years old and could smell whiskey on his breath.

"Me and my misses are headed to Fort Yuma to live with my son. He is a captain in the Army. My name is Richard Maddox and this here is my wife LuAnn," the elderly man said.

"My name is Rafael Reyes and this is my wife, Ana Teresa. We are going through to El Paso," Rafe returned their greetings.

The men exchanged handshakes and the women

smiled at each other. Rafe sensed the three Anglos were surprised both he and Ana Teresa spoke English.

"Are you from El Paso?" LuAnn asked Ana Teresa.

"No I grew up in California. We were going to Santa Fe to return home, but the passes are closed. We are going to El Paso instead," she replied.

"Santa Fe?" Rudy Cannon asked. "Been there several times. What do you do there Mr. Reyes?"

"You can call me Rafe. I am a horse breeder. I have a ranch and raise blooded horses," Rafe replied.

"Saw that Appaloosa tied to the back. He sure is a beauty. That one of yours?"

"Yes sir. He is one of my studs."

"I'm a whiskey salesman. Travel all over the southwest. Been on these damn rickety coaches more times than I'd like to admit. Sorry for the swearing ma'ams," Rudy tipped his hat to the ladies.

"Rafe, how would you like to play a little poker?"

"Afraid I don't know much about poker or any card game for that matter," Rafe told him.

"Don't worry about that son. I'll be glad to teach you and we'll make it a friendly game just to pass the time," he replied and pulled out a deck of cards and shuffled them. "What about you sir, would like to play?" he asked Richard Maddox.

"Sure, I don't mind since it's a friendly game. I can't afford to bet. My wife and I are going to live with my son because we lost our ranch. Just getting too old to keep it up anymore and LuAnn here has been sickly."

"Before we start, would either of you like a sample? It's the best Bourbon all the way from Kentucky." Rudy pulled a flask from his pocket and offered it to Rafe first.

"None for me, thank you sir," Rafe replied.

"I was a whiskey drinker, but gave the devil up thirty years ago and haven't touched it since," Richard stated.

Rudy shrugged and took a long drink from the flask, then shuffled and dealt out five cards each to Rafe and Richard. "Now, you do know about suits in cards?"

"Yes," Rafe answered.

Rudy went on to explain how to make various poker hands. The three men played for more than an hour before they felt the coach slow and then stop.

"Why are we stopping?" Ana Teresa asked.

"A waystation to change horses. You can take a quick break here," Rudy told her.

For two and a half days they traveled from Warner's Ranch southeast toward Fort Yuma. The long hours on the stage were boring and dusty. One part of the trip was so bumpy, the lighter weight women were bounced high off their seats. At least twice a day the stage stopped at a waystation to change horses and give the passengers time to use an outhouse or get a meal. When they stopped at Cook's Well to change horses, Rafe untethered Rayo. Without saddling him, Rafe rode around the waystation giving Rayo a well-deserved break from the back of the churning wheels.

When they were back in the coach Rudy said to Rafe, "That is a fine example of horse flesh. What kind of a breed is he?"

"Appaloosa. He was bred in Mexico from fine Mexican stock," Rafe replied.

"Are all Appaloosas so big?" Rudy asked.

"He is a bit taller than normal, though the breed is touted for its slender body. They make excellent riding horses for that reason. They are also very smart and easy to train."

Rudy continued discussing horses and from time to time, the three men played cards. The women mostly kept to themselves. On the third day, a woman joined their group sitting beside Ana Teresa.

"*Soy señora Olivia de Martinez,*" she spoke her name. In Spanish she said she getting off in Tucson, then going to her home in Nogales, Sonora, Mexico.

"*Me alegro de conocerte, mi nombre es Ana Teresa,*" she responded a greeting and gave her name.

Olivia was talkative and grateful to have someone fluent in Spanish. She and Ana Teresa carried a conversation most of the morning. Olivia lived in Nogales, just over the Mexican border. She had been visiting her sister in San Diego who just birthed twin girls. She went to help with her sister's other eight children.

"I do not know what they will do with two more mouths to feed," Olivia said. "Though she is younger than me, she looks much older. I told her husband to stop giving her babies. He only laughed at me."

At mid-afternoon they were nearing Fort Yuma. Rudy told the travelers the layover stop was situated here because of the large fort. "Was a time when Indians frequently attacked stages and passengers," Rudy explained. "Sometimes Fort Yuma had to send troops to protect the stage lines."

LuAnn Maddox gasped. "Indians?"

"Not any more ma'am. Things are quiet nowadays."

"Well then quit scaring people," she retorted in a huff.

When they stopped, it was explained the eastbound stage did not leave until the following morning, giving the horses and drivers a rest. Ana Teresa was happy to have the longer time off the bumpy coach. She asked about a bath and was told she could have the bathtub in about an hour.

The stage stop owner retrieved a telegram when Rafe checked in. George had wired him Christmas greetings and was glad they were going to El Paso. The news from home was that Carlos and Bibiana announced they were expecting a child in the summer. All the news in the telegram was happy and joyous and his family wished them both a Merry Christmas.

After a warm bath and a hot meal, Ana Teresa felt completely refreshed. She was enjoying Olivia and their conversation, which helped to pass the time. Olivia was much older than Ana Teresa, more her mother's age, and had a keen sense of humor. She told Ana Teresa she thought Rafael was *"muy guapo,"* which made Ana Teresa giggle. She too thought Rafe was very handsome. Ana Teresa asked Olivia to sit with them at their table for the evening meal.

The following morning, the passengers traveling east were bumping along in the coach. The windy colder weather was gone, replaced by sunny skies and warmer temperatures. At the first waystation, some thirty miles east of Fort Yuma while the horses were being replaced, the passengers went into what looked like a small shack. A man wearing an almost clean white apron guided them to sit at the small tables. He was a friendly sort with a toothy smile and gray curls poking out from under a folded paper sack cap.

"Yew have yer choice of beef an taters or stew. I do have fresh rattlesnake I can grill fer yew, if'n yew like," the cook offered and grinned after he added rattlesnake to the menu.

Ana Teresa was surprisingly hungry and ordered the beef with potatoes. Rafe ordered the stew. They were finishing their meals when the door to the shack banged open. A tall, husky bearded man stood in the center of the doorway brushing desert dust off his shoulders with crossed hands and then slapped at his pants. Ana Teresa thought it was humorous since the dusting seemed of not much help to his disheveled dirty look.

The man's lips were parched and his cheeks ruddy or perhaps sunburned. Rafe noticed the man's blue cap with a leather bill. It was the same type the soldiers at Fort Yuma wore. The man had a pistol tucked in his waist under a rope holding up his filthy pants.

"My name is Desperate Billy," the man said in a loud booming voice. "I just survived a trek in the desert after escaping from the Army stockade at Fort Yuma. I want a steak, a bottle of Red Eye, and I'm horny as hell. Now, get going on that steak while I look around for a woman who'll take care of my lust," he growled and gave a belly laugh.

The large man put his hand on his pistol as he walked into the room and looked at each woman. He stopped at Rafe's table, looked at Olivia and said, "You're too old." His eyes then fell on Ana Teresa. "Now this is what I need." Walking around the table, he grabbed her left wrist. "You're coming with me sen'o'rita. I saw us a nice

Appaloosa waiting for us outside," he said as he pulled her out of the chair. "Hurry up with that steak and Red Eye!" he yelled.

Ana Teresa screamed and tried to pull away from him as he held on tight and pulled her toward the door. She kept struggling and looked back at Rafe with desperation in her eyes.

All the rage of Rafe's life flushed through his veins stinging his heart and blanking his brain as he watched Ana Teresa being pulled away from the table. He then saw the image of his fifteen-year-old sister, María, after she was raped by the *haciendero, don* Bernardo. The image of the Reynolds brothers taking his Indian ponies and shooting him in the shoulder popped up in his mind. Image after image of the injustices of his life flicked in his brain. The image of Benicío shooting his beloved Chiwiwi was replaced with Diego de la Torre lying dead under his horse. Diego had attacked Rafe for wanting to marry Ana Teresa. Now she was helplessly being dragged by this brute of a man.

He put his hands near his guns wanting to come up and shoot the *desgraciado*. He knew he could easily best him, but he held Ana Teresa firmly in front of him. Rafe did not have a clear shot at the desperado.

Desperate Billy saw Rafe reach for his guns. "Don't try nuttin," he grumbled pointing his pistol and waving it in Rafe's direction.

Rafe put his hands up in a calming way, but nodded at Ana Teresa. He wanted her to know he would not let the man take her, but felt completely helpless. Studying the situation Rafe focused on calming his breathing. The seconds ticked by slowly. Rudy Cannon coughed behind Rafe and he could hear one of the women sniffling. Rafe waited, watching the man carefully for a time when he could shoot Desperate Billy without hurting Ana Teresa.

"Put the steak and whiskey in a sack," Desperate Billy yelled at the cook while pointing the gun at him.

The cook nervously did as the outlaw said. He dropped the bottle of whiskey and it broke spilling the liquor all over the kitchen floor. Hurriedly, he grabbed another bottle and put it in the sack, handing it toward the outlaw.

"Sen'o'rita, you take the sack," Desperate Billy ordered Ana Teresa.

As she reached for the sack, he squeezed her left wrist tight. Rafe saw her wince in pain. She grabbed the sack and glancing back at Rafe she quickly slung it with all her might at the man holding her. As the force of the glass bottle struck Billy, his eyes widened with surprise and he loosened his grip. As Ana Teresa started to squirm free, Billy wobbled and almost lost his balance trying to keep his hold on her.

Seeing Ana Teresa break free of Billy's grip, Rafe came up with his guns aimed at the wretched man, "Drop that gun or you are a dead man."

CHAPTER 8

When Rodolfo and María got the telegram from her uncle saying Rafael wanted them to come to El Paso, María was elated. They owed Rafael everything. Because of her brother, she and Rodolfo had a life. The last time she saw Rafael, she had treated him terribly. Angry after he took her to Santa Fe, she blamed him for what she thought were the tribulations of her life – killing *don* Bernardo, kidnapping her and the children from Mexico, and even the inevitable death of her baby. She now understood Rafael only had her best interest in his heart. She wanted to set things right with him.

Since returning to Mexico, María found a new life. She and Rodolfo lived as free *peóns*. At first they were outlaws, living off the land and the meager items they stole from *haciendeeros*. Then more peasants joined them, almost seventy now, and more came each week. They came following her husband's dream of freedom and self-sufficiency for everyone. Because of her brother Rafael, they no longer had to steal or sleep on the hard ground. Rafael inherited and then gave them the Reyes *hacienda* in Torreón so they could live in peace.

They and their gathering of peasants settled the vast *hacienda* last fall. It needed much work to rebuild, but the people were joyous in the efforts. Here they were building a future free of servitude – a future as free men and women. The children were learning at the school María started in the living room of the main house. Several new families joined them last month and two babies had been born.

She had so many reasons to want to see her brother, the biggest to thank him for giving them the *hacienda* and to tell him of the life he gave to all of them.

She and Rodolfo discussed several options. "If we leave today, we should be able to be in El Paso on Christmas Day," María said thinking they could make the trip in four days.

Rodolfo convinced her to have Christmas Day at the *hacienda* to celebrate their first Christmas with the people who chose to live here and who helped them work the *hacienda*.

"I guess you are right. We have many arrangements to make if we are leaving and Rafael will wait until we arrive. Besides this is our first Christmas as husband and wife. Gloria and Roberto have worked so hard to decorate the house for us, and the pig has already been slaughtered."

"Can you get our things ready?" Rodolfo asked her putting his hand on her bulging stomach. María was five months pregnant though it hardly showed under her loose *camisa*. Unlike baby Bernardo's pregnancy, María felt wonderful. The baby was kicking stronger every day. Secretly she was praying it was boy. If so, she wanted to name the baby, Rafael.

"Of course. Who will look after things here?" she asked him.

"Maxorro and Javier. The people look to them for guidance when we are not around."

That night Rodolfo and María lay in bed. María curled in his arm lazily rubbing her hand across his chest.

"Maxorro and I talked and decided we should take the silver to El Paso. I will ask your cousin Martín to talk to his friend Jerry Carr. Maybe he can help us sell the silver," Rodolfo told her.

"No, we cannot! What if we get caught with it? What about *bandidos* on the road? You know they will kill us for it," she pleaded.

Rodolfo and three members of their outlaw band stole silver ingots from a silver shipment outside of Zacatecas last summer. It was a rash plan at a desperate time when the group of free *peóns* were starving and Rodolfo was convinced it would be the answer to their prayers. Pepe was killed in the raid, but they escaped with fifteen ingots of solid silver. Only after the heist did Rodolfo realize the roughly formed ingots were marked with the silver mine's mark, making them easily identified. The small fortune of silver lay buried behind the barn of the *hacienda,* useless to their needs. Rodolfo now rued the day he thought it a good plan.

"I do not see any other way to get money for the silver. We have to take the chance we can make it there and cross the border with it," he tried to assure her.

"No, I'm afraid. If we are caught, then all will be lost," she implored him.

Her words fell on Rodolfo's deaf ears. The silver was wasting away, while the *hacienda* needed so much. If they were to make a go of it here, they needed more livestock, wagons, horses, cattle, and seed to plant for the spring crop. Every day he watched the people go hungry. The pig which had been butchered and hung for the upcoming Christmas feast was the last hog, though two piglets were born several months ago. Even the piglets were having a hard time scratching out enough scraps to eat.

The following morning, Rodolfo asked Maxorro to help him build a false floor under the wagon, just tall enough to slide the ingots of silver into place. "It must be made in a way where the ingots are completely safe and tucked soundless in place," Rodolfo told him. "We can use weathered boards stripped from the outside wall on the western side of the barn. Nothing must look tampered or new."

The wagon was the same rickety wagon Rodolfo and María took to El Paso to buy guns last year. Once again, they would travel as poor *peóns* on the road to find a better place to live. They would take only old clothes and wornout pots and pans. He decided not to tell María of the silver. It would only worry her if she knew, besides if they were caught she would have nothing to hide.

"Use two of the young mules," Maxorro suggested. "Any of the better horses might catch attention."

"Yes, you're right. Pick the two mules you think will be best," Rodolfo replied welcoming the older man's opinion. "Perhaps you should come with us?"

"I have to admit your offer is tempting, but my place is here. I will watch over things while you are gone."

Maxorro had been the muleteer for the silver mine.

His mules carried the heavy packs of silver ingots between the mine and the Mexico City Mint. Of Cazcanes Indian heritage, the muleteer had been treated only slightly better than the indentured miners. When he had the opportunity to join Rodolfo during the heist of the silver, he took the chance to live free. It was a decision he never regretted.

He was forty-two years old. Following in his father's footsteps, he started helping with the mule trains when he was eleven. The next thirty year took a toll on his body leaving him feeling like an old man. That was then and this was now. Rested and happy, Maxorro enjoyed working at the *hacienda*. It seemed as if years shed from both his body and soul. Two months ago, he started helping a woman who came to the group with two teenage children. Her husband had died of an untreated illness. She caught Maxorro's eye and he enjoyed the children. Soon he hoped they might marry.

On Christmas Eve, the men built a huge bonfire in the middle of the courtyard. The woman and children danced. Paco strummed an old guitar. Maxorro sang and everyone was surprised at his deep melodic voice.

The roasted pig was served with sweetened squash and potatoes. Several of the women made tortillas and Benita made a bread pudding of stale pieces of bread soaked in milk. The mood at the *hacienda* was elated. María rested her head against Rodolfo's shoulder, happy with the world.

On Christmas morning, Rodolfo loaded the larger open-backed wagon with as many people as it could carry. Others walked alongside. They drove and walked the twenty miles to the church in Torreón. It was the first time many of the people had been to the large town. Spaniards in the town gawked and pointed at the ragged group. María held her head up high, daring anyone to refuse their passage.

Two days after Christmas, they readied for the trip to El Paso. María and Rodolfo loaded personal belongings on the floorboard while Maxorro harnessed two mules to the old wagon. María carried the food she packed in sacks and placed it under the seat. Rodolfo helped her up on to the wagon and then turned to his old friend Maxorro. "I told Javier to rely on you if there is any trouble or if the police or government comes. Have Pablo talk to them. He has all the official papers saying we own the *hacienda*," Rodolfo told him.

Maxorro handed Rodolfo a rifle. *Peóns* in Mexico were not allowed to own firearms, but Rodolfo and his outlaws owned many. "You may need protection," Maxorro told him knowing of the precious cargo. Rodolfo stowed the rifle under the canvas tarp as he got up on the seat.

"Via con Dios," Maxorro blessed them and started the mules.

Rodolfo took the main trail from Torreón to Chihuahua. The day was chilly and the sun hidden by heavy clouds. María pulled her shawl tightly around her head.

Rodolfo kept the mules at a steady pace. Even with María pregnant, he hoped to make the trip in four days. He worried about her condition and would not have let her come if she was further along. Though not her first child, it was Rodolfo's first time to be a father. She teased him when he fretted about her condition, treating her as if she was helpless.

Well north of Torreón they caught up with a caravan of four fully-loaded wagons carrying heavy loads. As they approached, Rodolfo saw four armed guards riding along side of the caravan.

"María look, we will be safe if we stay close to this caravan. They must have precious cargo. All we have to do is keep up with them," he whispered to her.

This time of year between Christmas and the New Year not many wagon caravans traveled north on the Chihuahua Trail. One of the guards noticed them and dropped back.

"Hola," Rodolfo greeted him. He held up his empty hand as the man approached. The guard had his rifle in hand, but not in a threatening manner.

"Where are you coming from?" he asked.

"We are from a *hacienda* south of Torreón. My pregnant wife and I are going to El Paso to seek a better life for our child. She has an uncle there," Rodolfo explained.

The guard's eyes appraised the *peón* couple. The woman's long dark hair flowed out from under her shawl and down to her swollen belly. The young man had clean shaven cheeks on a lean face. The back of the wagon contained only a few rusty tools strapped to the sides and the wagon itself looked like it might fall apart. Surely these two were not outlaws.

"I'll ask the wagon master if you can join us. There is always safety in numbers," he said and rode off.

When the caravan stopped for the night, Rodolfo and María stopped and parked their wagon a short distance away. After the nightly tasks were completed, a rotund man walked toward them.

"I am Alejandro, the wagon master. Armando tells me you are traveling to El Paso?" he said as a question.

"*Sí señor,*" Rodolfo said humbly. "I am Rodolfo Guerrero and this is my wife, María."

The man looked at the meager meal María was preparing over a tiny fire and felt sorry for the young peasant couple. "Come, join us. My cook has prepared a beef stew. You are welcome," he said.

"*Gracias señor,*" Rodolfo thanked him.

Later that evening as they sat by the fire, they learned the caravan was carrying a late order of steel and iron to a foundry in Pueblo, Colorado. Alejandro was from Zacatecas. He and his wife had four children and his wife was pregnant with their fifth child. They talked well into the night, until the wagon master dispatched the evening guards.

"*Buenas noches.* We leave at sunup," he wished them a goodnight.

Rodolfo and María could not believe their luck. They felt safe traveling with the caravan and the wagon master told them he would look out for them. Curled together under the heavy quilt in the back of their wagon, Rodolfo kissed her gently, then with more passion. Though pregnant, she did not resist his advances. She shivered and he pulled her close.

Her breasts were swollen from the oncoming child. Cupping one, he heard her groan slightly in response and she kissed his neck and nibbled on his earlobe. His *pene* stiffened into a rock.

"Mi amor. I love you so much. I could never want for anything else as long as I have you," he whispered to her.

"Show me," she giggled and wrapped her hand around his stiff manhood.

CHAPTER 9

"Don't shoot mister, don't shoot. This gun is old and it don't even work," Desperate Billy begged when he saw the young Mexican pointing two pistols directly at him.

"Drop it and kick it over here," Rafe told Desperate Billy. The man's face dripped of whiskey and a cut was bleeding from his cheek where a piece of the whiskey bottle cut him. After heaving the sack into the would-be kidnapper, Ana Teresa ran to safety behind Rafe.

Desperate Billy dropped the gun and kicked it toward Rafe. "Don't shoot me, mister. Please don't shoot me. I'm just hungry, that's all." Billy put his hands high up above his head as he backed up against the wall near the door.

"I'm sorry ma'am," he said looking at Ana Teresa. "I'm really sorry ma'am. I didn't want to hurt you."

"Is there a sheriff around here?" Rafe asked the cook.

"No law round here," the cook answered.

"No law, what are we going to do?" Rafe asked.

"I'll go get the stationmaster," the cook said and rushed out the door.

Meanwhile Rafe kept his guns pointed at the man calling himself Desperate Billy. He looked about thirty-five with a tall, husky build and large hands. His clothes were filthy and did not fit him well. On his head, he wore the hat of a Union soldier, which was so dirty it hardly looked blue anymore.

A shaken and trembling Ana Teresa came up to Rafe from behind and hugged him around the waist and laid her head on his back. Rafe felt her shaking, but he did not take his eyes off the man who tried to kidnap her.

Billy thought himself an unlucky man. Why he came barging into the stage stop was just part of his continuing stupidity. He was put in the Army stockade for similar foolishness. All he really wanted was something to eat.

Rafe saw Desperate Billy's eyes dart from him to where the door was located. Rafe could see him calculating his odds.

"You just stay there and keep those hands above your head," Rafe warned him.

A few moments later, the stationmaster pushed open the door and walked in taking off his gloves. "What's going on here?" he asked sternly.

"This man came in here, demanded food and whiskey, and then tried to kidnap my wife. What do you want to do with him?" Rafe spoke out.

"Yes, that's right. What are you going to do?" Rudy Cannon spoke up.

"We don't have any law around here. All I can do is lock him up in the barn until the U.S. Marshall comes around. Don't know when that'll be," the stationmaster replied. He did not need this type of trouble. He had trouble enough with outlaws and bandits who tried to rob the Wells Fargo stagecoaches. Two of his drivers were shot in the last month and one died. It was getting harder and harder to find tough men who were willing to take that kind of risk. Now this fool accosted his passengers right here at the station.

"I could just shoot him and be done with him," Rafe grumbled and was angry enough to do it. Desperate Billy now stood unarmed and though everyone in this room probably would support him doing so, it was cold-blooded murder.

"No, no, don't let him shoot me. Please don't let him shoot me. I didn't mean it," Billy begged, but everyone looking at him knew he meant to do exactly what he demanded.

The remnants of the steak were lying in the whiskey soaked bag on the floor. The stationmaster shook his head.

"Let him have the steak and I'll lock him up in the barn. No use wasting good food. Don't give him any whiskey and clean up this mess," the stationmaster told the cook.

The cook picked the broken bottle of whiskey out of the sack and handed the steak to Billy. The stationmaster pushed Billy out the door and led him to the barn.

Thirty minutes later, the passengers were told the stage would be leaving shortly. Rafe comforted Ana Teresa and the other passengers praised her bravery.

"Never seen anything like that in all my travels," Rudy said. "Can't wait to tell my wife Alice about the excitement."

Rafe thought he could do without any more excitement on this trip. He especially did not want to shoot anyone, even Desperate Billy. Before they left the waystation, Rafe put his arm around Ana Teresa. Surprisingly, she seemed less upset than he.

"You were very brave when you hit the man with the sack. If you missed, he could have hurt you," Rafe told her.

"I don't think he wanted to hurt me. I think he just wanted a hostage to escape, but I think he may have taken Rayo," she said.

"How can you say that? The man was dangerous and had a gun. You amaze me that you are not more upset with him or me."

"You? Why would I be upset with you?" Ana Teresa looked confused.

"He was dragging you toward the door and I did nothing. I could have jumped at him or tried to get off a shot." Rafe was feeling a bit clumsy about the way he handled the situation.

"How could you know the gun didn't work. Besides I know you would have rescued me."

"He could have gotten you on Rayo and taken off. I'm not sure I could have caught up and rescued you. I'm glad you hit him with the sack," Rafe said and laughed.

"There was something about him, like he was acting mean and tough, but in his eyes I could see he was just scared. I could be wrong, but it was in his eyes," she said.

"Well, you're safe now and I promise to never let you be put in a dangerous situation again." Rafe held her in a firm hug, thankful the incident with Desperate Billy was over.

"There was nothing you could do to prevent it."

"Still, I promise to always take care of you." Rafe

pledged again.

Each day since Rafe and Ana Teresa had left Rancho Simi, he felt guilty about taking her away from a comfortable and safe place. Though she never complained, Rafe could tell the trip was hard on her. Now he could add almost being kidnapped to the list of unpleasant incidents. "Please God, let it end now," he prayed silently as the stage was loaded.

In the small barn, Desperate Billy devoured the steak. He sure missed the whiskey, but he had not eaten much of anything for two days and the steak was mighty good. He was thankful the young Mexican did not shoot him, though he deserved it. He had done plenty of stupid things in his life, trying to act tougher than he was.

Billy could hear the stage being readied. The stationmaster yelled a last call for the passengers. Once the stage departed, Billy thought the stationmaster might kill him to be rid of him. He needed to somehow get out of this barn. Looking around he spotted a pitchfork and there was a small window in the back.

Picking up the pitchfork, he broke the window at the back of the barn. It took several strikes to demolish the window and he stood on a couple of hay bales to hoist himself up and out. Sprinting away from the back of the barn, Billy hoped no one saw him escape. He stayed near the road where the stage would come by. About a half mile down the road a small grouping of boulders created a good place to hide.

Crouching, he waited for the stage to round the bend. As it passed, he sprinted and grabbed ahold of the rear boot and pulled himself up. Like a piece of luggage, Desperate Billy hitched a ride, his legs dangling off the back. The big Appaloosa tied to the back of the stage snorted and whinnied at him, then quieted.

After many miles of riding the boot, Desperate Billy quietly crawled to the top of the coach. The canvas shades were pulled down. Holding onto the luggage straps, Billy swung his legs into the door window and slid into the coach.

"Howdy folks!" Billy announced himself as he landed between the bench seats. Along with Rafe and Ana Teresa the only other passengers were Olivia Martinez and Rudy Cannon.

Ana Teresa and Olivia gasped and recoiled away from the desperado. Rafe pulled one of his guns and pointed it directly at Billy's face. "What the hell are you doing here?" Rafe growled at him.

"Sorry folks, but I couldn't stay back there at the station. The Army would have found me and taken me back to Fort Yuma. I need to get as far away as I can from that place," Billy said humbly.

"Ma'am, I want to apologize for treating you badly back there. Honest. I wasn't gonna kidnap you, I just didn't want to get shot for robbing the place for whiskey and food. I was gonna take the Appaloosa, but I must say you were mighty brave hitting me with the sack."

He saw Ana Teresa's arm linked through Rafe's. "I owe you an apology too," he said looking directly at Rafe. "I didn't know she was your wife."

Billy remained sitting on the floor of the coach. Rafe and Rudy knew he was unarmed, nonetheless he was a big man.

"You . . . you come up mighty fast with those guns. I thought you was gonna shoot me right there on the spot," Billy spoke in a friendly voice hoping the young Mexican man would not shoot him for sure this time.

"I am not a killer mister, but if you had taken her I would have hunted you down and killed you slowly to make you pay for taking my bride," Rafe told him.

"I would do the same, if I was you. I ain't no kidnapper. Like I said, I was just trying to protect myself. Not that you ain't pretty ma'am. You sure are mighty pretty. All I want to do is get to Texas and from there I can get myself to Michigan some way"

"Well what are we going to do with him now?" Rafe asked looking at Rudy.

"I won't be no trouble. I promise I'll behave myself," Billy begged.

"We should help him," Ana Teresa told Rafe. She did not know why, but she felt sorry for him. Though he smelled awful, his eyes did not hold any evil in them. They were a light grey-blue color and they twinkled when he smiled. She thought he might even be somewhat handsome if he shaved and took a bath.

"We can't trust him," Rafe said giving her a concerned glance.

"You have every right not to trust me after what I did back there, but I tell you all I want is to get back to Michigan."

Rafe sighed and holstered his pistol. He had a mind to try to push Billy out the coach's door, but doubted he could move the large man. Billy leaned back against the door stretching his legs out in front of him and relaxed.

"Why did they have you in the stockade? What did you do?" Rafe asked keeping his hand near his gun still nervous about Billy.

"Well, since you asked. You see I'm a blacksmith and I was the smithy there at Fort Yuma and I tell you I was the best they ever had at that fort. There was this young lieutenant, fresh out of West Point. That boy was from Connecticut, spoiled like an only child. Every time I shod his horse, he gave me a hard time saying I didn't do it to his satisfaction. There were other times he got in my face about something or another. He just did it because he could. Finally, I went kinda crazy one day after he complained I was too slow at fixing his bent bit. Well, I punched him. Broke his nose and knocked him down. It got me put in the stockade waiting for a court martial. I knew my time with the Army was over, so some friends helped me break out during the night. I was lucky to get to that stage stop. My canteen was empty and I hadn't any food for two days. That Arizona desert is mean," Billy finished his story.

"How long were you in the Army," Rudy asked after hearing the tale.

"Most part of nine years. That's the devil of it, I could have been out and gone, but I stayed in. I like blacksmithing and like I said I am good at it. The Army needed me. If that lieutenant busted me with a court martial . . . well I guess it don't matter now I busted out of the stockade."

For the next four hours of the long and bumpy stagecoach ride, Billy entertained the passengers. Many times he made them all laugh with his stories and his wit. When the coach stopped for a quick break, Billy helped the other four passengers step out of the coach.

"Where'd he come frum?" the driver fumed. "He weren't in there when we left Boggs Station." Putting his hand on his holstered gun, the driver stepped toward Billy.

Rafe stepped up and placed himself between them. "He jumped on at the last minute. I'll vouch for him." Rafe was not sure why he decided to defend Billy. It was instinct. Perhaps Ana Teresa was right and Billy was not a bad man, just a man with bad breaks.

At the evening stage stop, Rafe paid for Billy's fare to El Paso and also paid for Billy to get a bath and bought him clean used clothes. Billy joined Rafe and Ana Teresa and Olivia for dinner. As he walked up to their table, they almost did not recognize the tall, clean-shaven man.

"Billy Swanson, at your service," he said, bowed to the ladies, and smiled a huge grin before he sat down. Since Rafe knew Billy was a blacksmith, the talk turned to blacksmithing and Rafe asked him about metals. Along the conversation, Rafe told Billy he was a gunsmith.

"I noticed those guns of yours right off and not just because they was pointed at me," he said with an easy laugh. While he talked, Ana Teresa studied his face. He had nice features. A shard from the whiskey bottle had cut his cheek, but it probably would not scar. His teeth were slightly crooked, but it appeared he still had a full set. His hair was medium brown cut short and his eyes twinkled when he smiled. The only thing Ana Teresa found completely comical were his enormous hands.

The following day Billy graciously helped the ladies into and out of the coach at each waystation and helped the driver with luggage. Ana Teresa could not believe the change in him. It seemed impossible this good-natured man, Billy Swanson, tried to kidnap her just a few days ago calling himself Desperate Billy.

CHAPTER 10

The hours bumping along in the cramped coach were long and boring. Because of the dry terrain, the passengers agreed to keep the canvas window blinds pulled down to minimize the dust. When conversation ran out Ana Teresa dozed on Rafe's shoulder, if he was not playing cards with Rudy and Billy.

On the second day out of Yuma, the driver told the passengers they were entering the land of the desert Indians. He said the Indians were peaceful tribes, scattered for many miles in this barren part of the Arizona Territory. At the mid-morning stage stop, Ana Teresa stepped from the coach expecting more of the barren landscape, where plants struggled to live. Surrounding the stage stop, tall green tree trunks stood, some with arms stretched high. They were like nothing she ever saw before. Barren like the land, the tall trunks had no leaves, gave virtually no shade, and grew in funny shapes.

"What are those?" she asked as she stood near the coach.

"Well, those are the giant cactus of the desert called saguaros. They grow all over the Sonoran Desert in southern Arizona," Rudy Cannon replied.

Ana Teresa had never seen anything like the tall cactus. Their green trunks, if you could call the base a trunk, was a foot or wider in diameter. The outer skin of the trunk was folded in and out like an accordion as it circled the trunk all the way to the top. At odd intervals, arms which came out sideways and then turned toward the sky made some of the giants look like thin men with their arms reaching up.

Ana Teresa walked closer to the nearest tall giant. Along each rib, one inch or longer thick thorns stuck out of little bumps in the green skin. She reached out and touched one of the thorns carefully. Rudy and Rafe walked up beside her.

"I've never seen anything like this before," she said turning to them.

"Nor I," Rafe agreed.

The cactus soared at least twenty feet up and this one had three arms. Each arm was about half the diameter of the main trunk. About ten feet above them, they could see a two-inch hole in the green trunk, then Ana Teresa noticed more holes.

"What are those holes?" she asked pointing up.

"Small birds nest inside. Their nests are well guarded," Rudy replied. Ana Teresa thought well guarded was an understatement.

"Come, the stage will be leaving soon," Rafe said taking her arm.

As they walked into the stage stop's small dining area, the skin of a six-foot rattlesnake hung from a nail by the door. The rattles on the tail stretched for at least ten inches. Ana Teresa shuttered at the sight of the snake.

When they returned to the coach, Ana Teresa asked for a seat next to the window. She opened the canvas covering enough to look out. As the coach began to roll, she watched in fascination as the giant cactus dotted the landscape. Below on the desert floor, scraggly bushes grew along with a few squatty trees. The trees were sparse of leaves and the bushes looked mostly dead. It was then she started to notice the dirt. The dirt looked hard and littered with small pebbles. It was light tan, almost whitish in color and looked bone dry. This was not the fertile dirt of California.

The land looked eerily unable to sustain any life and yet bushes and especially the tall giant cactus grew. As she watched, she tried to see if there was a pattern to their shapes. Each cactus looked unique. Some had no arms and grew straight and tall. Others had many arms, and some only a few. Sometimes she saw the small birds flitting in and out of the giants.

She watched out of the window until the driver pulled up the team and stopped the coach. He opened the coach door. "One of the horses is limping some. I want to

check it out. You can get out and stretch," he told the
passengers.

With the coach stopped, everyone stepped outside
and stretched their legs. Rafe and Billy went to see if they
could help the driver. Near to where the coach stopped,
several low-growing furry plants grew. Ana Teresa headed
toward one to investigate.

"Don't touch it. Don't even go near it," Rudy's voice
warned her.

"It looks so furry," she replied.

"They're called jumping cactus and the fur is really
barbed needles. If you even get close to one, they will jump
on you and catch in your skin and clothes. I knew a boy
once who got caught in one and got a thousand needles
stuck in his leg. It took days to get them all out."

"All's okay folks," the driver called to them. "Just a
stone."

At the afternoon stage layover, at a place called
Maricopa Wells, Ana Teresa talked incessantly about the
desert and especially the giant cactus. Rafe found her
intrigue amusing, though he admitted he had never seen
anything like it before.

Maricopa Wells was a long adobe building. Along
with the typical dining room, tables of blankets, jackets,
pants, shoes, and just about anything someone might need
on their journey were stacked by size. On a pole, a few
women's dresses hung and on another hats of various
types. On the far wall, food staples were available. It looked
more like a large general mercantile store. Indian women
hovered over the goods. One had a baby strapped to her
back. The women smiled and pointed to the blankets and
jackets. "You want?" one asked Ana Teresa.

Besides their stagecoach, several large wagons were
parked in the open area near the buildings. Not far away, a
caravan of five covered wagons and livestock were camped.
On the other end, a large corral had many horses and mules
waiting for stages or for sale.

Suddenly the sound of hooves filled the air. A loud
voice boomed, "COMPANY HALT!"

Ana Teresa peeked outside as a line of Army cavalry stopped in front of the building. "Water your horses and attend to your needs. You have thirty minutes," the captain called to the troops.

Her mind immediately flicked to Billy thinking they must be after him. Out near the coach, Ana Teresa saw Rudy Cannon walk near Rafe and speak to him. Rafe nodded his head up and down. Wildly, she looked around for Billy.

Rafe walked to where the Army captain had dismounted.

"Good afternoon. Warm day," Rafe said striking up a conversation.

"Warm? Well yes I guess you could call this warm, but then I guess you have never been here in the summer," the captain replied with a smile.

"How hot does it get?" Rafe asked.

"Well over a hundred and very little rain."

"Over a hundred degrees!" Rafe could not imagine.

"You should be glad to be traveling in the winter. Summer is brutal."

"Where are you coming from?" Rafe asked casually. He hoped this was not a regiment sent to find Billy.

"Our outfit is out of Benson. We're always patrolling between here and the New Mexico border on the lookout for Apache raiders."

"Apaches? Are they hostile?"

"Can be. They usually keep holed up in the Chiricahua Mountains, but there was an attack near Rita Ranch, south of Tucson. We'll be riding the stage trail for the next several days."

Rafe breathed a sigh of relief. Not only would the stage be protected, but they were not here looking for Billy.

"Well I guess we'll be seeing more of you then. My wife and I are traveling east."

Rafe walked to the building. Seeing Ana Teresa, he took her arm and led her to a corner. There he relayed the captain's words. "Find Billy. I'm going to buy him a new hat and a bandana. Tell him to meet me in the barn."

For the next three days, the Army captain and the eight troopers rode near the stage. At first Billy was obviously nervous and kept his hat pulled low, but as the days wore on he relaxed. Apparently, news of his escape had not reached this regiment of soldiers.

Luckily for the passengers, they reached Tucson on the day before Christmas. The driver suggested several hotels in the town and said they would not be restarting the trip until two days after Christmas. Rudy wished them a Merry Christmas as he left to find his horse at the livery. His small ranch was several miles north of town and he was delighted to be home for the holiday.

On Christmas Day, Rafe and Ana Teresa attended Mass at the nearby church and enjoyed strolling the plaza. Although no shops were open, walking and not riding on the bumpy coach was a joy. They enjoyed their first Christmas dinner together at a small restaurant on the first floor of the hotel.

CHAPTER 11

Two days after Christmas as the stage was preparing to leave Tucson, Rafe overheard the Army captain talking to the driver.

"I'll leave two troopers as an escort as far as Benson," the captain told the driver. The driver replied, grumbling something about trouble.

"Can't be helped. I've been assigned to guard the Wells Fargo coach heading west. It's carrying the Army payroll for Fort Yuma."

As Rafe and Ana Teresa waited impatiently to board, along with Desperate Billy and three new passengers, they watched the Army captain and six troopers ride away with the westbound stage.

Billy helped the driver load the passenger's bags to the top of the coach, securing the luggage with straps. With two troopers on horseback, and a guard riding shotgun, the coach departed. The passengers introduced themselves. Rafe, Ana Teresa, and Billy were joined by two businessmen who sold ladies dresses and a quiet older man who introduced himself as Harry Simpson.

Once out of town, the stage ran at full speed as the road from Tucson to the next station was in good condition. The morning was cold, so the passengers agreed to keep the canvas shades drawn down tight. As the stage sped along, the two businessmen were discussing their trade, Harry appeared to be sleeping, Billy seemed lost in thought, and Ana Teresa had her arm tucked tightly through Rafe's arm.

Rafe was daydreaming about getting back to Santa Fe and his horses. Although he had only been gone for six months, it seemed much longer. In the distance, Rafe faintly heard coyotes yipping. It was a sound he had heard often in his life, both in Mexico and Santa Fe. The yipping usually meant a pack had made a kill. All was quiet for several moments, then the yipping started again, closer and louder.

Suddenly a shot sounded and then another hit the side of the coach. Ana Teresa screamed. "Ye'haa," Rafe heard the driver yell to the team and the coach lurched forward picking up speed. Billy pulled up the window shade and peered out.

"Indians," he said. An arrow struck the door of the coach near him, forcing him to jerk back inside.

"Yiiii, yipp, yipp, hooot, hooot," Ana Teresa heard an Indian nearby yelling a war call. Several rifle shots resounded from behind them. Then they heard a rifle report from the coach's guard.

Instinctively Rafe pushed Ana Teresa to the floor of the coach. "Stay down," he told her and pulled his pistol. The two businessmen and Harry Simpson looked stricken.

Not knowing how far until the next waystation nor how many Indians were in the attack party, Rafe pulled out his second pistol handing it to Billy.

"It will shoot if you keep pulling the trigger but is hard to control. Take time between shots and you will get the feel of it," Rafe instructed. "Use your shots wisely, we don't have much ammunition," he added.

More rifle fire suddenly erupted. Rafe pulled the canvas window shade aside and saw four Indians riding alongside.

Billy peered out of the window on the other side of the coach. "Apaches. Got three on my side," he said as he pointed the pistol and waited for them to get closer.

Rafe peered from the small window and got a good look at the Apaches. They wore faded cloth headbands over their long black hair. One brave had his hair braided. Two of them wore black leather vests over their cotton shirts. All wore leather moccasins reaching almost up to their knees. The horses they rode were decorated with feathers and paint.

"Yiiii, yiiii, yiiii, eeeyipp, eeeyipp," one of the Apaches screamed and raised a rifle in Billy's vision. Billy aimed carefully and took his first shot, dropping the screaming Indian who was closest to the coach.

Kneeling by the window, Rafe took a shot but missed as the coach's lurching made his aim on the warriors difficult. The trailing warrior pulled an arrow and it hit the coach just below Rafe's window. Another Indian was aiming at the drivers above. Rafe took aim and fired. The Indian jerked and almost fell, but managed to turn his horse and ride off.

Billy took three more shots, but all missed their mark. The Apaches circled the coach firing intermittently and Rafe heard the driver yell, "Bart, you hit?"

"Yeah," another voice said. "It's not too bad."

The driver yelled to the horses and the coach swayed erratically, almost knocking Rafe off his knees. Two more shots came from the top of the coach as the guard attempted to defend the stage. Rafe thought about the unprotected troopers and hoped the Indians had not picked them off.

Peering again through the small window, the Apaches were a fearsome sight. They seemed adept at firing both rifles and arrows from horseback. Rafe braced himself and fired four rapid shots at them, but with the speed of the horses and the erratic bumping of the coach no bullets hit the marauders.

"Rafe, I need more ammo," Billy yelled. Ana Teresa reached over and popped six bullets from Rafe's gunbelt and quickly handed them to Billy.

Rafe reloaded and tried to steady his breathing. Taking careful aim, he squeezed off two shots at the lead rider. The warrior fell from his horse. Peering back, Rafe saw another Indian stop near his body. Quickly he reloaded the used chambers.

"Billy, on the count of three, empty your chambers. We'll try to scare them with our firepower," Rafe told him.

A rifle report sounded and they all heard a voice from the top of the stage yell, "Got that one."

"One, two, three," Rafe counted aloud and then he and Billy let loose with the GSW double-action pistols. Shots flurried from the coach on both sides.

A few return shots came from the Apaches, but Rafe

could tell the shooters were getting out of range. Suddenly it was quiet again and a short while later they felt the coach ease up and slow down to a more normal traveling speed.

Rafe helped Ana Teresa up to the seat. He could tell she had been crying. It was almost another hour before the coach slowed and arrived at the Cienega Stage Station.

"Looks like you got hit?" the waystation worker said to the driver as they pulled into the yard.

"Yeah, them damn Paches again. Bart's been hit."

"Ah, it's a flesh wound," Bart said. "I'll just clean it up."

Opening the side door, the driver asked, "Who did all the shooting?"

"We did," Billy spoke out.

"Thank you boys. That was a close call. Apaches usually don't run this far west of the Chiricahua Mountains. I hope we don't run into more trouble before we cross into the New Mexico Territory."

"We'll be ready for them," Billy told him.

Rafe walked back to where Rayo was tied to the boot. After double checking Rayo had not been hurt in the skirmish, he pulled more ammunition from his saddlebag and his rifle from the scabbard. He put both inside the coach.

Only one of the troopers came riding into the waystation a few minutes after the coach. Rafe heard the trooper tell the driver his partner was killed in the raid. He asked for someone to go retrieve the body and take it back to the Fort in Benson.

Ana Teresa could not stop shaking. Twelve arrows were embedded in the sides of the wood coach. One stuck out of the suitcase tied to the boot. When the coach got started again, she clung to Rafe's arm and prayed for God to keep them safe.

CHAPTER 12

For four days María and Rodolfo rode along with the caravan. At night, they shared their meager provisions and María helped with the cooking for the caravan's workers and guards.

"Hey Alejandro, you should keep her to cook for us. We haven't eaten so good in a long time," one of the guards called to the wagon master. María made homemade tortillas and spicy chili with meat. The men asked for second helpings of both.

Though the heavily laden caravan moved at a slow pace, Rodolfo thought the additional travel time well worth it. By traveling with the guarded iron ore, they felt protected from *bandidos*.

On the fifth day when they arrived at the border in the late afternoon, they were passed along with the convoy with no questions asked by the border guards. Being the last day of the year, only a small crew staffed the border checkpoint. Rodolfo breathed a sigh of relief as they slowly followed the caravan into the south side of El Paso.

Pulling beside the lead team, he called to the wagon master. "Alejandro we are stopping to get supplies and then will be going to our uncle's ranch. Thank you for the hospitality."

"Nice to know you. Take care of that little one when it comes," Alejandro replied.

As Rodolfo drove through the town, Christmas decorations still hung from the gas streetlamps around the plaza. It was New Year's Eve and a special Mass was in progress at the church.

"We should go say our thanks," María said to Rodolfo. "God has been so good to us."

"It will be dark soon and we still have almost an hour before we get to the ranch. Perhaps thanking God when we get there will be enough," Rodolfo told her. María nodded knowing he was right.

Following the road north from El Paso, it was after sundown when they arrived at the ranch. As they drove into the courtyard, the family burst from the front door. When Ita and *tía* Lupe saw María's swelled belly, they cried and laughed.

María expected her brother to be there. "Where is Rafael?"

"We have not heard from him since we got the wire from Fort Yuma. I expect he will be here any day now," *tío* Jose told them. "How was your trip," he asked.

"All went well *tío*. We traveled with a caravan and the wagon master took care of us. He even fed us at times."

"Francisco, Tomás take care of the wagon," Jose called to two of his sons. The boys drove the wagon toward the corral behind the house and Rodolfo followed. María followed her aunt into the house.

"María, sit down. You look weary," her aunt said.

"No *tía*, let me help."

"No. I have plenty of help. Go cleanup and rest. I will call you for supper."

Though María wanted to stay in the kitchen and chat, she did not argue. After washing her face in a basin, she stretched out on the bed in the back room. The five long days on the bumpy trail left her back aching and uncomfortable pains in her stomach persisted for the last three days. She said nothing to Rodolfo, knowing it would only make him worry. Closing her eyes, she fell asleep.

Rodolfo walked with Tomás and Francisco to the corral behind the house and helped them strip the mules of the harnesses. Tomás made sure each mule had a large helping of grain and water. They manually pushed the wagon to the back of the barn.

"This old wagon sure is heavy," Francisco said.

Rodolfo shrugged. He knew why the wagon was exceptionally heavy, but could say nothing. Beneath the floorboards, hundreds of pounds of silver ingots lay hidden.

He was relieved they had an easy trip and were now over the border. The only remaining problem was how to engage Martín. He hated to admit the silver was stolen, knowing María's cousin would think badly of him.

Rodolfo met Martín on their last trip. It was Martín who engaged Jerry Carr to help them buy the guns and ammunition and get them across the border. Martín knew of Rodolfo and María's outlaw life in the Mexican mountains, but somehow admitting he was a thief robbing a silver mule train seemed more wicked.

Later around the supper table, the talk was lively. The family was elated about the news from the *hacienda*. Lupe's eyes widened when she heard there were around seventy *peóns* living there, many women and children.

"How do you feed everyone?" she asked.

María explained how everyone worked and shared skills. "The children go to the school every day for three hours," she told the family feeling proud of their accomplishments in Torreón. "George Summers helped with initial supplies, but sometimes there is not enough food. We need seed for next year's plantings. We are hoping Rafael will help us."

"*Sí,* I am sure he will help. It was through his generosity we were able to get this ranch back and buy the cattle we needed. He is a good man," Jose said and he crossed himself adding a blessing.

In Rodolfo's mind, asking Rafael for help to sell the silver made his stomach churn. Telling Martín about the silver heist was one thing, telling Rafael was another. Rafael would not be pleased Rodolfo put his sister in such danger.

Toward the end of the dinner, Jose quieted the family. "It is almost the new year," he said. "We must give thanks to God for all he has done to help us this past year." Everyone around the table bowed their heads and Jose said a prayer of thanks.

"Amen," everyone repeated.

It was getting late. Ita's youngest child was already asleep on her shoulder. Her other young son was having trouble keeping his eyes open. María was also feeling the long days on the road and the weariness in her bones.

"Rodolfo I'm tired," she said. "Stay and enjoy the

evening."

Rodolfo stood and gave her a kiss on her cheek. "Goodnight my love. Are you sure you are all right?"

"Yes, I'm just tired."

The celebrating continued until well after midnight. Rodolfo wanted to talk to Martín about the silver, but needed to talk to him alone. His feelings about the silver waffled. He was glad to have the stolen silver out of Mexico, but it still felt like a noose around his neck. Perhaps he should just bury it somewhere until a good plan could be worked out.

However, the provisions and money left by George Summers were only keeping the people barely fed. Unfortunately when *don* Bernardo died, vandals took almost everything. In the midst of their fervor they damaged and destroyed many of the houses and the corrals. Only one young mare was found running alone in the hills. Rebuilding the *hacienda* into a viable ranch was a monumental task.

The last time he and María came to El Paso, they left thirteen *bandidos*. A little less than one year later, sixty-eight people waited for their return. *Peóns* heard about their efforts and came looking for a better life. Rodolfo was not sure how much better it was, yet. The people still had meager rations and roofs on most of the *jacals* leaked when it rained. When he complained María always reminded him the people were free. "You cannot put a price on freedom," she would always tell him.

María was hoping her brother could add more funds to help them. Rodolfo thought perhaps Rafael could use the silver ingots to repay the debt. However, it seemed inappropriate to pay a debt with stolen silver.

After midnight, Jose brought out the tequila and they toasted the New Year. "Salud, and bless us in coming year," Jose said.

It was the first of January 1873 and Rodolfo was twenty-five years old. In previous years the change of the years meant little to him. When he was a *peón*, life dragged along from day to day with little change. When he was an outlaw, every day brought a new a dilemma or strife. Now by the grace of God and the generosity of Rafael, he and María owned the large Reyes *hacienda*. This year was going to be a good year. It was the year he was going to become a father.

CHAPTER 13

María and Rodolfo spent the first day of the New Year attending church with the family. It was a Holy Day of Obligation, a Mass dedicated to the Virgin Mary on the eight day of the birth of Jesus. Padre Serrano gave the Mass honoring the Mother of Christ.

After the Mass the padre greeted the family. He hugged the younger children and then recognized María. "*María, mija.* You have returned to us. Your uncle told me you went to Mexico."

"*Sí Padre.* This is my husband, Rodolfo."

Rodolfo bowed slightly and took the padre's extended hand. Padre Serrano could not believe the change in María. The last time he saw her she was sad and pessimistic. The young woman standing in front of him holding the man's arm was radiant. The padre blessed them and moved on.

After Mass, the family gathered around the large dining room table to celebrate. The family was thirteen since the addition of Ita and Martín's third child. Lupe served tamales made with spicy meat covered in corn *masa* and wrapped in cornhusks. Rodolfo had not eaten tamales since his youth when his mother made them for the family's Christmas dinner.

Lupe's were spicy and tender. Rodolfo added extra of the rich red chili sauce over the tamales to add even more spice. Along with the tamales, she served beans and a sweet bread pudding. Rodolfo ate second helpings of everything, praising Lupe on the meal.

After supper Rodolfo invited Martín to take a walk. "Let's walk off some of this food, then perhaps we shall come and have another helping," Rodolfo teased Lupe. She beamed at his compliments.

As Martín and Rodolfo walked away from the house, Rodolfo mustered the courage to discuss the silver. "Martín, I want to tell you something, but you cannot tell anyone, especially Rafael."

"What is so important that I cannot tell anyone?" Martín replied warily. Though he liked Rodolfo and now he and María were expecting a child, the last time they were in El Paso they wanted to buy guns. It put Martín in a very difficult position. At that time they were living like outlaws, now Rafael had given them the Reyes *hacienda* and they were living on the *hacienda* as farmers and ranchers.

"We have fifteen silver ingots we want to sell here in El Paso before we leave. Will you talk with your friend Jerry Carr to see if he will sell them for us?" Rodolfo just came out and said it. Relief swept over him after exposing the secret of the silver.

"What? Where did you get that much silver?" Martín asked shaking his head in disbelief.

"You do not want to know. We need horses, cattle, and many supplies at the *hacienda*. There are over sixty of us now. It is many mouths to feed everyday and the crops will not be harvested until summer."

"You stole it!" Martín accused him in a whisper.

"Yes, but now I wish I had never done it. Believe me it was much easier stealing the silver than it will be selling it, and one of my good men died. The silver was buried in Torreón, useless to our needs. I brought it across the border hoping . . . " Rodolfo let the sentence hang between them. He could tell Martín was angry.

"I cannot get involved with this. If I get caught, it is the end of me and my family here in El Paso. Talking to Jerry Carr about the guns was not right either. I had to keep it a secret from Ita and it is not our way," he huffed crossing his arms.

"I understand. I did not tell María I hid the silver in a secret compartment in the wagon, because it was dangerous for us to bring the silver across the border. Can you get a message to Jerry Carr? I will meet with him. You do not need to get involved. We are desperate for money to get the *hacienda* going."

Martín looked hard at Rodolfo. He had compassion for their circumstances. "Yes, I will do that much for you, but be warned, Jerry runs with a dangerous crowd. If anything happens, you are on your own. I will not be able to help," he warned him.

Later in their small room, Rodolfo decided he needed to tell María about the silver. She would want to know what Martín said about Jerry Carr. She had been the one who trusted Jerry to get them the guns and had given him her stash of silver and gold coins. Jerry had not swindled them. He expected she would agree with his decision to bring the silver.

He turned to her. *"Querida,* I need to tell you something."

"What my love?" she said dreamily. Sharing New Years with her uncle's family and knowing Rafael would probably be here soon left her feeling elated. The pains in her belly had subsided, probably just stress from the wagon trip, and the baby was kicking normally again.

Her pregnancy had awakened her heart to her other two children, Antonio and Alicia. They were living in Santa Fe with her mother, their grandmother. It had been more than a year since she saw them. Antonio would be in school and Alicia four years old. She was sure they were well tended and happy living at George Summers' large home with proper shoes and warm clothes. The Summers graciously took them in with open arms, like family.

It seemed another life. She had been broken and angry. *Don* Bernardo fathered her children, using her as his mistress and treating her like a *puta*. She was only fifteen when he first raped her and she became pregnant with Antonio. *Don* Bernardo was the *haciendero,* she a *peón*. It was common for the master to abuse and mistreat the peasants. In the years after Rafael shot *don* Bernardo leaving him crippled, he forced her to tend to all of his needs including his sexual desires.

Even though *don* Bernardo often treated her and the children with some form of kindness, her eyes were opened after she fell in love with Rodolfo. His fight to be free of servitude and oppression from the ruling upper class of Mexico's *hacienderos* became her fight. Rodolfo loved all of her – her mind, body, and soul. Rodolfo awakened both her sexual passion as well as the passion for helping peasants obtain a life worth living.

Almost seventy people now lived at the *hacienda* in Torreón. The people worked together sharing everything. She watched them blossom as she had, learning to make their own decisions about a future. She and Rodolfo worked side by side as equals with the rest who shared their vision. They never took more than their fair share, sometimes taking less.

She only wished her mother and the two children living in Santa Fe could be here to share these days with her. She was toying with the idea of suggesting they go north for a visit, even though the weather was cold and snowy.

Rodolfo interrupted her thoughts. "I hid the silver in a compartment under the wagon and brought it here with us. I had to get it out of Mexico," Rodolfo admitted. At first his words did not register. They had talked about the silver and had agreed to leave it buried in Torreón.

"You did what!" she exclaimed.

"The silver is hidden in the wagon. Please do not be angry. I did not want you to worry on the trip. It was lucky we came up on the caravan with the guards. It made the trip safer."

"You took a huge chance with our lives and our baby's life," María fumed. The silver had been their only disagreement. She had not wanted him to go to Zacatecas in the first place. He promised her they were only checking out the situation. Instead, he and three of their band of outlaws stole fifteen ingots of silver. It was reckless and dangerous. Pepe was killed.

The silver ingots were useless to them in Mexico. Each ingot was marked with the insignia of the mine and if ever located would mean certain prison or even death.

"I wish you had never gone to Zacatecas. You put us all in danger. Now you brought this scourge here to my uncle's house. What were you thinking?"

"Lo siento querida," he told her he was sorry. "I did it only for the people. They need to eat. We need so many supplies at the *hacienda.*"

"Dejame sola," she grumbled telling him to let her be and turned her back to him in a huff. He knew she was angry and he understood. Hopefully tomorrow, she would think differently about it.

The following morning, María was out of bed before Rodolfo woke. When he walked into the kitchen and said good morning, he could tell she was still mad. After downing a cup of coffee and scrambled eggs, he walked outside. He and María argued occasionally, but never had they not spoken and not gone to bed in each other's arms.

"Mierda, soy un idiota" he cursed himself as an idiot.

CHAPTER 14

"We should be in El Paso by this evening," the man riding shotgun told the weary passengers when the coach was changing horses at Prado Verde waystation. Rafe and Ana Teresa had been on the stage for almost two weeks, celebrating Christmas in Tucson and the New Year at a stage stop along the way. Both Rudy Cannon and Olivia Martinez departed at the stop in Tucson six days ago, so the days since Tucson were boring and long, though they had no more trouble or Indian attacks. Arriving in El Paso would be a huge relief.

Billy was sitting beside Ana Teresa leaning against the side of the coach snoring softly. Rafe paid for Billy's ticket through to El Paso. Ana Teresa told him she had forgiven Billy for his attack and actually felt sorry for him. He agreed, but warned her Billy had no money and might revert to his desperate ways.

The late afternoon sun blazed through the right side windows as the coach rumbled along the rutted path. Ana Teresa dozed on Rafe's shoulder. The two businessmen who sold ladies dresses sat across from them. In some ways it reminded Rafe of his frequent trips to sell GSW guns. He and George Summers had many times travelled from town to town demonstrating and selling the double-action firearms.

George Summers invented the GSW brand of double-action about eight years ago with his partner Frank. They were traveling on a sales trip the day Indians attacked their small wagon east of El Paso. Rafe happened upon George's overturned wagon the following day.

Closing his eyes Rafe remembered that day. Frank was dead, George near death with an arrow in his leg. After burying Frank, Rafe treated George's wound and took him to El Paso. Rafe was seventeen then, riding Rayo after fleeing Mexico. That one day changed Rafe's life forever. No doubt it was God's hand that led him to the very spot.

Rafe now considered George his adopted father and George's family, his family.

A few hours later, Rafe could tell they were getting close to the city. More riders and wagons plied the road. He heard the driver greet another coach heading north.

"Ana Teresa, wake up. We are getting near El Paso," Rafe whispered to her and moved his shoulder a bit.

Opening her eyes, she smiled at him. "I can't wait to have a hot bath and a good meal and most of all a soft bed," she whispered in his ear. She covered his hand with her gloved hand and squeezed.

"Yes, my love. It won't be long now," he said and gave her a big smile.

As a courtesy, the coach stopped in front of the Hotel Stratton, since everyone on the coach was staying there. Billy jumped out and helped the shotgun rider unload the passenger's luggage off the coach while Rafe tethered Rayo to the rail in front of the hotel. He took Ana Teresa's hand helping her up the steps and into the hotel lobby.

"Mister Ortega, good to see you again sir, welcome," Henry the clerk behind the desk greeted him. Rafe was not surprised Henry remembered him since he and George Summers frequented the hotel on all their trips to El Paso. Rafe had also been to El Paso alone several times on business.

"Thank you, Henry. I need two rooms. Your best," he said. He and Ana Teresa had been traveling as husband and wife over the course of the long stagecoach journey. It seemed easier and more appropriate. No one questioned it, but here in El Paso, news of their wedding would be known and he wanted no gossip to taint them.

"Henry, this is my fiancée, Ana Teresa de Soto. Please have a bath prepared for her and have our belongings taken to our rooms," he requested.

"Of course, Mister Ortega. Pleased to meet you miss," the clerk said.

Rafe signed their names on the hotel registry. On all of his past trips to El Paso, he was Rafael Ortega. He was

Rafael Reyes now and after he signed in, he turned the book toward the clerk. "I am Rafael Reyes de Estrada now." Though the clerk looked surprised, Rafe was not sure how to explain the change.

Billy was standing near the door with their bags. He looked uncomfortable in the elegance of the hotel's furnishings.

"You go ahead my dear. I'll take Rayo and Billy to the livery. I have an idea." Rafe kissed her cheek.

"Billy, come with me," Rafe said walking to the doorway.

Rafe walked out, unwound Rayo's reins from the rail and headed down the street with Billy tagging along beside him. Billy prided himself as a blacksmith and he needed a job. As they walked into the livery, Rafe called out. "Charlie! Hey Charlie are you here?"

"Yes sah, here I is." The old black livery man shuffled out from behind one of the stalls. "Ah be danged but if it ain't my yung pistolero friend frum Sante Fey. How yew doin Rafe?" he stuck out his hand.

"I'm doing just fine Charlie, how about you?"

"Cain't complain fo an ole black livry man," he replied and gave out a big belly laugh. "Yew here on bidnezz?" he asked.

"No not this time Charlie. I'm getting married."

"Married! Well I'll be a sow's ear. She be a lucky lady."

"No I think I'm the lucky one, Charlie. I need you to take care of my horse. We've been on a great adventure and he needs rest and good feeding," Rafe told him and handed him the reins.

Charlie took the reins and stroked the horse's face. "Mighty fine hoss, boy. Like I's axed yew last time I sees yew, yew shur yew dun wanna sell im to me?" he asked and again laughed about it.

"You know I won't Charlie but I'll tell you what my friend. Rayo has sired many Appaloosa foals. Next time I come to El Paso, I'll bring one of them and sell it to you," Rafe promised.

"Yes sah that would be mighty fine, mighty fine. Dun yew worry none bout yer hoss. Yew knows I take good care of im. Who be dat man?" Charlie asked about Billy seeing him standing behind Rafe.

"This is my friend, Billy Swanson. Billy needs a job and he's a right good blacksmith. Do you need help around here?" Rafe asked.

Charlie's dark black eyes appraised Billy. "He shur is a big feller. I shur cud use im fer sum heavy work round here. I cain't pay yew much, but I kin give yew vittles and a place to lay yer head to start. What yew say?" Charlie stuck out his hand crushing Billy's just to let him know he was the boss.

"I can do whatever you need done and I can start with this Appaloosa," Billy said taking Rayo's reins.

"Shur nuff, glad to knows yew Billy."

Rafe knew Charlie was a good man. If Billy worked well, old Charlie would be good to his word. Sticking out his hand, Charlie took it and pumped it hard. "Bring the missus by. I likes to meet her."

"Don't worry, you will. I'll be needing a buggy tomorrow. Can you get one hitched up and brought to the hotel in the morning?" Rafe asked.

"Shur thing," Charlie replied. Rafe turned and walked out of the livery heading back to the hotel. He was relieved Billy had a place to stay and a job. Hopefully Billy would make good with it.

Billy walked Rayo back to a stall and stripped the saddle. Picking up a brush, he started at Rayo's neck brushing down his flanks. He could not believe his good luck. He was in Texas, out of the reach of the Army for now or so he thought. His belly was full and he had a job. Rafe's generosity amazed him. By rights, Rafe should have shot him dead that day at the waystation east of Fort Yuma. Instead, he treated him with kindness and Billy could not understand why. For Billy, Rafe's actions hit him deep in his soul. He owed the young Mexican big time and hoped he could repay the debt someday.

Not many times in Billy's life had luck or kindness shined on him. Usually it was the other way around. His mother died when he was ten after the birth of his sister. It still hurt awful bad. He did not blame his father for going to the drink after that. Billy was the oldest and tried his best to mother and father the youngsters. Some days his father would come home blinded by the whiskey and start beating on his younger brother, Sam. Billy was big for his age and would intervene, more than once knocking his drunken father down.

When he was fourteen his grandfather and grandmother must have realized his father's anguish had turned him into a drunk. Grandmother helped with the younger girls. Sam was good in school and his grandparents encouraged him. Billy received a letter some years ago that Sam had finished medical school and was a doctor.

His grandfather took Billy to work with him in his blacksmith shop. Billy took to the work finding it interesting and easy. His big frame made pounding the metal effortless. He loved the way metal could be shaped and he still did.

At first when the Civil War started, Michigan sent some volunteers. Everyone thought the war would be over quickly. Two years later Billy was drafted into Lincoln's Army. It just did not seem right he was now on the run because of some wet behind the ears lieutenant.

Rayo kicked his back foot when Billy brushed his underbelly. Billy was not sure if the spirited horse was happy or upset. Taking a gentler touch Billy brushed Rayo's rump. While he brushed he watched Charlie work. Physically the old man looked bent and he shuffled about the livery in a slow way, though judging by his handshake and the way he lifted hay bales Charlie was stronger than he looked.

CHAPTER 15

Ana Teresa lounged in the hot water of the bath. It was the first luxurious bath she had for several weeks. Scrubbing off the dirt and grime from the many stagecoach hours, she then washed her hair.

Traveling as husband and wife on the long trip proved difficult for both of them. At most of the stage stops, sleeping arrangements were communal. Several of the stops had private rooms and of course they shared one bed. She loved falling asleep in Rafael's arms and found herself longing for his touch.

She had loved Rafe since last spring, believed he was lost to her, and then they found each other again. Had it not been for the Los Angeles vigilantes, they would already be married. As she ran the soap over her breasts, her sexual awareness heightened. It was the same feeling as when Rafe held her in the small beds, wrapping his arms around her tight. He usually slept shirtless. Often she ran her hands on his chest or pressed her breasts tight up against his side.

If he had pressed, she would have given herself freely to him with abandon. He kept them in control telling her they needed to be right with God since her parents would disapprove. Her brain knew he was right, but her body craved him.

Rafe promised they would be married here in El Paso. It was already almost dark out and she knew they would not be riding to the mission tonight. She ran the soap between her legs and around her groin. A small groan escaped her lips.

Rafe strode down the boardwalk toward the Hotel Stratton humming a tune. They were finally in El Paso and his future bride was on the second floor having a well-deserved bath. The last two weeks of pretending to be man and wife and yet keeping virtuous had luckily been helped by the awkward sleeping arrangements at most of the stage stops. Had they more privacy, Rafe doubted either of them could have waited.

In reality before their adventure, he only knew Ana Teresa in short exchanges during parties, several riding excursions, and dinners at the de Soto *hacienda*. He fell in love with her dancing the Fandango at the de Soto Easter fiesta. Her golden brown eyes melted his heart.

Now he was more sure than ever. Though raised in an aristocratic Spanish family, Ana Teresa embodied his American ideals. She looked forward and not back, embracing what would be the spirit of the new American southwest. Her father's loss of their Spanish Land Grant in Rancho Simi birthed a new and open-minded understanding of reality. She no longer believed in the superiority of the Spanish ruling class.

Ana Teresa told him Diego de la Torre tried to rape her near the stream one day when she was riding alone. She fought him off and escaped, but knew she could not tell her family. Men like Diego, an elite Spanish *caballero,* would always be believed over a woman. Rafe thought it was a good thing Diego's horse killed him the day they fought on the plaza in Santa Fe. Now knowing the truth, he would be determined to return to Santa Fe and kill the *desgraciado caballero* in cold blood, if he was still alive.

When he reached the hotel, Rafe jumped the four front steps two by two and strode to the front desk.

"I'll be needing my bath now," he told the desk clerk.

"Yes sir. I believe the young lady has just finished. I will send up more hot water directly."

"Much obliged," Rafe responded.

Taking the stairs in leaps, he put his key into the door of room twelve at the end of the hall and opened it. It was not a room he had ever been assigned on his many stays. It was large and had windows on two sides. The large four-poster bed was layered in stuffed quilts and four pillows. On the far wall, a large armoire stood open with his satchel sitting in front of it. Rafe thought it would make a perfect room to consummate their vows.

Bathing and shaving, Rafe dressed quickly and knocked on Ana Teresa's door. "Are you dressed?" he asked as she opened it.

She was a vision of loveliness in a light green dress. Her freshly washed hair was still damp and shining in the light. He could not resist but to pull her close and kiss her. She pulled him into her room and out of the hallway.

Rafe found himself lost in her kisses. Alone in her room, all he wanted was to feel her naked body next to his. He kissed her cheeks and worked to her neck. Her arms encircled him and they clung to each other.

His heart was full and his body ached for this woman in his arms. The smell of her freshly shampooed hair filled his nostrils with a light lavender scent. His mouth found hers and he parted her lips with his tongue, searching for hers. She eagerly returned his kisses with a fervor matching his. Her breasts were pressed against his chest.

Every part of him ached for the sensual release of their bodies being intertwined. He knew she would not deny him.

"Rafael, I love you so much," she said softly near his ear.

His heart soared at her words. He loved her fiercely and she loved him in return in spite of his humble origin. This was the woman he wanted to be the mother of his children, the woman standing by his side, and the woman who would grow old with him. His body hungered after her with the fire of pure passion. His soul knew it was wrong. He wanted no regret to ever come between them.

Tenderly he broke their embrace and held her by the shoulders. "We have waited to be married in the sight of God. We must wait just until tomorrow. We will go to the mission in the morning and ask Padre Serrano to marry us. You will thank me someday."

Rafe led the way downstairs to the restaurant off the lobby. When he and Ana Teresa finished dinner, he walked her upstairs to her room and kissed her on the cheek goodnight.

In the morning, the buggy stood waiting for them in front of the hotel. Snapping the reins Rafe headed the buggy down the road and then on a road heading north out of town. Seven years ago, the padre at *la Misión de Socorro* had saved his life. Padre Serrano and the brothers at the mission nursed him back to health and hid him from Roy and Eldon Reynolds and their mean spirited father, Henry Reynolds. The Reynolds had put a price on his head after Rafe cut off part of Eldon's ear in a fight.

Rafe was shot in the shoulder and probably would have died without the padre's help. Rafe repaid the padre a number of years ago with money to fund the mission school, but some debts never die. He was elated it would be Padre Serrano, who would hear their marriage vows.

"You will love the padre," he told Ana Teresa. "Perhaps *doña* Chana will make us a feast."

Ana Teresa snuggled against him. Her long brown hair was flowing with the movement of the buggy. It had been such a long trip to El Paso waiting and wanting Rafael so much. She smoothed her dress against the wind and prayed for a short ride.

As Rafe drove the buggy into the courtyard of the mission, a brother in a brown robe walked down the front steps. Rafe jumped to the ground and strode to meet him.

"Buenos días, soy Rafael Ortega de Estrada. Estoy buscando al Padre Serrano," Rafe greeted him and told the brother he came to see the padre.

"You are Rafael? You are the one who gave the mission so much. I am new here, but the brothers and the padre talk about you all the time and give thanks daily," the brother replied. Turning quickly the brother ran back into the mission yelling loudly for everyone to come outside.

In a few minutes, brown-robed monks surrounded them. Rafe found it amusing the normally quiet and reserved monks were all talking and laughing at once. Padre Serrano walked down the front steps and wrapped Rafe in a huge *abrazo*. They hugged and the padre said, *"Bienvenido mi hijo.* We are overjoyed you have returned to us," the padre said calling Rafe, my son, as he always did.

"Padre, this is Ana Teresa de Soto. We came to be married."

The padre looked at the beautiful *señorita* taking her

gloved hand. *"Bienvenido señorita.* So you wish to marry this *pistolero?"* he asked with a twinkle in his eye.

"Sí padre, very much."

"Come to my office," the padre said wrapping and arm around each of them. "Tell *doña* Chana to prepare us a feast," he told one of the brothers.

After the padre seated them in his office he asked each of them, "What has brought you to this decision to marry?" Though the padre knew Rafael's heart was pure, he was determined to perform his priestly duties. He recognized Ana Teresa as a well-bred *señorita.*

"You are here alone with this man. Where is your family *mi hija.* Do you have permission from you father for this marriage?"

Rafe responded, "Her parents are in Spain, Padre. They lost their land grant in California and have gone to Spain to locate their family documents. You know her father would never give us permission. She is *Californio* and you know I am *mestizo."*

Ana Teresa and Rafe held hands tightly. Rafe was sure Padre Serrano would not require permission knowing Rafe's past.

"Rafael is correct. My father would never allow this union, but I do not believe in the Spanish caste system anymore. Rafael is a better man than most *caballeros.* I want to marry him Padre, with all my heart," Ana Teresa said.

"I see," the padre responded. "You are of age and I can see you are in love, though I fear you must reconsider marrying in such a way. You would be married in the sight of God, but you need to have family to witness your vows. Only then will you be able to move forward with your lives."

He then turned to Rafe. "Have you been to your uncle's ranch? Your sister and her husband and the family came to Mass on New Year's Day. They mentioned you were coming to El Paso, but nothing about a wedding. Why have they not come with you to witness the marriage?"

Rafe realized in their haste to be married today, he overlooked the obvious. His aunt, uncle, and their family lived only miles from the mission. María and Rodolfo had arrived from Torreón. If Ana Teresa had no family, at least he had family to witness the vows. He also needed the thirteen gold coins for presentation to Ana Teresa. The coins represented Jesus and his twelve apostles and his willingness to provide for his new bride. Symbolically, the coins reinforced the groom's love and admiration. It was a very important part of any Hispanic Catholic wedding. He had the coins ready in Los Angeles. Now he only had eight in his pocket.

He turned toward Ana Teresa. "The padre is right. We have waited to make this marriage acceptable to both God and society. We must wait until my family can attend." He thought she was going to start crying at his words. Instead, she nodded in agreement.

"*Bueno*. Come eat with the brothers before you ride to your uncle's ranch. *Doña* Chana is expecting you," the padre invited them to stay.

CHAPTER 16

The meal served by *doña* Chana did not disappoint. The brothers talked avidly during the meal about the mission's school. Forty-three children came to the school daily. Rafe knew without explanation the children were of Mexican origin from the surrounding small ranches and children of the local miners. These were young minds, who like their fathers and uncles before them, would not have the opportunity to learn to read and write except at the mission. It was as it had been in Mexico when Rafe was a boy. The children of peasants only learned life skills and were not educated in reading and numbers.

The brothers accredited the school's success to the money Rafe donated. Rafe had repaid the brothers kindness to him with several thousand dollars. The brothers used the money well. Padre Serrano begged Rafe to tour the classrooms.

"We need to go to my uncle's house and see the family," Rafe said. "I promise we will come and see the school soon."

As Rafe helped Ana Teresa up and into the buggy, Padre Serrano put a hand on Rafe's shoulder. "Send me a message when you want to have the wedding."

"*Gracias Padre*. I hope it will be tomorrow." The padre's face broke into a grin and he patted Rafe on the shoulder.

Jumping up on the buggy seat, he snapped the reins and the buggy lurched forward down the lane. Rafe headed northeast toward his uncle's ranch.

"Padre Serrano and the brothers are wonderful," Ana Teresa said to him. It made her proud to hear the brothers talk about Rafael. According to the brothers, God's hand reached them through Rafael to help them with the school.

"They said you gave them money to start the school several years ago. Was the money from your horses?" she asked.

"No, the money was a gift." Rafe had told Ana Teresa about Chiwiwi, his first love, but it was difficult to discuss that part of his life with her. "I saved Chief Letoc's only son and heir from a flash flood at the Isleta pueblo. Letoc gave me rolls of Spanish gold coins, which the tribe had from long ago. I used some of the money to help the mission and some to buy my *tío* Jose's ranch."

"It was Chiwiwi's tribe?" Ana Teresa asked.

"Yes. Chief Letoc was her uncle and it is how I met her."

Instinctively Ana Teresa put her hand over Rafe's. He had told her how he loved the young Indian girl and how Carlos' brother killed her. She accepted a piece of Rafe's heart would always be reserved for his first love.

"Padre Serrano said your sister María and Rodolfo are at your uncle's ranch. I can't wait to meet them," she said changing the subject.

"Yes I can't wait to see them myself. We will be there soon."

Rafe urged the horse a bit faster. His sister had been through hell, but now was married to his boyhood friend, Rodolfo Guerrero. He wanted to hear the news on how they were faring at the *hacienda* he gave them.

"It's curious how life works. I hated and wanted to kill *don* Bernardo for raping María. Now I own all that belonged to him including his name, because he raped my mother. Even you will carry his name once we are married and our children will be Reyes," Rafe said.

"How horrible for your mother being raped and then knowing the same man raped her daughter. It is very sad."

She knew Rafael had been born in Mexico as a *peón*, a peasant in servitude to *don* Bernardo. It was a world foreign to her in many ways. She grew up in privilege and wished she better understood parts of his life that still seemed murky to her.

"Such is the life for *mestizos* and *Indios* in Mexico. *Peóns* have few options. The *hacienderos* own the land and keep the *peóns* in servitude. My sister and Rodolfo were fighting for the freedom of *peóns*. They were living as *bandidos*. Rodolfo led a band of *peóns* and they robbed from *hacienderos* in order to live. It was why my mother finally told me the truth, so I could inherit the *hacienda*. My mother was afraid María and Rodolfo would be killed or taken to prison," Rafe attempted to explain life as a *peón*.

"What do you mean *bandidos?* Was your sister doing that?" Ana Teresa asked.

"Yes, but they have stopped stealing and are living on the *hacienda* I inherited from *don* Bernardo. They are now responsible for running it. My mother feared for their safety. It is the reason she told me what *don* Bernardo did to her and of my true birthright. Please don't think badly of them. Life is very hard in Mexico for *peóns."*

"I won't. You know it is hard for me to understand. All I know is the dreadful violation *don* Bernardo did to your mother had only one blessing. I now have you," Ana Teresa squeezed his hand harder.

"Yes. We can forget about all this history. You and I will start a new life in Santa Fe," Rafe told her.

It was shortly after noon when Rafe drove the buggy to the front of his uncle Jose's house. Martín was the first to greet them, *"Hola Rafael."* He grabbed Rafe in an *abrazo*. The rest of the family flooded from the house and gathered around them. One by one they hugged Rafe and the younger children looked shyly at Ana Teresa.

"Everyone, I present to you my future wife, Ana Teresa de Soto," Rafe said proudly.

María hugged Ana Teresa, then everyone else followed, greeting her and welcoming her to the family. Rafe had not seen his sister since she left Santa Fe for El Paso, almost a year ago. He could not believe how healthy and cheerful she appeared and she was showing a pregnancy. Her sparkling eyes reminded Rafe of the young girl he knew before *don* Bernardo raped her. It brought a smile to his face seeing her happy again.

Ana Teresa was overwhelmed with all the attention. The young children tugged at her and pulled her by the hand toward the house. Rafael's family was warm and welcoming. She found his aunt delightful. She noticed

Rodolfo hung back a bit, only shaking hands with Rafe and shaking her hand politely.

Rafe's aunt Lupe shooed the young children away. "Come, my dear. We are overjoyed to meet you. Rafe did not wire us of your upcoming wedding so this is a wonderful surprise. Come, I will make us coffee."

The afternoon was chaotic. Ana Teresa did her best to remember their names. She often confused the younger children as they darted and played. It did not matter as they surrounded her with joy and love and she was happy to be so warmly accepted.

"When is the wedding?" *tía* Lupe asked.

"Padre Serrano said as soon as the family can come."

Lupe made a thoughtful face. "I need to get the boys new suits and Olivia has outgrown her shoes, and I will need to buy food for the feast. We can go to town tomorrow and go shopping."

Ana Teresa groaned internally. It seemed as if something was always usurping their marriage. "I'm sure whatever they wore to church last Sunday will be fine. Tomorrow is Saturday and we could send word to the padre we can come in the afternoon," she suggested.

"There, there, my dear. It will only make Rafael more fervent to wait a few days," Lupe said. Ana Teresa wanted to laugh, but did not want to appear rude. All she and Rafael had been doing was waiting.

"If we can find the proper clothes on Saturday, then perhaps Monday or Tuesday. Would you like another cup of coffee?" Lupe said oblivious to Ana Teresa's disappointment.

Jose and Rafe sat talking in the living room. "How long will you be staying?" Jose asked.

"Until there is a clearing in the weather, then we plan to go to Santa Fe. At the hotel, they told me the roads to Albuquerque are icy and treacherous. They say it is worse to the north on the road to Santa Fe. Meanwhile I want to enjoy our stay with everyone as long as we can," Rafe answered.

"Why don't you come and stay with us," Jose asked Rafe. "The boys can sleep in the barn."

"I appreciate your offer *tío,* but Ana Teresa and I will need time alone."

After supper with the family, Rafe and Ana Teresa headed back to the hotel before dark. Stopping at the livery, Rafe told Billy they would not need the buggy in the morning.

On the following morning, Rafe and Ana Teresa met the family in town. Ita and María chose new clothes for the children and shoes for Olivia. She was thirteen and a budding young woman now. She reminded Rafe of the Summers' girls, Lolo and Lizzy, at that age.

Rafe told Ana Teresa to do some additional shopping. She had only packed a small suitcase when they left Los Angeles. She bought two more dresses and a warm sweater.

While the women were in town shopping, Martín had a chance to talk to Rodolfo. Martín contacted his friend Jerry Carr and set up a meeting with him for María and Rodolfo to discuss the silver.

"He'll meet you Sunday afternoon in a wooded area with large cottonwood trees near the Rio Grande," Martín told Rodolfo.

"Does he speak Spanish?" Rodolfo fretted he would not be able to communicate with the Anglo without Martín.

"Jerry was raised here in El Paso. He speaks enough Spanish. When we were kids, I taught Jerry Spanish and he taught me English. Remember what I told you though, he can run with some very bad characters. You must be careful not to cross him. I have done all I will do," Martín finished with a warning.

CHAPTER 17

Saturday evening Charlie paid Desperate Billy his first weekly pay.

"Tis only fer da three days werk yews gives me, so tain't much," Charlie told him.

"Mighty happy," Billy replied. He liked working along with Charlie. The old black man was easy going and made pretty good grub. They fixed a spot in the loft with soft straw and several blankets where Billy slept at night. Billy helped with the heavy work and any blacksmithing that came in.

"Where's the best saloon in this here town?" Billy asked.

"Well, deys be da Gem. Dey got em a dancin show and the saloon girls are uppty. Word in town heah the Gem draws a lot of card cheats. Then deys be Lilli Jean's. It's not far over ta thatta way. Lilli's be an okay place."

"Does she got gals?" Billy asked.

Charlie looked at Billy knowing he meant whores. "Shur nuff. Yews mightta go git a bath down in Chinee town afor yews gos to Lilli's. She'da give yews one of her better girls iffn yews do."

"Thanks Charlie," Billy said determined to get himself a girl tonight. It had been too long since Billy had himself a woman and the money jingling in his pocket was calling his name.

About an hour later, Billy Swanson walked through the batwing doors at Lilli Jean's Saloon. It was Saturday night and dusty cowboys lined the bar. Cowboys surrounded a Faro table near the front of the room. Poker games were playing on three other tables.

Billy walked to the bar and ordered a beer. The sign said beer was a nickel, whiskey fifteen cents. He wanted a whiskey, but settled for the beer. He was not sure how much a poke was going to cost him.

He paid for the beer and turned sideways to enjoy the

action. A man sat at a piano near the back plinking out a tinny tune. Billy scanned the girls working the floor. A cowboy held a young girl tightly in his grasp on the small area near the piano. Her blond hair was curled up on her head. Billy liked blondes better than redheads. As the couple turned, Billy saw the girl was not all that pretty and not young either.

Another dark haired girl was moving between the poker tables checking drinks and making small talk. She wore a blue ruffled dress draped over lacy white underskirts. Her stocking covered legs ended at high top shoes. Billy thought she was pretty. One of the poker players pulled her into his lap and tried to kiss her. She slapped him and sauntered away. The other players laughed and grinned.

"You be new round here," a woman said as she walked up toward Billy. The woman was well dressed, older, and had an air of authority. She made a motion and the bartender immediately filled another glass with beer and sat it in front of Billy.

"Billy Swanson, ma'am. I hail from Michigan."

"You're a long way from home," she replied. Lilli could tell the big hunk of a man was not a cowboy.

"Well I've been around some."

"I'm Lilli Jean. This here's my place. So what have you been around doing?" Lilli always liked to size up new customers. She ran an honest place and tried to ward off trouble before it started.

"I'm a blacksmith, ma'am. I just started working for Charlie in the livery."

"Charlie's a good man. You treat him right, he'll treat you right." Lilli relaxed knowing Charlie Hastings was a good judge of character. If Charlie approved of this Billy Swanson, then Lilli had no concerns.

"So what are you looking for? A poker game or you just drinking for awhile?"

"I appreciate the beer, ma'am. I was kinda hoping to get me a girl to talk to, you know upstairs talk." Lilli thought the man polite. He called her ma'am and seemed a bit embarrassed to ask outright for a whore. He was clean and freshly shaven.

"Well I have several girls who could talk to you upstairs," Lilli replied. "Just what kinda gal you looking for? I got blondes, brunettes, darkies, Mescans, and one Chinese gal. What's your pleasure?"

Billy was not picky, especially not tonight. He was horny as hell and the beer was fueling his needs. "I only got two dollars. I know it's not much. What can that get me?"

Lilli usually wanted five dollars for any of her girls, however it was winter and business was slow. The cowboys on the cattle drives were not on the move.

"I'll tell you what. I'll give you credit."

"Credit, what's that?"

"Well you give me your two dollars. I'll loan you another two dollars for a nice girl tonight. You'll owe me the two dollars from next week's pay. I'll even throw in another beer afterwards on the house."

"That's a deal," Billy said.

"Look around and take your pick of the girls. When you decide you let me know."

"I want that one over there. That one in the blue ruffled dress," Billy blurted out. He did not need time to think about it. The dark haired girl in the blue dress already caught his eye.

"Cathy," Lilli Jean called out to the young woman. As she walked up, Billy noticed her blue eyes, about the color of her dress.

"Cathy, this here's Billy Swanson. He's a blacksmith working down at Hastings Livery. He's looking to go upstairs and do some talking."

Lilli strolled off and Cathy moved up beside Billy at the bar. "Hello Billy," she said. He smelled clean and was freshly shaven. His lips curved a bit crooked when he smiled.

"Howdy ma'am. You sure are pretty."

"Where are you from Billy?"

"Michigan. It's not like here. We got big lakes up there. I'm on my way back north real soon."

"Why don't we go upstairs and you can tell me all about those big lakes in Michigan."

Upstairs Cathy closed the door to her room. Billy stood a bit awkwardly near the bed. Cathy pulled her hair clip out and her dark hair fell around her shoulders. Carefully she took off her dress and hung it over a chair. Billy gaped. Her stockings ended high on her legs. Around her waist the top of a corset was pushing her large breasts up. She pulled off her short bloomers and started to unlace the corset.

"You can undress," she said to Billy.

"Yes ma'am." Billy quickly peeled his trousers and shirt. Underneath them he only wore long johns. His hard penis made the pants of the long johns stick out.

"Looks like you don't want to do much talking after all?"

"No ma'am."

Cathy stood in front of him only wearing a garter, her stockings, and her high top shoes. "Do you mind the shoes? They are such a pain to hook and unhook. It takes about five minutes."

Billy grabbed her and pulled her to him. "No kissing on the lips," she said. "I'll do just about anything else."

Billy let his hands wander her breasts. They looked larger with the corset on, though he thought they were nicely shaped. He cupped one in each hand. He bent and snuggled his face between them. Carefully he took one nipple into his mouth and sucked and licked it. Cathy worked her hands to the buttons on the long johns and started to undo them.

"How much time I got ma'am?" Billy asked.

"About a half hour."

"Okay, let me take you quick to take the edge off, then I want to enjoy it," Billy said.

Cathy lay back on the bed and Billy quickly jumped out of his long johns. He was rock hard, engorged with his pent up need. He spread her legs revealing a patch of dark hair. Cathy reached down and grabbed it. Her touch almost made him explode.

She guided him into her and after one big push into her softness, Billy exploded. He howled in delight, pumping her in and out until his sexual release was spent.

Billy began to caress her breasts again, touched her gently and kissing her belly. Cathy thought him an interesting man. He was a big man, but was gentle and freshly bathed. He was polite, even calling her ma'am. She could tell he was the type of man who would not strike her or hurt her. Many of the cowboys used whores both for sex and punching boards. When they got drunk, some got mean as snakes.

"Come here Billy," she said. Cathy moved further onto the bed and patted a space beside her. Billy obliged. His wet penis lay limp. Cathy stroked her hands on his chest. He had a nice amount of hair, not too much. She licked at his neck and nibbled his earlobe. Before long Billy grabbed her by her waist and rolled her on top of him. He was hard again and as he slipped it into her, she leaned down and kissed him on the mouth.

CHAPTER 18

Saturday night Rodolfo turned to María and took her arm. María ignored him for the past two days because he brought the silver to El Paso. *"Querida,* we need to talk about this. I know you are mad at me and I understand. Martín has arranged a meeting with Jerry Carr tomorrow afternoon. Jerry helped us buy the guns and this is our chance to see if he will help us sell the silver."

María looked into his eyes. She knew he only had good intentions, though had put them in danger. She was more upset he kept it a secret from her.

"Rodolfo, I have been thinking about how we can get the money back to Torreón. I will ask Martín to wire the money a little at a time until we get all of it. That way we do not take a chance of being caught with all of it crossing the border back into Mexico or robbed by bandits," María told him.

"No querida, Martín wants no part in this. It is too dangerous. He has setup the meeting for us with Jerry Carr and that is all he will do."

María sighed. She did not blame her cousin. Though the silver ingots could probably not be traced to the silver robbery in Mexico by the Texas authorities, just the amount of silver would be questioned.

"Rodolfo, I trust Martín and from what I remember he told me he grew up with his friend Jerry Carr. We have no other choice, we need the money," María said.

"I have been thinking, perhaps we should talk to Rafael. He is a businessman and would be able to exchange the money in smaller amounts. He could wire us money from time to time and also reimburse himself for all he has done for us," Rodolfo suggested.

"Never! I do not want my brother to know about the silver."

"But, he is family. We can trust him," Rodolfo argued.

"Do you want to tell him how you stole the silver? How Pepe died and you killed Sancho? Is this how you want Rafael to look at you?" María spoke vehemently and a scowl crossed her tan face.

Rodolfo felt defeated. He and Rafael had been childhood friends, both born and raised on *don* Bernardo's *hacienda*. He did not want Rafael to think he was still an outlaw and always putting María in danger.

"We will meet with Jerry Carr tomorrow and then decide what to do," Rodolfo conceded.

Sunday morning María and Rodolfo went to Mass with the family at the mission. Arrangements were made with the padre to hear Rafe and Ana Teresa's wedding vows on Monday afternoon. The entire family was enthralled with the plans, giving Rodolfo and María a chance to slip away for several hours. Rodolfo asked to borrow Jose's buggy to take María on a Sunday drive.

"Of course. Use the brown mare. She does not mind pulling the buggy," Jose answered.

Rodolfo took out only one ingot from the false floor of the wagon and hid it on the buggy seat under María's skirt. Martín had given them directions to the meeting place and told them it was a heavily wooded area with large cottonwood trees near the Rio Grande. No one was there when Rodolfo parked the buggy between two large cottonwoods and tethered the horse.

"Buenos días," they heard a voice coming from behind the buggy. They turned to see Jerry Carr walking up from behind them.

"Buenos días," they both replied.

"Martín tells me you want to talk to me?" he asked in almost good Spanish. "Do you want to buy more guns?"

"No, we do not want guns. We have silver to sell," Rodolfo told him.

"Silver, what do you mean silver? Silver coins? I can get those anywhere. I don't need silver coins," he said and laughed.

"No, not coins. We have ingots," María broke in.

"Ingots, what do you mean ingots?" Jerry asked.

"Yes, look," she answered and moved her skirt to show the oblong bar. Rodolfo took the ingot and placed it into Jerry's outstretched hand.

The eight inch long bar was dull gray, roughly formed, and very heavy. On the top was a symbol created when the metal was hot and molten. Jerry thought if it was silver, the ingot was in its primitive form. He tested the weight and turned it over several times. "Where did you get this?"

"That is not important. We have more of them. Can you sell them for us?" Rodolfo asked him. Martín warned him not to trust Jerry and Rodolfo was not feeling comfortable – something in Jerry's eyes.

"I may know a man here in El Paso who deals in smuggled precious metals. How many do you have?

"We have fifteen," María blurted out before Rodolfo could stop her.

"Are they on the other side of the border? I cannot get these across the border for you, if that's what you have in mind." Jerry suspected the silver was still in Mexico, hidden somewhere.

"It is already over the border," María spoke up. She did not sense Rodolfo's unease.

"They are somewhere safe," Rodolfo said not wanting to tell Jerry Carr too much.

"I see. You need to sell the bars for cash? Guns?" Jerry asked.

"For money," María spoke out of turn.

"Hmmm." Jerry turned the heavy ingot over and over several more times. "Give me a couple of days and I will see the man and find out if he is interested. I need to take this to him. He will know its value."

Rodolfo almost denied the request. He hated to give up one of the precious ingots, but saw no way to say no.

"Very well. You must protect it with your life," Rodolfo warned Jerry.

"Sure," Jerry responded with a grin. "I'll keep it real safe. If the man wants to buy them, you know I get my cut of ten percent," Jerry told them.

"Yes we understand," Rodolfo replied.

"If you can do this we will reward you with a bonus," María said and gave him a big smile.

Jerry smiled broadly at her. Her innocence was obvious.

"I will contact Martín as soon as I know," Jerry said. After stuffing the ingot into his saddlebag, he mounted up and rode away through the trees.

"María, do not be so hasty. I do not trust this Jerry Carr. You told him too much. Martín warned me, Jerry is a dangerous man. From now one, I will do the talking," Rodolfo said to her in a gentle manner.

On the way home, Jerry mulled over how to approach the man who dealt in smuggled precious metals. A smuggler himself, Jerry knew there was no honor in his profession. He guessed the weight of the ingot as maybe more than fifty pounds. There was an old scale at home he could use to verify his assumption.

Doing a mental calculation, Jerry saw dollar signs. Lots of them. His business running guns and ammunition to Mexicans across the border was dwindling. The Mexican government was cracking down on border inspections and the guards who took bribes were getting scared. He had several narrow escapes recently that might have landed him in federal prison, if caught. This new deal was a godsend and the two peasants were obviously desperate to unload the silver. Both worked in Jerry's favor.

With the gunrunning business failing, Jerry had been toying with the idea of buying a racehorse. Racing was legal and impromptu races happened all over El Paso and Juarez. However, quality racehorses were expensive and the silver could be his ticket to leaving the gunrunning business and becoming a gentleman racehorse owner.

"Thank you Lord," he said looking up as he rode to his home.

As Rodolfo and María drove away, there was both relief and tension in their faces.

"I don't trust him," Rodolfo repeated. "He knows nothing about silver. We may never see that ingot again."

"He's our only hope," María replied.

"No he's not. I think we should talk to Rafael."

"Please don't involve my brother. He and Ana Teresa are getting married tomorrow and he has given us so much. I could not face him if he found out about this."

Yesterday María was able to get Rafael alone for a short while. They walked outside after supper. She apologized to her brother for her vehement anger toward him. She thanked him for avenging her honor and killing *don* Bernardo. He reminded her *don* Bernardo died of a heart attack and not by his hand. They talked about the *hacienda* and about life in Torreón. Rafael told her about her children, Antonio and Alicia, and the house he was building in Santa Fe.

"You have done so much for us, not only for Rodolfo and me, but for all the *peóns,*" she told him.

"*Don* Bernardo owed us both so much more," he responded. "Look at you now. Pregnant with Rodolfo's child and making a life for the other peasants. I am very proud of you María."

CHAPTER 19

Monday afternoon did not come soon enough for Rafe and Ana Teresa, but now they stood in the mission's chapel. Padre Serrano dressed in his formal robes was standing in front of them. Rafe's family sat in the pews behind them. All of the mission's monks in their brown robes sat behind the family with the exception of Brother Leonard, who was helping Padre Serrano with the Mass.

Ana Teresa wore the cream dress and Rafe his best traveling suit. Ita and María weaved small wildflowers in her braided hair and made her a small bouquet of flowers.

"Who offers this woman?" Padre Serrano began the customary service.

"I do," Jose said. Though not formally a relative, Ana Teresa felt happy to have Jose present her.

"What do you give for this woman," the padre said turning to Rafe.

Rafe handed him thirteen gold coins. Padre Serrano accepted the coins and performed the blessing ritual. The coins represented Jesus and his twelve apostles and Rafe's willingness to provide for his new bride. Symbolically, the coins reinforced the groom's love and admiration. When the bride accepted the coins, she was communicating her unconditional love, trust, and dedication to her new husband. It was a tradition steeped in the Spanish Catholic religion.

As the padre continued the Mass, Ana Teresa's knees felt weak. Finally, she and Rafael were marrying. It made her sad her parents were not sitting in the pews. They were in Spain and Ana Teresa had not seen them for almost two years. Even though she knew they would not approve of Rafael, she wanted them to see how happy she was.

Rafe stood beside Ana Teresa staring at the altar. Behind it, a large wooden cross with a sculpture of Jesus hung on the wall. Before the Mass both he and Ana Teresa made their confessions. He confessed killing *don* Luis' gunman in Mexico and shooting *don* Luis. He asked for forgiveness for his part in Diego de la Torre's death. Padre Serrano absolved him.

As the padre continued with the wedding Mass, Rafe's mind wandered. He wished George and Josefina Summers were sitting in the pews. He owed George everything he was today. Without George Summers' help, Rafe would still be a Mexican *peón* or probably dead. Instead, he was an American horse breeder with a future in Santa Fe. He knew George would deny that notion. George believed Rafe saved his life. Rafe never quite understood why he helped George Summers the day he found him almost dead from an Indian arrow in the Texas desert. George believed it was the hand of God. Rafe only knew he now loved George like a father.

Padre Serrano was reading the scripture. When he finished he turned toward them saying, "Praise be to God."

Ana Teresa and Rafe were kneeling at the short bar in front of the altar. The padre motioned everyone to rise.

"We are gathered in the sight of God to join these two in holy matrimony," he began.

Ten minutes later everyone was hugging them and laughing. Lupe had tears in her eyes. Ana Teresa felt as if it was a dream. The padre introduced them as *Señor y Señora Rafael Reyes de Estrada*. When she was a little girl, she played pretend with dolls dreaming of this moment. Though this simple ceremony was not as she dreamed, the man standing beside her was more than she could have ever imagined.

"Felicitaciones mi hija," Padre Serrano wished her congratulations.

"Gracias padre."

Later that evening, Rafe stopped the buggy in front of the Hotel Stratton. He helped Ana Teresa down from the seat. It seemed unbelievable he was finally married to this beautiful *señorita* from California.

They walked into the hotel and to the desk. "Please have *Señora Reyes'* belongings taken to my room and return the buggy to the livery," he told the clerk.

"Well congratulations. I'll take care of it immediately.

Is there anything else you'll be needing?"

"No thank you."

They climbed the stairs and Rafe opened the door to his room. He sensed Ana Teresa was nervous, her hand trembling slightly. As they waited for her belongings to be brought from her room, Rafe busied himself making space in the armoire for her clothes. He checked to make sure there was water in the pitcher and clean towels.

Only a couple days ago, they clung desperately in each other's arms longing to have this moment. Now he nervously paced hoping he would not fail her. When Rafe closed the door behind the young man who brought Ana Teresa's belongings, he turned to her. She was standing in the soft glow of the oil lamp with the light catching glints in her brown hair.

"Do you want anything?" Rafe said as he stepped to her.

"No I have everything I need."

Rafe took a deep breath wrapping his arms around her. He tried his best to relax, but at the same time he felt his lust respond at the thought of taking his bride for the first time. He kissed her tenderly.

He had been with other women in his life, both making tender love with Chiwiwi and drunken sex with Elena. He knew Ana Teresa was a virgin, pure and no doubt unsure.

The butterflies in Ana Teresa stomach embodied her nervousness. She wanted to please him, to be able to accept his love without trepidation, though her hands quivered. "I love you Rafael."

He took her trembling hands in his. "I am nervous too. We will take our time tonight, because from this day forward we have all the time in the world," he reassured her.

"I'm not afraid. I just hope I will please you," she told him.

"Please me? Everything you are pleases me. I fell in love with you the first time I saw you. You were wearing the red and black dress at the fiesta and after we danced the

Fandango you had me under your spell," he teased.

"I remember that day well. Bibiana had introduced me to many of the Santa Fe *caballeros* on the *paseo,* but most of them were dandies. When you looked into my eyes and held me in the dance, my heart skipped a beat. In those first days, I was not sure how long I would stay in Santa Fe. Then, I knew for sure I loved you the day you came to the abandoned *hacienda* near the river. Do you remember?" she asked.

"You mean the day you wielded my sword and saved my life!" Rafe said with a grin. "I believe you are not as helpless a *señorita* as you pretend."

"Nor am I any longer a *señorita*. I am your wife."

Rafe took her in his arms. His lips found hers and suddenly the butterflies disappeared. He was her husband, she his wife. She responded to his kisses as the butterflies were replaced by a passion growing inside her.

He kissed her neck and shoulders. Ana Teresa helped him remove his suit coat and tie. She hung the coat on a hook in the armoire. He unbuttoned his shirt and she pulled it off his shoulders. A pattern of small scars resembling a star caught in the glow of the oil lamp.

She reached out and put her hand over the star-shaped scars, which covered his heart.

He put his hand over hers. "I give this heart to you," he said.

"I will take good care of it," she replied.

Gently he started to unbutton her dress. At the fifth button it fell from her shoulders and she stepped out of it. He kissed her bared neck and the tops of the breasts. She wrapped her arms around him. The skin on his back was bumpy with scars. Her fingers traced one of the longer scars, which stretched from almost his shoulder blade to his waist.

Rafe smoothed her unruly hair off her shoulders, then kissed her neck. His touch excited a fire within her racing down between her legs.

"Would you like me to turn down the lamp?" Rafe asked her.

"No. I want to see your face," she replied.

Rafe's hands began to fumble at the laces on her chemise. The laces untied and the bodice opened exposing her breasts. He cupped one in his hand touching it tenderly then dipped his head to kiss her pink nipples.

A small groan of desire escaped Ana Teresa's lips. She pulled his chest to hers feeling her bare breasts touch the bareness of him.

It was Wednesday evening before they exited the room to have supper at the restaurant down the street. Ana Teresa's face glowed in the late afternoon sunlight. She held Rafe's arm and he walked tall and proud down the sidewalk.

Rafe found out over the last two days he had not really ever known true love. He thought he loved Chiwiwi, his first love. It was young and pure love. A Tiwa Indian maiden, Chiwiwi had sparked a passion in him. It was love, but not the kind of love he now felt for Ana Teresa. Theirs was a deep, mature love between a man and woman. They gave themselves without reservation over the past two days, exploring every inch of their bodies.

Rafe now knew the bottoms of her feet were ticklish. She giggled uproariously when he ran his finger down the arch of her foot. She knew the reason for each scar on his back and the star-shaped scar on his chest. She made him tell her everything. When she learned he took the scar across his shoulder for helping another man lift an exceptionally heavy agave, tears formed in her eyes. She cried when he told her the other man had died. However, he stuck to his promise to Longwei and did not tell her about the opium, which was also grown on the agave *hacienda*.

Rafe ordered steaks after they were seated in the restaurant. The owner brought coffee.

"Rafe, Rafe." He heard a voice from across the room. Terry Howard, the banker from the El Paso Republic Bank was walking toward them. Rafe stood up and extended his hand.

"Hello Mr. Howard. May I introduce my wife, Ana

Teresa," Rafe said. Ana Teresa stretched her gloved hand to the man.

"I heard you were in town and also heard you got married. Congratulations to you both," he said.

"Thank you Mr. Howard."

"Come on Rafe. You know you can call me Terry. Mind if my missus and I join you? I have some things to discuss with you, so it is lucky I saw you."

Terry Howard resettled his wife at their table and they exchanged greetings. Rafe had never met Nancy Howard. She was a tall woman with an easy smile and big teeth. She made a few comments to Ana Teresa quietly while he and the banker were talking, but allowed Terry to control the conversation.

The waiter brought all four dinners to the table shortly after the Howards seated themselves. Terry Howard concentrated on his steak, only making small talk during the meal. When they finished, the waiter cleared the table of the plates and brought coffee.

"I get out to see your uncle from time to time," Terry said. He seems to be making good progress on making the ranch profitable again. Those Reynolds really let the place go." The banker had been instrumental in helping Rafe repurchase the ranch for his uncle. He managed an account Rafe kept with the bank to help his *tío's* family to purchase stock and supplies.

"Yes. The barn is in good shape and his cattle are fat. I appreciate you have been sending me updates on the money I left under your care," Rafe said.

"Well, well something has come up. I was going to write to you, but now that you are here we can discuss it in person."

"Is there a problem?" Rafe asked.

"No, no problem, no problem at all. It is just that a property may become available adjacent to your uncle's ranch and I wonder if you might have any interest in buying it. It would almost double the size of the ranch and there is a nice house on the land."

"Oh, I had not thought about anything like that."

"It is the Lazy H Ranch. The owner is having health problems and his wife died a few years back. He has a son, but he is in San Francisco and I doubt wants to come back to El Paso. The owner still owes a mortgage to the bank and he is overdue," the banker explained the situation with the property.

Rafe thought about how the bank foreclosed on Henry Reynolds and the old man had to leave. Rafe felt no sorrow for old Mr. Reynolds because he stole the ranch at gunpoint from his uncle. Rafe had bought the foreclosed ranch so his uncle and family could live in peace. However, throwing an ailing man off his property did not seem right.

"Your uncle has been prudent and the account you left him has been earning interest. You could buy the Lazy H and still have funds in the account," the banker explained.

Rafe had not thought about the account for some time, though to his recollection his uncle only used about a third of the money. The banker's comments made Rafe ponder his own finances. He had been gone from his horse breeding business for more than six months. George Summers wired him money to Los Angeles, but now Rafe was unsure whether George had just loaned him funds. He also needed to help Rodolfo and his sister with money to fix the *hacienda* in Torreón. Perhaps he was broke and did not know it.

"I will need to think about it and talk to my uncle. We will be here for a few more days until the passes to Santa Fe are clear. Perhaps I can come to the bank on Thursday or Friday and we can go over the property in more detail."

"Yes, yes, that would be fine," Terry responded.

Chapter 20

By Thursday morning the weather turned colder and windy, after several days of mild temperatures. Rafe asked the desk clerk to check on any news about the northern passes. By the time they came downstairs, the clerk told them a new storm was battering northern New Mexico and Colorado. The news was disappointing.

Rafe and Ana Teresa dressed warmly and drove the buggy to his uncle's ranch for a visit. The boys and his uncle were out on the range checking on the livestock when they arrived. Lupe hugged them in hearty *abrazos* with repeated congratulations for their marriage. Rafe left Ana Teresa in the kitchen with his aunt and went to the barn to check on Rayo.

The spirited Appaloosa stood quietly in a stall until he heard Rafe's whistle. The horse perked his ears and whinnied.

"Hello my friend," Rafe spoke to the horse. Rafe could tell his cousins had ridden the horse and he was thankful for their help. The Appaloosa needed exercise regularly.

While he was in the barn, Martín walked in and greeted him. The silver hidden in the rickety wagon was worrying him. He knew Rodolfo and María were no match for Jerry Carr's cunning and he thought the silver could be a danger to them all.

"How is married life?" he asked casually with a grin.

"I can't believe how lucky I am," Rafe replied.

"She seems a good match for you," Martín said.

They made small talk until Martín told Rafe what was bothering him. "Rafael, I have to tell you something. María and Rodolfo may be in trouble."

"Trouble? Trouble at the *hacienda?*" Rafe asked.

"They brought a load of stolen silver ingots here to El Paso. They want to try to sell them. They asked for my help." Martín quickly gave Rafe an account of how he helped them buy guns on the previous trip through his friend Jerry Carr.

Hearing his cousin's words, Rafe's anger burned at his sister and Rodolfo. He gave them the inherited *hacienda* in Torreón so they could be safe from the police and this was how they repaid him, by bringing stolen goods across the border.

"I promised to keep this a secret, especially from you, but I'm worried Jerry Carr will either swindle them or try to rob the silver for himself. He is a friend, but this is a huge amount of money at stake," Martín continued to explain the dilemma.

"I should never have trusted Rodolfo," Rafe grumbled. Though a childhood friend, Rodolfo apparently had not given up his outlaw ways.

"Rodolfo told me he stole it before you gave them the *hacienda*," Martín explained. "They have many needs trying to get the *hacienda* repaired and to feed the people."

"How much silver?" Rafe asked trying to calm his anger.

"Rodolfo said they have fifteen ingots. He said each one weighs fifty or sixty pounds."

Quickly calculating the amount of silver staggered Rafe. "How did they get it over the border?"

"I assume it is hidden in the wagon." Martín pointed to the rickety wagon sitting at the back of the barn. "Jose and Tomás said the wagon was very heavy when they pushed it back there."

"They took a terrible chance bringing it here. If they had been caught, they would both be in jail and my sister is pregnant," Rafe complained angrily. "Where are they?"

"They went to town to meet with Jerry Carr again. They should be back anytime."

When Rodolfo and María arrived at the ranch, Rafe was waiting for them in the barn.

"*Hola,*" Rodolfo called out as they rode into the barn.

Rafe strode purposely until he was almost upon them and growled, "Martín told me about the silver."

"What silver?" María asked innocently.

"Do not play with me María. The stolen silver you brought here to El Paso to sell. I gave you the *hacienda* and *don* Jorge setup accounts for your needs. Still you two have not given up your thieving way." Rafe's voice rose as his anger burst through.

María and Rodolfo looked at each other and Rodolfo began to talk. "Rafael, you know I turned outlaw after I got out of prison. I did it because no one would hire me after I was accused of being a thief, when I was not. It was Joaquin Moreno, the *desgraciado* from town, who robbed the store. He and his friends came to hide near the lake where you and I fished as boys. I was there when the police came and arrested Joaquin and his friends, including me. Joaquin told them I was part of his gang, so I went to prison along with them."

Rafe knew of his childhood friend's misdeeds and always thought it was true. After he heard Rodolfo turned to be an outlaw, he never questioned his guilt.

"But you turned to the *bandido* life and took my sister with you," Rafe continued accusing Rodolfo of his wayward ways.

"Yes that is true. After looking for work and not finding any, I was starving until I met up with some *peóns* who were raiding *haciendas* for food and what they could sell to stay alive. We became *bandidos*. At times we gave part of our food to poor peasants we met along the way and before long more people joined us. Then María came back to Torreón. I did not expect to fall in love with her. She chose to join me. I wanted her to return to Santa Fe."

"I chose to stay in Mexico. Rodolfo is good to the people and they follow his dream to be free. You know how *peóns* are treated in Mexico, slaves or worse," María interjected supporting her husband's actions.

Unfortunately, Rafe did know how *peóns* were treated, because he too had been one. The *hacienderos* abused them and treated them with no regard. They died with an empty belly.

"What about the silver? You stole it." Rafe brought the conversation back to the question at hand.

Rodolfo told Rafe how María stole gold coins from *don* Bernardo over the years. With her money they had bought guns and ammunition here in El Paso from Jerry Carr. It was before Rafe gave them the *hacienda* and they were living in the hills outside of Torreón.

"When we got back to our campsite with the guns, more people had found us and stayed. It was becoming more and more difficult to provide food for the people and the children were going hungry. The local *hacienderos* were becoming more watchful of their stock. One of my friends, Paco, told me about small silver mines around Zacatecas and thought we could rob one of them. Four of us went to Zacatecas and came back with fifteen ingots of pure silver. I admit it was stupid and dangerous. I thought it would solve our problems and did not realize the silver would be useless to us. There is no way a *peón* can sell it in Mexico."

"You should have thought about that sooner," Rafe grumbled.

"Yes, it was stupid. I guess I was desperate," Rodolfo admitted his folly.

"You don't understand what it feels like to watch the children go hungry. We needed money to feed the people. We were living on what we could hunt or steal from the *haciendas,*" María said defending Rodolfo and trying to make her brother understand.

"Yes, the people look to me for protection and food. They are my responsibility now," Rodolfo finished.

Rafe listened to their story trying to put himself in Rodolfo's shoes. He had known Rodolfo since they were kids and knew he was not a bad man. Now, after hearing what he and María had gone through, he began to realize their dilemma. He looked at his sister, with her eyes shining when she spoke of what they believed and understood their need to feed the people.

"What did Jerry Carr tell you about selling the silver?" Rafe asked.

"He said he knew a man in El Paso who bought precious metals. He said the man will pay thirty cents an ounce. We were going to ask Martín to help us figure out how much the silver is worth, but I think that's a lot of money," María answered.

"Martín thinks Jerry Carr will swindle you. He is probably right. When are you to meet with Jerry again?" Rafe asked.

"We are to bring the silver on Saturday to the grove. Jerry will lead us to the buyer where we will exchange the silver for money. I told Jerry to come alone. I told him that because I do not trust him," Rodolfo said.

"What is your plan after you get the money?" Rafe asked.

"We need to take the money home as soon as possible. The people are waiting for us. María and I think we should head home right away after we sell the silver."

"Did Jerry ask you anything about your plans?" Rafe asked.

Rodolfo stared for a moment trying to remember the conversation with Jerry Carr.

"You told him we were going directly back to Mexico." María nudged Rodolfo who then nodded in agreement.

Rafe pondered the news about the meeting with Jerry Carr. The situation bothered him and it could mean life or death for Rodolfo and María dealing with Jerry Carr and the buyer. He would have to go with them and give them protection, but maybe there was a better way.

"Let me find out how much the silver is worth. How heavy is each ingot?"

Rodolfo reached into the saddlebag of the horse and pulled out a grey-colored bar about eight inches long and two inches high. He handed it to Rafe.

The weight of the silver brick surprised Rafe when Rodolfo put it into his hand. He estimated it weighed fifty pounds. "You have fifteen of these?" Rafe asked.

"Yes, they are hidden in a secret compartment in the wagon."

"Here, put this one away. Tell no one else. I need to make some inquires and will talk to you again tomorrow."

Rafe saddled Rayo and then walked to the house to find Ana Teresa. He found her in the kitchen with his *tía* Lupe peeling apples.

"I need to go to town. I'm taking Rayo. You stay here and I'll return in a few hours," he told her.

"We have much to do," his aunt replied.

"Do you need any supplies from town, *tía?*"

"I could use several pounds of coffee and a slab of bacon if you can stop at the mercantile," she replied.

CHAPTER 21

Rafe swung up onto Rayo's saddle and kicked him to a gallop. The cold wind bit at his face. At first he was angry about the silver, but now he understood. Rodolfo stole the ingots before Rafe inherited the *hacienda*. Perhaps he would have done the same in Rodolfo's shoes.

While he was enslaved at the agave ranch in Jalisco, Rodolfo and his sister were trying to make a go of it at the *hacienda*. The house and buildings were vandalized and deteriorated and now the people were rebuilding. Rafe realized he had not transferred any money for them to buy provisions, though Rodolfo said George had helped them with supplies.

Uncle Jose had similar problems here in El Paso after Rafe bought the Reynolds ranch, but Rafe had left money in the El Paso Bank for their needs. As he rode, ideas and questions floated through his mind. Reaching town, he rode directly to the bank. As he walked in, Terry Howard's door was open and he was sitting at his desk with papers strewn across it. Rafe tapped on the door.

"Rafe, Rafe, come in," the banker said. "I'm glad you are here. I have just been going over the details of the property I told you about and your current account. Close the door and sit down."

Terry turned a map toward Rafe. "Here is your uncle's ranch." The map had pencil marks around an area and Tecolote Ranch was written inside the marks. "This is the Lazy H." Terry pointed to another area circled with Lazy H marked on it. The two properties shared a common boundary on the east side of his uncle's land.

"Hiram Harper owns it. Like I told you he is many months behind on the mortgage and in poor health. I hate to foreclose, but I have no choice."

Rafe and the banker discussed the property and the mortgage. Mr. Harper was five hundred dollars behind in mortgage payments with no way to pay. The entire mortgage was approximately thirty-five hundred dollars. The eighty-five acres included a small lake, a decent house, a barn, and several corrals and outbuildings.

"I was out there not long ago and the house and buildings are in good shape. Old Hiram used to raise quality cattle. I remember several prized bulls he raised," Terry told him.

"How much do I have in my account?" Rafe asked.

"Well now, let me see." Terry ruffled through several sheets until he found the one he wanted. "The account started with over six thousand. Your uncle has asked for draws of about two thousand and there is some interest. The current balance is four thousand, two hundred and thirty-three dollars and a few cents. As I told you, your uncle has been very prudent."

Rafe had enough money to buy the Lazy H outright. He thought it might be a nice property for Martín and Ita and their three children as his uncle's house was getting quite crowded. His uncle and cousins could run the properties as a single ranch, sharing time and effort. Though options about the Lazy H Ranch was the topic of conversation, Rafe's intention was to find out about silver. As Terry finished telling Rafe the details about the Lazy H, Rafe changed the subject.

"Do you know what the going rate for an ounce of raw silver might be worth?" Rafe asked the banker.

"Silver? Silver? Well I'm not exactly sure. I don't deal in raw silver, only coins," he responded looking confused at the question.

"Could you find out? I have several bars of raw silver and would like to exchange them. Then I would feel more comfortable making this transaction."

"Oh I see. I guess I could find out from the assay office. I can ask there and get back to you."

"I'll be in town for awhile. Can you find out and I'll come back in a couple hours?"

"Come back after one and I should be able to tell you," the banker told him. They shook hands and Rafe walked outside into the chill. He headed to the telegraph office down the street. He needed to send George a telegram and hoped the lines were not down from the winter storm.

Jerry Carr sat in the Gem Saloon with Bo Preston. A half-drunk beer sat in front of each of them.

"I'm telling yew, this deal's worth a shitpot of money." Jerry chuckled to himself at the thirty cents per ounce he quoted the greaser Mexicans. The buyer was giving him sixty cents an ounce and he still would get his ten percent off the top. It was a lot of money.

Yesterday he went to see Tom Hussmann, a respected racehorse breeder in El Paso. Jerry had his eye on a two-year-old red mare. Tom showed him she came from good stock and put her through her paces on the racetrack. After looking the two-year-old over, Jerry decided to buy the horse and gave Hussmann a one hundred dollar deposit. The silver deal would easily bring the remainder of the money he needed to buy the horse and much more.

"So what do you need me for?" Bo asked. "You said the stuff is already over the border and sounds like you have this deal in hand." In the past, Bo Preston worked with Jerry running guns across the border. Handy with his guns, Bo was the muscle and Jerry the brains.

"Well this here deal is worth a fortune, not the petty stuff we usually do," Jerry replied. "I want you to wait for the greaser couple across the border. They're heading back to Torreón after the deal, carrying their share of the money. They should be easy pickins for yew."

"Well I won't come cheap in this deal. What's my share?" Bo asked him.

"We'll split the greaser's share fifty-fifty. The way I see it, it's over fifteen hundred dollars each."

Bo whistled. "For that kind of money I'll kill the buyer and the Mexes for you." Jerry knew Bo would take the deal.

"We can't kill the buyer. We need him. I don't know how to exchange the ingots for money."

Jerry pondered killing the greasers before he paid

them their share, but he would now leave that up to Bo. The extra money would go a long way. No one in Mexico would care about a poor young Mexican couple being robbed or killed. It nagged him they were related to Martín Ortega, a friend he grew up with and called Marty. If Marty asked about them, he would just say he sold the silver for them. They could have been held up by bandits on their way home. Hell, it happened all the time down there.

Rafe stopped at the barbershop for a shave and went to the mercantile for the items his aunt needed. It was almost one-thirty when he walked back into the bank. Terry Howard greeted him with a handshake.

"Come into my office." Terry closed the door behind them. "I met with Bert in the assay office. He said he sends silver bars to the bigger office in Tucson. The mines send any smelted ore there also."

"Did you ask about the value?" Rafe asked.

"Well, he said it would depend upon the quality. He did say quality raw silver could fetch around a dollar an ounce."

The news disappointed Rafe. He hoped to be able to have Terry Howard transact the sale of the silver here in El Paso, but the value of the silver astounded him. Quickly he calculated the fifteen ingots of silver lying in the rickety wagon were probably worth almost fifteen thousand dollars. It was enough to buy the ranch here in El Paso, create an account for supplies at the *hacienda* in Torreón, rebuild his house and refill his bank account in Santa Fe, which surely had dwindled in his absence.

"I could arrange for the silver to be transported to Tucson on a Wells Fargo coach. I have connections on the other end," Terry suggested.

"I'll have to think about it, Terry. I have heard Wells Fargo is a target for bandits."

"Yes, yes that true. Have you given any more thought to the property?"

Rafe thought about it and liked the idea. It would help his uncle and almost double their land here in El Paso.

The only thing bothering him was the owner's predicament. Terry said the man had lost his wife and was ill. Rafe could not throw him out in the cold.

"Can you ask the owner if he would sign over the deed to me if I pay his outstanding debt? I will allow him to continue living in his home and I will pay the mortgage each month. I only ask that he keep the house and barns in good condition and he will let my uncle's family begin to graze cattle and plant the fields. He can live there until he dies."

"My, my that is more than generous. I'm sure Hiram will agree," Terry said.

"Put the paperwork in my uncle's name, as you did for his ranch. Take the money from the account here as you have done in the past. If I am not still in town when this transpires, my cousin Martín speaks English now and can act on my behalf."

Rafe and the banker shook hands. As Rafe walked out the door, Terrence Howard shook his head. The young Mexican never ceased to amaze him.

CHAPTER 22

No matter how Rafe thought it through, no good plan to sell the silver in El Paso seemed practical. Rodolfo told him how stealing the silver was so much easier than finding a way to sell it and now Rafe understood. He could drive the rickety wagon to Tucson where Terry said he could sell the silver. Besides the danger of the drive, he wondered if selling that much silver in one transaction would raise questions. Rafe noticed the ingot Rodolfo showed him was stamped with a mark on the top side, obviously the mark of the mine. It could be traced. Rafe wondered if burying it somewhere until he could figure out a way to sell it might be the best alternative.

Rafe rode into the barn and found Tomás and Little Jose mucking the stalls.

"Can you unsaddle and brush Rayo for me?" Rafe asked the boys.

"Sure," Tomás replied.

Walking to the house, Rafe tried to forget the silver. He wanted to talk to his uncle and tell the family about the Lazy H Ranch. He found his uncle in the kitchen and gave the supplies he picked up in town to his aunt.

"*Tío*, I made a deal with the banker today," Rafe began.

"A deal for what, *mijo?*"

"To buy the Lazy H Ranch to the east of your land. The owner is behind in the mortgage and the bank was going to foreclose. It will double your land."

"But Rafael, we do not need more land. We already have enough. Besides, we know *Señor* Harper and he is a good man."

Rafe imagined his uncle would be happy with the news. "I know *tío*, but the property has a good house and barn. Martín and Ita could have a house of their own. What about the boys when they grow up and marry? Tomás is almost sixteen. I am looking to the future *tío*," Rafe explained.

"That is true *mijo*. I know Ita would like a house of her own, but I could not do such a thing to *Señor* Harper. Lupe helped nurse his wife when she was ill."

"I agree *tío*. I told the banker to pay up the mortgage and allow *Señor* Harper to stay on the land. You and the boys will be allowed to farm and ranch the property until *Señor* Harper dies or can no longer live there, then it will be yours."

His uncle pondered the idea and then smiled. "It is a good plan. We will tell the family at supper."

Later that evening after supper, Rafe drove the buggy back to the city and Ana Teresa held tightly onto his arm dreaming of the night to come.

"Your family has made me feel so welcome. I think what you are doing for them, buying the new property is wonderful," she said to him. When he told them at supper, everyone had ideas about the new land. Ita was especially excited as someday soon she and Martín could have their own home, yet be close to the family.

"When my mother and the children come to visit, my uncle will have more room for guests," Rafe told her.

"Or we can come to visit again," Ana Teresa commented.

Thoughts about the new land nagged at Rafe. He knew trouble waited for him back in Santa Fe. The local Spanish aristocrats wanted revenge for the death of Diego and their swords pointed directly at him.

Perhaps purchasing the new ranch in El Paso was a prudent idea. Should he be found guilty of Diego's death or the Spaniards killed him, Ana Teresa, his mother, and the children could come here to El Paso to live. He tried to shake those fears off, though they percolated in his subconscious.

They arrived at the livery and Billy greeted them when they pulled in. "Hello folks," he said.

"Hello Billy. We'll need the buggy again tomorrow."

Charlie walked from the back of the barn. "Hallo mista Rafe, missus. Yew be lookin well," he said with a huge grin stretching across his white teeth.

"How's it going here with Charlie, Billy?"

Charlie answered, "Billy be doin good werk. We's juss fine, ain't we Billy?"

"Yeah. Ol Charlie here cooks a mean chili. Spices it up with them red Mexican chilis."

"I's learnt me frum a Mexcan woman I be sweet on a long time ago."

"Glad to see it's all working out for the both of you. We'll see you in the morning," Rafe said turning and taking Ana Teresa's arm.

They strolled down the sidewalk toward the hotel. Piano music wafted down the street from the several saloons and mixed into an unintelligible sound. Ana Teresa shivered as the night chill descended like a blanket and a light wind blew in their faces. She clutched closer to Rafe.

They were passing in front of Lilli Jean's Saloon when a door slapped open across the street and someone yelled, "Told yew not to be cheatin round here."

Across the street a ruckus spilled out of the Gem Saloon. "Who yew calling a cheat? Yew juss spreading filthy lies." A cowboy in the street was dusting his hat on his pants leg as he stood up.

"Yew go on and don't yew come back any time soon," a man who threw the cowboy out of the Gem, yelled back.

Knowing his guns were in the hotel room where he left them this morning, he pushed Ana Teresa behind him and stood protecting her with his body against the wall of Lilli Jean's Saloon.

"Oh yew juss go to hell," the cowboy hissed and weaved as he walked off down the street. The ruckus reminded Rafe he should not leave the hotel without his guns again.

"It's safe now, let's go." Ana Teresa grabbed Rafe's arm even tighter as they walked the short distance down the street to the Hotel Stratton.

In the morning, Ana Teresa told Rafe she wanted a bath and wanted to go shopping for a new dress and a pair of warmer shoes, if possible. Rafe decided to ride to his uncle's ranch and discuss the silver again with Rodolfo and María.

"I'll be back before supper and we'll go to the restaurant," he told her. "Tell Clive at the mercantile to put the bill on my account at the bank," he told her. "Buy whatever you need."

Before he left, he held her in a tight embrace. He kissed her cheeks and neck. She giggled and squirmed, though her mouth sought his. She felt tingles in her nipples and groin as he let his tongue touch her lips. "You are a devil, *señor.* Come back later after my bath."

In the livery, Rafe asked Billy to saddle a horse instead of using the buggy. Rayo was at his uncle's corral. He thought it a safer place, though felt no threat against him or the horse here in El Paso. He had trouble in the past however, and the trouble last night in the street heightened his good sense. Today his GSW pistols were in the gunbelt around his waist.

He rode directly to his uncle's ranch hoping to find Rodolfo and his sister. They needed to discuss ideas concerning the silver. He had not told Ana Teresa about the silver, still hoping there was a resolution, which did not involve him directly.

Rodolfo met him as he rode into the yard.

"I'm glad you came," he said.

"Why?"

"We had a visit from Jerry Carr last night. Martín thinks he was looking for the silver. He made some threats about it," Rodolfo said.

"Did he threaten you directly?"

"No, but he demanded to know where the silver was and how we planned to transport it to his buyer. Martín knows him well and said he did not like his attitude. He said Jerry seemed like he had been drinking. María's scared." Rodolfo was scared too, but too manly to show it.

"Where's Martín?" Rafe asked.

"He and Little Jose are checking the stock. He'll be back soon."

Rafe realized Jerry Carr would not let the valuable silver slip through his hands easily. He probably suspected the silver was here at the ranch, putting the entire family at risk. The next time Jerry came to the ranch, it could be with a gun.

"I think you and María need to go back to Torreón immediately. You will be safe over the border."

"What about the silver? We can't take it back," Rodolfo said.

"No the silver stays here. Martín and I need to make a plan to keep it out of the hands of Jerry Carr. He's trying to swindle you, maybe worse."

"We are supposed to meet him tomorrow afternoon at the meeting place by the river. He will be angry if we do not show up."

"Yes he probably will be, but he's not going to get his hands on the silver."

Rodolfo looked at Rafe with his eyes wide. "What about you and Martín?"

"Don't worry, we'll think of something and I can protect myself. Go tell my sister to get her belongings together. As soon as Martín returns, we'll decide what to do."

While he waited for Martín, Rafe studied the old wagon with the secret panel. It appeared more rickety than it was in reality. Rafe located the well-disguised compartment. It was not visible to the naked eye, except from underneath. Rodolfo had done a good job. About an hour later Martín rode into the barn.

"Martín, Rodolfo and María need to get away from your friend. I think they need to go back to Torreón as soon as possible. Your friend Jerry Carr means trouble," Rafe said to his cousin as he was getting off his horse.

"What about the silver?" Martín asked.

"I've been thinking about taking it to Santa Fe. I can smelt it at the foundry and remove the mine symbol. Then, well I'm just not sure, but I'll think of something."

CHAPTER 23

Later that night Ana Teresa snuggled with Rafe in their room at the Hotel Stratton. Her hand was lazily moving across his chest. Making love to him was heavenly. It tickled her from the inside out and made her feel so alive. All she wanted now was to feel his nakedness beside her.

She wondered if every woman felt the way she felt. Did they want their man in the way she wanted Rafe? She wanted to ask Ita, but it was embarrassing. Tonight after they made love, Rafe seemed somewhat preoccupied.

"What are you thinking?" Ana Teresa asked running her hand down his arm.

"I have a problem and I don't have an answer," he replied.

"A problem? Tell me about it."

Rafe knew he needed to tell Ana Teresa about the silver and his dilemma on what to do. It was something he hated to admit, and yet the outcome might also help his own financial future and hers. Selling the silver ingots in Santa Fe could provide him enough funds to finish the house and recoup any money the months away from his business had cost. He owed George Summers money loaned to Rodolfo and María for getting the *hacienda* setup.

"Rodolfo robbed a silver mule train out of Zacatecas. He's brought the silver here to El Paso."

"What? You told me they quit the *bandido* life?" she asked very surprised.

"Yes they have, but they stole the silver before they knew I inherited the *hacienda*. They did it to buy food and ammunition for the freedom fighters who joined them. There are more than sixty people now to house and feed."

"Why didn't they use it in Mexico? Why did they bring it here?"

"The silver is in ingot form, not coins. *Peóns* could never use such silver to buy supplies in Mexico. They are lucky to have a few *pesos* in their pockets," Rafe tried to explain the situation in Mexico, though not sure he could make her understand.

"So what does this have to do with you?"

"Rodolfo took a chance and brought the silver here to El Paso. Martín's friend offered them thirty cents per ounce. We believe he wants to cheat them. I know I can get over a dollar or more per ounce in Santa Fe."

"Can't you sell it here in El Paso?"

"No. I could take it to Tucson to sell, but I think it is a better idea to take it to Santa Fe."

"Are we taking it with us on the stagecoach?" she asked still not understanding the complexity of the situation.

"No, an ingot weighs about fifty-five pounds, so fifteen ingots weigh over nine-hundred pounds."

"Madre de Dios," she said wide eyed as what Rafe was telling her sank in.

"Is it a lot of money?" she asked not readily able to calculate it in her head.

"Yes it's a lot of money."

Ana Teresa pondered quietly. If he said he needed to take the silver to Santa Fe, then she trusted him.

"We can take a wagon," she suggested.

"No, you are going by stagecoach. It is too dangerous, and besides it is winter and you know how cold it will be in the north."

"I don't care. I want to be with you," Ana Teresa pouted. She was finally married and now Rafe wanted her to go to Santa Fe alone, without him.

"It will only be for several days. I will ask Martín to go with you on the stage. I will not leave you alone, even on a stagecoach. Remember I promised to keep you safe."

"There's your solution. Martín can drive the silver to Santa Fe and we can go by stage."

"No, I need to protect it."

"And who is keeping you safe?" she asked.

Rafe had not even considered that he might need someone to help him with the load of silver. He felt confident with his pistols and he was a dead shot.

"You cannot go alone. I will tell the sheriff about the stolen silver, if you even think about going to Santa Fe alone," Ana Teresa warned him in a huff. It was a false threat, but she hoped he would think about what she was saying.

Rafe sighed. Ana Teresa was right. Rodolfo and María needed to return to Mexico. Martín would take the stagecoach to protect Ana Teresa. He should have a second gun on the wagon if there was trouble.

"You must know someone? Your uncle or one of the older cousins?" she asked.

"I do not want my uncle to be involved in this scheme. He has a family to feed. The boys are too young and green. I need someone tough and good with a gun, in case there is trouble."

"What about Padre Serrano. Surely he knows someone?"

Rafe gave her a sideways glance. "Am I to ask the padre if he knows someone who would ride with me and a wagon of stolen silver to Santa Fe?"

"There must be someone," she pleaded.

"There is no one," Rafe replied to her. "You are right I should not go alone, but there is no one I can trust."

Rafe sat up off the edge of the bed. At first it upset him Rodolfo stole the silver, but then he understood. For all the misery Mexico's aristocrats caused poor peasants, this was a small price to pay and the money would help the people who came to work the *hacienda*. Remembering his awful childhood, he was glad Rodolfo robbed the miner's silver muletrain, even though it was now his problem.

"I'm sorry. I need to do this for Rodolfo, María, and the *peóns* at the *hacienda,* and for us. It is something you cannot fully understand."

"I refuse to let you go alone," she said adamantly while she wildly tried to think of a way to stop the dangerous plan.

"You refuse?" Rafe said confused by what she meant. How could she refuse?

"I am your wife. You promised to love and honor me, or have you forgotten? It was only five days ago."

"I . . . I . . . " Rafe could not finish. She was upset and rightfully so. After only five days of marriage, he was plotting a dangerous trip for stolen silver that was not even his.

"You can take Billy with you," she blurted out as the idea popped into her head.

"Billy?"

"Yes Billy Swanson, Desperate Billy," she said with emphasis.

He had to admit as crazy as it sounded, Desperate Billy was a big man, tough enough to escape the stockade in Fort Yuma, and he fearlessly tried to accost the waystation with a broken gun. If Billy had anything, he had plenty of guts to attempt such things. Though a blacksmith by trade, he was an Army soldier and proved himself when the Indians attacked the stagecoach. He would probably also be obliged enough to agree.

Rafe nodded his head. "I'll ask him to go."

CHAPTER 24

The next morning, Rafe bought a wagon from Charlie at the livery along with a team of horses to pull it. He also stopped at the mercantile and filled the wagon with staple supplies and tools. When it was loaded, Ana Teresa followed him in a buggy to his uncle's ranch.

Making excuses to the family, Rodolfo and María hastily packed their belongings to return to Torreón.

"We have been gone too long," Rodolfo told Jose.

"The people need Rodolfo's guidance to keep the *hacienda* protected," María said to her aunt. "We must get home."

Martín and Rodolfo loaded food supplies, blankets, and baby clothes into the wagon. As the sun was almost straight up in the sky, María hugged everyone and Rodolfo shook Martín's hand.

"What about Jerry Carr? What do you think he will do?" Rodolfo asked.

"He will not be happy and will be looking for you, so you better get to the border crossing as soon as you can. Do not linger in Juarez, because Jerry has many friends there too," Martín warned Rodolfo.

Rodolfo understood and turned to Rafe and gave him a big hug.

"Come to Torreón and see us soon, you and Ana Teresa," Rodolfo said.

The family watched as the couple rode away south toward the town of El Paso and the border to Mexico. María turned and waved several times.

Several hours later Jerry Carr paced back and forth in the meeting place near the Rio Grande. He kept a sharp eye watching down the path to the river looking for the Mexican couple on their rickety wagon. Agitated, he invented reasons for their delay.

Another hour went by and he knew they were not

coming. Red-faced angry, he mounted up and rode hard to Martín's ranch. His dreams of being a racehorse gentleman were rapidly vanishing from his mind and it only added to his boiling anger.

On the dirt road leading to the ranch, Jerry passed a one-horse buggy carrying a young man and woman. Jerry took a good look at the driver, but it was not the young greaser couple, though they were Mexican. The driver of the buggy took a good long look at him as he rode by.

Rafe saw an Anglo man riding hard in the direction of his uncle's ranch. The man scowled in anger and only slowed down for an instant to study them before he spurred his horse on. Rafe assumed it might be Jerry Carr, the buyer of the silver. The man looked angry and must be wondering why Rodolfo and his sister did not keep the appointment. Hopefully they were well south of the border by now.

Rafe steered the buggy to the livery and helped Ana Teresa down. Billy walked up taking the reins of the horse.

"Is Charlie around?" Rafe asked. He wanted to tell Charlie he needed Billy before asking Billy to go with him. It was only courteous.

"Charlie ain't here Rafe. Said he needed an afternoon off to spend with his grandson. Think they went fishing," Billy told him.

"Ana Teresa, go on to the hotel. I need to talk to Billy. I'll be there soon." As Ana Teresa walked out of the livery, Rafe looked at Billy Swanson.

Billy was solidly built and taller than Rafe's six-foot frame by several inches. His beard was scruffy with a several day's growth, but Rafe noticed he wore new clothes since he saw him last.

"How's it going here Billy?" Rafe asked.

"Ol Charlie's real nice and I sure do appreciate you getting him to hire me for a little while. I get three square meals a day and work to keep me busy."

"What do you mean a little while?"

"Well now, he don't really need me all that much. I think he's keeping me on just because you asked him."

The news relieved Rafe's mind a bit. Charlie would not be mad if Billy went with him to Santa Fe.

"I need to drive a covered wagon to Santa Fe and I need someone to ride shotgun. I will be carrying precious cargo and it could be dangerous," Rafe warned him.

"What do you mean precious cargo?" Billy asked.

"Let me just say, it's valuable. Can you shoot a rifle?"

"Yes sir, I sure can. Just because I'm a blacksmith don't mean I didn't learn to shoot. The Army taught me well. I was one of the best riflemen in the regiment."

"So you'll go with me?"

"Sure. I owe you. When are we leaving?"

"Tomorrow morning. Early. We'll take the buggy to my uncle's ranch before sun up, so tell Charlie to leave it ready. Take warm clothes. If you need anything, go to the mercantile and tell them to put it on my bill. See you then," Rafe told him before heading to the hotel.

Jerry reached the Ortega ranch and quickly dismounted without bothering to tether his horse. "Marty! Marty! Where are yew?" he yelled out.

Martín was just coming out of the barn as Jerry barged his way in. "Jerry, what are you doing here?" Martín asked trying to sound nonchalant, but noticed Jerry was packing a pistol.

"Where are your cousins? They were supposed to meet me at two, but they never showed up," Jerry growled. He pushed Martín aside and looked into the small barn for the rickety wagon.

"Jerry, calm down and quit shouting. The family doesn't know anything about this," Martín said. "They loaded their wagon and told me they were going to meet you and then head home to Mexico. Are you telling me you never saw them?" Martín's stomach flopped as he formulated lies in answer to Jerry's angry questions.

He was thankful Rafe asked his younger brothers to hitch up the team of mules and pull the wagon to the grove of trees behind the house. Rafe suspected Jerry would come to the ranch when his sister and Rodolfo did not show at the appointed time.

"That's right they never showed."

"They told me they were scared, maybe they just headed back to Mexico Jerry," Martín continued with the lies.

"Hell, why would they do that. I told them I had a buyer for the silver. Why would they be scared?"

"They're just poor people, Jerry. You must have scared them." He could see Jerry was in a rage, but was believing him.

"If they are poor, where the hell did they get that much silver?" Jerry growled.

"They told me they stole it from a silver mule train headed to the mint in Mexico City. Did you tell anybody about the silver?" Martín asked.

"No, I just told the buyer," Jerry grumbled. He had also told Bo Preston. He wondered if perhaps Bo could have outsmarted him and taken the silver for himself. Bo offered to kill Marty's cousins and Jerry knew he was not above doing it.

"Did you tell the buyer who they were?"

"I told him they were cousins of yours from Mexico."

"Perhaps he got greedy. What if the buyer was scouting the ranch and spotted them heading out to meet you? Maybe he got to them first and undercut you. I better go out looking for them and you better go see the man you made the deal with," Martín told him.

Jerry grumbled at Martín's suggestion. Quickly he turned and walked back to his horse.

"When yew find your cousins, tell them that thirty cents is a good price for black market silver," Jerry shouted and mounted up. Martín watched as he left the ranch.

It was late in the afternoon when Jerry Carr rode up to Hastings Livery and dismounted. If anyone knew the comings and goings in El Paso, old Charlie knew. A big man came out of the back to greet him.

"Hey, where's Charlie?" he asked the big man gruffly.

"Charlie took a day off. Can I help you?" Billy asked.

"Well, maybe yew can. Looking for an old rig driven

by a Mexican couple. Yew seen anything like that lately?"

"Naw, I ain't seen it," Billy replied.

Jerry walked toward the back of the barn and spotted a buggy parked as if it had been driven lately. Charlie kept several buggies and wagons for rent, but when they were not being used he parked them behind the barn.

"I saw this buggy coming from the north side of town this afternoon. Who was driving it?" he demanded.

"That was my friend Rafe and his wife. Why do you want to know?" Billy asked.

"Well, is he related to the Ortega family? They have a ranch just north of town."

"Maybe. I don't rightly know."

"Where's he staying? I want to talk to him," Jerry snapped at the big man. His questions and comments were coming quick and short-tempered. Billy did not like his tone, but felt obliged to answer. Perhaps Rafe needed to see this man.

"He's at the Hotel Stratton," Billy told him.

Jerry asked nothing more and jumped to his horse. Billy thought it a bit odd the man was asking about Rafe and seemed angry, but then Rafe asked him to ride shotgun on the trip to Santa Fe tomorrow and said it might be dangerous. This man was heeled with what looked like a Remington-Rider revolver and he wore it in front with the grip pointing to his right. Billy knew the pistol well, because he used the same type when he fought in the Civil War. It shot true and got him out of trouble many times. They took it from him when he was arrested at Fort Yuma and since then he felt naked without it.

Riding the short distance, Jerry stopped in front of the Hotel Stratton. He felt sure the young Mexican couple in the buggy were related to Marty, but did they know about the silver? Marty told him the family did not know. For several long minutes he sat on his horse vacillating what to do. Finally, he turned his horse back down the street and hitched it to the rail in front of the Gem Saloon.

CHAPTER 25

Just as the sun lightened the Sunday morning sky, Rafe arrived at Hastings Livery. The previous evening with Ana Teresa was bitter sweet. She smelled of soap and lilacs as she clung to him all night. This morning as he packed to leave, she made him promise to be careful. He could still taste her lips on his from a passionate kiss before he walked out of their room.

He had already bought two tickets for the stage. She and Martín would leave on Thursday morning. He and Billy would not make as many miles as Ana Teresa would riding in the stagecoach and Rafe wanted to get to Santa Fe before her.

"Mornin Rafe. Yew be takin my man?" Charlie greeted him with a handshake and Charlie's smile denied he was angry Billy was leaving.

"Yes sir, it's time I get home and I asked Billy to come to Santa Fe and work for me. Much obliged you gave him work while he was here."

"Yer man Billy did a good job fer me. I got me sumtime with my granchillen," Charlie said and went over and shook hands with Billy.

"Here's yer last pay. Anytime yew come to El Paso, yews gots a job here wit me." Billy shook Charlie's hand and dumped his few belongings into the buggy.

"I'll have Martín return the buggy on Thursday," Rafe told him. Charlie stuck out his hand and Rafe shook it, then jumped up to the buggy seat and snapped the reins.

When they arrived at the ranch, Martín had the small covered wagon with the silver in the secret compartment hitched and sitting behind the barn ready to go. Martín was surprised to see a tall ruddy faced man sitting on the buggy seat beside Rafael.

"Who are you?" he asked.

Rafe made the introductions. "Martín, this is Billy Swanson."

"Glad to know you."

"I loaded food and extra wool blankets," Martín said.

As they loaded the final items into the wagon, neither Rafe nor Martín heard Jose walk into the barn. "Why are you taking that old wagon?" he asked.

It was a question Rafe was not prepared to answer. He knew his uncle would not believe anything he said. *"Tío, I can't explain it to you now. I'm just asking you to trust me."*

Jose nodded in response. He knew something was amiss. Rafael was leaving his new bride to drive this rickety old wagon to Santa Fe, while Rodolfo and María drove a new wagon back to Mexico. Martín told him last night he would be accompanying Ana Teresa to Santa Fe by stage on Thursday. None of this made sense, but he trusted Rafael had his reasons.

"Give Lupe and the children my love, but we must be leaving," Rafe said and gave his uncle a hug.

"Via con Dios," Jose told Rafe.

Rayo was tied to the rear and Rafe took the reins, as he and Billy pulled out of the barn.

"Here keep this close," Rafe told Billy as he handed him the GSW rifle. Billy pulled a six-shooter from behind his jacket and stuffed it under the tarp. Rafe gave him a quizzical glance.

"Well I thought I needed to replace that old broken down gun I used on you at the stage stop," he said with a sheepish grin and put the rifle between his legs.

"We got a long way to go Billy and it's going to be cold when we get up north," Rafe said.

"Not to worry Rafe. I grew up in Michigan. I can tell you about cold."

Rafe took a shortcut across the north field of the ranch. It was winter so the grain his uncle grew was cut and the ground hard and bumpy. About an hour later they connected to the wide path called the Chihuahua Trail, which led north and south through New Mexico along the Rio Grande.

As the miles started to grind behind them, Billy and

Rafe talked about life. Billy did not ask about their valuable cargo. He saw nothing but supplies and warm blankets in the back, though he wondered why two young mules were pulling the wagon and not two horses.

The day was bright and clear with the sun warming the desert chill. Rafe had driven a wagon or ridden Rayo along this road between El Paso and Santa Fe dozens of times. It was a road, which held both good and bad memories. He wondered which would be the case for this trip. Several hours later dust was visible in their backtrail.

"Billy, keep a sharp eye on whatever that is behind us," Rafe said as he snapped the reins to the young mules. They picked up speed slightly.

The large dust trail was gaining on them, but slowly. Billy scanned his eyes frequently keeping tabs on whatever was behind them. Finally a wagon popped into his view, then another.

"Looks like a wagon train," Billy said. Rafe sighed in relief.

About two hours later a small caravan of loaded wagons caught up with them. The wagon master called a greeting and Rafe hollered back asking if they could join up.

"Sure. We're going to Albuquerque. Always can use a couple extra guns," he yelled back.

The small caravan of loaded wagons slowly passed Rafe and Billy until they were bringing up the rear. Rafe urged the two mules to keep up.

Jerry Carr talked to the silver buyer late Saturday afternoon asking him if the greaser couple came to him directly. "Of course I have not seen the young Mexican couple," the man groused at Jerry when asked. The buyer was angry Jerry thought he would be a double-crosser and told him to forget any future deals.

Jerry spent most of the day on Sunday talking to guards along the border crossing and some of his friends in Juarez. No one saw a young Mexican couple driving a rickety old wagon pulled by two mules. He had not seen Bo since early Saturday morning, when they made the final plans to rob the greasers. It made Jerry wonder if Bo double-crossed him, taking the silver all for himself.

From all he could gleam, Marty's cousins and the silver just up and vanished and nothing made sense. The only plausible idea revolved around Bo Preston.

Sunday night Jerry Carr walked into the Gem Saloon with a bad feeling.

Bo Preston was sitting with friends at a table near the backdoor of the saloon. His right arm was wrapped around one of the saloon girls and a bottle of whiskey sat on the table. The girl was giggling and squirming as Bo moved his hand up her dress, but she did not protest too hard. Bo spotted Jerry when he came through the batwing doors. He pushed Clare off his lap and met Jerry as he crossed the room and led him to a corner in the back.

"What the hell happened to the greasers? They never showed," Bo groused. Jerry knew Bo well and could tell Bo was genuinely annoyed about the greasers.

"What the fuck Bo, why didn't yew come to me right away? I thought yew took the silver for yourself," Jerry replied.

"Fuck you Jerry. I waited until late this afternoon watching the border. Where the hell have you been? Did you get the money?"

"The greasers stiffed me and never showed with the silver. I don't know where the fuck they are."

"What about the buyer?"

"I went to him and they never showed there either. He's mad and the deal's off."

"We need to find that silver. Let's go down there and find those fuckers," Bo grumbled.

"I'm not sure they ever crossed the border. That's what I have been trying to find out."

Jerry needed Bo now more than ever. All his dreams about the racehorse were evaporating. Bo was a gunman and one of the few men Jerry trusted here in El Paso. He had saved Jerry from several dangerous situations in the gunrunning business. Bo was fearless and quick to the draw. On one incident, he and Jerry delivered a load of rifles to the leader of Mexican *bandidos* over the border. Trying to steal the guns, the Mexicano pulled his gun and was about to shoot Jerry. It was Bo who saved his life and shot the outlaw. Two *bandidos* riding with the leader pulled on him and Jerry thought they were dead men. Bo grabbed Jerry's arm and pulled him behind the wagon. Bo was fearless as he shot it out with the outlaws.

After the shootout, Jerry and Bo became trusted partners. Bo told Jerry he had been born in New York and came to El Paso when he was twelve years old. His father got in trouble with bootleggers and was run out of New York City. He got as far as El Paso and resettled the family.

Bo tried hard not to show his disappointment. The seventeen hundred dollars he planned on getting from his part of the transaction would have been easy money. "You never told me how much silver they had," Bo said.

"Well, they told me they had fifteen ingots. The one they showed me weighed about fifty-five pounds."

Bo whistled, "Man that's a lot of silver and heavy too. It can't just have disappeared."

"I would have made a pretty penny. Fuck, I already put up a deposit on that racehorse I've been wanting." Bo noticed Jerry used the term I, not we, in regards to making a pretty penny, but let it pass.

"I think that silver is still here in town. I checked at the border crossing and no greaser couple in a rickety wagon went over the border in the last couple of days."

"How do you know it was rickety, maybe they got a new wagon. They had a ton of silver to haul."

"I saw the wagon and mules in my friend Marty's barn a couple days ago. I know it because it was the one they drove over the border last year. Now it's gone."

Bo pondered Jerry's words. "We're gonna go to see this friend of yours tomorrow. That fucker must know where the silver is. Friend or not, we'll make the greaser talk," Bo bragged.

CHAPTER 26

Rafe and Billy ate the caravan's dust for what now seemed like long miles, but it was a good plan to travel with the wagon train where there would be safety in numbers. Indian attacks were rare anymore, but highwaymen sometimes plied the trail plundering wagons and stages. It was not many years ago Carlos' brother plundered along this very route.

In an attempt to be inconspicuous, Rafe borrowed an old pair of *pantalones* and a jacket from Martín rather than travel in his suit. Billy was dressed in a warm woolen coat and an old hat. Rafe found it was not hard to get Billy talking to pass the time.

"Billy, how long did you say you served in the Army?" Rafe asked.

"Almost nine years. I was drafted a year after the Civil War started. I was twenty-five years old, older than most of the boys who were taken from Michigan. Just my luck our regiment ended up at Gettysburg under the command of a young general named Custer. He had just been promoted and that galoot wasn't afraid of nothing. I can still picture him sitting atop his horse leading the charge. I lost a couple good friends and took a ball on my upper right thigh on the third charge. They say Custer kicked ass in that fight and I believe it is true. Spent the rest of the war in a hospital in Washington D.C. Last I heard, that crazy General Custer is up in Montana wanting to tame them Indians up there."

"I thought you were a blacksmith?" Rafe asked him.

"I could have mustered out. I liked the Army and I didn't have much to go back to in Michigan. My grandpa was a blacksmith and he taught me a thing or two, so I stayed in and was able to work my way into blacksmithing. I know a lot about metals."

Rafe told Billy about the Summers' foundry in Santa Fe. When he told him they made guns, like the rifle and

Rafe's pistols, Billy whistled.

"You mean your father makes these guns?"

"My adopted father. Yes. He invented this type of double-action mechanism."

"I surely would like to see all about that. Maybe he can teach me," Billy said.

"I thought you wanted to go back to Michigan?"

"Well now, I really don't have much reason to go back home to Detroit. Only one left there is my sister, but I'm sure she has enough work taking care of her family. My grandpa is gone too. My sister sent me a letter about six years ago telling me so. I'd like to try Santa Fe with you," Billy said and really meant it.

Watching their back trail Billy wondered about the weight of the wagon. It was later that afternoon before he asked directly about their cargo. "By the way Rafe, I noticed the wagon wheels are leaving a deep imprint on the road. What are we carrying that would cause that?"

Rafe's eyes widened a bit. He had not thought about the weight of the cargo leaving deep tracks so easy to follow. He decided Billy should know the truth. "We're carrying fifteen ingots of Mexican silver and I need to get them to Santa Fe."

Billy whistled. He thought it might to be some kind of metal, because it did not take too much space in the wagon and was obviously heavy.

"Did you steal them from those uppity Mexican fuckers?" Billy asked.

"No I didn't, my sister's husband stole it in Mexico. They brought it to El Paso to sell."

"Fifteen ingots. That's a shit load of silver. How much is it was worth?" Billy asked.

"You seem to know about metals. Do you have any idea how much it's worth?"

"Well let me see. Last year the Fort Commander asked me to forge an Army belt buckle for him out of silver. I went to Yuma and bought a couple ounces of silver at two dollars an ounce. If you have fifteen ingots, that's more than a bucket full of money," Billy answered and laughed.

"Two dollars? I hope I can get that much up in Santa Fe. I was hoping for about a dollar an ounce. First thing I have to do is recast them to get rid of the Mexican mine markings."

"Well hell, that's easy," Billy said and proceeded to give Rafe a few ideas on how to melt the silver into new molds. From Billy's description, Rafe knew the equipment at the foundry in Santa Fe could easily do the job.

Jerry Carr spent Monday trying to make the pieces fit. The greaser couple was nowhere in El Paso, unless someone was hiding them well. Going back to the border, one guard thought he remembered a young couple fitting their description, but the wagon was newer and pulled by a team of horses. As he remembered, the wagon contained supplies and clothes, nothing more.

He spent several long hours watching Marty's ranch from a knoll not far away. Nothing seemed out of the ordinary as Marty's family went about their chores. He thought about roughing Marty up to get an answer, but Marty saved his ass from the other Mexican boys when Jerry first moved here to El Paso. For many years, Marty was his only real friend.

Riding back to El Paso, he stopped at the livery.

"Hey Charlie," he called when he rode in.

"Hallo Jerry. Whatcha need? That there hoss needs a shoe. I kin tell frum his step," Charlie told him.

Jerry ignored the old black liveryman's comment. "Yew seen an old rickety wagon lately, specially one driven by a young greaser couple?"

Charlie hated when Jerry talked about Mexicanos with contempt. He was poor white trash from Oklahoma and Charlie knew Jerry did lots of illegal things here in El Paso.

"Well now, let me see. Cain't rightfully member. I's getting old and my eyesight and memery ain't so good no more."

"Where's that big feller, the one that was here a

couple days ago? Maybe he'd remember," Jerry asked.

"Well now Billy ain't here no mo. Going on his way to Sante Fey," Charlie said.

"Santa Fe! Why would he go to Santa Fe this time of year? I heard the passes are still closed," Jerry grumbled.

"Well I tell yew, he's a goin to Sante Fey wit a man who's got a biddnez up there."

"What kind of business?"

"He makes guns. Brings em here frum time to time and sells em at the genral store. Thems those fancy double-action type."

Jerry remembered Marty's cousin was a gunsmith from Santa Fe. "Yew meanin Marty's cousin from Santa Fe?" Jerry asked.

"That be the one. That boy be a *pistolero*. He be the one who dun kilt em Reynolds boys and their Pa. Anyone thinkin bout messing with im will run into a heap a troubl," Charlie warned.

Later Monday night Jerry sat nursing a beer at the bar in Lilli Jean's Saloon. He was so deep in his thoughts he did not hear Bo Preston walk up behind him.

"Hey Jer, whaddaya you got for us?" Bo asked. Bo's straggly brown hair was disheveled and his clothes rumpled after spending time with one of Lilli Jean's whores upstairs. Bo paid extra for several hours with Roxie. The whore had the biggest breasts he ever saw and Lilli charged extra for her fee.

"I know the greasers did not cross the border with the silver. I think maybe they left the old wagon here in El Paso and took a new one back to Mexico. Charlie is missing a buggy and his new blacksmith is gone, too. He left with Marty's cousin on their way to Santa Fe. I scouted at Marty's house and the old wagon is not there." These were the only facts Jerry knew for sure.

"I told you we need to rough up that Marty friend of yours. He must know what's going on," Bo said.

"And I told yew, I don't want Marty hurt."

"What about the blacksmith and Marty's cousin? Maybe they are taking the silver to Santa Fe," Bo asked.

"Don't know much about the blacksmith. Saw him once in the livery a couple days ago. Big man with big hands. Marty's cousin is a businessman from Santa Fe. I heard he just got married and that's why he was in town. Oh yeah, and Charlie said he was the Mex who killed Eldon and Roy Reynolds a couple years back. Everyone talked about how fast he was with a gun."

Bo pondered the information. He remembered when Eldon and Roy Reynolds had a showdown with a Mexican *pistolero* and Sheriff Watkins. Word on the street was the Mex had special guns and was lightning fast. Nathan Peters, the deputy at the time, blabbed the story for weeks after the killings. Despite any reputation, Bo trusted he could best the greaser.

"Tomorrow we'll scout the roads leading out of town. If that heavy wagon left here, we should find tracks," Bo replied.

CHAPTER 27

At twilight Rafe saw the lights of Las Cruces up ahead getting more clear. He urged the tired mules as they trailed the caravan of wagons in front of him. About twenty minutes later Rafe pulled behind the large stage stop near the center of town. The facility offered protection and food as there was constant activity with wagon caravans traveling north and south on the Chihuahua Trail.

"Billy go in and get us supper," Rafe told him. Billy understood Rafe's unease at leaving the wagon loaded with the silver unguarded.

The meal of stew and biscuits was simple, though tasty and hot. Billy ordered a beer for each of them and Rafe started a small fire for the coffee pot. As the chilly desert night enveloped them, Rafe pulled the wool blankets from the back of the wagon and handed one to Billy. "I'll take first watch," he told him.

Rafe watched Billy curl under the blanket near the fire and soon heard snoring. His thoughts wandered to Ana Teresa. She would be safely sleeping at the Hotel Stratton in the big bed they had shared. When he worked out this trip, he planned to be in Santa Fe ahead of her. She and Martín were scheduled to leave El Paso on the Thursday stage. By Rafe's calculations, he and Billy were only making about half the miles any stage would or maybe less.

Rafe pondered trading the mules for a four-horse team to pull the wagon. It would allow them to pick up speed, but they would lose the protection of the traveling caravan. Several hours later, Rafe woke Billy to pull his turn at guard duty. They took three-hour intervals of sleep and guard duty throughout the night.

Billy woke Rafe when he heard the wagon train master shouting from the stage stop to get the train rolling. Daylight was just creeping over the eastern mountains.

"Does anybody know we're carrying the silver?" Billy asked when they got on the trail behind the caravan.

"My cousin Martín and my sister and her husband, and my wife knows too, but my sister and her husband are well on their way to Torreón, Mexico. They were going to sell the silver to a man named Jerry Carr. He offered them thirty cents an ounce," Rafe responded.

"What do you know about Jerry Carr?" Billy asked.

"He is a friend of my cousin Martín. Last year my sister and her husband bought guns from Jerry and he smuggled them back across the border into Mexico for them."

"Guns? Are they outlaws?" Billy asked.

Rafe sighed. He did not want to tell Billy everything about his sister's past. Now though, it seemed to make no difference.

"Yes they were outlaws. Not like you think. They are peasants, and in Mexico peasants work like slaves for the rich *hacienderos* or miners. My sister and Rodolfo are fighting for peasants to have more freedoms, so they needed weapons."

"What's a *haciendero?*" Billy asked.

"A *hacienda* is like a very large farm or ranch. The *haciendero* owns the land. In Mexico in the past, land was allotted by the King of Spain to loyal people born to the noble class. Only rich aristocrats born in Spain would be granted theses large parcels of land." Rafe tried to explain three hundred or more years of the caste system of Mexico in simple terms. Then he added, "People born in Mexico of mixed blood are considered peasants. They work like black slaves do here in the United States."

"Are you one of those aristocrats?" Billy asked because Rafe certainly did not dress or act like a poor peasant. He spoke good English and told Billy he owned a horse breeding ranch in Santa Fe.

"I was born a peasant on a *hacienda* in Torreón," Rafe admitted. For the next hour Rafe explained how he was raised, how he ended up in Santa Fe with George Summers, and how he inherited the *hacienda* in Torreón where his sister and husband now lived.

"Dang. That's quite a story," Billy said. "So your

sister's husband stole the silver and brought it to El Paso?"

"Yes, peasants could never sell anything like that in Mexico. They stole it before I inherited the *hacienda*," Rafe told him. "My sister thought Jerry Carr could help them sell the silver here in El Paso. He offered them thirty cents an ounce and they thought it was a good price. I think he wanted to swindle them. Like I told you, they are peasants and do not know of such things."

As the hours past slowly, Rafe and Billy took turns driving the team. When the caravan rested, they rested the mules. The friendly wagon master offered them meals and made sure they had enough water.

Over the next two days, Billy and Rafe filled the long hours with lively talks. Rafe found Billy entertaining with his stories about his time in the Army. He told Rafe he was almost thirty-six and had never married. Rafe explained how he met George Summers and how the man he now considered his father had changed his life. By the time they stopped south of Monticello on Wednesday night, Rafe found he truly liked Billy Swanson. It seemed almost impossible the rough and dirty man, calling himself Desperate Billy who tried to kidnap Ana Teresa, was this same man. What seemed even more impossible was that Rafe had an idea Desperate Billy could be an asset at the foundry in Santa Fe.

Early Thursday morning Martín drove the buggy to the livery, then met Ana Teresa at the hotel. She was waiting for him in the lobby of the hotel. At ten in the morning, they boarded the stage for Santa Fe. Four other passengers boarded the stage with them.

Ana Teresa was thrilled to be finally leaving El Paso. The last five days were long and boring without Rafe. Every morning and night she prayed for his safety. She wondered how he and Desperate Billy were getting along. Whenever she thought about them, it made her smile. Rafe was shocked when she suggested he take Billy along for protection. Even though he had threatened to kidnap her, she knew in her heart Billy was not a bad man.

Suddenly she heard the snap of the reins and the driver yell to the horses. The stage gave a jerk and they were moving. Ana Teresa smiled and folded her hands in her lap.

On Thursday morning around ten, Jerry waited for Bo on the road north of El Paso. Jerry spent the last two days trying to figure out what happened to the silver. Yesterday he made a visit to Tom Hussmann and explained he might not be able to buy the racehorse as he promised. Jerry asked for his deposit back and Tom cursed at him saying, "What the fuck do you think a deposit is you dumbass? If you don't pay me the rest I keep your hundred and the horse."

For all his effort, Jerry only knew four details – the young Mexican couple with the silver had probably gone back to Mexico, the rickety wagon was missing, Martín's cousin bought a new wagon from Charlie, and both he and his wife had checked out of the Hotel Stratton.

Last night he and Bo met at Lilli Jean's to discuss ideas. Bo would not let him forget how he let the silver slip through his fingers.

"Fuck you Bo. It's not my fault," Jerry retorted.

"Yeah, well what are we going to do about finding it?" Bo groused.

"Well, have your fun tonight, cause tomorrow we're going to see about finding that wagon."

After drinking at Lilli Jean's for a while, Bo suggested they join a poker game at the Gem Saloon. Bo considered himself a card sharp, usually winning handily over many of the cowboys who tried their luck at the Gem.

By four in the morning, Bo lost over three hundred dollars and Jerry quit playing after losing fifty and spent the rest of the night watching Bo lose while he drank whiskey.

While waiting for Bo to arrive, Jerry located some deep tracks on the north road. The tracks joined the Chihuahua Trail from the direction of Marty's ranch, though Jerry thought the tracks could be from any of the many local ranches.

When Bo arrived, he suggested they follow the trail north for a while. The Chihuahua Trail was well used by riders, stagecoaches, and wagons of all types. It was the main route north and south from Mexico City, through El Paso to Santa Fe. Many sets of tracks, some deeper than others, were visible. Horse prints and the thinner tracks of stagecoach wheels were intermingled with other tracks.

"This is stupid," Bo finally said. "We have no idea if these are the tracks of the silver wagon or just some wagon loaded with supplies."

Jerry's head pounded with his hangover and Bo was sullen. "We need to get your friend to talk," Bo told him. Jerry did not want Marty hurt, but he agreed.

"Come on, we'll try to find him at the ranch," Jerry said turning his horse south.

They rode up to the Ortega ranch about two in the afternoon. Lupe and Ita were busy in the kitchen and saw them ride up. Jose was over at the Lazy H talking to Hiram Harper about the deal Rafael struck with the banker. Lupe walked out of the kitchen door to greet the strangers, though she thought she recognized one of them as a friend of Martín.

"*Hola, bienvenidos,*" Lupe welcomed them.

"*Soy Jerry Carr, ¿dónde está Martín?*" Jerry asked Lupe in Spanish if Martin was around.

"*No está aquí,*" she told him Martín was not there.

"What the hell is she saying," Bo hissed. He had no tolerance for the stupid greasers here in El Paso who could not speak English.

"Marty isn't here," Jerry translated.

"*¿Cuándo regresa?*" Jerry asked her when he would be back.

"*No lo sé,*" she replied she did not know shaking her head back and forth.

"*Gracias,*" Jerry said tipping his hat.

"Why didn't you press her for more information?" Bo grumbled at him.

"I'm not going to rough up a woman," Jerry grumbled.

After Lupe went back into the house, Jerry slowly walked his horse to the back door of the barn. Deep rut tracks led out and away from the barn and off to the far trees. Jerry and Bo followed the tracks. Where they ended, they looked for any sign of digging.

"It doesn't look like they unloaded the wagon here. See, the tracks leading back to the barn are just as deep." Bo pointed to the several sets of wagon ruts.

As they rode in circles, Bo spotted a set of deep tracks leading away from the barn heading north. The tracks cut across an empty field. "That could be it," Jerry agreed.

They followed the tracks north, losing them at times in the hard ground, then finding them again. Finally the tracks ended at the Chihuahua Trail and headed north.

"It's got to be it," Jerry said.

"Yeah, but who's driving?" Bo asked.

"I don't know, but we're going to find out."

Night was falling as Jerry and Bo turned south back toward El Paso after finding the deep ruts leading from the Ortega ranch. Jerry wanted to ride immediately to find the wagon, but Bo talked sense to him.

"That heavy wagon will be slow. It will take almost a week just to get to Albuquerque," Bo said.

"I don't care how many days it will take them, we need to get after them," Jerry protested hotly. His brain could only think about the silver and he imagined with every delay it was slipping away.

"Calm down Jer. You always go off half-cocked and that's why you get into trouble," Bo told him. "We still don't know who's driving the rig and if he has help. You want to walk into an ambush?" Bo continued.

Jerry quieted. Bo was right and the weather could also be an issue this time of year. Though today was milder, a winter storm could catch them on the trail.

"All right. We can leave in the morning," Jerry finally agreed.

Chapter 28

Billy took the last watch and woke Rafe who was huddled under a blanket in the back of the wagon. It was Saturday morning and they were keeping up with the caravan of wagons traveling to Albuquerque. Rafe fell asleep last night worrying about the two mules. He could tell the heavy load and fast pace was taking a toll on them. By the time Rafe crawled from the wagon, Billy was already walking back from the stage stop with hot coffee.

Though the caravan stopped at waystations along the trail, Rafe and Billy did not leave the wagon untended. It meant colder nights and guard shifts. Rafe was impressed Billy did not complain.

When they were back on the trail later that morning, Rafe recognized the terrain.

"We should get to San Marcial by this afternoon. I've been thinking we need to give these mules a day's rest. They have a hotel there or we can stay with my friend Carlos' cousin, Tomás. It will be safe for us there," Rafe told Billy.

"I real bed would feel mighty good," he replied with a smile. "Do you still think there is danger from that Jerry Carr feller?"

"I'll only feel safe when we get to my home in Santa Fe. Even if no one is following us out of El Paso, we still have to be on guard for highwaymen."

At the next rest stop, Rafe untied Rayo and pulled his saddle out of the back of the wagon.

"I think I'll ride the rest of the way to San Marcial. Rayo needs a break from eating our dust," Rafe told Billy.

While Billy drove the wagon, Rafe decided to check on a thin dust cloud he noticed behind them. Urging Rayo to a gallop, he headed south back down the trail. It was not long before he spotted two heavily loaded wagons slowly making their way north. Rafe rode to meet up with them.

"What do you want?" the driver asked gruffly

narrowing his eyes when he saw the young Mexican's two pistols. His rifle was perched beside him, though he kept his hands on the reins.

"I'm guarding my back trail. My wagon is up ahead with a larger caravan," Rafe told him.

"You be smart mister. I've been on this trail on many trips and been robbed several times. It's more dangerous closer to the border, but I know it could happen anywhere on this trail," the man told him.

"The caravan ahead is going to Albuquerque. Where are you headed?" Rafe asked.

"Headed to the Santa Fe Trail and then on east to Fort Madison. Carrying a load of parts for the railroad. Fort Madison is the hub for supplies right now." The man relaxed and spoke easily after realizing Rafe was not a bandit.

"We will be stopping at San Marcial. How about you?" Rafe asked.

"Naw, I want to make it to Socorro if I can. I need some supplies from there."

Rafe wished the man a good trip and turning Rayo headed north toward Billy and the wagon.

"Everything okay back there?" Billy asked as Rafe rode up.

"Yes."

Jerry and Bo spent the first night heading up the Chihuahua Trail in Las Cruces. Much to Jerry's annoyance, Bo got drunk and went with the only pretty *puta* working the cantina. Jerry got a bed at the stage stop. In the morning Jerry questioned the stable boy.

"You seen any rickety old wagon pulled by two mules come this way," he asked the boy.

"*Yo no hablo ingles,*" the boy responded he did not speak English.

"*¿Viste vagones con mulas?*" Jerry asked him if he had seen a wagon pulled by mules. The boy shook his head no.

Frustrated, Jerry waited impatiently for Bo at the stage stop. He muttered to himself about bringing the gunman with him. Perhaps he should just ride on without him. The sun was high before Bo rode up.

"Where the hell have yew been?" Jerry groused at him angry about their delay. Bo was treating this trip like a holiday.

"Keep your pants on," Bo said.

"If I'm right, that wagon has a five or six day jump on us and you're messing with some whore."

"Calm down Jerry. How come you didn't do the same. The whores were cheap back there."

Bo always noticed Jerry was not big on the ladies. In fact, he had never seen Jerry go with a whore when they drank at the Gem or Lilli Jean's.

"Because we're on a business trip, not a holiday," Jerry responded.

"Speaking of business, I've been thinking about our split," Bo said.

"Our split. What the hell do yew mean, split? First we gotta find the wagon with the silver, then we gotta sell it. Ain't no split until we do that."

"Don't you fucking worry Jerry, we're gonna find that silver."

"I still get the biggest share. Without me, yew would not even have the job," Jerry grumbled.

"Bullshit, we get equal shares," Bo looked Jerry squarely in the eyes and put his hand near his gun.

Jerry muttered under his breath, but did not outwardly argue. Half of the silver fortune was still a lot of money. It would be enough to buy the racehorse and more.

"Come on we're wasting time. Let's go find that wagon and get rich," Jerry said. Jumping to the saddle, he spurred his horse into a gallop.

Later that afternoon Rafe told Billy, "Follow me." He turned Rayo off the Chihuahua Trail and with the wagon following rode up the road to San Marcial. As they reached the small village, Rafe noticed everything looked in good repair. A few locals were walking casually along the street heading to the mercantile. Several dusty horses were tied to the rail in front of Big Ed's Saloon. His mind flashed to the time when the Sutton cowboys terrorized the small hamlet, shooting out windows and taking pot shots at the locals. Everything about the town now seemed peaceful.

Carlos' cousin, Tomás Armijo, was the mayor and Ed Seeley owned Big Ed's Saloon. Rafe considered both his friends. He led the wagon pulled by the tired mules up the main street. He was sure Tomás would not mind if they secured the wagon and spent the night.

At the end of the street, Rafe turned toward the river and the Armijo *hacienda*. Just as Billy made the turn onto the path leading to the main house, one of the rear wheels made a funny noise. Billy heard it.

"Whoa," he yelled and jumped off the wagon.

"Doesn't look good Rafe. Something is wrong with that back wheel," Billy reported.

Rafe jumped down from Rayo to have a look. "Do you think we can get to that barn up ahead before it completely breaks down?" Rafe asked.

"Not sure, maybe, then again maybe not."

"Stay here. I'll let them know we are here," Rafe said.

Rafe walked to the house and knocked on the door. A maid opened it, *"¿Tomás está en casa?"* he asked if Tomás was at home.

"Sí, por favor entra." Yes she replied, please come in.

"Rafael bienvenido, we did not know you were coming," Tomás welcomed Rafe and stepped up and gave him an *abrazo.*

After the greeting and hug, Rafe told Tomás about the wheel coming loose on the wagon and explained it was blocking the road to the main house. "I'd like to get it to the barn," Rafe told him.

"Come, I'll get some men and see what we can do to move the wagon," Tomás said and led the way to one of his out buildings.

By the time they got to the wagon, Billy already knew it was the wheel hub.

"I can fix it with a new hub, but if we can't find the part here we may need a new wheel," Billy said as they walked up.

Rafe introduced Billy, "Tomás this is Billy Swanson. He's a blacksmith by trade and is helping me with this load." Rafe did not say what was in the load, though he knew Tomás well enough to know he would not ask.

As they were discussing the wheel, several men walked up. One carried a large toolbox and another a jack. They talked to Billy about the wheel.

Tomás' foreman ordered one of the men to get a spare wheel from the barn. "The wheel is a bit smaller, but it will get the wagon moving," he told Rafe and Tomás.

"My men will take care of the wagon," Tomás told him. "Come into the house and rest. Teresa will be happy to see you. How are Carlos and his new bride? You must tell us everything."

Rafe left Billy with the wagon and followed Tomás into the house. As they walked inside, Teresa Armijo, Tomás' wife, came from the kitchen and wrapped her arms around Rafe in an *abrazo*.

"Bienvenido Rafael. We are so pleased you have come to visit. Go sit in the parlor and I'll bring the tequila."

Sipping the tequila with Tomás, Rafe told them all the news. Carlos and Bibiana were expecting a child and he had been married in El Paso last week.

"Where is your wife?" Tomás' wife asked. "Why did she not come with you?"

Rafe explained she was taking the stagecoach and how the trip in the wagon would have been grueling for her. He left out the part about the silver. Surely, if Jerry Carr planned on chasing them, he would have caught up with them by now. Perhaps because of the tequila or perhaps because of the familiar town of San Marcial, Rafe finally relaxed.

CHAPTER 29

Several hours later, the maid showed Billy into the parlor.

"Is there a place in town where I can get a new wheel or maybe a blacksmith shop where I can fix the hub?" Billy asked.

"Yes, there is a livery in town. Monday we can go there and see what they have," Tomás told him. "Meantime we can keep the wagon in the barn."

Rafe had lost track of days. Tomorrow was Sunday and all the businesses in San Marcial would be closed. It nagged him it was another day's delay, but thought the rest for the mules was a good thing.

"I have to take Billy to Big Ed's Saloon and get a room for him," Rafe said.

"He can stay here. We have plenty of room," Tomás offered graciously.

"Billy deserves a night off," Rafe said. "Besides I wouldn't mind seeing Big Ed."

"Yes, I will go with you. I would not mind having a drink with Ed tonight, but first Teresa has dinner ready for us," Tomás said. "We will go to town later."

After supper, Tomás, Rafe, and Billy headed to the town of San Marcial. Rafe rode Rayo and Tomás loaned Billy a horse. They rode directly to Big Ed's Saloon in the center of town. As they walked into the only saloon in San Marcial, Rafe looked around the familiar room. Two cowboys sat a table with a bottle and a deck of cards. Three locals sat at another table playing Monte. Against the bar two cowboys, one Anglo and one Mexican, were in a discussion with beers on the bar in front of them.

The mood in the room was serene, not at all like when the Sutton cowboys harassed the local Hispanics and not at all like the day Rafe killed John B. Sutton in a gunfight. Sutton pulled on him and Rafe shot him dead near the spot where the two men now talked and drank beer.

"Hey Ed," Tomás called out as they got to the bar.

"Hey Thomas," Ed Seeley said. As Rafe took off his hat, Ed recognized him. "Rafe it's good to see you again," Ed greeted him and reached across the bar to shake Rafe's hand.

Ed would never forget the young Mexican *pistolero* who was instrumental in protecting this town from John Sutton's out of control cowboys several years ago.

"Ed, this is my friend Billy. Do you have a room for him?" Rafe asked.

"Sure do. How you doing Billy." Ed stuck out his hand and Billy shook it. Reaching back behind him, Ed got a key off a hook on the wall and handed it to Billy. "Room four. It's the last one down the hallway."

Ed's hotel was now completed with six rooms and he was planning on adding six more in the coming years. Life had been good for Ed since he married Cynthia, John Sutton's widow. Besides being exceptionally happy in his married life, she helped him finance the completion of the hotel.

"Is Cindy here?' Tomás asked thinking she would want to say hello to Rafe.

"She's at the house. I was just fixing on letting Roberto finish up for the night and heading home, but let's have a drink first," Ed offered.

They talked and laughed for the next several hours. Ed told Rafe how things calmed here in San Marcial since Cindy took over the ranch. The locals and cowboys made peace at last. He and Cindy were happily married and Cindy was pregnant.

"I'm gonna be a father," Ed said beaming. "I never thought I'd ever have a wife let alone children. Cindy says she wants at least three or four," Ed said with a grin.

Ed poured several shots for each of them as the talk continued.

"I got married Ed. Last week," Rafe told him.

"Well where is she?"

"She's coming by stagecoach. Speaking of which, she

left El Paso Thursday morning. Do you know when it would get here?" Rafe knew his original calculations concerning the time he and Billy needed to drive the wagon and the time for the stagecoach to reach Santa Fe were wrong. Now, the wheel on the wagon needed fixing adding another day's delay.

Ed rubbed his chin. "Well I don't rightly know, but I think it is a three or four day trip. Depends if they have any trouble. It did not stop today, so it may come tomorrow."

"Does it always stop here or would it go onto Socorro directly?" Rafe asked. Rafe wanted to see Ana Teresa and make sure she was safe. He also was trying to figure out a new plan so she would not reach Santa Fe before him.

"That depends, if any passenger wants to stop here, they stop, or if they have any supplies for me. I do have a couple orders coming, but not sure when they left El Paso." Ed's less than specific answers left Rafe unsettled. If the stagecoach did not stop, Ana Teresa would reach Santa Fe before him for sure.

They spent another hour talking before Tomás said they better get home soon. "Me too, Cindy is probably worried already," Ed said.

"You want a drink before you go up Billy?" Rafe asked.

"Thanks, but I'm tired. I think I'll go get some shuteye," Billy said and went up to his room.

"You want another shot before you go?" Ed asked Rafe and Tomás.

"No, Teresa is probably worrying. We better get home," Tomás responded.

Stretching out on the bed, Billy thought about Rafe's conversation with Ed and Tomás. It was obvious they had mutual respect for each other and from the stories, Rafe was part of a big shootout here in San Marcial. Texas cowboys had moved into the little town and terrorized the locals, who were of Spanish descent.

Billy lived long enough in the west to know most

easterners and especially Texans hated Mexicans. They called them greasers. He saw it in towns and in the Army, too. The Anglos thought the greasers were stupid and slovenly, and hated anyone speaking Spanish. Billy believed it too when he first got to Yuma. He did not understand the locals and heard the other soldiers curse and grumble about it.

Over the years, Billy got to know the local liveries in Yuma. One elderly Mexican blacksmith became his friend. Edwardo took him to his home numerous times for supper and to meet his family. Billy found out everything he thought about Mexicans was untrue.

The blacksmith lived in a small house in the south part of Yuma where only Mexicans lived. The houses were small, but well kept. The inside of the blacksmith's home was immaculate. A small shrine to the Virgin Mary was tucked in the corner with lighted candles. On each visit Billy's respect grew. Edwardo's wife cooked beans and chilis with beef or pork. Her homemade tortillas were light and melted in his mouth. Several times she made a special Mexican dessert, which she called *capirotada*. The bread, egg, and raisin dish was spiced with cinnamon and sweetened with honey. Billy loved it and always ate second helpings.

Now he was traveling with Rafe. His respect for the young Mexican grew each day. Billy could not think of another man he knew who seemed to possess more integrity and grit. By all rights Rafe had every reason to hate him for trying to steal the Appaloosa and kidnap Ana Teresa. Yet, Billy could tell Rafe held no resentment toward him. Billy hoped someday he could repay Rafe for his compassion and swore to have his back, if ever he needed it.

Rafe slept fitfully in the bedroom at Tomás' home until the rooster crowed. He could not figure out a way to find Ana Teresa coming on the stagecoach to tell her what to do if she reached Santa Fe before him. The only plausible plan, which came to mind, was to wire ahead to Carlos and make sure he and Bibiana met her when she arrived. Bibiana was Ana Teresa's cousin and Carlos his best friend. They would welcome her and keep her safe until he arrived with the wagon.

The only problem with the plan was San Marcial did not have a telegraph. He would have to ride to Socorro to send one. He could make the trip in two days, but it meant leaving the wagon loaded with the silver here in San Marcial with only Billy to protect it.

When he came into the kitchen to greet Teresa and thank her for the hospitality, she was busy getting the children ready for church.

"We will leave soon," she told him assuming he would accompany them to church.

As the Armijo carriage arrived at the small Catholic Church in San Marcial, the bells were calling the people to worship. Rafe dipped his fingers in the holy water, then followed Tomás and his family down the aisle. They sat in a pew near the front.

At every opportunity during the Mass, Rafe said a prayer for Ana Teresa. He prayed Saint Christopher would keep her safe. He prayed she would forgive him for abandoning her six days after they were married for this somewhat foolhardy trip to get the silver to Santa Fe. In his final prayer, he asked the Virgin Mary to forgive him for his selfishness and help him figure out a way Ana Teresa would not reach Santa Fe before him.

At the end of the Mass, Rafe wandered outside. The sky was a clear aqua blue with only a few fluffy white clouds and the sun shone brightly. While the sun was warm on his face, the winter air had a chill in it. He was surprised to see Ed Seeley walk from the church with Cynthia holding his arm. The last time Rafe saw Cynthia, she was Cynthia Sutton, the widow of John Sutton. Rafe made her a widow and he wondered if she would be pleased to see him.

"Hello Cynthia," Rafe stepped up to her and Ed.

"Rafe. Ed told me you were in town. It is so nice to see you again." Unlinking her arm from Ed's she reached out and gave him a hug.

"She was angry I was late getting home last night until she heard you were in town," Ed added.

Cynthia's auburn hair was twisted into a bun at the nape of her neck. Her crystal green eyes glinted in the sunshine. She radiated joy from her entire being.

"Ed says you are married now, too," she said to him. "She is a very lucky woman, just as I am."

"Ed told me you are expecting a child," Rafe said. Cynthia beamed with delight and took Rafe by the arm. They walked down the church's walkway toward the numerous waiting carriages.

"Rafe, Rafe," he suddenly heard Ed's booming voice. "I see the stagecoach coming."

Fifteen minutes later when Ana Teresa stepped off the stagecoach in San Marcial, New Mexico, Rafe took her hand as she stepped from the coach.

CHAPTER 30

Ana Teresa's heart sang as she felt Rafe's arms surround her after she stepped off the dusty stagecoach. Once again he miraculously found her.

"Mi amor," she whispered, my love.

When Martín stepped out of the coach, he was surprised to see Rafael holding Ana Teresa. He did expect to see his cousin until they reached Santa Fe.

"Hello Rafael," he said. "We did not expect to see you here."

"The wagon broke a wheel. Billy is getting it fixed. Come, we'll go to the Armijo's home and have Sunday lunch.

Rafe had their suitcases unloaded from the coach and told the driver Martín and Ana Teresa would not be continuing today.

"They can take any stagecoach that comes through here," the driver told him. "They just need to show their tickets."

"Thank you." Rafe replied realizing his problem was solved. Martín and Ana Teresa could take another stagecoach a few days behind him and Billy. In the meantime, San Marcial was a safe place for them.

Ed and Cynthia offered to drive Rafe, Ana Teresa, and Martín to Tomás' home, where Teresa was already busy adding extra places at the table for the Sunday meal. Tomás greeted them on the porch.

"Tomás, may I present my wife, Ana Teresa, and my cousin Martín Ortega," Rafe introduced them.

"My honor," Tomás said taking Ana Teresa's hand. *"Bienvenidos,"* he welcomed them as he ushered them inside.

After introductions, Ana Teresa and Tomás' wife Teresa were instant friends. Rafe heard them laughing at the similarity of their names as Teresa took her back into the kitchen while the men headed to the parlor.

Jerry Carr and Bo Preston spent the night at the waystation north of Monticello about sixty miles south of Socorro. Over the past three days they passed numerous riders, three stagecoaches, and several small wagon trains. Today they passed two wagons pulled by four-horse teams loaded with lumber and metal rails. As they passed the second caravan today, Jerry began to wonder if the silver wagon turned off the trail. He was sure they would have overtaken the slow moving wagon by now.

The empty trail stretched out in front of them and Bo took to cussing at every annoyance, as they did not see any sign of a lone covered wagon carrying the silver. The deep ruts they followed north of El Paso had become indistinguishable from the many others.

"This is a crock of shit," Bo told Jerry. "We have no idea where the wagon went. It could be anyplace ahead or maybe it turned off."

"If yew want to go back to El Paso, go ahead," Jerry grumbled. He hoped Bo would take the advice and leave. Then if Jerry found the silver, he would not have to split the money.

"Go fuck yourself," Bo replied.

"Yew've been dragging us down since we started with yer drinking and whoring," Jerry growled back at him.

"Yeah, well maybe you should try it sometime. Beats sitting alone." Bo had known Jerry for many years and never saw him take a whore upstairs. It did not seem natural and Bo wondered about it some.

"If yew want to poke those woreout trollops, that's yer business. Just don't fucking do it on my time," Jerry cursed back at him. Jerry urged his horse a bit faster so he could end the conversation.

About an hour later, the sun dipped behind the western mountains. Bo rode to catch up to Jerry.

"My horse is almost done in. I think there might be something wrong with one of her back shoes," Bo told Jerry. Bo owned the tan mare for many years and knew her gait well. She wasn't limping, but the gait was not right.

"Maybe we should turn back to Fort Craig. We

passed the sign a few miles back," Jerry suggested.

"I think there are a couple small towns between here and Socorro. Can't remember the names, but I know there are markers. We should slow the pace and take the first sign we see," Bo replied.

An hour later Jerry and Bo rode along the main road of San Marcial. Long shadows covered the dusty little town as they rode up and saw the sign for Big Ed's Saloon and Hotel.

"Howdy," Ed Seeley greeted the two strangers when they walked up to the bar.

"Howdy, shots and beers and whatcha got for food?" Jerry ordered.

"I got steak and potatoes or beef stew," Ed told them as he poured the shots and filled two glasses with beer.

Both Bo and Jerry ordered the steak and potatoes. While Big Ed was in the back fixing the meals, Bo looked over the small saloon. It was quite nice for such an out-of-the-way place as this tiny hamlet in New Mexico.

It was Sunday night and cowboys sat at three of the six tables playing cards. They barely glanced at Bo and Jerry as they walked in and now paid them no mind at all. Bo noticed two of the men were Mexican, while the others were Anglo. It was an unusual sight to see cowboys playing cards with Mexicans.

When Ed served the meals Bo asked, "Nice place here. Who owns it?"

"I do. I built this place when I mustered out of the Army over at Fort Craig about ten miles south of here."

"So I guess you are Big Ed?"

"Ed Seeley, but everyone calls me Big Ed."

Bo and Jerry could see why. Ed Seeley was a broad-shouldered bear of a man over six feet tall and well over two hundred and fifty pounds. His short sandy hair was graying at the temples. He had an easy smile and seemed amiable, though probably not someone you wanted to rile.

"Hey Ed, bring another bottle," a cowboy yelled.

"Excuse me," Ed said. Grabbing a bottle from behind the bar, he headed to the cowboy's table.

Setting down the bottle, Ed glanced at the coins and bills on the table. Ed knew all the men well. They worked for his wife at the Circle B Ranch, the cattle ranch she inherited from her dead husband.

"You boys should be careful not to lose all your pay in one game," Ed chided them. Paydays were on Fridays and cowboys often lost everything playing poker before the weekend was over. It was good for his business, but Ed wondered how these men ever expected to have anything other than a bunkhouse over their heads.

"Yew ain't got no whores, Ed. All we got to spend our pay on is yer whiskey and poker," one of the men said in return. It was said in good humor. Though Ed knew the men wanted him to run whores here at the saloon, he refused.

Ed walked over to the table where Billy Swanson was playing with four other cowboys from the Circle B. Ed introduced Billy and the men were happy to let him play.

"You boys need anything?" Ed asked.

"Maybe later. We still got some in this bottle," Sam Jergins replied.

When he walked back to the bar Jerry spoke up, "We need a couple rooms for the night."

"That's not a problem. Pretty quiet around here after the New Year. The rooms are two dollars a night," Ed told them. "You want another shot?" he asked.

"Since I heard you don't run whores, you better give us a bottle," Bo said.

They took the bottle and their half-eaten plates of food to a table near the front. Jerry was surprised at the deep rich flavor of the well-cooked steak. He could tell the quality of the beef was excellent. A pile of boiled potatoes were stacked on the plate and covered in butter.

Ana Teresa enjoyed the evening as they talked and laughed with Tomás and Teresa and their family. Tomás recounted Rafe's previous adventures here in San Marcial and how Rafe had cleaned up the town.

"Before John Sutton's Texas cowboys came to town, San Marcial was a quiet place. After the Texas cattleman bought the land and brought his cowboys here, a war almost broke out. The cowboys terrorized the locals and the villagers were scared for their life and property," Tomás explained what happened. "The Texans had no respect for anything or anyone here. They thought the people were stupid and inferior. No one was spared their spite, even me," Tomás fingered a scar on his chin from a fight in the street with one of the cowboys.

When he talked about a poor woman who was raped and murdered by two of the cowboys, Ana Teresa shuttered. It left her with a knot in her stomach knowing how it felt to be helpless against a much stronger foe.

"Rafe killed them both in a gunfight. They bushwhacked him on the road north of here trying to steal Rayo and the black stallion for their boss, John Sutton," Tomás retold the story.

"I was only protecting my life," Rafe interjected.

"You protected the entire town," Tomás replied. "When he brought the two bodies back to town, Sutton accused him of murdering them. Sutton drew on Rafe in anger over the deaths of his two men and Rafe had no option but to kill the bitter cattleman," Tomás recounted.

Ana Teresa remembered Billy wanting to steal Rayo and Rafe told her how Carmela had stolen the horse in Mexico. Now she learned Rafe had killed three men over the horse. The Appaloosa was remarkable, though Ana Teresa wondered why it was such a target.

Later that evening Rafe held Ana Teresa in his arms. As she lay with him in the small bed, Ana Teresa's hand caressed Rafe's bare chest and traced the star-shaped scar. "I wonder if you love me as much as you love Rayo," she teased.

"How can you even ask me such a question," Rafe sputtered thinking she was serious.

"Then show me how much you love me."

CHAPTER 31

Monday morning Billy was up early and when he walked down the stairs at Big Ed's Saloon he smelled bacon cooking. "Mornin," Billy called out as reached the bar. "Sure smells good," he added.

Ed Seeley walked from the kitchen. "Go and sit Billy while I fry up some eggs for you," Ed offered as he poured him a cup of coffee.

"Thanks Ed."

A little while later Ed arrived with two plates of bacon, eggs, and biscuits. After pouring more coffee, he sat down.

"How long you known Rafe?" Ed asked.

"I met him west of Fort Yuma right before Christmas," Billy said. It sounded like a plausible story and better than he tried to rob him and kidnap his wife.

"You were in the Army? You got one of those short Army haircuts just like mine," Ed asked and laughed. The comment surprised Billy. He almost forgot he was a fugitive from the Army stockade at Fort Yuma and Ed's comment made Billy think he should let his hair grow longer.

"Yeah, I did a hitch. You did time in the Army?" Billy asked not wanting to answer Ed's question directly.

"Yeah, my last station was at Fort Craig, just south of here. When did you get out?"

"Oh a couple months ago. My hitch was up and I'm getting older," Billy said somewhat vaguely.

"I was cavalry. How about you?"

Billy wanted to change the subject, but found it hard not to answer Ed's questions.

"Been doing blacksmithing for the last six years. Got winged by a bullet at Gettysburg. Probably should have mustered out then, but I stayed in. General Stephens sent me to Fort Yuma."

Billy concentrated on eating the breakfast hoping to

end the questions about the Army. The eggs were cooked with the yolks still a bit runny and the bacon was thick and crisp.

"You want another cup?" Ed asked.

Billy nodded absentmindedly to Ed as something was nagging him about last night. One of the two men who came in looked familiar. When they first arrived his back was to them, but later Billy saw them sitting at a table. Something about the thinner man reminded him of someone who came into the livery in El Paso.

After Ed finished pouring the coffee Billy asked, "Hey Ed, I saw two men come in last night. Do you know them?"

"Naw, just a couple of strangers. Said one of their horses has a bad shoe so they stopped. Hey maybe you can get some business. You said you're a blacksmith," Ed told him.

"They still here?"

"Yeah, they're up in their rooms. Why?"

"Just thought I recognized one of them. Rafe suspected someone might come after us from El Paso. Could be them," Billy told him.

"Why would anyone be after Rafe?"

Billy searched for an answer. "He tangled with someone."

"I'll tell ya Rafe is quick on the draw. If I was them I would not want to tangle with him," Ed said.

"I hear you. I've seen him in action with those double-action pistols of his. He had me dead to rights when I tried to steal his horse and take his wife hostage," Billy blurted out without thinking.

"What! You tried to take his wife and the Appaloosa? Hell, he gunned down three men here in San Marcial who tried to bushwhack him and take his horses. You're lucky to be alive."

Ed shook his head in disbelief. The story seemed completely impossible. Rafe introduced Billy as a friend yesterday.

"Yes very lucky. I was really acting stupid. It's all

good now and we're friends. Hey Ed keep an eye on those two jaspers for me just in case they're the ones coming after Rafe."

"I'll do that."

"Soon as I eat I'm gonna see about the wagon wheel," Billy said.

"The livery's down the street thataway. Ask for Pedro," Ed told him.

Ed mused over the story Billy told him. Rafe was not a hot-head, but Ed was pretty sure if Billy tried to steal Rayo and Rafe's wife, Billy was a very lucky man to be alive. Ed could not wait to hear Rafe's version of the story.

Billy walked down the street and found the livery.

"Good morning. I'm looking for a twelve spoke wheel for a covered wagon. The hub broke and it looks like it can't be fixed," Billy told the man at the livery shop.

"You can look *señor.*"

Billy followed the man to a shelf where bins contained hubs segregated by size. Billy found two which might fit the broken wheel. Hefting them, one in each hand, he turned to Pedro.

"I need to take these to the mayor's house can you take me there?"

"*Sí señor.*" The man helped Billy load the heavy hubs into a buggy and they rode off to the mayor's house.

Jerry got up earlier than Bo though it was still late in the morning. He smelled bacon as he walked down the stairs into the main room of the saloon. Ed Seeley was not in sight. Spotting a pot of coffee behind the bar, Jerry walked around and poured himself a cup.

A few minutes later Ed walked out of the kitchen surprised to see one of the strangers drinking a cup of coffee.

"I helped myself," Jerry said.

"Oh, that's fine. I'm cooking up some more bacon and eggs in the back. Do you want some now or are you waiting for your friend?"

"Don't know when Bo will get his lazy ass out of

bed, so bring me some breakfast."

Thinking about what Billy told him Ed asked, "I never did get your names last night. I should add them to my register."

"I'm Jerry Carr and Bo Preston's upstairs."

"Nice to meet you Jerry. I'll be back with them eggs and bacon in a few minutes."

Ed was stuck at the bar without any help until later in the morning. He wanted to find Billy or Rafe and ask if either of these men were the ones from El Paso.

Bo was still not down by the time Jerry finished his breakfast. He asked Ed about their horses.

"I unsaddled them and put them in my barn out back. That's included in the two dollar fee," Ed told him.

"I gotta see to the mare. Bo thinks she's throwing a shoe."

"The livery is down the street thataway. Ask for Pedro," Ed said.

A Mexican was unhitching a buggy in the livery when Jerry walked the horse through the front doorway.

"Hello *señor,*" the man greeted him.

"Yew Pedro? Can you check her shoes?" Jerry asked.

"*Sí. Un momento,*" Pedro responded while finishing with the buggy.

After checking the mare, Pedro pointed to the left back hoof. "The shoe is bad," he said in broken English. "I fix."

"*¿Viste vagones con mulas?*" Jerry asked him if he had seen a wagon pulled by mules. Pedro looked surprised as Jerry spoke to him in Spanish.

"*No vi ningún vagón de mulas,*" Pedro said he had not seen a wagon pulled by mules, but told him there was a wagon with a broken wheel at the mayor's house that he never saw before.

Jerry told him to fix the shoe and quickly walked from the livery back to Big Ed's Saloon. Bo was still not downstairs. Jerry had an idea the wagon carrying the silver was somewhere here in San Marcial and he needed Bo to help him find it. Taking the stairs in twos, Jerry banged on

Bo's door.

"Whatcha want?"

"Get up. We got work to do," Jerry called through the door.

When Bo opened the door, Jerry was waiting leaning against the upstairs railing.

"Let's go," he grumbled.

"Hey, I'm not going anywhere without coffee and breakfast."

"Okay, it's downstairs, but hurry it up or I'm leaving yew behind."

Thirty minutes later they walked into the livery. Bo's mare was standing quietly in a stall.

"¿Dónde está la casa del alcalde?" Jerry asked where he could find the mayor's home.

"Norte, en la hacienda Armijo," Pedro answered the Armijo home was to the north of the town.

While Pedro worked on the mare's shoe, Jerry walked the short distance back to the hotel's corral. He saddled his horse and rode back to the livery. Hopefully the greaser would have Bo's horse shod and ready.

At Tomás' barn, Billy pulled the broken hub off the wheel and replaced it with one he brought from the livery. One of the ranch hands who helped yesterday, was helping him to jack up the wagon and replace the small temporary wheel with the fixed wheel. They greased all four hubs and axles and inspected them for flaws. Billy walked to the house still somewhat greasy and dirty from his work.

"The wheel's fixed," he told Rafe. Rafe and Ana Teresa were in the dining room with Tomás and Martín having an early lunch.

"Good, I'll get my things together," Ana Teresa said.

"I told you, you and Martín need to take the stagecoach to Santa Fe. Nothing has changed. You cannot ride with us on that old wagon. Look what happened with the wheel. We were lucky it happened somewhere where we could get it fixed easily."

Last night Ana Teresa told him she was not taking the stagecoach and insisted on going with him to Santa Fe on the wagon. They argued, but he could not sway her desire nor could he convince her of her folly. It was winter and a breakdown or highwaymen could be fatal.

Ana Teresa huffed and folded her arms across her chest. Rafe looked at Billy.

"I think we need to take it for a drive. Go hitch the mules and we'll test it by going to town to pick up supplies," Rafe said looking at Billy.

"I'm going with you," Ana Teresa demanded. Rafe did not argue. It was only a trial run to town. He would have to change her mind before he and Billy left for Santa Fe.

Billy put the extra hub in the back and jumped on the tailgate. Ana Teresa sat on the seat next to Rafe. Snapping the reins, Rafe started the mules and the old wagon creaked forward.

It was a little past noon when the wagon rolled down the main street of San Marcial. Rafe stopped the wagon at the livery.

"Can you lift it?" Rafe yelled back at Billy.

"Sure," Billy laughed and picked up the metal hub.

"Meet us at the mercantile," Rafe said. Billy hefted the heavy hub in his left arm and walked off toward the livery.

Rafe snapped the reins and the wagon continued down the main street. The wagon seemed to be rolling steady as Rafe made deliberate turns to test the wheels. He pulled to a stop in front of the mercantile.

"Have Arturo load a slab of bacon, lard, a bag of coffee, beans, and jerky," Rafe told Ana Teresa. "I need to talk to Big Ed."

While Ana Teresa headed into the mercantile, Rafe walked across the street to Big Ed's Saloon. He found Ed behind the bar.

CHAPTER 32

Billy walked into the livery with the heavy hub on his shoulder. Two men were in the back, one of them was saddling a horse.

"Pedro, I'm returning one of the hubs. The other one worked. Tomás Armijo said to put it on his bill," Billy called out thinking Pedro must be somewhere in the barn.

"That's the big man from Hastings Livery in El Paso. I'm sure of it," Jerry hissed quietly to Bo.

"If he's here, then the wagon must be here too," Bo whispered.

"Pedro, you here?" Billy called out again.

"Pedro's not here right now," Jerry answered as he walked toward Billy towing a horse. His face was shadowed by his hat.

"Do you work here? I need to tell him about the hub."

As Jerry talked to Billy, Bo walked quietly up from behind. He pulled his pistol from the gunbelt.

Billy was holding the hub on his shoulder as Jerry walked up. Something about the man was familiar as if Billy had seen him somewhere before.

"Hey mister," Billy started to say.

Bo swung the gun against the back of Billy's head. As if in slow motion, the heavy hub fell off Billy's shoulder as he crumpled to the ground.

"Come on," Jerry said as he jumped to his saddle.

Rafe found Ed Seeley cleaning the bar when he walked into the saloon.

"Ed, I want Ana Teresa to take the stagecoach to Santa Fe. She wants to ride the wagon, but it is too dangerous. Besides, it will be freezing up north. Here's her ticket, but I need a favor."

"Anything Rafe," Ed said.

"After she leaves, can you send someone to Socorro

to send a telegram? I'll write it out. I need to tell Carlos to meet the stagecoach when she arrives, in case we get delayed again," Rafe told him.

"Sure. I'll take it myself. Cindy likes to go shopping in Socorro. She's welcome to stay here until she leaves," Ed offered.

"Thanks Ed, but she and Martín will stay with Tomás and Teresa." At least Rafe hoped he could get her to stay here in San Marcial. She was not listening to him and demanding to go with him.

"Come to the kitchen. I have some paper and a pen back there," Ed said.

In the mercantile across the street from Big Ed's, Arturo took Ana Teresa's order and was busy organizing it behind the counter. Ana Teresa walked outside and hopped up on the wagon. She ducked under the small canopy. The bed of the small wagon was covered with blankets and cooking supplies. The large barrel of water was tied to the inside because of the colder weather. She could see Rafe's point. The wagon was hardly big enough for two people, let alone three. Pushing aside a sack of flour, she made room for the new supplies.

"There's the wagon," Jerry hissed at Bo as they came out of the livery onto the main street. As they approached, the mules stood quietly in front and no one was around.

Suddenly Ana Teresa felt the wagon shift as someone stepped on the wheel. She assumed it was Arturo. "Bring the supplies back here Arturo," she called out.

Jerry jumped up on the seat of the wagon. He was surprised when he heard a woman's voice, but he was sure the old wagon pulled by the mules was the one owned by the young Mexican couple. He snapped the reins and the mules started to pull.

The jerk of the wagon toppled Ana Teresa to the bed of the wagon, too startled to scream. The wagon swayed erratically back and forth, as the mules began to gain speed. Bo picked up the reins of Jerry's horse and followed the wagon south out of the town of San Marcial.

Ana Teresa tried to regain her footing in the rocking

wagon, finally working her way toward the front and pulled back the wagon's canvas flap. An unfamiliar man was in the seat holding the reins.

"Who are you," she demanded to the man's back.

Jerry heard the woman's voice behind him and turned his head. A lovely young woman's face peeked from the canvas. It was not the face of the young Mexican woman who came with Rodolfo to sell the silver. This woman was fair skinned and had brown hair.

Ana Teresa could tell by the sun they were traveling away from the town. "Where are you going? Take this wagon back to San Marcial."

"Shutup and maybe you'll live." Jerry shoved the woman back into the wagon with his hand. Ana Teresa fell backwards hitting her head against the large water barrel.

Rafe and Ed walked out of the kitchen talking and laughing. "Cindy can get headstrong too," Ed said. Rafe had been telling him how Ana Teresa was insisting on riding in the cramped wagon instead of taking the comfortable stagecoach. "If it does not come tomorrow, we'll invite your bride to have supper with us at the ranch. Cindy would love to have female company. We don't often entertain."

"Much obliged, Ed. I was worried Cynthia might harbor ill will toward me for shooting John," Rafe admitted.

"If she ever did, she doesn't any longer. We are very happy together."

The batwing doors banged open and Arturo ran inside the saloon.

"*Señor,* the wagon is gone," Arturo said.

"What do you mean the wagon is gone?" Rafe demanded.

"I was inside packing the supplies. When I came out it was gone," he explained.

"Where is Ana Teresa? *¿Dónde está la señora?*" Rafe demanded in both English and Spanish.

"*No lo sé,*" Arturo said he did not know.

Rafe quickly strode to the doorway of the saloon.

The spot where the wagon had been was empty. "Damn Billy," he muttered thinking if Billy wanted the silver, he could have done it along the trail when no one was around.

"Perhaps she drove the wagon to the back door thinking it would be easier to load," Ed suggested.

"*No señor* Ed, I already checked the back door," Arturo said.

"Go check again," Ed barked at him as he and Rafe headed out into the street.

"Billy must have taken the wagon," Rafe said calming down. "Perhaps he decided to take the wagon to the livery to check the wheel again." There was no other explanation which made any sense. They turned right and down the street heading toward the livery.

Before they reached the livery, they saw Billy stumbling near the doorway holding his head.

"Billy! Where's the wagon? Where's Ana Teresa?" Rafe yelled at him.

"What do you mean? Someone knocked me over the head. I think it was that man who came to the livery in El Paso looking for a broken down wagon. I'm not sure. His hat was pulled down, but I think it was the same man," Billy said. "Come to think of it I saw him at Big Ed's last night with another man."

"Two men came in last night, strangers. One said his name was Jerry Carr and the other he called Bo. Can't remember the name, but I wrote it down. They drank some and stayed the night in the hotel," Ed told Rafe kicking himself he forgot to tell Rafe sooner. "The man named Bo wore his gun like a gun hand; the other was thinner and sandy haired."

Rafe had never met Jerry Carr, but the brief description reminded Rafe of the man he and Ana Teresa passed on the road south of his uncle's ranch.

"Ed, I think Ana Teresa has been kidnapped with the wagon. Jerry was following us from El Paso," Rafe said.

"Yes, Billy said you tangled with someone there."

"Not exactly tangled. He wants to steal the wagon."

"Why would he want that old wagon? It's not worth anything," Ed said.

"No not the wagon, but the load of silver it is carrying."

Ed whistled. "I see. Take my buggy. It's in the shed out back of the hotel."

"No, I need Rayo and I need my guns. They're both back at Tomás' ranch."

"Then let's go get them. The wagon can't travel fast with that load," Ed said. "I'll get my rifle."

"Just take us to Tomás'. We can handle this. You have a pregnant wife at home."

Martín greeted them in the courtyard when they rode in.

"Where's the wagon?" he asked.

"I think Jerry Carr stole it. Ana Teresa was inside," Rafe spit the words out bitterly.

Martín hung his head. "Let me get my things," he said.

"No you stay here. Billy and I are going after them."

"But I know Jerry," Martín protested.

"Ed said it was two men. A man named Bo is traveling with Jerry. Do you know who that might be?" Rafe asked.

Martín pondered the question a few moments. "I'm not sure, but sometimes a gun hand named Bo Preston works with him. I've heard he has a nasty temper and is quick to the draw."

It was several hours after the wagon was stolen before Rafe and Billy were ready to ride. Tomás loaned Billy a young buckskin.

"Thank you for the horse, Tomás. I'll get it back as soon as we find the kidnappers," Rafe told him. Rafe mounted Rayo and Billy rode the borrowed buckskin.

"*Via con Dios,*" Tomás gave them a blessing. Ed Seeley reached up and extended his hand as did Martín. Rafe quickly turned Rayo down the path, then spurred Rayo to a gallop. Billy followed.

Wasting no time, they rode through town and then south toward the Chihuahua Trail. Rafe could see the deep wheel tracks of the covered wagon. One thing was in their favor, the mules would not go fast pulling the weight of the silver load.

CHAPTER 33

Ana Teresa sat up. She had a knot on her head and her head throbbed from hitting the water barrel. The wagon bumped and swayed unsteadily and she knew the man was driving too fast. Rafe told her the trip was dangerous and she had not believed him. Terrified, she wondered what happened to Rafe and Billy. She was in the back of the wagon making room for the new supplies, when the man drove off.

As the wagon swayed, she carefully peeked out of the canvas. Another man rode along side, with a saddled horse in tow. Both men were Anglos wearing denim pants and wool coats.

"Hey there Jerry, can't you get those mules to go any faster? That guy in the livery may come after us." Bo now thought he should have shot the man, but at the time did not want to make noise. Instead, he gun butted the back of the man's head with his pistol.

"They're fucking mules and this wagon is heavy. I can't push them any faster," Jerry retorted.

When they reached the Chihuahua Trail, Jerry turned south toward El Paso. If he knew another route, he would have taken it, but the main trail was the only road connecting El Paso to the cities in northern New Mexico.

"Go check our back trail," Jerry grumbled at him.

Ana Teresa's mind churned trying to formulate a plan of escape. As the man on the horse rode off, her mind swirled with ideas. Perhaps now with only the driver around, she could jump off the back of the wagon and he probably would not even hear her fall. She worked her way to the tailgate and looked down. Though the wagon was not moving extremely fast, it was still a fair jump off the back. She thought she might get hurt in the fall and the trail offered no places to hide. The second man would surely be back soon and find her on the road. Then what?

Quietly she searched the contents of the wagon for

anything she might use as a weapon. The cooking supplies were stowed in the back and she found a cast iron pan. Testing the weight in her hand, she thought a swift and mighty whack to the back of the driver's head would knock him out or at the very least give her an edge.

"No one's coming," she heard the other man's voice say as he rode up.

When Rafe and Billy reached the main trail, Rafe held up and stared at the ruts as they made sure the wagon headed south. He was sure Jerry Carr would take the wagon back to El Paso. Any other plan made no sense. He stared at the ruts, then kicked Rayo to a gallop.

The most important concern on his mind was Ana Teresa. Perhaps they did not even know she was in the wagon. He tried to make sense about why she had not stayed in the mercantile with Arturo when he went to talk to Big Ed and he cursed himself internally for agreeing to this trip in the first place. He should have told his sister to sell the silver to Jerry Carr and be done with it. If not for Ana Teresa, he would forget the wagon and the silver, and let Jerry Carr have the problem.

This was not the first woman Rafe loved who he put in harm's way. Rafe could not stop his mind from seeing the images of Chiwiwi lying in a pool of blood, dead by Benicío's bullet. The scene had been a recurring nightmare, which used to haunt him. He had loved Chiwiwi and she was dead because of his actions as much as Benicío's gun. Now because of his own greed, his beloved wife was in danger or worse.

"Por favor, Dios, que no le ocurra ningún daño." Rafe asked God not to let any harm come to Ana Teresa, then spurred Rayo faster.

"Rafe, they can't have gone too far. The mules will not take the punishment of hauling the weight of the silver before they wear out," Billy spoke shaking Rafe from his thoughts.

"I hear you Billy. We just have to find them before nightfall. I am afraid of what they might do to Ana Teresa,"

Rafe choked on his words.

"We'll find them Rafe. Hopefully all they want is the silver," Billy said to calm him down.

"Those mules are starting to fade," Bo yelled to Jerry. "You better pull up."

Jerry knew Bo was right, but was trying to push the young mules as far as possible south of San Marcial.

A short time later, Ana Teresa felt the wagon turn left and the mules slow. The wagon bumped erratically as they turned off the main trail, so badly she had to hold on to the side rail to stay sitting. Finally the wagon stopped.

Ana Teresa grabbed the heavy pan in her hand and stayed inside the wagon. Wildly she tried to think of a plan. If she could knock out one of the men with the pan, then perhaps she could escape the other. There were two horses and she knew how to ride.

She could hear the mules braying as they were unhitched from the wagon.

"Jerry, I'm going to check on the silver. It must be in the back." Ana Teresa heard one of the men say to the other, calling him Jerry. Suddenly the back flap of the canvas opened and light flooded in. The second man's face popped into her view.

"What the fuck!" Bo yelled as he saw the woman in the back of the wagon. "Jerry, who the fuck is this woman?"

"I don't know. She was in the back when we took the wagon."

Bo saw the woman was holding a heavy cast iron pan. She did not look Mexican, though he thought she looked of Spanish heritage. Bo pulled his gun and pointed it at the woman. "Put down the pan," he grumbled.

"If you hurt me, my husband will kill you," Ana Teresa responded with as much emphasis as she could muster.

"Hurt you? *Señorita,* what I want to do to you won't hurt a bit." Now that he had a chance to study her face, the young woman was beautiful. She was probably Spanish, or part Spanish, with delicate features and long brown hair. It had been a long time since Bo had a lovely woman and not a wornout whore.

"Stop it Bo, we can use her for a hostage. I'm sure her husband is Martín's cousin. He must be the one who was driving the wagon to Santa Fe. He will gladly trade the silver for her."

"You mean that big guy is her husband?" Bo asked.

"No, her husband is Mexican. The one Charlie Hastings told me was a *pistolero*. Yew'll have enough money to get all the women yew want when we get back to El Paso," Jerry continued trying to convince Bo to leave the woman alone.

"Fuck you Jerry. If you were a real man, you'd take her and dump her in the river when you got your fill," Bo grumbled to Jerry as he walked off to see to the horses.

Ana Teresa knew the man who just walked away would be back for her. She saw it in his evil eyes. Picking up the heavy pan gave her some comfort, though knew it was no match to the evil man's gun. Rafael miraculous found her twice before and she prayed he could again.

"Por favor Dios, envíame a Rafael," she prayed to God to send Rafael to find her.

Rafe was keeping a sharp eye on the ground as he rode. He was sure the wagon was traveling south and he knew from the days driving the mule team, they would be getting tired. Surely Jerry Carr knew you could not drive the mules to exhaustion.

Long shadows started creeping over the trail as the sun dipped behind the western mountains. Rafe knew they had to find the wagon before dark. If night fell without finding it, he feared what they might do to Ana Teresa and they probably would kill her when they were finished with her. Bile soured his stomach at the thought.

Something caught Rafe's eye. A set of deep tracks veered off the road toward the river.

"Hold up Billy," he called. Circling several times he was sure the silver wagon pulled off the road. "Come on, this way."

"Just ten minutes," Bo whined several times implying his desire for the woman.

"What the fuck Bo, leave the woman alone. We can't be worrying about yew getting yer nuts flushed. Think about the silver. Yew can get all the whores yew want when we get back to El Paso," Jerry admonished Bo again.

Ana Teresa sat in the wagon holding the pan on her lap. Her mind wildly searched for an idea. If she could just subdue the mean man, perhaps she had a chance. The mean man wanted his way with her, but the other, the man who drove the wagon was keeping him back. From what she could understand, the driver's name was Jerry and evil one was Bo.

"Ah come on Jerry, it won't take long. Then we can just leave her here and we won't have to worry about her," Bo begged.

"Fuck you Bo. Go get some kindling for the fire." Jerry hated to make a fire, but the chill was already descending upon them hidden under the trees near the river.

As the evil man named Bo walked away, Ana Teresa thought it was her chance. "Jerry, can you help me down," Ana Teresa called to the driver.

Jerry heard the woman and realized she probably needed to get down from the wagon. Walking over, he pulled the back flap.

Ana Teresa swung the pan as he moved the flap. She aimed high hoping to hit him in the head. The pan swung through the air, then made contact.

"What the fuck," Jerry growled as he ducked the pan and it hit his left hand holding the canvas flap. "Yew bitch, yew tried to hit me," he growled. Grabbing the pan he threw it on the ground, then pushed her hard back into the wagon.

Rafe and Billy followed the wagon tracks away from the main trail toward the river. They moved slowly and quietly, not wanting to alert the kidnappers.

"Billy, whatever happens make sure not to hurt Ana Teresa," Rafe expressed his fear.

"I hear you Rafe. All I can say is I'll kill those ruthless jaspers for you, especially if they've hurt her."

They slowly followed the deep wagon tracks. Suddenly Rayo perked his ears and Rafe signaled Billy to stop. Rafe was familiar with Rayo's movements. The well-trained horse could hear things Rafe could not. Rafe stopped and listened, but everything was quiet.

When Bo got back with a load of kindling, Jerry was grumbling and rubbing his sore left hand.

"What happened to you?" Bo asked.

"Fucking bitch hit me with a pan," Jerry said.

Bo realized Jerry did not care anymore about the woman. "Start the fire Jerry. I got something to take care of."

Ana Teresa heard the two men arguing and heard Bo's voice. She knew he was coming for her. She scrambled toward the front of the wagon when the back flap opened.

"You can't get away that easy," Bo sneered.

Ana Teresa turned and grabbed at the supplies under her. Frantically her hand searched for anything to throw at the man, anything to stop him from getting into the wagon. She knew his intent. Her mind flicked to the story Tomás told about the woman raped and killed by the two cowboys in San Marcial. Rafe had killed the two, but it was too late for the woman. It gave her only momentary peace thinking Rafe would also avenge her with these two men's lives.

Time seemed to float into slow motion. She saw a lustful look spread across the evil man's face. He moved the flap aside as he stepped on the tailgate. The wagon swayed with his weight. He was not a big man, but solidly built. He took off his hat to show a receding hairline and flung it beside him.

"Don't worry. You'll like what I give you. All the girls say I'm good. You'll probably be begging me for more when I'm done with you," Bo gloated.

Ana Teresa's hands groped behind her. She was sitting on a blanket with her back against the front seat.

Bo unbuckled his gunbelt. She could smell him from where she sat. His body odor was foul and his clothes were dirty and stained from days on the trail. Bo placed the gunbelt on his right, not far from Ana Teresa's feet. She made a move to kick at it, but they were just out of reach.

"Now, now. That won't do," he said as he grabbed her ankles. She struggled but he held her tight in his strong grip. "But I do like a woman with a bit of spunk," Bo sneered.

CHAPTER 34

Rafe and Billy continued slowly moving toward the river. Rayo's ears perked again. "Rayo hears something. Get ready," Rafe said. Pulling one of his pistols, Rafe took Rayo's reins in his left hand and gently nudged the horse. With guns ready, they slowly rode following the wagon tracks. Rafe heard a branch crack as Jerry broke a limb for the fire.

Jerry knew what Bo would do to the woman in the wagon. He poked a few whores in his time, but Jerry found it not very sexually exciting and sometimes could not get it up. Bo probably thought he was queer, but Jerry always wanted a nice woman, like the one in the back of the wagon. A woman who would love him and not just spread her legs to anyone for money.

As Rafe walked Rayo slowly, the wagon suddenly popped into his view. The man he thought was Jerry Carr was standing near the fire. Ana Teresa was nowhere in sight. He put his hand up to stop Billy who rode behind him.

Ana Teresa's hands worked behind her back desperately searching for something, anything to throw at the man coming toward her. She knew screaming would do no good. He reached her and straddled her legs with his.

"Now let's see what you have," Bo snickered. Roughly, he tore at her blouse and ripped it away from her shoulders. The tops of her breasts popped into his view. "Now that's more like it."

She felt his hand on her breast as he pulled at her blouse. "Stop," she begged him.

Bo tore again at her blouse until her breasts were bared. Seeing her creamy breasts and pink nipples only aroused Bo even more. His penis swelled in his pants. He put his knees over hers to hold her in place.

Leaning back, Bo started to unbutton his trousers. Suddenly Ana Teresa's hand, which was searching behind her, felt something hard and cold. Frantically, she wrapped her hand around the barrel of the pistol Billy had hidden under the canvas.

Bo was intent on working the buttons of his pants and having trouble with one button. "Shit," he muttered.

Finding the gun's handle, Ana Teresa worked it into her right hand. She had little experience with guns, but had fired her father's pistol several times. The hammer was tight and she was afraid he would hear the click.

Jerking her legs up, she momentarily wobbled her foe. Bo cursed at her and the button of his trousers popped exposing him.

Bo grabbed at her flaying legs trying to spread them. Ana Teresa cocked the hammer of the pistol and whipped it around from behind her back. Without thinking, she closed her eyes and pulled the trigger.

The gunshot echoed in the trees and all around them. Rafe kicked Rayo hard to close the short gap to the wagon. He took a shot at Jerry who was standing by the fire, but missed.

"What the fuck? Bitch!" Bo screamed at Ana Teresa as he grabbed his balls and blood flowed through his fingers. Pain shot through his face as the realization hit his brain. Ana Teresa looked into the evilness in his eyes and cocked the pistol again. This time she kept her eyes on him when she fired at his chest. Bo Preston buckled back and fell over.

Jerry went for his pistol as Rafe and Billy rode up. Billy cocked the rifle and aimed at Jerry, "Drop it."

Shaking, Ana Teresa heard a gunshot outside. "Drop it," she heard a voice say.

She cocked the pistol again and aimed it at the back of the wagon. Her hands trembled and tears flooded her eyes, but whoever came for her would get the same fate as the dead man at her feet.

Rafe jumped from Rayo and walked toward the wagon. His heart jumped and skipped beats as he approached, not knowing what he was going to find in the back. Slowly he pulled at the canvas with his pistol aimed and ready.

"You come in here, I'll shoot!" Ana Teresa screamed out.

Hearing his wife's voice, Rafe called out, "Ana Teresa, don't shoot, it's me."

Rafe opened the canvas flap to find his bare-chested wife sitting holding a pistol and a man covered in blood lying dead at her feet.

"Rafael!" Ana Teresa cried out when she saw him.

Tears flooded her face as Rafe climbed in to her side. "I'm so sorry Rafael. I'm so sorry."

"Don't be sorry you killed this man," Rafe said to her. "His kind deserve to rot in hell," Rafe told her.

"No, I'm sorry I didn't listen to you. I was so stupid wanting to go with you. Can you ever forgive me?" she asked then fell into his arms sobbing.

A gunshot rang outside the wagon. "I told you not to move," Billy told Jerry. He shot into the dirt just to make the kidnapper dance. Billy was itching for the man to move or to make any kind of threat. He would be happy to plug him for what he did to Ana Teresa.

Rafe wrapped a blanket around Ana Teresa after she tried to fix her clothes. "Are you sure you are all right? He didn't hurt you?"

"No. He was going to, but I found the gun under the blankets."

"I didn't know you knew how to shoot."

"I just pulled the trigger," she admitted.

When Billy saw Ana Teresa come out of the wagon in one piece, he looked at Jerry and said, "It's a really good thing she is okay."

"Please don't shoot me," Jerry whined. "It was Bo. I didn't want to hurt your woman."

"He's right. It was the man in there, in the wagon, who wanted to . . . " she could not finish the sentence.

Billy pulled Bo's body out of the wagon and laid it to the side. Jerry was sitting on a log with his hands up on his head. He stared at nothing on the ground in front of him. Taking the silver proved to be difficult, more difficult than he imagined. All he wanted was to get back to El Paso alive.

"You are the same man who planned on cheating my sister out of the silver," Rafe said still trying to get his emotions under control.

"I was giving them a fair price for the stolen silver, but they left me hanging. When I figured yew were taking it to Santa Fe, I got Bo to help me take it from yew. I was wrong," Jerry admitted.

"Should I kill him and leave him for the buzzards for what they did to you?" Billy asked while looking at Ana Teresa. He was still itching to kill Jerry.

"No. He didn't know I was in the wagon when he stole it. He tried to protect me from the other one, the one I killed," Ana Teresa said.

"I'm sorry about Bo, ma'am. I didn't mean yew no harm."

"Don't kill him Billy. Ana Teresa is right. No more killing, unless we have to," Rafe told him.

"Take your friend and leave," Rafe told Jerry.

"Now, tonight? It's almost dark," Jerry whined.

"Yes now. Be thankful to God I'm not letting Billy do what he wants to do to you," Rafe told him.

Billy helped Jerry loaded the body onto the horse and Jerry Carr rode south into the darkness towing Bo's dead body. Rafe added logs to the fire for the long cold night ahead.

CHAPTER 35

"Billy wake up, we're in Santa Fe!" Rafe nudged Billy who was huddled under a blanket while Rafe took his turn at driving. Rafe stopped the wagon on a hill south of the city at the point where he had first seen Santa Fe on a cold and snowy day not unlike today. Rafe remembered the cold and snow amazed him that day when he was only seventeen. George Summers was driving the wagon bringing Rafe to Santa Fe for the first time.

Today, the squatty adobe houses with a thick layer of white snow made them look like iced cakes. The snow clung to the short pines trees and the wagon was covered with a layer of ice and snow.

Since leaving San Marcial, Rafe and Billy were able to spend nights at waystations and stage stops, instead of sleeping in the cold wagon to protect it. They no longer worried about Jerry Carr or his gun hand, Bo Preston.

Billy shaded his eyes to look at the city. It was a small town, not a city by eastern standards. The low buildings of the town were nestled in the valley of a large snow-capped mountain range to the north. Mostly all he could see was white.

"Detroit is a lot bigger, but it looks a lot like this in winter," Billy said.

About two hours later Rafe drove the wagon down the road leading to the Summers' ranch and foundry. Rafe thought it was the twentieth or maybe twenty-first of January. He had not seen Santa Fe or his family for nine long months.

Gray smoke drifted from all the chimneys of the house and foundry's chimney spewed black. He sighed at the sight. As Rafe drove the team into the courtyard, the front door opened and the family spilled out. George reached them first.

Jumping from the seat, Rafe wrapped George in a tight hug. Excitedly, the Summers' teenage daughters, Lolo and Lizzy, grabbed him from their father and Lolo had tears in her eyes.

Rafe saw Celiá and Josefina bundled up with wool blankets standing on the porch and waving. Rafe introduced Billy to George and the girls.

"Bienvenido Rafael," Rafe heard Esteban welcome him home. Esteban was the stable man at the Summers' ranch and saw the wagon driving in.

"Gracias Esteban. Please drive the wagon into the barn and unsaddle Rayo and feed him and the mules."

"Come into the house. You two must be freezing," George said.

Reaching the porch, Rafe wrapped his arms around his mother, Celiá, and adopted mother, Josefina, one arm for each and walked them through the door and into the house. The warmth and familiarity of the Summers' home enveloped him. He was finally home.

In the parlor, the family gathered excitedly to greet him more fully. A fire blazed and crackled in the large fireplace warming the entire room.

Josefina kissed his cheek and let go of his arm, but his mother clung to him, not letting go as tears flowed down her cheeks.

Rafe pulled off his heavy wool coat and hat. After days on the trail, his clothes were dirty and his beard scruffy. It was Lolo who took his coat.

"Rafe, you stink," Lolo blurted out and laughed. "Good," Rafe said and grabbed her in a hug. "Eeek," Lolo screeched.

"I'm not getting near you until you have a bath," Lizzy said as she backed away.

George and Josefina's two daughters loved him like a brother and he relished the teasing and fun they shared as siblings.

Billy watched the family from the hallway. He could feel the family's joy at having Rafe home. He never had a family like this to come home to and thought Rafe was a very lucky man.

"Come you must be dying to have a bath and put on

something clean," Josefina said. "Billy can take Carlos' room. I'll have Juanita heat the tub."

"Thank you kindly ma'am. I wouldn't mind cleaning up," Billy said.

Rafe and Billy climbed the stairs to the second floor and Rafe showed him into the bedroom where Carlos slept before marrying Bibiana. His heart ached to see Ana Teresa, but exhaustion and filth took priority. After the incident with Jerry Carr, Ana Teresa gladly took the stagecoach from San Marcial. Rafe wired Carlos and Bibiana to meet her and take her to their home. When he brought her here to introduce her to the family, he wanted it to be special.

Later Rafe joined George in the parlor where he sat in the big chair sipping brandy to ward off the chill. George thought Rafe looked thin, but otherwise in good health.

"I'm sorry I have been away so long, *don* Jorge," Rafe said using the personal name he called his adopted father.

"We've missed you terribly. Especially your mothers," George told him. Rafe thought it funny he called the two women, his mothers, but it was fitting. He thought of both of them in that way.

George and Rafe talked of Mexico. George was glad to hear Rafe saw Rodolfo and María. Rafe told him of the sea voyage from Manzanilla to Los Angeles and how the storm at sea was very scary. "I huddled with Rayo in the belly of the ship," he admitted.

"I've crossed the Atlantic several times. One trip hit such a storm and I remember it was very frightening," George agreed.

"I had trouble in Los Angeles with a gang of vigilantes," Rafe told him about the Citizens Security Patrol in the city who were harassing Mexicans and who wanted to steal Rayo and hang him. George shook his head. It seemed trouble haunted his young adopted son. The story nagged at George. He knew the sheriff wanted to jail Rafe here in Santa Fe and bring him to trial for Diego's death. George had tried hard to sway the sheriff from the plan, but the sheriff thought it the only way to make peace with the aristocrats. Sheriff Johnson assured George there were enough witnesses to acquit Rafe. George was not so confident. He decided not to mention the trial until later when he and Rafe had more time to discuss it. Tonight he only wanted to enjoy having his son home and safe.

Billy finally joined them in the parlor, clean and shaven. Juanita found some clothes which almost fit his large frame. Rafe thought he would send him to town in the morning to buy clothes more suitable.

"Billy, come in and sit. Rafe tells me you are a blacksmith by trade," George said and handed him a glass of red wine.

"Well sir, my grandfather was a blacksmith back in Michigan where I grew up. He taught me how to work different types of metals. I was drafted into the Army during the Civil War and when it was over, I worked my way into becoming a smithy. I've worked with most metals over the years, I guess," Billy answered.

"Well, we can sure use you here. I forgot to tell you Rafe, I received a large order from Fort Bliss and Carlos has been helping me, but he has limited time. Perhaps Billy can help us meet the Fort Bliss order," George said.

"Yes I can sir," Billy said with a smile. "I'll do anything you need."

Lizzy came to the door of the parlor and announced dinner. George led Rafe and Billy into the large dining room. Rafe's nose caught a whiff of Juanita's green chile stew, which was one of his favorites. He wondered if Billy would think it too spicy.

Lolo walked into the room dressed in a gold colored gown. Sheer sleeves came down just above the elbows. The gold dress had embroidery patterns around the floor length skirt. At the neck a square opening with no collar came just above her breasts and the waist had a silk sash. The dress reflected her golden brown eyes. Her dark brown hair was gathered on top of her head, as was the latest fashion. Rafe gasped at the girl who just a few years ago was a skinny teenager, all arms and legs, and now was a beautiful young woman.

"George, you better lock her up. The young men of Santa Fe are definitely not ready for such beauty," Rafe said.

"Thank you Rafe," she dipped demurely in a small curtsey.

"We're too late Rafe. She has several suitors already banging at the door," George said with a grin.

"I'll kill them!" Rafe said jokingly and everyone laughed.

"There are several *caballeros* calling, but nothing serious. I want father to take me to New England where he grew up so I can meet some Eastern gentlemen before I make up my mind," Lolo spoke up ignoring Rafe's comment about killing her suitors.

"Well, aren't you the snooty one. Aren't you a bit young to be looking for gentlemen or *caballeros,*" Rafe said and everyone laughed.

"Shush Rafe, I will be eighteen this year and if I don't start looking and find a suitor I will be an old maid," she responded sternly.

"I seriously doubt that! What about you Lizzy?" Rafe asked.

"I just want to grow up and have fun." Lizzy was always the less serious of the two girls, full of giggles. Her looks favored George, with light brown hair and freckles. She was the one who liked to go riding and asked her father to teach her how to shoot.

"We are so excited to meet Ana Teresa," Josefina said.

"Tomorrow I'll go and fetch her from Carlos and Bibiana's house. "I will invite them all to dinner," Rafe said.

Eight candles lighted the long Spanish colonial table in the Summers' dining room. The family stood behind their high-back chairs and George gave the blessing over the meal, the same blessing Rafe heard so many times before.

"Lord, bless us your humble servants. We give thanks for this food which you have provided. We give you thanks for returning Rafael safely. Keep us safe in your arms and let us be servants of your will, Amen."

"Amen," they all chimed in.

Billy enjoyed the meal of spicy green chili. The tender chunks of beef melted in his mouth without much chewing. The stew was spicy, but Billy thought it delicious. A stack of hot tortillas circulated several times around the table. Billy observed Rafe and the dynamics of what he perceived to be a good family. They made him feel welcome and offered him work in the foundry.

Billy noticed the woman introduced as Rafe's mother, Celiá, was quieter than the rest of the family. When she was introduced to him she smiled shyly and said, "I please to meet you," in a thick Spanish accent. Billy watched her over the course of the meal thinking she was a handsome Mexican woman. She was younger than he might have guessed. Rafe told him he was twenty-three, so Celiá must be close to forty, but she looked much younger. Her brown skin was firm and her body slender. Her hair showed a few wisps of gray glinting in the otherwise long black braid down her back. Her dark eyes flashed when she smiled.

The family was still seated at the dining table when the maid answered the door. Several moments later, Carlos, Bibiana, and Ana Teresa entered the room.

"Ah, there you are. I sent a messenger to Carlos and asked him to come," George said.

Rafe jumped up and moved to Ana Teresa's side. She was dressed in a traditional Spanish gown of green and gold. Her long hair cascaded down her back. Shyly she took Rafe's hand and stood next to him. No one said a word awestruck by the young woman's beauty.

"Everyone, I am pleased to present Ana Teresa, my wife."

CHAPTER 36

George was having coffee when Rafe and Billy came downstairs the next morning. Outside, last night's storm dumped several additional inches of snow leaving a pristine sparkling white blanket covering the yard. For as long as Rafe had been in Santa Fe, he still could not get used to the snow and cold, but Billy said it reminded him of his days growing up in Detroit, Michigan.

"Good morning," George greeted them.

"Good morning," they chimed together in return.

"How about some breakfast? Juanita will bring it shortly. We have a full day ahead of us."

"You surprised me last night with Ana Teresa, father," Rafe said as he sat down.

"I assume you slept well." George gave a knowing look at his son and Rafe blushed. George remembered seeing Ana Teresa at Bibiana and Carlos' wedding, though not formally introduced. She had carried Bibiana's veil. She was beautiful, though somewhat quiet last night, and he hoped she would be a good partner for Rafe.

When George married Josefina, she too was a beautiful young woman. Born in Spain, Josefina had been raised in a fairly wealthy family. He brought her to America and several times in the first few years, he thought he had made a mistake, especially when their infant son died of influenza. She was heartbroken for many months, but George learned of her inner strength. Over the years she provided him with love and support for the ranch and business, standing strong beside him.

When he brought young Rafe home from Texas, it was Josefina who immediately began his studies and taught him the social graces he needed to survive. Never once did she question his decision to bring him home. She opened her arms and heart to the young Mexican boy.

Last night the family surrounded Ana Teresa with questions and laughter, telling stories about Rafe, and good-naturedly teasing the newlywed couple. Rafe's new bride took it all in stride. George caught Celiá and Josefina looking at the couple with tears of joy in their eyes.

Not only had Rafe brought a wife, he brought Billy home from this trip. Billy was a big man with thick arms and looked to be in his mid thirties. Rafe said Billy was a blacksmith and George trusted Rafe's judgment of men.

"I hope you are ready to get to work Billy, because you are going to earn your pay for the next several weeks," George told him.

"Yes sir, never been afraid of work. I just hope I can help and not get in the way," Billy answered.

"You will not be in the way Billy. I know you can learn the machines and work the furnace. It will help free us to do the fine work of assembling the weapons," Rafe added.

"Yes, managing the furnace is very important and the quenching process for the various parts of the guns is precise. You know metals, so you know what I mean. We're lucky to have you Billy. It took Rafe a good while to learn quenching. I'm sure you'll understand my methods in no time," George said confidently.

After breakfast, they headed to the foundry several hundred yards behind the house, stomping through over a foot of snow. The snow stopped overnight, but the sky was dark and ominous as if it could start again at any moment.

Rafe and George introduced Billy to the other workers and left him with Jose to learn the workings of the furnace. George headed back toward his office. Rafe followed and closed the door after them.

"Father, I have something to tell you before we get started. The wagon in the barn, the one Billy and I drove here is loaded with silver ingots."

"Silver? I thought it odd the wagon was pulled by mules. How much silver and why?" George asked.

"The silver is from a mine in Mexico. Rodolfo stole it from a miner's mule train on the way to Mexico City. It was before they knew about the *hacienda*," Rafe added.

"Why did you bring it here?" George asked. Rafe

could hear aggravation growing in his voice.

"Being *peóns* in Mexico, they have no way to sell or exchange it there. Rodolfo created a secret compartment under that old wagon and drove it to El Paso. They tried to sell it there, but they were going to be swindled. I couldn't find a way to sell it in El Paso."

"So you drove it here? That was foolhardy, Rafe." George was both perplexed and upset. As if Rafe did not have enough problems here with the Spanish aristocrats, now he had a wagon loaded with stolen silver ingots.

"I'm sorry father. Rodolfo was desperate to get money to buy guns and food to feed the *peóns* who live with them. All this happened before they knew I was giving them the rights to the *hacienda* in Torreón. They were offered thirty cents an ounce by a crook in El Paso, but I decided to bring the silver here. I believe I can get a better price and use the money to help them get the *hacienda* running and repay you whatever I owe you," Rafe said.

George remembered well the empty shelves at the *hacienda* in Torreón and the lean hungry people living there. He had done what he could to buy supplies for them when he was in Mexico, but it would not surprise him if the people were not once again starving. George knew Rafe's intentions were good. He was not a thief nor would he condone Rodolfo's treachery, if not for the people starving at the *hacienda*.

"Well, your bank account has gone down to almost nothing. This will help you and pay me back for what I donated for the *hacienda* and what I have paid to rebuild your house, but don't misunderstand me. I don't condone Rodolfo's thievery nor your foolhardy trip to bring it here," George said. "Now, show me what you have."

They walked to the barn and Rafe produced an ingot from the secret compartment handing it to George. The gray ingot was heavy and in rough form. "It has the mark of the silver mine stamped on it. We have to do something about that," George said. "How many do you have?"

"Fifteen," Rafe answered. "Billy says he can recast them to remove that mark."

"Yes, that is the first step."

"How can we sell these, father?" It was a question George pondered as he looked at the ingot. Though he had the tools and equipment to recast the ingots here at the foundry, he had little knowledge of selling silver in this form.

"I'll wire Bill Moore and ask him what to do. Leave it here for now. We have work to do for the order from Fort Bliss," George said thinking his mining friend in Elizabethtown would have ideas about the silver.

Returning to the foundry, Rafe checked on Billy. Jose was pleased with Billy's grasp of the huge furnace. Billy said the foundry was amazing.

George asked Rafe to help him complete the buffing on the pistol parts so they could finish assembling them. They worked until suppertime taking a short break for lunch. Ana Teresa was in the kitchen with Josefina and his mother when they walked inside. The women scurried to get them a quick meal.

"She lovely," Celiá whispered to Rafe in broken English as she put a bowl of stew in front of him. Rafe knew she meant Ana Teresa. As he ate, he felt blessed to be home and blessed to have Ana Teresa as his wife.

When the hard day was over, Jose told George he was pleased with Billy's work and grateful Rafe brought him. George thought Billy's expertise with metals and blacksmithing would be an asset to both the foundry and Rafe's budding horse breeding business. For some time now, George had been thinking about the future. He was getting older and Rafe was like a son to him. His two daughters would marry and leave with their husbands. Someday he wanted to turn over the foundry business to Rafe.

CHAPTER 37

For the next two weeks, George supervised Rafe and Billy on the work needed to complete the Fort Bliss weapons order. Each day George became more impressed with Billy's knowledge and willingness to learn and work. He was pleased with Rafe's judge of character. Rafe did not leave the Summers' ranch, working extra hours during the day in the foundry and spending each night engrossed with his new wife.

George was thankful Rafe was sticking close to home. He promised to alert Sheriff Johnson when Rafe returned, knowing the sheriff wanted to hold the trial. It was something George dreaded with all his heart. He knew Rafe was innocent of any wrongdoing; however the Spanish aristocrats had power and money to corrupt the system. George feared they would try to hang his innocent son for Diego de la Torre's death.

Several times George planned on talking to Rafe about the situation, but the deadline for the huge order for Fort Bliss was looming. He decided to wait until after the order was complete and hoped no one knew Rafe had returned.

Though busy, one milder afternoon Rafe saddled two horses for himself and Ana Teresa to show her the new house. His original house had been burned to the ground by Diego's friends. At the time Rafe wanted revenge, but now all he wanted to see was his new house rising up at the top of the hill.

Ana Teresa loved the view from the porch. She could see the horse barn below them and could also see the rooftop of the Summers' home. A long snow covered pasture stretched out to the south and down the hill. She could picture young horses running in the pasture during better weather. She had toured Rafe's horse barns and the yearlings were adorable. She picked a young long-legged mare that Rafe promised to train for her use.

"The house is perfect Rafael. When will it be finished?" she asked.

"Surely by summer. Hopefully work can start again after this terrible winter weather subsides. Maybe in March they can get started again."

Near the end of the second week, a casting mold with the Mystic Lode Mine mark on it arrived from George's friend Bill Moore.

"Bill has a gold mine. Can we recast the silver in this mold without trouble?" Rafe asked.

"Bill sent the mold, so I believe he understands what we need," George replied. Rafe appreciated George did not reprimand him again for bringing the silver to Santa Fe. He seemed convinced they could sell it here for a good price.

They enlisted Billy to recast the ingots. George felt it better not to involve any of his other workers in the process. Billy recast four ingots so far. He did the work early before anyone else arrived at the foundry. George wanted to be as cautious as possible when trying to sell the silver. Thus far, his only idea was to have his friend Bill Moore sell the silver for them.

Ana Teresa found the Summers' family embraced her in every way. She was only a few years older than Lolo and the two girls became instant friends. She and Lolo experimented with new hairstyles and laughed and giggled uproariously at the family's expressions. The girls were the same size and Lolo allowed Ana Teresa to share several of her gowns, as Ana Teresa only brought a few belonging with her.

The first week of February brought a break in the weather. The skies cleared to a bright teal blue and the sun melted away a lot of the snow. Lolo asked her mother if she and Ana Teresa could ride to town to go shopping.

Just after the noon meal, Esteban drove Lolo and Ana Teresa to Santa Fe in the carriage. Josefina asked Esteban to pickup several items at the mercantile while they were in town. When he dropped them off in front of the dressmaker's shop, he promised to return later in the afternoon.

Lolo had ordered several new dresses and was excited to have a final fitting. *"Buenos días, señoritas,"* the dressmaker greeted them as the girls walked into the shop. She led Lolo to an area in the back of the store where she did fittings, leaving Ana Teresa to browse.

Lolo emerged from the back in an almost finished dress. The beige dress was trimmed in a teal blue ruffled collar and buttoned down the front with matching blue buttons into a V-shape over the skirt. The end of each sleeve had a matching blue bow.

"What do you think of this one?" Lolo asked twirling around in circles and almost tripping on the unhemmed skirt.

"I love it. You look so grownup in it."

"Have you found anything you like?" Lolo asked her. The dress shop had a number of finished dresses for immediate sale as well as the styles the dressmaker could make by hand. Ana Teresa was used to having her dresses custom fitted, but she was in dire need of clothes. She picked up a simple frock of cream with red polka dots and held it up.

"No, no that's not for you," Lolo shook her head and frowned.

"How about this one then?" Ana Teresa held up a purple taffeta with purple brocade down the buttons in the front and matching brocade on the sleeves.

"That's better. Let's go try it on," Lolo said and led her to the dressing room.

After several hours, Lolo and Ana Teresa walked from the dressmakers shop. Ana Teresa purchased three dresses and the dressmaker was going to get the one hemmed over the next hour so they could take all three dresses home today.

"Let's have a hot chocolate while we wait," Lolo said and led them across the plaza toward a small restaurant. It was bright and sunny and the plaza was busy with many people taking advantage of the good weather.

As the girls walked across the plaza, Ana Teresa let the sun warm her face. Santa Fe felt like home to her. After her father lost the land grant in California, she was sent here to live with her uncle Pedro and cousin Bibiana. She and Bibiana had ridden the plaza in their carriage and flirted with the *caballeros*. They rode as available unmarried *señoritas*, wooing the young dandies and hiding their faces behind fluttering fans. Now both she and Bibiana were married women and she smiled picturing the ritual as rather frivolous.

For the past two weeks she saw little of Rafe, since he and Billy were working hard at the foundry and machine shop. By the time they finished dinner, he was already exhausted and several times he fell asleep beside her in bed as his head touched the pillow. However, she loved him even more, if that was possible, seeing him being responsible with his foundry work and horses. He told her the work would slow down as soon as they finished with the large weapons order.

As the girls crossed the plaza, Alvaro Gutierrez and Benjamin Pacheco were on horseback riding on the *paseo* headed to the Palacio Cantina. Alvaro rode distracted in his thoughts. Virginia Barceló Verdugo, the owner of the cantina, was beginning to succumb to his advances and he thought perhaps he would taste her lovely lips tonight. Virginia had been Diego de la Torre's woman until he was killed by the *mestizo* dog. Now, Alvaro was the only one of the young *caballeros* she allowed to woo her.

"Alvaro, is that the *señorita* from California?" Benjamin asked shaking Alvaro out of his thoughts.

"I do not know. It looks like two gringo girls to me," Alvaro replied annoyed with the interruption. Alvaro's thoughts about Virginia prevailed. "I do not have time for foolishness now. Virginia is waiting for me." Alvaro spurred his horse down the *paseo*.

"Wait, you better look. I think it is her," Benjamin insisted.

Alvaro reluctantly paused again and turned his horse around to take a better look at the two young women crossing the plaza.

"She is the one Diego wanted. I thought she was sent

away in shame after the *peón* murdered Diego and her reputation was tarnished," Benjamin said.

"I saw her at Bibiana de Soto's wedding last spring. Look at her now, she is not dressed like a proper *señorita*," Alvaro said recognizing Ana Teresa.

"Who is that young girl she is with?" Benjamin asked.

Without answering, Alvaro spurred his horse and rode down the plaza and waited for the young women to walk in front of them. As they approached, Alvaro urged his horse to block Lolo and Ana Teresa's way as they walked toward the restaurant. Annoyed the girls tried to walk around, but Alvaro backed his horse to block them again.

"Hey what's wrong with you, let us pass!" Lolo yelled at the man blocking them.

"You be quiet!" he yelled back at Lolo. "What are you doing in Santa Fe *señorita?*" Alvaro asked coldly looking down at Ana Teresa.

She recognized the men on horseback as Diego's friends, some of the Spanish dandies here in Santa Fe. She remembered the one glaring at her was named Alvaro Gutierrez.

"It is none of your business why I am here, now move away and let us pass and do not bother me again," Ana Teresa told Alvaro with a defiant look.

"I make it my business *señorita*. You are the reason Diego is dead because you chose to be with the *mestizo* dog. You will pay for your mistake," Alvaro threatened her.

"Do not threaten me *señor*. I tell you again to move aside or I will call for the sheriff." Her words did not deter Alvaro, though she saw the other dandy back his horse a few steps.

"You have not seen the last of us *señorita*. I tell you again do not let us see you with the *peón*, because we will finish the job we started that day at the abandoned *hacienda*," Alvaro warned her.

"You were lucky that day *señor*. If Rafael had his guns you and your friends would be dead just like the *picaro*, Diego de la Torre. The next time my husband sees you harassing me, you will not be so lucky!"

Alvaro's eyes glared at her and she defiantly stared right back at him. She did not back away from the two horse-bound *caballeros,* but stood her ground.

Benjamin hissed at Alvaro, "We better leave them alone. People are watching." Not one for a fight, Benjamin did not want the gossip around Santa Fe to say he was harassing two young *señoritas.* Benjamin turned his horse and trotted away. Alvaro glared at the girls, then followed him.

"Who was that?" Lolo asked when the two left. She knew they were *caballeros* by the style of their silver-studded *trajes* and the elaborate silver adornments on their horses, but did not know their names.

"Those men are the same ones who hurt Rafael once and I believe they are the same ones who burned down his house. They think we are still living under the old Spanish traditions. They hate Rafael," she said. Trembling a bit from the encounter, Ana Teresa followed Lolo inside the restaurant.

Chapter 38

Alvaro caught up to Benjamin and cursed him as a coward. "You cannot harass young girls in the street," Benjamin retorted. They arrived at the Palacio Cantina and Alvaro was still in a rage. The *mestizo* was back in Santa Fe and the sheriff did not have him in jail. The gringo named George Summers was supposed to deliver the *mestizo* to the sheriff, but was no doubt protecting him.

Alvaro walked to the bar and ordered tequila, ignoring Benjamin. While he drank several shots, he pondered what to do with the information. Oscar Peralta and Vicente Vargas sat at a Monte table playing cards.

"Tell Oscar and Vicente we will go and kill the *mestizo* dog. We will make him pay for Diego," Alvaro ordered Benjamin. Alvaro thought of himself as the *jefe*, ordering the others to do the dirty work, while keeping his *grandee* hands clean. Alvaro's conceited attitude infuriated Benjamin.

"We should tell the sheriff. If we kill him, the Americano laws will hang us. I do not want to die for such a killing," Benjamin said shaking his head and downing a shot of tequila. He had tangled with Rafael in the past and knew the young Mexican was brave and heard he was deadly with his guns. Benjamin wanted no part of the *mestizo's* wrath nor the Americano law.

"No one will care if we kill a *mestizo,* besides we can do it where no one will see us. After we kill him, you can have the used up *señorita,* unless you are a *culón* and won't take her," Alvaro taunted him. He thought of Benjamin as a chickenshit who would run from a fight.

"*Chingate Alvaro,* I hope he kills you and I will get Virginia," Benjamin told Alvaro to go fuck himself, sick of his demeaning attitude toward him. He knew Alvaro wanted the cantina owner, Virginia Verdugo, but she was putting him off.

"You are not man enough for Virginia, *pendejo.* She

will not go for a *maricón* like you," Alvaro called him a dummy and a queer and laughed at him.

Benjamin was tired of Alvaro always making fun of him calling him a chickenshit. When Diego de la Torre was alive, he treated him the same, always belittling him just to have fun and making the others laugh at him. Benjamin was twenty-seven and not married. He treated young *señoritas* with respect as his parents and the church taught him. Diego used to call him a *maricón,* a man who liked men instead of woman, but it was not true.

"I'm leaving. Maybe Oscar or Vicente will do your bidding." Benjamin tossed the last shot of tequila down his throat. Placing a coin on the bar, he went to get his hat and coat.

"Cinga tu madre, maricón," Alvaro called him a mother-fucking queer to his back as he left and Benjamin heard the others laugh.

Benjamin bristled at Alvaro's taunts. For more than a year now, his father had been demanding he quit hanging around with the useless Santa Fe dandies and take over responsibilities at the family *hacienda.* With Alvaro's curses lingering in his mind, he swore he would no longer be a part of the young *caballeros* who had followed Diego de la Torre and now thought of Alvaro as their leader. This was the last time he would be called a *culón* by the puffed-up arrogant dandies. It was time to grow up and take responsibility for his father's *hacienda* and take a wife.

Alvaro paid no attention to Benjamin's departure in a huff because he did it many times before when they made fun of him. All Alvaro wanted now was to go upstairs and find Virginia. The last time he saw her here at the cantina, she promised to let him come up to her bedroom. It was late afternoon and Alvaro turned his attention to a game of Monte. The card game would fill his time while he waited for her to come down.

Benjamin trotted his horse north out of Santa Fe tormented in his thoughts about taking disrespect from Alvaro. Last year he met Valentina Marquez de Archuleta, a *señorita* from a prominent family in Albuquerque. Over the past six months, he had seen her several times and he thought she encouraged his advances. She was twenty-three, a bit older than most available *señoritas*, but Benjamin found her intelligent and since she was not from Santa Fe, she did not know how the other dandies treated him. He spurred his horse toward his *hacienda* north of town and decided to go to Albuquerque to see her soon.

Heading north, he came to the road leading to the Summers' ranch. His own *hacienda* was not far, located west and north of the Summers' ranch. He paused at the road heading to the house and pondered what he knew about the *señorita* from California. She told Alvaro to stay away from her or her husband would kill him and his friends. He could only assume the *señorita* married the *mestizo*. Benjamin heard rumors about the *mestizo's* expertise with guns and how he had killed some *Tejanos* in San Marcial and El Paso. The rumors warned of both his speed and accuracy.

If the *mestizo* was back in Santa Fe, Benjamin wanted no part of going after a man who was good with his pistols. He wanted the *mestizo* to know he was no longer out for his neck like the other *caballeros*.

He decided to go and make amends with Rafael for being a part of the dandies who burned down his house and who tried to kill him at the abandoned *hacienda*. Spurring his horse, he rode down the path under the GSW Ranch sign and toward the large house at the end of the road. When he arrived, Esteban came out and took the reins of his horse and greeted him.

"Bienvenido, can I help you?" Esteban asked.

"Yes, my name is Benjamin Pacheco. I would like to speak to Rafael," he said.

"He is in the foundry, *señor,"* Esteban said and pointed to the large building with the smokestack.

Benjamin jumped from his horse and headed toward the foundry. As he walked in, George Summers saw him and walked up to meet him in the hallway.

"Why are you here?" George asked. He recognized Benjamin as *don* Ramon Pacheco's son and one of Diego's friends. He was sure Benjamin was one of the dandies Rafe accused of burning his house.

"I know Rafael is here. I mean him no harm. I just want to talk to him," Benjamin said. He removed his gloves and extended his hand to George.

George did not see any anger or animosity in Benjamin's eyes. After a few moments, he said, "Very well, come with me." George led him to the machine shop where Rafe was working.

Rafe and Carlos were assembling rifles on the long assembly table and looked up when George led Benjamin in. Carlos looked surprised and Rafe gave the man a steady look. Carlos dropped the rifle barrel and walked up to Benjamin.

"What are you doing here? Where are your friends?" Carlos demanded.

"I want no trouble Carlos. I am here to tell him Alvaro knows he is back in Santa Fe and will either go to the sheriff or come after him," Benjamin said looking over at Rafe.

"Why are you telling me this?" Rafe asked him directly.

"I want no trouble. I came to apologize for burning down your house. I know Diego attacked you on the plaza and you did not murder him. I no longer want to be part of what Alvaro and his friends want do to you. I am just here to tell you that," Benjamin said.

"How did you know I was here?" Rafe asked.

"We saw Ana Teresa in town and Alvaro confronted her."

"What? Did he hurt her?" Rafe demanded.

"No, she told him not to come looking for you, because if he did you would kill him. I do not want any part of their ways anymore."

"Why are you doing this Benjamin? Is this some kind of a trick to lure Rafael into looking for Alvaro?" Carlos asked him still suspicious.

Benjamin had been friends with Diego and the young Spanish dandies for many years. He was with Alvaro the day they confronted Carlos and cut his neck as a warning against Rafe. Though Benjamin was not the one who cut him, Carlos was wary of the Benjamin's motives.

"No Carlos, this is not a trick. I am tired of being with those *pinche caballeros* and I know Rafael is innocent. My father wants me to take over the family *hacienda* and we will be neighbors. I plan to marry soon. You will no longer see me with Alvaro and his friends, but hear me Rafael. Be aware. Alvaro knows you are back. That is all. I must leave now." Benjamin turned and walked away.

Later that afternoon when Ana Teresa and Lolo returned from town, she ran to find Rafael. "Rafael! Alvaro knows you are here," Ana Teresa told Rafe as she rushed into the machine shop.

Rafe put down the weapon part and went to her and held her by the shoulders. "I heard you were brave again and you told him I would kill him and his friends."

"What? How did you know that?" she asked startled he knew about her encounter with Alvaro and Benjamin.

"Alvaro's friend, Benjamin, came here and told me what Alvaro did and how you stood up to him."

"What are we going to do? Alvaro is out for revenge. I know he wants to kill you or have you hang for Diego's death. Bibiana told me her father talked about it all the time before you left for Mexico. Now because of me they know you are back . . . " she left the sentence unfinished.

Rafe wrapped his arms around her. "Do not be afraid my love. I have many witnesses who saw I did not murder Diego. Even Benjamin said so when he was here."

"We should go back to California. They cannot do anything to you there," she pleaded temporarily forgetting the Citizens Security Patrol who tried to hang Rafe and ran them out of town.

"I must clear my name here in Santa Fe. While it is tempting for us to make a life in Rancho Simi and we may someday, I must face the law here and clear my name."

"Rafe is right Ana Teresa, he must clear his name here or there will be no safe place for you to live. They can reach you even in California. I will get the best lawyer to represent him. We will win this. We just have to be patient," George broke in.

Benjamin's visit and his revelation nagged at George. He promised the sheriff to alert him if Rafe came home. Because of the large order and the weather, George had not notified the sheriff.

"No. I don't trust the *dons,* like my uncle Pedro. He hates Rafael. The *dons* can manipulate the law. I am afraid they will pay off the witnesses and they will hang Rafael," she pleaded with George.

"Ana Teresa is right *don* Jorge. The *dons* will do whatever it takes to have Diego de la Torre pronounced innocent and find Rafael guilty of murdering an aristocrat," Carlos spoke up.

"Like I said, we will hire the best lawyer. This is how the American system works. It has to be done with lawyers, not guns or swords," George told them.

"I agree we have to fight this within the legal system. I want to be part of this city. I want to raise my family in Santa Fe, so I want my name cleared from the charge of murder. There were many witness the day Diego was killed by his horse after he attacked me," Rafe agreed.

"All right, let's get this job finished and delivered and then we'll go see the sheriff and start the process of getting Rafe's name cleared. Rafe, you and Billy will deliver the order to the Army depot in Albuquerque," George said. He thought if Billy was tough enough for Rafe to trust him riding shotgun over the load of silver, he certainly could protect the gun shipment to Albuquerque.

Ana Teresa did not like the option of relying on the American law. She thought leaving New Mexico for California where they would be safe was a better option.

She did not trust the Santa Fe Spanish aristocrats would give him a fair trial, including her uncle *don* Pedro. He spouted nothing but hate for the so-called *mestizo* dog, as he often called Rafael. Now she was being asked to trust the American legal system to protect Rafael against the power of the Spanish elite. No, she did not like it at all.

She kissed Rafe on the cheek and returned to the main house. Rafe and Carlos got busy assembling the last of the double-action rifles and Carlos packed them in the shipping box. Rafe sensed Ana Teresa's anguish in her voice and eyes. He would have to console her when they were alone tonight. In the meantime, there was work to be done.

CHAPTER 39

Alvaro Gutierrez sat with Oscar Peralta and Vicente Vargas playing Monte after Benjamin walked out. The simple Spanish card game allowed his mind to wander. Not only did the *mestizo* return, he married the beautiful Spanish *señorita,* Ana Teresa. It was against all Spanish traditions.

Several times he glanced at the old *dons* who were drinking at tables on the far side of the cantina. They or their fathers were part of Governor Manuel Armijo's Army who should have destroyed the Americanos in 1846, but Governor Armijo turned tail and ran, ordering the New Mexican Army to retreat to Santa Fe. General Kearny marched into Santa Fe and took New Mexico without firing a single shot. Now the *dons* spent most of their time at the Palacio reminiscing about old times, sipping brandy, and taking a *puta* when they could get their old *penes* to cooperate. Their inaction left their sons and grandsons with only a flimsy, prideful delusion of power in the New Mexico Territory.

Alvaro and his friends played Monte for three or four hours before Virginia Verdugo floated down the stairs of the Palacio Cantina. Tall and well proportioned with raven black hair, alabaster skin, and gray-blue eyes, Virginia had an ageless beauty. She was rich and unmarried and Alvaro believed she was the desirable prize for avenging Diego's death. Several other *caballeros* had died in duels over her hand, but it was Diego's death, which hurt her terribly. She admired his power. Diego exuded machismo and dominated the young *caballeros* in Santa Fe and now Alvaro wanted that coveted position.

"Alvaro!" Virginia called out as she floated downstairs. She was dressed in a black, old fashioned, high-collared Spanish dress. The elaborate black bustle crowned a rippled red underskirt. A long lace *mantilla* hung past her waist. Although the style of the dress was old fashioned, Virginia looked anything but. She wore a heavy gold necklace around her slender neck and several jeweled gold rings.

Alvaro stepped to the bottom of the stairs, bowed, and complimented her before taking her hand. He led her to a table and the bartender brought brandies in stemmed crystal glasses for them. Her perfume wafted to Alvaro's nose as he helped her into the chair.

"I was told you ran that *culón,* Benjamin, out of here for sullying Diego's death," she purred. Alvaro was the only *caballero* fueling the anger of the Spaniards against the *mestizo* who killed her Diego. Even the older *dons* were tired of complaining and refused to take their vengeance. Virginia had been stoking Alvaro's aspirations for power as well as his desire for her.

"I learned the *mestizo* dog has returned to Santa Fe," Alvaro told her. "Now is our chance to take our revenge."

The news caught Virginia a bit by surprise. She had spies and patrons who usually kept her immediately informed of any news in the city. "And you have not already done so?" Virginia responded.

"I have just learned this news. It will take time to formulate a plan to take him without the Americano sheriff's knowledge," Alvaro told her.

"You are a *culón* Alvaro, if you are afraid of the *pinche* sheriff. My Diego would have already bested the *peón* and brought me his *cojones.*" Virginia called him a chickenshit for his inaction, touting how Diego would have brought her the *mestizo's* balls, and a rage swelled in the pit of Alvaro's stomach. He wanted to remind Virginia that her beloved Diego did not best the *peón,* but instead died fighting him. The *peón* was not only a talented foe, but had a superior horse.

"I promise you I will take the *peón* and bring you both his head and his balls," Alvaro swore to her taking her hand. She gave him a guarded look and he knew by her demeanor he would not be going upstairs with her tonight.

"If you want me, you will make it so. Only a true man will share my bed," she responded before standing and walking off toward two tables where older *dons* were playing cards. As she walked away, she knew Alvaro was seething. She orchestrated her behavior to extract his anger into action, knowing he wanted her. Though Alvaro was better looking than Diego, he was only half the man and she was only toying with him. He would never reach her bedroom.

First Benjamin disrespected him and now Virginia's cooling attitude intensified Alvaro's rage. Raised in a respected Spanish household and steeped in the traditions of the Spanish caste system, Alvaro believed he and his kind were superior. Before New Mexico was a United States Territory and new Americano laws were enacted, the *mestizo* would have already been dead. It was the sheriff who was a *culón,* wanting to bring the *mestizo* to trial. Alvaro swore under his breath it would never happen. The *mestizo* would die by his hand.

Alvaro walked to the Monte table and barked at the young *caballeros* playing the card game. *"Vámonos."*

Oscar Peralta moved his chair, but Vicente Vargas just looked up at Alvaro. "I am on a winning streak. I will meet you later," he grumbled. Vicente disliked how Alvaro tried to act like Diego. In truth he disliked Diego, but Diego was mean and spiteful and Vicente feared rebuke for any disloyalty. Alvaro was just a pompous *pendejo."*

"I said we go now," Alvaro said pulling the sword by his side and putting the tip next to Vicente's neck. Vicente felt a prick on his neck, but remained steady.

"I will meet you later," Vicente grumbled. He knew Alvaro would not run him through here in the cantina.

A moment hung between them before Alvaro backed off and sheathed his sword. *"Vámonos,"* he said looking at Oscar.

Rafe stood in George's office the day after Alvaro recognized Ana Teresa in town.

"I know you should not have to go to trial. You are innocent," George said.

"I must face the law and clear my name. I cannot live here always looking over my shoulder," Rafe replied.

George was somewhat surprised the news had not

spread into town to the sheriff over the last several weeks since Rafe came home. He attributed it to the bad weather.

"Billy and I will take the order to the Army Depot in Albuquerque and when I get home we'll go see the sheriff," Rafe said.

"All right. In the meantime I will speak to Ron Iverson. I contacted him when you were in Mexico. He is my friend and a good lawyer," George told him.

"Do you think I can get a fair trial?" Rafe asked. It was the question continuing to nag at him. Perhaps Ana Teresa was right and they should leave and go back to Rancho Simi.

"I believe so. You heard Benjamin. Even he knows you are innocent."

"Yes, but he may still side with the Spaniards. You know how they band together against Americans and they would definitely stand together against me."

George could not disagree. He observed that behavior for years. The Spanish clung to their traditions and were angry at losing their power when the American laws took over. Though he knew Rafe was innocent, he too feared whether justice could prevail here in Santa Fe. Part of him wanted to tell Rafe to leave, but he knew it would be no life for him and Ana Teresa.

"I have to trust the law," George finally said putting a hand on Rafe's arm. "Just be very careful until we can get you safely in the jail. One of Diego's friends may try to take his own revenge."

The following morning Alvaro ordered Oscar and Vicente to take turns watching the Summers' ranch. "I want to know immediately if you see the *mestizo*," he told them. Alvaro kept an eye on the plaza hoping to see Ana Teresa again. He toyed with the idea of kidnapping her to bring her husband, the *mestizo*, out of hiding.

He left the Palacio last night angry after Virginia threatened him. He decided he would not approach Virginia until he dangled Rafael's head and balls from his sword.

By the end of the second day with no news, Alvaro was getting impatient. Oscar suggested they storm the Summers' foundry where Alvaro was sure the *mestizo* was hiding. "Let us go and burn it down like we did his house. When they attempt to put out the fire, we will kill them all, even the gringo who shelters him."

"Perhaps. Let us give it a few more days to catch the *peón* alone," Alvaro responded. He agreed with Oscar's plan, but killing Americans, perhaps women, would definitely put a rope around their necks.

Everyone at the foundry worked feverishly to complete the Fort Bliss order on time. When the order was loaded and the wagon made ready, Billy climbed up on the covered wagon to take it to the Army Depot in Albuquerque. Rafe saddled Rayo making the excuse the horse needed the exercise, when in fact riding the powerful horse settled his nerves.

Rafe held Ana Teresa in his arms. Tears glistened in her eyes as she tried hard not to cry. The morning sun crested the mountains lighting the clouds in an orange, pink, and gray sky just over the eastern peaks of the Sangre de Cristo Mountains promising good weather.

Billy felt content with his new position working for George Summers. He considered himself lucky to be learning a new job. He only hoped the Army would not find him here in Santa Fe. When they were alone, he told Rafe he should not be the one to deliver the order to the Army Depot. Rafe understood and told him he would make the actual delivery while Billy waited in town.

Billy appreciated neither Rafe nor Ana Teresa recounted the story to the family about how he burst into the waystation brandishing a broken gun and calling himself Desperate Billy. It seemed so long ago, though only several months had past. He did not believe he deserved being locked up in the stockade and facing a court marshal for striking the arrogant lieutenant. However, he now knew the charge of escape would be added to his other charges and no Army jury would overlook that.

Though he was letting his hair grow and usually sported a scruffy beard, Billy wondered if he would be recognized. Was Santa Fe far enough from Fort Yuma to be safe?

As Billy snapped the reins, he looked back at the house. The family was standing on the porch and waving. Josefina and Celiá stood together waving at them. At the evening meals Billy took the opportunity to study all of the Summers, as well as Rafe's mother, Celiá. He believed her quiet nature was more because of a minimal knowledge of the English language. He noticed when she smiled her entire face lit up and her dark eyes gleamed.

He found little resemblance between Rafe and his mother. Her complexion was darker and her hair almost black. He knew Rafe's father was a Spaniard from Mexico and assumed Rafe resembled him. Billy waved in return and turned the horses down the lane.

Oscar Peralta sat on a knoll watching the trail to and from the Summers' ranch according to Alvaro's instructions. Oscar grumbled unhappy at getting up before sunup and in the cold. He pulled at the collar of his coat to ward off the cold morning air. He and Vicente Vargas were taking turns watching the house, hoping to see the *mestizo* called Rafael leave the property. Today it was his turn to watch the morning's activity at the ranch.

As the sun came up, a covered wagon pulled into the courtyard from the foundry. It was not the usual activity. Oscar shaded his eyes against the rising sun. A man in a hat drove the two-horse team, but he could not tell if it was the *mestizo*. After a few minutes, a short older man walked the big Appaloosa out of the barn. A man in a black Stetson walked out of the front door with several women. He hugged the women and then strode toward the Appaloosa. Another man stood in the courtyard. The man in the Stetson jumped onto the Appaloosa. Stepping the horse a few feet, he reached down and shook the man in the courtyard's hand. There was no doubt in Oscar's mind the rider of the Appaloosa was the *mestizo*.

As soon as he saw the wagon followed by the *mestizo* on the Appaloosa pull out of the courtyard, he turned his horse and rode to where the Summers' driveway met the main trail. He kept in the shadows of the trees. Once he saw the wagon turn south, he rode hard to Alvaro's *hacienda*.

CHAPTER 40

Alvaro was still asleep when Oscar rode into the courtyard. Banging on the door, Oscar told the cook to go wake him. About fifteen minutes later, Alvaro walked into the kitchen in his sleeping gown. Oscar was sitting drinking coffee and eating Mexican pastries.

"Why are you not watching the house?" Alvaro grumbled angry at being awakened so early.

"Alvaro, the *mestizo* and a gringo are headed south. The gringo is driving a covered wagon and the *mestizo* is riding the Appaloosa."

Alvaro was suddenly attentive. "You are sure they are headed south?"

"Yes, I followed them to make sure."

"Go get Vicente and meet me on the trail south of town. Tell him to bring his rifle. They cannot be too far driving a wagon. Go now," Alvaro ordered him. He told the cook to get his breakfast ready immediately as he headed upstairs to dress.

Alvaro formulated a plan as he rode to meet his friends. Vicente was the best shot with a rifle, so they would simply pick off the *mestizo* from a distance and be done with him. He knew he promised Virginia the *mestizo's* head, but all that was necessary was his death. A rifle shot from a distance was untraceable to his hand. He would take the credit and would be a hero in the eyes of Santa Fe's elite. He would be the man who avenged Diego de la Torre's death and got rid of the *mestizo* dog. Then he would go to the Palacio Cantina and claim Virginia as his prize. Puffing his chest at the thought, he spurred his horse and hurried to meet his friends south of town.

Billy urged the team to an even but fast pace after they merged onto the main trail. Rafe was riding Rayo beside him. As they entered the main town of Santa Fe, Billy noticed Rafe kept watching their back trail and eyeing movements near them. Billy wondered if Rafe was just nervous about the gun shipment or the gossip he heard at the foundry about how Rafe was involved in the death of a young aristocrat here in Santa Fe. According to the story, they battled on horseback with swords and the other man's horse fell on him. Billy thought the story odd as he never saw Rafe wear a sword, only his guns. He decided he would ask Rafe the details on the long hours of this trip.

The plaza in Santa Fe was just awakening as Billy slowed the wagon down the main street. The mercantile was setting out the items it displayed on the sidewalk. The owner was moving a large barrel near the front door. Today on the plaza, only a little snow remained in the shadowed areas, not like the day when they arrived in Santa Fe. On that day everything was covered in a thick coating of white.

Billy felt the sun begin to warm the left side of his face as it fully crested the mountains. They passed the center of town and Billy snapped the reins to put the horses back to the faster pace. About an hour later they caught up with a caravan of wagons just south of La Cienega Stage Stop. Rafe told him to join the caravan while he went to find the wagon master.

"Hello," Rafe greeted the man riding near the front wagon. "Are you the wagon master?"

"Yes, name's Homer Jackson. You traveling alone?" Homer eyed the young Mexicano and watched his hands carefully. Two guns rested in the rider's holster.

"My name is Rafe and I have a wagon trailing you. Mind if we tag along for safety?" Rafe asked.

"Sure, I always welcome extra help. Started traveling in a caravan because of highwaymen. Got held up several times. I assume you can use those pistols?" he asked.

"Yes. I will defend the caravan as well as my own wagon," Rafe assured him.

Rafe stayed up with the wagon master for about an hour talking and passing the time as the caravan traveled south toward Albuquerque. Billy kept the wagon following the trail, though passed several of the slower wagons of the caravan.

Alvaro arrived about an hour after Oscar told him the news. Oscar and Vicente were waiting for him on the south side of town just off the main trail. "Have you seen him?" he demanded as he rode up.

"No. They must already be ahead of us," Vicente responded. I checked in town and they are not there.

Alvaro pondered the possibility the *mestizo* and the wagon might have headed east on the Santa Fe Trail, instead of south. However, he thought it unlikely because of the winter weather in the mountains. South was the obvious route. Though it took almost an hour to assemble his friends here south of the city, Alvaro was not worried about losing the *mestizo* on the Appaloosa. Since he was riding with a wagon, he was going to be making less distance.

"Come on. There is a pass at Black Gulch Mesa where we can hold up and wait for the wagon to come by. Vicente, you will be able to shoot him from there and we will not be seen," Alvaro told him.

They took a trail along the Rio Grande where they would not be seen from the main trail, riding at a fast pace. It was an old trail, but well known to those families who lived in Santa Fe for generations. They made good time and reached the spot known as Black Gulch Mesa. The desert mesa stood against the sky and the foothills created a natural rise where the Chihuahua Trail was easily visible. Alvaro led the way to a vantage point where boulders created shadows and were large enough to hide them.

Oscar felt the temperature drop as he settled behind a shadowed boulder and out of the sun. "How long do we wait," he grumbled.

He knew Vicente would fire the fatal shot and Alvaro would claim the glory. Oscar would get nothing for his trouble. It had been the same with Diego. When he was alive, Diego never dirtied his hands unless necessary, always making demands of the other dandies. Commanding respect, Diego exuded power over the young *caballeros* of Santa Fe, in a manner Alvaro could not.

Vicente set himself up where he could get a clear shot at anyone on the main trail. He balanced the rifle on a crook in the boulder aimed down the trail. Alvaro paced nearby as they waited.

The sun was finally warming the air and Billy shrugged out of his heavy jacket. A little while later he saw Rafe riding in his direction.

"You tired of driving?" Rafe asked him.

"Naw, the team is easy. Did you find the wagon master?"

"Yes. He's happy to have us tag along. Said he started to only travel in a caravan because of highwaymen. I think we better stick with them for safety, though it will make the trip a bit longer."

Rafe rode up beside Billy staying on his eastern side. Rayo pranced keeping step with the team horses.

"Hey Rafe, I been meaning to ask you. I heard you had some trouble in Santa Fe. Somebody died and they're saying you might have murdered him," Billy asked him about the gossip.

"Yes I had some trouble and no I didn't murder anyone. I told you about how the wealthy Spanish run Mexico and treat the peasants badly. Well it is not so different in Santa Fe. There are old Spanish families who think they still hold the power. They don't respect people like me who were born peasants. They lost power when New Mexico became a territory of the Unites States."

Rafe stopped talking while he reined Rayo tighter. One of the team horses was catching the stallion's attention. Perhaps she was getting close to going into heat.

"One of the young aristocrats wanted Ana Teresa and hated me because he believed I was low class. He attacked me on the plaza with his sword and we fought. I was on Rayo and he was on his black stallion. Lots of people were there that day and watched the fight. His stallion bit Rayo and Rayo bucked up. Before I knew what was happening, the horses were clawing at each other, but Rayo was taller and stronger. Diego slipped off his saddle and his horse fell on top of him."

"And the horse killed him?"

"Yes he was pinned under the horse and died, but the Spaniards still want to blame me. When I go back to Santa Fe, I'll have to go to trial," Rafe finished.

"That's not fair. You shouldn't have to go to trial if everyone knows you're innocent. It was self defense!" Billy exclaimed.

"The local Spaniards don't care about innocent or guilty. They want revenge."

Minutes dragged slowly with nothing popping into view. Oscar was freezing and stiff sitting behind the cold boulder. "This is stupid Alvaro. We should have taken him at the foundry like I told you."

"So you think trying to kill him at a gun foundry would be a good idea. You are more *estúpido* than you look," Alvaro retorted hotly.

"And if you had killed him last year instead of letting a woman scare you with a sword, Diego would be alive," Oscar grumbled.

Alvaro burned inside at Oscar's insult. He, Vicente, and Benjamin caught the *mestizo* at an abandoned *hacienda* last year. They encircled him with their horses and the *mestizo* was unarmed. Diego had sent them to kill him, but Ana Teresa defended him with a rapier. Alvaro shied from harming the young woman and let the *mestizo* dog escape.

"Come here. I see wagons coming," Vicente called out.

The three shaded their eyes into the sun. "Look, there they are."

It was not the lone wagon with the *mestizo* riding the Appaloosa, but a line of wagons and riders traveling as a caravan. Suppliers had begun to use this method as protection from highway robbers.

With the bright morning sun in their eyes, it was hard to make out much from their vantage point. Alvaro scanned his eyes looking for the Appaloosa.

"Look there at the middle of the caravan; there is a

covered wagon with a rider nearby. Yes, it's the Appaloosa," Alvaro said excitedly pointing to the caravan.

"Yes, that's him. They must have joined up with a caravan leaving Santa Fe," Oscar agreed.

"Shoot him," Alvaro said excited having the *mestizo* in his vision. "Shoot him now."

Vicente tried to get a clean sight on the rider of the Appaloosa. The image of the rider kept ducking behind the wagon.

"What are you waiting for?" Alvaro demanded.

"I can't get a clear shot."

"Culón, shoot or I swear I will kill you now," Alvaro growled.

Vicente took aim and squeezed the trigger on the rifle.

A shot rang from the foothills and Rafe heard a bullet whizz nearby.

"Damn, that was close," Billy said.

"Keep the wagon in formation," Rafe told him.

Reaching back, Rafe pulled his rifle from the scabbard on the saddle. Ahead of him he saw six caravan guards do the same. Another shot rang out. Two of the guards turned toward the sound and started riding hard. Rafe pondered only a moment deciding whether to stay with the wagon or follow the two guards in the chase.

"Billy, keep your pistol out and ready," Rafe told him and kicked Rayo to a gallop.

Alvaro saw the rider on the Appaloosa turn from the wagon and follow several other guards with rifles coming in their direction.

"He's coming. Take him now," he growled at Vicente.

Vicente saw the riders coming toward the foothills after his second shot. He stood and headed toward his horse.

"You die for his head," Vicente stowed his rifle and jumped to his horse. Oscar was already mounted and riding off.

As Rafe and the guards rode toward the foothills, Alvaro spouted a Spanish curse into the wind. *"Me cago en ese hijo de puta."* The curse, saying he would shit upon the son of a whore, was directed at Rafe, but his words blew away in the wind as he mounted and rode after his comrades.

CHAPTER 41

Two days after Rafe and Billy left with the gun order for the Army Depot in Albuquerque, George was sitting in his office trying to catch up on some paperwork. His door opened and Mayor Billy Thornton and Sheriff Johnson walked in.

"Good morning gentlemen," George said with a smile.

"Good morning George. We've heard your son is back in town," the mayor spoke first.

"Well yes and no. He was here for a few days, but he is making a delivery for me and has gone to Albuquerque."

"You promised to turn him in as soon as he came back to town," the sheriff gruffed. "I thought I could trust you George."

"Gentlemen, you surely would let us have a few days to have my son home after an extended leave. He has just been married and after all you know he is innocent." George was working hard to keep his voice calm and his irritation at the whole situation under control.

"Well yes, but *don* Pedro came to my office yesterday and is upset about it. He was told Rafe married his niece, the Spanish girl from California, and you know how the *dons* feel about that too," Mayor Thornton replied.

"Do I need to remind you that New Mexico has American laws and not Spanish. My son is entitled to marry anyone he wishes. If *don* Pedro is upset, then that is his business."

The sheriff was frustrated by the whole matter. He believed in his heart Rafe was innocent and interviewed numerous witnesses who swore to him Diego started the fight. Diego's horse killed him, not Rafe, so charging Rafe with murder was a long stretch. Nevertheless, the *dons* were in an uproar and Diego's friends were likely to start trouble. Sheriff Johnson convinced himself he was only trying to keep the peace by arresting Rafe.

"When will he be back?" the sheriff asked.

"About a week, maybe a bit longer. It will depend upon the weather," George replied.

"I expect you to bring him in, George. Immediately. It is not just for a trial, but it is also to keep him safe. We can't have him running around Santa Fe and have the *caballeros* trying to kill him. I won't be able to stop them."

"I understand. As soon as he gets back, I'll have him turn himself in," George replied.

After the sheriff and mayor left, George sat at his desk staring at the ledger. Part of him wanted to wire Rafe in Albuquerque to tell him to head directly to El Paso. He would be out of the reach of Sheriff Johnson in Texas. Yet, Rafe told him he wanted to clear his name. He had not done anything wrong, but everything hinged on American law and the ability for a judge to get the entire story.

When George discussed the case with Ron Iverson, the lawyer harbored some doubts. Normally to prove guilt, the sheriff would have to produce witnesses who saw Rafe stab or kill Diego. However, Ron seemed a bit unsure about the role Rafe's horse played in the matter. Rayo and Diego's black stallion were clawing at each other, raised on their hind legs. He thought it possible a judge might interpret the horse under Rafe's control. He was looking for legal cases to use in Rafe's defense.

Regardless of the law, George was more worried about Diego's friends. They had already burned Rafe's house to the ground. If Rafe was acquitted, he could still be a target here in Santa Fe at any time.

Arriving in Albuquerque, Rafe delivered the weapons order at the Army Depot after dropping Billy in the older part of town. Billy promised to stay around the plaza until Rafe completed the delivery. The captain at the depot required a short training on the features before he would sign the acceptance for the order.

He and Rafe spent more than an hour shooting at targets. By the end of the training session, the captain was thrilled with the balance and accuracy of the rifles. He thanked Rafe and told him he expected another order might be coming in the next few months.

Rafe drove the empty wagon back to the plaza. It was a pleasant winter day in Albuquerque with the sun warming his back as he drove. He circled the plaza twice looking for Billy, then parked the wagon near the saddle shop. Though Albuquerque reminded him of Santa Fe with its mostly adobe buildings, Rafe thought Albuquerque showed little charm by comparison. The *paseo* was packed dirt and the plaza was brown and sparse.

Albuquerque was built near the Rio Grande. Cattle pens created more of the town than houses. Rafe had been to Albuquerque when the pens were full of Texas cattle coming north on the Goodnight-Loving trail. Thousands of cows could be held here while the cowboys took a break drinking and gambling in the town. Today the pens were empty and the town quiet.

Down the sidewalk, he saw the sign for John Grady's Mercantile. Rafe often delivered guns to John's store over the years. On one of Rafe's deliveries, John explained how the Army Depot was located in Albuquerque to keep control over the cattle drovers.

Rafe jumped off the wagon. Billy was nowhere in sight. Rafe planned on making the delivery and reaching the Placitas stage stop on their way home before nightfall. They had no reason to stay and Rafe wanted to get back home as soon as possible. No doubt Billy was somewhere in town, drinking or gambling.

Heading down the sidewalk, Rafe looked for the nearest saloon. Pushing in the door to the first saloon, Rafe was surprised to see Army soldiers at most of the tables, though he knew the Army had a full garrison stationed here. A few cowboys stood at the bar, and three Spanish *vaqueros* sat at the table in the back. It did not surprise him Billy was nowhere to be seen. No doubt the sight of the soldiers scared him.

Rafe checked the other two saloons with the same result. Walking from the last saloon, Rafe's path led him past the Sheriff's office. He stopped dead in his tracks as he glanced at the poster board in front of the office.

WANTED. Deserter from the U.S. Army, Fort Yuma, California.

A drawing of Billy's face, his name, and the reward of $50 completed the notice. Rafe thought the drawing was of a much younger Billy with a beard and doubted he might be easily recognized. Still, the poster was a warning and Rafe was sure Billy saw it.

Rafe searched Albuquerque for the rest of the afternoon, trying to imagine what happened to Billy or where he might hide. Unable to ask many questions, Rafe checked the livery, the mercantile, walked the alleyways which connected to the main plaza, and even checked the church. Finally, he sauntered into the sheriff's office convinced Billy must already be in jail.

"Hello sheriff," he greeted the man sitting behind the desk.

"Hello young man. Can I help you?"

"I . . . I am Rafael Reyes de Estrada from Santa Fe. I just delivered a load of rifles to the Army Depot and wondered if you had any need for new firearms?" Rafe easily fell into a sales pitch he learned while traveling with George Summers.

"You from that GSW foundry in Santa Fe?" the sheriff asked.

"Yes sir. Do you know George Summers?"

"Met him several times. You say you delivered a load of guns to the depot?"

Rafe edged closer to the door leading to the cells. It was pulled closed so he could not look inside.

"Yes sir. Delivered the load this morning." Rafe pulled one of his pistols and put it on the sheriff's desk. "I bet you have a lot of trouble in this town when the cattle are on the move."

The sheriff picked up the pistol, turning it in his hands and testing the feel. "Yeah, summer is a whole lot busier. Sometimes them cowboys get mighty twitchy. Why last fall we had a big dustup when the Kinney Gang rustled several hundred Double B stock."

"The Kinney Gang. I've never heard of them. How come I don't see a poster outside for them? I only saw the one for the Army deserter?" Rafe asked.

"Can't pin anything on them. Sometimes they call themselves the Rio Grande Posse. Try to pass themselves off as vigilantes, but theys just rustlers. Say, this pistol sure is a beaut, but I can't afford one on my salary," the sheriff told him and handed it to Rafe.

"Did they catch the deserter?" Rafe asked. He kept his voice casual and disinterested trying to keep the sheriff talking about Billy.

"Naw. The soldiers here don't care none about deserters. Now if Cochise or some of them Apaches get on the warpath, then they get excited. Otherwise, they're more interested in drinking and gambling. But, they send me the posters and I hang em up."

"Well, thanks sheriff. I'll see if I can get you a discount on one of our guns and let you know." Rafe stuck out his hand and the sheriff shook it.

Relieved, Rafe walked out of the office with no idea where to find Billy. Around the plaza, gaslights were beginning to shine as twilight was setting over the city. Rafe walked to the wagon and jumped to the seat. It was too late to make Placitas. Snapping the reins, he started the horses and drove the wagon to the livery.

"I'll pick up the wagon and the Appaloosa in the morning," he called to the man.

"Sure. I'll take care of everything."

Rafe saw no options to finding Billy. He made one more pass checking at the saloons, before obtaining a room at the hotel and having a meal in the lobby's cafe.

The following morning dawned with gray clouds on the eastern horizon. Overnight Rafe formulated no plan to find Billy and decided with the oncoming weather he needed to head back to Santa Fe. Perhaps Billy saw the wanted poster and hopped the boot of a stagecoach just like he had when Rafe first met him.

Walking to the livery, Rafe paid the daily fee and jumped to the seat. Snapping the reins, he pulled out of the livery towing Rayo and within a half hour was well north of Albuquerque. He was almost to Placitas when he heard a rustling in the back of the wagon under the canvas tarp.

"Keep driving. I'm going to keep hidden back here until we're far away from Albuquerque," he heard Billy's voice.

"Billy? Where have you been? I looked all over for you."

"I saw the poster and been hiding out. I was afraid you were going to leave me yesterday, but I crawled in here late last night."

"I think you can come out. I saw the sheriff yesterday and he said the Army regiment here doesn't go chasing deserters. I think you're safe."

"No matter. I'll stay under this tarp for a while longer," Billy replied.

CHAPTER 42

By the time they were driving into Santa Fe two days later, Billy was once again riding up on the seat next to Rafe. They spent many hours of the trip discussing options for Billy. Though Rafe wanted him to stay in Santa Fe, Billy thought he should move on in the spring, far away from Fort Yuma.

"I best be getting on my way soon," Billy told him. Rafe found he was disappointed. Billy was a good worker and Rafe now thought of him as a good man and not Desperate Billy, though he understood his dilemma.

After supper that evening, Rafe and George talked for several hours in the parlor. A roaring fire crackled in the fireplace keeping the room warm. It was the room where they spent many hours in lively discussion after the supper meal. Tonight the mood was somber.

George told him about the sheriff's visit and how a trial seemed the only course of action. Still, George held reservations about whether the truth would prevail.

"You could ride off early in the morning. Go back to California or El Paso and I will arrange to send Ana Teresa," George told him.

"Like a coward or worse, like I'm guilty?" Rafe retorted.

George hung his head in shame for the thought, but he was not convinced Rafe would get a fair trial here in Santa Fe.

"I left Mexico on the run believing I was a murderer. I lived in shame for many years. I do not want that for Ana Teresa or my children. I am innocent *don* Jorge, and I intend to prove it."

"I understand," George said with a sigh.

"Don't worry. You said Ron Iverson is a great attorney and I believe God will see me though this ordeal," Rafe told him.

"We will go to the sheriff after breakfast in the

morning. Goodnight my son. You better go spend your last night of freedom with your wife."

George Summers stared into the fireplace with one foot on the hearth as Rafe walked from the room. He was proud of Rafe, more proud than he could say. However, George was afraid the Santa Fe justice system might hang an innocent man and it knotted his gut.

The following morning Rafe and George rode to the sheriff's office.

"I'm here as you requested," Rafe stepped up and said as they walked in.

"Please have a seat," Sheriff Johnson told him. He pulled out a file from his desk and handed the arrest warrant to Rafe.

Rafe scanned the paper. His eyes focused on the section labeled, Arrest Issued For, and read – for the murder of Diego de la Torre. The warrant was granted on behalf of Diego de la Torre's parents and *don* Pedro de Soto, Ana Teresa's uncle.

The sheriff allowed Rafe several minutes to say goodbye to George before he walked him to the back room and opened the middle cell door. George followed them to the cell. Rafe walked in and the sheriff clanged the metal door and turned the key. It broke George's heart to see his adopted son standing in the cell behind bars.

"This is as much for your protection Rafe," the sheriff said as he stood by the cell. "You are entitled to have visitors and I'll bring three meals a day from the cafe. You just tell me what you want."

"Keep him safe," George told the sheriff.

"Don't worry George. He'll get a fair trial and I won't let those Spaniards try for a lynching party. No sir. This will be completely on the up and up," the sheriff assured him.

When George arrived home, Josefina ran and fell into his arms. She prayed there was some mistake, or by some miracle the sheriff would end this nightmare.

She blamed herself for Rafe's trouble, thinking she had not taught him about Santa Fe's Spanish aristocrats and how they still held on to the Spanish caste system.

Growing up in Spain, Josefina understood the social order which gave aristocrats power over the people they perceived as inferior. Now they wanted to make Rafe pay for murdering one of their favorite sons simply because of his lower class bloodline.

"George, you must do something," she pleaded.

"I've done everything I can. Go pray," he said unwinding her arms. He left her in the hallway and went to the kitchen.

She knew he would go to the foundry and spend his days while Rafael was in jail working day and night. Josefina had learned over her years of marriage to George how he grieved privately and turned his grief into his work. It was so when their own infant son Gregory died of influenza when he was eight months old. She watched him walk away and then slowly gathered herself.

When George said the prayer for the evening meal, he added a prayer for Rafe. A somber atmosphere prevailed. Several times George saw tears well in Ana Teresa's eyes. She barely touched her food. Even Billy did not finish his portion of meat when he usually took second helpings.

After the meal the women were in the kitchen. Billy carried several large logs from outside and was stoking the fire as the nights were still very cold.

Celiá stood by the kitchen counter staring at the wall. Yesterday George and Josefina sat with her and explained in Spanish what was happening to her son. It was difficult for her to understand about the American laws. What she did understand was the Spanish caste system. It was a system where the aristocrats could do anything to the *peóns* including killing them for any grievance. There was no concept of justice in the Spanish caste system.

As Billy rose from stoking the fire, he noticed Celiá looked stricken. Walking to her side he spoke, "Your son is a good man. He spared my life and showed me only kindness. God will protect him." He did not know if she understood him, as Billy knew Celiá spoke little English. She tipped her face to look at him and Billy saw tears in her dark eyes.

Celiá did not understand Billy's words, except for the word God. Josefina taught her the English word. *"Mi hijo no ha hecho nada malo. Él es un hombre bueno,"* Celiá wailed her son was a good man and had done nothing wrong, though Billy did not understand her.

She turned and fell into Billy's arms as the tears flowed down her cheeks. He held her until the sobbing subsided and then carefully extracted himself a bit embarrassed by her sudden embrace.

"Ma'am," he tipped his head and walked away.

CHAPTER 43

For the first two nights while Rafe was in jail, Ana Teresa cried herself to sleep. George told her both Diego's parents and her uncle Pedro signed the arrest warrant charging Rafe with the murder. At breakfast on the third morning, she told George she was going to see her uncle and plead for him to drop the charges and then talk to Diego's family to do likewise.

"I don't think it is a good idea Ana Teresa. You know how they feel about *mestizos*. They will never agree to do it," George told her.

"I must try, *don* Jorge. I cannot stand to see Rafael in jail for something he did not do. Diego attacked him because of me. I must try."

"Very well, I will go with you. I promised Rafe to make sure you stay safe." Rafe made him promise not only that, but to give Ana Teresa a home, if the worst happened to him.

"It would be better if you go with me," she agreed.

It was mid afternoon when Ana Teresa and George arrived at the de Soto *hacienda*. The stableman came to take their horses as they dismounted in the courtyard. George used the door knocker to announce their arrival. A maid opened the door and recognized the young woman with the older gentleman. *"Ah, Ana Teresa, bienvenido,"* she welcomed her and escorted them to the entryway.

Removing her gloves and coat, Ana Teresa handed them to the maid and said, "Tell my uncle I wish to see him."

The house was familiar. She had lived in this house with her uncle's family for many months. She and her cousin Bibiana danced in the courtyard at the fiesta when she first met Rafael. Now however, she stood nervously waiting for the maid to fetch her uncle.

When she thought about her uncle accusing Rafael of murder her heart pounded in fear. She remembered vividly the day Rafael came to confront her uncle and asked for her hand in marriage. Her uncle Pedro yelled at Rafael, "No! You will have to kill me to get into this house. You will never have Ana Teresa. She will marry Diego." On that day she thought her life was over and she thought she would never see Rafael again. Thankfully God had a different plan.

"Why are you here?" Pedro de Soto yelled at Ana Teresa as he walked into the entry way of the main house.

"Why did you sign the warrant to arrest Rafael?" she blurted out. "You know he is innocent!"

"Have you no shame woman? You come to my home a married woman to that *mestizo* dog. You are now a tainted woman. Leave my house at once!" the old *don* growled at his niece. Her impertinence grated at him.

"*Señor,* you are wrong. I assure you Rafael is a man of integrity and is innocent of the charges you have brought against him. I ask you to reconsider for the sake of your family and the innocence of my adopted son," George stepped up and tried to reason with *don* Pedro. George had met *don* Pedro a number of times, the last time when Carlos and Bibiana were married. He thought of him as a hard man, but thought he would be reasonable.

"My family has been disgraced! The *mestizo* pretended to be a *caballero* and tricked me into letting him talk to my niece. He is only a *mestizo* dog and my niece and my family have been shamed. Now, leave my house!" *don* Pedro screamed at George and Ana Teresa. The anger welling inside him turned *don* Pedro's face red and his hands trembled. George could see the *don* was visibly shaken.

"I feel sorry for you *señor.* The American court will see my son is acquitted of this injustice and there is nothing you or the other *don's* will be able to do about it," George told him.

"I tell you now, if the *mestizo* walks free we will take care of him in other ways," the *don* threatened, turned his back, and walked away.

Ana Teresa remained stoic through her uncle's tirade. She thought him a mean and spiteful man. She and George mounted their horses and rode from the courtyard.

"I'm sorry Ana Teresa. I did not expect we could change his mind," George finally broke the silence.

"Oh *don* Jorge, what are we going to do?"

Alvaro was sitting with Virginia sipping a brandy at the Palacio Cantina. Though he missed his chance to kill the *mestizo,* the sheriff now had him in jail awaiting a trial.

Virginia was keeping him at arm's length, toying with him and it riled Alvaro. He thought she would be grateful the *mestizo* dog was finally going to see a rope around his neck.

"You promised to bring me his head," she complained. "Now you are happy to let the Americano sheriff hang him. You should have killed him like you promised."

"He will be dead either way and you can have your revenge," he tried to appease her.

"I do not trust the Americano law. It is not like the old ways. How can you be sure?"

"We have enough witnesses to hang him. Diego's father and *don* Pedro have arranged it."

"Are you sure the witnesses will remain silent?" she asked.

"Yes, I am sure. I was there at the *hacienda* when *don* Pedro bought them off. They will do as he says or he told them if they do not, they will get a special visit," Alvaro said with a sneer.

"And if he is acquitted regardless of these witnesses, then what? Perhaps they are not as afraid of you as you think," she whined at him. Virginia knew Alvaro desired her and she was leading him on, flaunting her body in return for seeking revenge against the *mestizo.* Though Alvaro was handsome, she had no desire for him. He was not her Diego. He was not a man who exuded machismo and commanded respect from the other *caballeros.*

Alvaro stood up beside her and grabbed her arm tightly. Her disrespect rang in his ears. For months she had been flirting with him, grabbing and stroking his leg under the Monte table. She teased and toyed with him and he saw himself as Diego's replacement. Had he not taken control over the local Santa Fe dandies? Was he not handsome and rich, richer than Diego?

"I told you, he is in jail and we have fixed the witnesses. The *mestizo* will hang according to Americano law. There is no doubt about it. Come take me upstairs now. You owe me Virginia. Come on," Alvaro demanded.

Virginia was stunned by Alvaro's demand and quickly responded. "I told you before. The *mestizo* must die. You should have already taken care of him. Until he is dead, you may have one of my whores." She got up and left him at the table fuming to think about what she said.

"I will go to the jail and kill him now, then you better be ready to take my *garrancha*," he swore to her as she walked away.

Alvaro surveyed the cantina. Several older *dons* played cards at the back table. He saw *don* Emilio nudge *don* Hector and smile in his direction. They probably heard the conversation as Alvaro realized he and Virginia were shouting.

"*¡Hijos de putas!*" he snarled, calling the old *dons* sons of whores, before he turned his back and strode with his head held high out the cantina's door.

CHAPTER 44

Getting his horse from the corral, Alvaro rode out to Benjamin Pacheco's *hacienda*. Benjamin was not there and the maid offered him a seat in the warm kitchen to wait. He had been to the home many times so the maid treated him informally, offering him coffee and a sweet biscuit. About an hour later, Benjamin and several *vaqueros* rode in from the west trail to the stables. They had been out looking for stray cattle and were cold to the bone after being out all day searching the hillsides.

"Alvaro, what are you doing here?" Benjamin asked surprised when he walked in the kitchen. Hungry and cold, all he wanted was something to eat and a hot drink or a brandy to warm him. He did not want to deal with Alvaro. Trying to act calm and friendly as if their previous argument was forgotten, Alvaro stayed seated and waited until the cook went to the stove to warm up a stew for Benjamin before he spoke out.

"I want you to come with me. We will stop for Vicente and Oscar, then we will go to the jail and kill the *mestizo*. I want you to call the sheriff out and distract him while Vicente and I go in and kill the *mestizo* dog."

Benjamin should not have been surprised by the arrogant plan, but he was. "And the sheriff will hang you. He does not care for the color of your skin or for your heritage. A killing is a killing," Benjamin retorted.

"What do you care? You will be innocent, because you will be outside with the sheriff."

"Innocent or not, there will be blood on my hands," Benjamin replied.

"I think you are just a scared *culón*. What is the matter with you? It is our chance to finish off the *mestizo* and avenge Diego." He knew Alvaro was goading him, calling him a chickenshit, insulting him like he always did. Benjamin did not let it annoy him.

"You are on your own Alvaro. I have responsibilities

here. I have taken over for my father to run our *hacienda* and I will be getting married soon. I do not have time to play like boys with you and the *caballeros* any more. I will not help you," Benjamin told him.

"You are a *pinche maricón,*" Alvaro called him a fucking queer and laughed at him as he stood up to leave. "I will spread that lie and no one will marry you."

"Call me what you want, but I will not help you kill anyone, *mestizo* or not. You should go now," Benjamin told him.

Alvaro was stunned by Benjamin's refusal. Well, he did not need him, Oscar and Vicente would help him kill the *mestizo.*

Now on the fifth day of Rafe's incarceration, although he was treated well and Ana Teresa had been visiting him every day, he was restless and claustrophobic. The lawyer, Ron Iverson, came twice to see him, discussing every detail Rafe could remember. Ron took notes and promised to talk to anyone who might have been a witness.

Yesterday Carlos came for a long visit. They talked about their adventures together and how they met on the dusty road in El Paso. At one point Carlos thanked him for saving his life when Rafe found him bleeding on the Chihuahua Trail.

Last night a feeling of depression tried to overtake him, but he silently chanted an Aztec prayer Xihuitl, the Healer in Mexico, had taught him. Xihuitl taught him the chant to help him overcome his depression during the time he had amnesia for the many months he wandered the hills of Mexico not knowing who he was or where he came from.

"Remember this – there are incomprehensible powers on this earth. Never forget that," Xihuitl taught him. It was only one of the lessons Rafe learned from the Healer, but one he truly believed. It matched his own Catholic belief that anything is possible as God directs.

Through the small window he saw snow falling and a little stuck on the windowsill. Thankfully Ana Teresa brought wool blankets and a warm heavy coat to ward off the draft. Yesterday when she came to visit, she told him how she and George went to see her uncle *don* Pedro to ask him to drop the charges. Rafe was not surprised when she told him the old man refused and threw them out of his house. He told her not to go again.

Today he was looking forward to seeing his wife again. She promised to bring Lolo and Lizzy. He lay back on the small cot and stared at the walls. Several days ago he counted the bricks. He counted 742. To keep his mind sharp, he started the count again.

"Rafael!" he heard Lolo shout out when she, Lizzy, and Ana Teresa were let into the jailhouse. "We brought food for you," Lizzy announced as she raced back into the cell room empty handed. Her exuberance made him laugh.

Lolo and Ana Teresa came up behind her with their arms full. The deputy opened the cell door and let the girls inside.

"Thank you," Rafe said and took the sacks of food and placed them on the small table in his cell. "How are you girls doing? Are you back to school?" Rafe asked.

"Yes, I wish I was graduating this year, like Lolo," Lizzy said with a frown. "Father and mother are giving her all the attention just because she says she wants to go back east."

"Yes and I can't wait for summer. Father has promised to take me to Boston," Lolo added.

Rafe was used to the bickering between his adopted sisters and somehow today it brought him joy.

The girls brought chicken and tortillas and crispy cooked potatoes dusted in red chili. Rafe took one and let the flavor waken his mouth. The food from the cafe was good, but nothing was better than Juanita's cooking.

As he ate, Ana Teresa studied her husband. She thought he looked thin and there were dark circles under his eyes. She decided to hide her true feelings and put on a brave face each time she came to see him. Only after she got home in the privacy of their bedroom would she allow herself to break down and weep. Today was no different as she smiled and laughed with the girls.

Rafe looked at his wife. He knew she was trying to act brave for his sake. He would have preferred she wept in his arms, so he could comfort her.

"You didn't notice Ana Teresa's new dress," Lolo said chiding him.

"Oh yes. It is very pretty. Stand up and let me see it better," Rafe said.

Suddenly gunshots rang out and voices shouted. The deputy ran to the door leading into the inner cells. "Keep away from the window," he ordered.

"Where is the sheriff?" Rafe called to him.

"He was called out to stop a ruckus out on the plaza," the deputy said.

Three more shots rang from outside the jail, then Rafe heard yelling.

"Give us have the Mexican!" one of the voices yelled out in broken English.

"Diego's friends," Rafe called to the deputy. "They've come for my head."

"I'm warning you. Don't come closer or I'll shoot to kill," Rafe heard the deputy yell.

A bullet whizzed though the neighboring cell window and made a dull thwack as it hit the brick wall.

Lolo screamed. Rafe quickly pulled the girls to the floor of the cell. Lizzy started to cry.

Three shots came through the window hitting the cell next to Rafe's.

"Get down on the floor over here by the cot," Rafe told them pointing to where he thought was a safe spot. Ana Teresa pulled out Rafe's double-action pistol from under her dress and handed it to Rafe.

He looked at it in disbelief and then into her eyes. She stared steadily at him.

"Thank you," Rafe whispered to her. "Get down with the girls," Rafe told her and crouched to a spot where he could see the raiders if they broke down the door.

The deputy stuck the rifle barrel through a peephole and fired twice then slid behind the jail's thick wall. Two more shots came through the door.

"Give us the Mexican!" the men on horseback yelled toward the jail.

From the deputy's limited view through the peepholes, he saw two men dressed in street clothes with burlap hoods covering their faces. He fired five shots at them, but doubted he hit either one.

"No, go away. The sheriff will be back shortly." Two more shots echoed outside and the deputy flinched. Peeking through the peepholes, he saw nothing. Quickly he drew back behind the wall and waited for the shooting to start again.

"Deputy Morgan, open the door," the sheriff called out.

"Are you alone?"

"Yes, open the damn door Morgan."

Reluctantly the deputy opened the door and the sheriff came in. "Is everyone all right in here?" he asked.

"Yes, where are those men on horseback? They shot up the place trying to get the Mexican."

"I placed a couple of well placed shots near them and they scattered. There were two of them on horseback," the sheriff said.

The sheriff opened the door to the cell area and found Rafe in his cell with a gun aimed at him and three women huddled in the far corner.

"What happened sheriff?" Rafe asked standing up.

"What are you doing with that gun?" the sheriff asked as he pulled his out and pointed it at Rafe. "Drop it son, I don't want to shoot you. Did you give him the gun, Morgan?"

Ana Teresa stood up and spoke out boldly, "I did sheriff. I brought the gun for protection and when those men came I gave it to my husband."

"I was only protecting the women," Rafe said. He dropped the pistol and pushed it toward the cell door with his foot.

"Morgan, get that gun," the sheriff ordered.

"Ma'am, don't ever bring a gun to this jailhouse again. If you do, check it in when you get here. Morgan, why didn't you check them for weapons when they came?" the sheriff asked.

"Sheriff, I was not trying to escape. My wife gave it to me to protect myself and the girls. You have to believe me, sir. Remember, I turned myself in to you. I want to be cleared of this mess, but now you know they want me dead, with or without a trial."

CHAPTER 45

Alvaro and Vicente rode the back roads to Oscar's *hacienda* after the sheriff thwarted their plan to get the *mestizo*. Oscar left the plaza after creating a disturbance to distract the sheriff and now paced the courtyard waiting for them.

"Did you kill him?" Oscar asked as they rode up.

"Where the fuck did you go?" Alvaro growled at Oscar. "You left us there like a *pinche culón,* just like Benjamin."

"I . . . I was only supposed to distract the sheriff. When the deputy started shooting . . . it was not the plan," Oscar whined. He knew Alvaro was mad that he left them, but Oscar was not going to risk his neck for the *pinche peón.*

"So you didn't kill him?" Oscar asked.

"No, the sheriff came back before we could get the deputy to open the door. The son of a whore is still alive," Vicente complained. The two raiders changed into their *trajes,* put the burlap hoods they used to cover their faces into a trash bin outside, and set it on fire.

After the raid on the jail, Alvaro realized he had few options except to let the Americano law hang the *mestizo.* Virginia would not be pleased, but he was growing tired of her games with him. After the *mestizo* was swinging from the noose, Alvaro would go to the Palacio and claim Virginia.

When Lolo, Lizzy, and Ana Teresa returned home later that day, Lolo ran to find her father in the foundry.

"Father, they tried to kill Rafe," she came running up to him. George was working with Billy and Jose near the furnace.

"What? Who?" George asked her.

"We took Rafe his lunch and then they came and bullets started to . . . one hit the wall in the next cell," Lolo was slightly breathless from running to the foundry and excited to tell the story.

"Is everyone safe? Is Rafe safe?" George demanded to know.

"Yes father, we are all safe, just scared. The sheriff and deputy were able to make them leave."

The news hit George hard. "Come Billy, follow me. We're going to go see the sheriff."

Billy was surprised to be asked to go, but stepped up after hearing Rafe was threatened and followed George without question.

It was about an hour later when George slammed open the door to the jail. "I heard there was trouble here today. I told you those *caballeros* would come for him. You have to stand up to them before the trial. They will stop at nothing," George yelled at the sheriff.

"Calm down George. Rafe is safe. It was just a couple of the dandies making trouble," Sheriff Johnson tried to minimize the situation.

"The girls were here! Lolo said bullets were flying in the cells. Anyone could have been hurt. I demand you release my son. He is innocent and you know it! I'm taking him home where we can protect him."

"You can't do that. Go home George. I'll double the guard here if that will make you happy, but Rafe must stay in jail."

"I'm warning you Johnson, if anything happens to Rafe, there'll be hell to pay," George warned the sheriff and stormed out.

On the way home Billy reflected on what happened at the sheriff's office.

"George, who do you think came to kill Rafe?" he asked.

"Friends of Diego de la Torre. They are claiming Rafe killed him, but it is not true. They want his head.

"Do you know which friends?"

"I can probably guess. Alvaro Gutierrez for one and also Oscar Peralta. Why?"

"I was just thinking perhaps we should pay them a visit as payback," Billy emphasized the word, visit, so

George understood his meaning.

"No Billy. I brought you today for my protection, but I doubt we can change the Spaniard's minds about this. I'm not sure anything short of killing them will help at this point."

Two days before the trial was scheduled to start Ron Iverson walked from his office to the jail. "Good morning, Rafe," the lawyer greeted him as the deputy let him into Rafe's cramped cell. It was his third consultation visit to continue formulating a strategy for Rafe's defense. Rafe found the lawyer knowledgeable and trusted he would be a great advocate to plead his case. Today however, he looked grim.

"Since I saw you last, I have interviewed many of the witnesses who claimed to be at the plaza when you and Diego de la Torre fought. I'm getting conflicting stories from the majority of them. They are claiming, you are the one who attacked Diego and urged your horse to attack his."

"I cannot believe it. What I told you is the truth," Rafe said.

"All I have right now are two Tiwa Indians who sell jewelry in front of the Governor's palace who will vouch for your story. I'm afraid the prosecution will eat them up and spit them out quickly."

"The sheriff took statements from many others who said it was a fair fight. What about them?" Rafe asked.

"Several have changed their stories or I think some are just too scared to testify," Ron said shaking his head.

Rafe jumped up from the cot and paced. "I knew the *dons* would do this."

"Do what?"

"Buy off the witnesses. They probably threatened them too," Rafe told him.

Ron flipped through his papers. "The owner of the Palacio Cantina, Virginia Verdugo, says you came to the cantina looking for Diego. She says you threatened to kill Diego."

Rafe wracked his brain trying to remember if he said those words to Virginia. "Yes, I did go there looking for him, but only to tell him Ana Teresa was in love with me and not him. I wanted to tell him she already accepted my proposal for marriage. I'm sure I never told Virginia I wanted to kill him. She's lying."

"Then what happened?"

"Diego was not there, so I went to the plaza looking for him. It was late afternoon and a few carriages with *señoritas* were circling on the *paseo*. I knew Diego would be there. He found me there calling me a *peón* and attacked me with his rapier. He was an expert swordsman and would have killed me, if not for my Appaloosa. I asked him to renounce his contract for marriage to Ana Teresa and he laughed and said I was unworthy of her. Then Diego slashed Rayo across the shoulder and the horse got upset. Rayo attacked Diego's smaller black stallion. It was all I could do to hang onto my horse. I even threw my sword away. Like I told you before, his horse fell on him and killed him, not me."

"Was the sword your only weapon?" the lawyer asked.

"No, I had a pistol, but as I told you before, I needed to best Diego on his terms in order to gain favor to win Ana Teresa's hand. I never pulled my pistol."

"I believe you, but everything is aligning against you. Without solid witnesses in your favor, we may have trouble swaying the jury. The fact you were armed may be used against you, whether you pulled your pistol or not. I will try to select the best jurors as possible and hope for the best. If there are any other details you can think of, have them ready for me. We only have two days until the trial and I need all the help you can give me."

The lawyer left and Rafe slumped on the cot. He was innocent. Now his entire life hung in a fragile balance and a lump formed in the pit of his stomach.

George Summers stopped by Ron Iverson's office later that day to check on the lawyer's progress. When George walked into the lawyer's office and shook his hand,

George could tell this was not going to be a happy conversation.

"I'm not feeling overly confident George," Ron began.

"What do we have?"

"Not much. Most of the witnesses are either refusing to testify for Rafe or have changed their story. A few have told me the fight was chaotic and they don't know who was at fault."

"Either way, Rafe did not murder Diego. The horse fell on him. How can that be murder?" George asked.

"The prosecution will claim Rafe was in control of the horse. He used it as a deadly weapon."

"That's preposterous! No jury could convict someone for what their horse does."

"Unfortunately there is some case law about someone deliberately using a carriage as a deadly weapon. It all comes down to intent. The witnesses are saying Rafe wanted to kill Diego. We need witnesses who will testify that it was Diego who threatened Rafe."

George's heart sank. He never should have agreed to the sheriff's foolhardy plan. He should have known the Spanish *dons* would stop at nothing to foil the law and now Rafe's life hung in the balance.

CHAPTER 46

The morning of the trial brought a heavy snow, though it did not deter people from lining up hoping to get a seat in the courtroom at the Governor's Palace. The day began with both lawyers interviewing potential jurors in front of the judge. Finally a jury of twelve men were seated on the right side of the room and the waiting citizens were let into the courtroom. Ana Teresa sat with the Summers' family who were seated directly behind the table where Rafe and his lawyer sat. Billy sat next to Celiá.

To the right of Rafe, Diego de la Torre's family were sitting behind the state prosecutor. The room was abuzz with excited conversation in both English and Spanish.

"All rise. The District Court of Santa Fe is now in session. Judge Henry Paddington presiding," the bailiff announced as the judge walked into the room.

"Please be seated," the bailiff instructed the people.

"Good morning, ladies and gentlemen. Today we will hear the case of the People of the Territory of New Mexico versus Rafael Ortega de Estrada. Are both sides ready?" the judge announced

"Yes your honor," they both answered.

"Then Mr. Luján, please proceed with your opening statement," the judge ordered the prosecutor.

Ernesto Luján, the state prosecutor, was himself a member of an original Spanish family who settled New Mexico with *don* Juan de Oñate. Though born in New Mexico, he was one of Santa Fe's aristocrats and a believer in the Spanish caste system. As a lawyer and schooled in the American legal system at the Saint Louis University School of Law, he considered himself a fair and just man, but the idea of a *mestizo* killing a pure-blooded Spaniard grated on him. Internally, he wanted the perpetrator to get the death sentence.

"Your honor, people of the jury, Diego de la Torre was murdered in the main plaza by the defendant, Rafael

Ortega de Estrada. I will prove beyond reasonable doubt, this man willfully went looking for Mr. de la Torre determined to kill him. You will hear from witnesses, how he came to the plaza on an Appaloosa, with sword in hand, looking for Mr. de la Torre. We will ask the court for the death penalty for the defendant," the prosecutor simply stated and returned to his seat.

Ron Iverson, Rafe's attorney got up and purposely adjusted the stack of papers in front of him before he walked over to the seated jury. "Your honor, gentlemen of the jury, what you heard from the esteemed prosecutor is completely opposite to what happened that day on the central plaza. I will prove it was Diego de la Torre who rode into the plaza with sword in hand to willfully attack my client. Yes, the two men battled, Diego with the intention of killing Rafael, and Rafael protecting himself. In the course of his zeal, Diego fell off his horse and the horse fell on him crushing him to death."

A murmur erupted in the courtroom. The judge banged his gavel to restore order.

"The courtroom is warned any outbreaks will not be tolerated," the judge demanded.

"The question which will be presented by the prosecution is not the reason for the fight of these two men. Diego de la Torre wanted to kill my client strictly because of his arrogant prejudices. You see my client is not a Spaniard; he is of mixed blood and was engaged to a young Spanish woman from California. Even though this is the law of our land, Diego was angry and determined to stop my client strictly because he considered Rafael of a lower class."

A softer murmur circulated in the room and then Ron Iverson continued. "In the United States of America all men are created equal. I will quote the second paragraph of the United States Declaration of Independence:

We hold these truths to be self-evident, that all men are created equal, that they are endowed by their Creator with certain unalienable Rights, that among these are Life, Liberty and the Pursuit of Happiness."

The lawyer paused a moment before he continued. "This is the law of the United States and all its territories. Diego was a believer of the ancient Spanish *casta* system. It drove him to want to kill my client and because of his own prejudices, Diego was accidently crushed to death by his own horse. Thank you." the lawyer returned to his seat next to Rafe.

A grumble started on the Spanish side of the courtroom after the lawyer finished his opening statement. They did not like what the lawyer spouted about their precious heritage.

"Order in the court," the judge called out while pounding the gavel.

"Prosecutor, call your first witness," the judge ordered.

"Your honor, I call Elias Sandoval to the stand."

Sandoval was the middle-aged owner of the leather shop on the north side of the plaza. His hair was graying and he wore spectacles with a habit of pushing them up with his right thumb.

"Please state your name and occupation."

"My name is Elias Sandoval and I own a leather shop."

"Now, where were you when Mr. de La Torre was murdered?"

"Objection, it has not been established the deceased was murdered," Ron Iverson stood and protested.

"Objection sustained."

"Very well your honor, I will rephrase the question. Where were you when de la Torre was killed?"

"I was returning from lunch and was about to unlock the door to my store when I saw a man riding an Appaloosa with a sword held up above his head riding hard toward a man riding a smaller black stallion. That is the man who was on the Appaloosa," Sandoval pointed at Rafe.

"Was the man on the black stallion armed? Did the man have a sword in his hand?"

"No, I did not see a sword."

"No further questions of this witness, your honor," Luján said.

"Mr. Iverson, your witness," the judge said.

"Mr. Sandoval, you say you saw this man on the Appaloosa with a sword in his hand and presumably attacking a man on a black stallion?"

"Yes."

"How far was the man on the Appaloosa from you when you saw him?"

"I do not know, not far, he was at the south end of the plaza, not far from me."

"What color was the Appaloosa?"

Sandoval thought about it for a short time and then answered. "The Appaloosa was black with black spots on white on its rear."

"No more questions, your honor," Iverson said. Rafe knew his lawyer caught the witness in a lie. Rayo was brown. He wanted to ask him why he did not press the issue.

Each witness for the prosecution testified with the same answer. The man riding the Appaloosa was the one who attacked Diego with a sword and evil intent. Each one identified Rafe as the man riding the Appaloosa. None of the witnesses saw whether Diego riding the black stallion had a sword or claimed they saw nothing at all.

Rafe stared intently at the witnesses trying hard not to show the emotion running through his veins. He thought many of the witnesses looked nervous and several glanced over toward the right side of the courtroom where Diego's friends, like Alvaro Gutierrez and Oscar Peralta sat behind Ana Teresa's uncle, *don* Pedro de Soto.

Later in the day the prosecution put Alvaro Gutierrez on the stand.

"Do you know why the defendant attacked Diego?" the prosecution attorney asked Alvaro.

"He wanted to marry the *señorita* from California, *don* de Soto's niece. She was engaged to Diego. He wanted to kill Diego so he could marry her," Alvaro lied.

Rafe's anger swelled to a fever. Everything was a lie.

He heard Ana Teresa gasp from behind him.

"It is not true," she cried out. "It is a lie; we were not engaged! Diego tried to rape me."

The courtroom erupted from both sides. BANG, BANG, BANG, the judge's gavel struck his desk. "I will not tolerate any outbursts."

When it was Ron Iverson's turn to question Alvaro he asked, "You have testified Diego wanted to marry Ana Teresa. Is that correct? He had made a contract with *don* de Soto?"

"Well, I am not sure if there was a contract, exactly. He thought the *mestizo* was not worthy of her hand."

"And why was the defendant not a worthy suitor?" Ron continued.

Alvaro huffed as if the question was stupid. "He is a *mestizo*. It is not allowed."

"Not allowed in a United States Territory. Not allowed by what set of laws?"

"It is just not allowed." Alvaro was beginning to get nervous and his hand twitched.

"Not allowed by the Spanish *dons* sitting over there? Not allowed by Diego de la Torre? So Diego decided to take the law into his own hands and kill the *mestizo* for what he perceived was against Spanish law?"

"No, I mean yes he did not want the *mestizo* to marry her." Alvaro pointed at Ana Teresa.

At 3:00 p.m. the judge ordered the session to end and to reconvene the next day. He told the jury not to discuss the case with anyone.

Rafe wrote a note and handed it to the lawyer. Sheriff Johnson and Deputy Morgan walked up to escort him back to jail. One walked in front and one behind as they threaded their way from the courtroom. Outside people jeered and called him names.

"Hang the murderer," someone yelled.

"Pinche peón, te colgarás," several voices yelled that he would hang.

CHAPTER 47

Shortly after the sheriff locked Rafe in his cell, Carlos arrived at the jail. The deputy showed him to Rafe's cell and opened the door. "Rafe, I got your note from Mr. Iverson," Carlos said.

"Carlos, I'm sure the witnesses have been bought off or threatened by the *dons*. I can see it in their eyes they are scared. I can't win."

"What can we do? If the *dons* did this, we cannot do anything about it. They have no respect for American law," Carlos said.

"What about Benjamin Pacheco? He came to warn me about Alvaro. Do you think he would help me now?"

"I don't know, but I will find him when I leave here and try to persuade him to help. He was part of the problem, but now something has made him change."

"Thank you Carlos. We do not have much time. My lawyer only has two witnesses who swore they saw Diego come after me, but they are Tiwa Indians and the jury will not believe them."

Carlos left the jail and rode directly to the Pacheco *hacienda* to talk to Benjamin. On the way, Carlos pondered why Benjamin had come to warn Rafe about Alvaro's plan to kill him. After Diego died, Carlos heard Alvaro took over as the leader of Santa Fe's dandies, *caballeros* who did little work and lived off their family fortunes. Usually they were all bluster and no action. Part of the elite Spanish society, Benjamin had been one of Diego's inner circle of friends, so his action to warn Rafe was confusing.

When Carlos arrived he was invited into the parlor and was greeted by Benjamin's father. *"Carlos, bienvenido a mi casa."*

"Gracias don Ramon," Carlos replied shaking his hand. Though not born an aristocrat in Santa Fe, Carlos Zuniga was a Spaniard from a well-known family in New Mexico and married to Bibiana de Soto.

"My wife and I enjoyed your wedding. How is your lovely wife?" *don* Ramon asked.

"Thank you for gracing our wedding, *don* Ramon. Bibiana is well, planning for the birth of our first child."

"Congratulations. Children are a blessing from God," *don* Ramon replied with a smile. "What brings you here today?"

"I came to speak to Benjamin. Is he here?"

"Yes, I will have the maid call for him," *don* Ramon said and left Carlos waiting.

A short time later, Benjamin walked into the parlor and greeted Carlos. "Benjamin, I wonder if we could discuss something? You came to warn Rafael about Alvaro. Can you tell me why?" Carlos asked.

Benjamin respected Carlos. With the exception he befriended a *mestizo,* Carlos was an honorable and educated man.

"It is true I used to be Diego's friend. Friend is not a word I think he would have used. Diego was not a gentleman, not an honorable man, but I followed him like the other dandies to have status here. Alvaro is trying to take Diego's place," Benjamin paused before continuing. "That life is not for me Carlos. I have responsibilities now. I am running the *hacienda* and plan to marry in the spring. I do not want to waste my life drinking, gambling, and fucking *putas* as I grow old. I want a home and a family, just as you do. I envy you and Bibiana."

"Alvaro is determined to have Rafael hang. Several men tried to take him from the jail at gunpoint. Were you part of that?"

"No, I can't believe they went through with their plan. Alvaro came and asked me to help them kill Rafael. I do not believe in killing. Diego always derided me as a coward and now Alvaro and the others do the same. They like to poke fun at me and call me a *culón or maricón,* but neither is true. I do not believe in killing, especially an innocent man. That is why I went to see Rafael to warn him." Benjamin was relieved to tell Carlos about Alvaro's unmerited treatment of him.

"You know Rafael is on trial for murdering Diego?"

"Of course," Benjamin said and lowered his head.

"I was at the trial today and all the witnesses for the prosecution swore it was Rafael who went after Diego. You were with Diego that day; is that what happened?"

"No, it was Diego who went after Rafael. Diego hated him and wanted to kill him, because the *señorita* from California favored Rafael and not him. He told us he really did not want to marry her, but agreed to *don* Pedro's offer of marriage. All he really wanted to do was soil and humiliate her, but most of all he did not want a *mestizo* to have her."

"Do you know if the witnesses have been paid off?"

Benjamin hesitated and walked to a table near the fireplace and poured two brandies. He handed one to Carlos. "I believe so, yes. I overheard my father talking about how *don* Pedro and Diego's family paid off or threatened the witnesses."

"Benjamin, will you be a witness for Rafael? You know he is innocent."

Benjamin took a sip of brandy before he replied. "Carlos, I can't. The *dons* will come after me and my family would be shunned from society. You know that."

"Yes I know and I cannot blame you, but I implore you. An innocent man will hang if no one who knows the truth steps up to save him."

"I am sorry, but I cannot. I have too much to lose."

"Thank you Benjamin. At least I know what I suspected is true," Carlos said, shook Benjamin's hand, and left.

Benjamin poured himself another brandy. Everything Carlos said was the truth. Rafael was innocent. His only crime was being born not of pure Spanish blood. Taking a sip of brandy, he knew what Diego and Alvaro said about him was true. He was a *culón,* a coward unable to stand up for what he knew was right.

CHAPTER 48

After the first day of the trial, the Spanish aristocrats spilled into the Palacio Cantina. Virginia Verdugo, the owner, had not attended. She rarely left the Palacio, which was both her business and home. Besides, she heard from the *dons* all the witnesses were paid off or threatened.

Tonight the cantina was full of activity and animated discussions. The Spaniards sensed a victory. Virginia circulated among the tables and overheard snippets of conversations. The witnesses identified the *mestizo* – he attacked Diego – the *mestizo* went looking for Diego on the plaza – he killed Diego. They called him a murderer.

Several of the older *dons* assembled at a table in the back. Their discussion grew louder and animated as the brandy started to flow. There was no doubt in their minds the *mestizo* was as good as dead. Virginia would have her revenge for Diego's death. Though it was not by a Spanish sword as she wanted, the *mestizo* would hang.

"Virginia, you should have come to the trial today," *don* Daniel Archuleta bellowed across the room to her.

Virginia slowly walked toward the table where the old *dons* sat.

"I did not need to, *don* Daniel," she purred. *Don* Daniel took in the scent of her expensive perfume. It was a pleasant scent overshadowing the cigar smoke in the room. If only he were younger he would woo her. *Don* Daniel knew Virginia and Diego de la Torre were lovers. He often watched them climb the stairs to her upper bedroom chambers.

"Come sit with us Virginia." *don* Antonio Peralta motioned to her. Virginia sat beside him and motioned to the bartender to bring more brandy.

The *dons* recounted the events of the trial for Virginia's behalf. "The prosecution's case is strong. You should have seen how the gringos were dejected when all the witnesses said the *mestizo* attacked Diego."

"Except for the *señorita* from California. She denied Diego was her fiancé and said he tried to rape her," *don* Daniel interjected.

Virginia's ears perked hearing Diego was engaged. Diego was hers and hers alone. He had professed his love for her many times. It was why he never married, but Virginia knew she and Diego could not formally wed. The prominent son of a Spanish family could not marry the owner of a cantina who ran whores for a living, even if she was pure Spanish, though Virginia hoped someday it could happen.

"He was engaged to this *señorita?*" Virginia asked.

"He had a contract with *don* Pedro de Soto for her hand," *don* Ricardo said.

Virginia held back the shock that hit the pit of her stomach. Diego never told her about any contract to wed. "Who is this *señorita?*" she asked.

"*Don* Pedro's niece from California. She was living with his family while her parents were in Spain. She is a beautiful girl. I can see why Diego was smitten. I would have married her myself if I were younger," *don* Juan Emilio said and laughed.

"I heard her parents lost their land grant in California. She was not rich," *don* Ricardo said.

"Rich or not, she is Spanish and Diego would have been envied if he took her hand. *Don* Pedro would have paid handsomely to be rid of her."

Virginia fought back tears as she stood up and bid the old *dons* a good evening. Their talk rattled her. Diego had lied. He had taken his pleasure with her, while courting a younger and more beautiful *señorita*.

The evening of the first day of the trial, the Summers' home was somber. George could tell Josefina was fighting not to break down and sob. Ana Teresa retired to her room upstairs. Lizzy, his youngest daughter, looked sorrowful but said little. Lolo on the other hand was animated in her anger at the injustice she witnessed and made it known.

"*Papá,* you can't let this happen to Rafe. You must do

something to get him out of this," she cried to her father.

"*Mija,* we must leave it to the lawyer and trust the law to work as it should. We all know Rafe is innocent. Carlos told me he is looking into some serious matters about the witnesses and thinks he has a reliable witness who may help," George tried to assure his daughter.

"I am afraid the Spaniards have fixed the witnesses. We saw it today, when every witness swore Rafe was the one who attacked Diego. Every one of them was nervous. I could see it in their eyes. They kept looking at the Spaniards sitting behind the prosecution," Billy spoke up. Normally Billy did not speak much around the family supper table, feeling he was an outsider. Tonight however, he could not hold his tongue. Rafe was being railroaded.

"Yes father, Billy's right. They were all lying. How can that be?" Lolo asked.

"Carlos and I think *don* Pedro and the other *dons* have paid the witnesses to lie," George responded.

"Perhaps we should pay these Spaniards another visit and threaten them to speak the truth. We could fight fire with fire," Billy spoke. He would be happy to reclaim his Desperate Billy persona to make sure Rafe was acquitted.

Billy sat across from Celiá, Rafe's mother. Her normally smiling face was solemn. He sat next to her in court and twice she grabbed his hand for support. He wondered if she understood much of the day's proceedings, as it was conducted in English. Nonetheless, she knew her innocent son was being tried for murder.

Celiá did not understand the Americano laws. Born and raised in Mexico, she was used to the Spanish caste system. The *dons* had all the power and the peasants had none. Apparently, nothing was different here in Santa Fe. She could only put her faith in God to save her son as she had done since the day he shot *don* Bernardo and escaped here to the United States.

Celiá rose and said she would go pray to God for help. Josefina offered to go with her, but Celiá shook her head no. "*Quiero estar sola,*" she said she wanted to be alone to pray.

George was visibly shaken, but tried to hide it so as not to panic the family. He was worried all the evidence was stacked against Rafe and there was nothing he could do about it. He and Ana Teresa already went to plead Rafe's innocence to *don* Pedro, but the *don* rebuked them and insulted Ana Teresa. There was true hate in the old man's heart, hate for mixed-blooded Mexicans and now for his niece, because she married one. All the years George had been around Spaniards, he still could not understand the fervent Spanish loathing toward the so-called lower classes of people.

George normally kept his emotions controlled, but there was a fiery anger building up in him. Try as he might he could not shake his fury at the Spaniards and his mind raced trying to think how he could get to the *dons* and make them realize they were wrong about the caste system and wrong about Rafe. The last thing he thought about before he went to sleep was to visit *don* Pedro's again in the morning before the trial and convince him at gunpoint to reconsider, for his niece's sake.

CHAPTER 49

When Carlos returned home after meeting with Benjamin, he was obviously distraught. It infuriated him that his father-in-law, Bibiana's father, *don* Pedro was one of the people who brought the charges against Rafe. He tried hard to separate those feelings from his wife, but tonight they boiled over.

Bibiana was sitting at her dressing table engrossed in brushing her hair. Noticing Carlos' obvious dark mood she asked what was bothering him. *"¿Qué te preocupa, querido?"*

"How can you ask such a question!" Carlos raised his voice. "Your father is accusing Rafael of murder and you ask me what is bothering me. You know Rafael is innocent. Ana Teresa told you Diego tried to rape her, and yet you said nothing."

She looked shocked at his harsh words. "I am worried about Rafael, but all the witnesses are all saying he was the one who attacked Diego. It must be the truth."

"You and I know it is not true. I spoke to Benjamin Pacheco. He told me it was Diego who wanted to kill Rafael and the *dons,* probably your father, have paid off the witnesses. I asked Benjamin to be a witness for Rafael, but he refused because he is afraid of retribution by the *dons."*

His words finally began to register in her brain. "My father is involved? I know he is unhappy about Ana Teresa marrying Rafael, but do you think he would do such a thing?" It was difficult for Bibiana to believe her father could be capable of treachery.

"Unhappy? Your father hates Rafael. He told him Ana Teresa was engaged to Diego, when it was a lie. He would do anything to see Rafael hang. He sent Ana Teresa back to California to ensure she did not marry Rafael."

"I heard my mother asking if she could ask Ana Teresa to come and visit. He got angry and cursed at her. My mother loves Ana Teresa and cannot understand why my father has disowned her."

"You know why, Bibiana. You know how the *dons* like your father feel about *mestizos*. Rafael will pay the price simply because of hatred by the Spanish aristocrats and I do not know how to help him."

Bibiana could picture the day Rafael came to the *hacienda* and asked her father for Ana Teresa's hand in marriage. Her father scorned him and forced him to leave without ever hearing what Ana Teresa had to say. She knew what Ana Teresa blurted out in the courtroom was true. Diego tried to rape her down by the stream when he caught her riding alone. Bibiana never told her father about it. Rafael was a good man and like a brother to her husband. According to Carlos, Rafael saved his life.

"I will go see my father tomorrow morning and try to talk sense into him. I know how to handle him and he has never refused me. Remember, he let me marry you even though you no longer had an inheritance. Now, go to sleep and do not worry," Bibiana told him confidently, but Carlos doubted his beautiful wife could change things. Like in a bullfight, the Spaniards were only waiting for the final blow to kill the bull before yelling *'¡olé!'*

Rafe slept fitfully through the night after the first day of the trial. Thoughts of Ana Teresa swirled in his mind. He was putting her through hell. Because of him, she was shunned and sent back to California, all because he was a *mestizo*. Now if he was found guilty, she would be the widow of a murderer.

Try as he might, he could not keep those thoughts out of his mind. He got up before daybreak and asked the deputy for pencil and paper. He wrote a letter to George.

George,
*   If I hang, sell the horses and property and give the money to Ana Teresa. Send my mother and María's children to my uncle in El Paso. Thank you for all you have ever done for me.*
*   Rafe*

At eight-fifteen in the morning, Rafe was cuffed and

shackled as the sheriff prepared him for the walk to the courthouse.

"Sheriff, why are you doing this?" Rafe complained about the rough treatment. Yesterday he simply walked with the sheriff and deputy to the courthouse.

"It's for your protection," the sheriff grumbled. Rafe wanted to curse at him, but held his tongue. It was obviously not for his protection.

The morning was clear and sunny and he enjoyed the sun hitting his face as he shuffled his way ahead of the sheriff to the courthouse. When he could see the court building, people were lined up waiting for the doors to open. The sheriff led him to a side door though an alleyway. Suddenly a he caught movement out of the corner of his eye and something came flying his way. Rafe ducked and a snowball hit the sheriff in the chest.

"Go on, stop that!" the sheriff yelled at several young men standing near the corner of the building.

"*¡Mestizo, hijo de puta!*" someone called him a mix-blooded son of a whore!

The sheriff kept his eyes on the crowd and hurried Rafe through the side door. He removed the handcuffs and leg shackles in the anteroom and ordered the deputy to watch the prisoner. About fifteen minutes later the court clerk opened the door and told them to enter. Rafe sat with Ron Iverson at the front table.

"Good morning Rafe. Did you get any sleep?" Ron Iverson asked. His mood was controlled, though he smiled at Rafe warmly.

"Good morning sir."

"Have you heard from your friend Carlos?" the lawyer asked.

"No, like I told you Benjamin Pacheco was there that day and knows I am not guilty. I hope Carlos was successful in convincing Benjamin to testify."

"I hope so. All we have is the two Tiwa Indians and I will try to discredit the prosecution's witnesses. Like I told you yesterday, the only absolute flaw I have is the color of the Appaloosa. I asked George to bring the horse today. It may save your life," the lawyer whispered in Rafe's right ear.

"All rise. The district court of Santa Fe is now in session. Judge Henry Paddington presiding," the bailiff announced.

CHAPTER 50

"This is the continuation of the case of the People of the Territory of New Mexico versus Rafael Ortega de Estrada. The jury has been sworn in and we will proceed where we left off yesterday. Mr. Luján you may continue calling your witnesses," the judge announced.

Luján called the first witness and again the witness told the same story, saying Rafe attacked Diego. The next witness denied seeing the fight entirely. Rafe thought the man looked very nervous. Finally Virginia Verdugo, the owner and madame of the Palacio Cantina was called to the stand.

Dressed in black and green with her tall *peineta* and veil, Virginia swept down the aisle. The men gawked. For many of the Spanish women it was the first time they ever saw the madame from the Palacio. Their husbands frequented her establishment often, but the sight of the beautifully dressed woman with the heavy gold jewelry shocked them. A murmur circulated around the room and several women slapped their gaping husbands.

"Do you swear to tell the truth the whole truth and nothing but the truth, so help you God?" the bailiff asked her to swear with her right hand on the bible and raised left hand. "Please be seated Madam Verdugo."

As Virginia sat, she scanned the courtroom. The *mestizo* sat in the front with his lawyer. Behind him sat a gringo family. With them Carlos, Bibiana, and a beautiful young woman sat to their left. Ana Teresa's light brown hair curled around her shoulders. Though her rather simple dress was not elaborate, Virginia felt old by comparison. At twenty years old, Ana Teresa exuded youth and innocence.

Luján approached the stand. "Please state your name and occupation."

"My name is Virginia Barceló Verdugo. I am the owner of the Palacio Cantina."

"Is it Miss or Missus Verdugo?"

"You may call me Madam Verdugo," she replied in thickly accented English. A small twitter was heard in the courtroom.

"Madam Verdugo did you know Diego de la Torre?"

"Yes, he was a frequent patron at my cantina."

"Do you know the defendant?"

"I only met him once. I do not know him."

"When did you meet him?"

"He came to my cantina looking for Diego."

"Did he say why he was looking for Diego?"

"He said he wanted to talk to him."

Virginia's statement paused the prosecutor because when he spoke to her privately she was adamant, Rafael was there looking to kill Diego.

"Was he armed?"

"I do not remember and I asked him to leave. Americanos are not welcome in my cantina," she replied, calling Rafe an American and not a *mestizo*.

Suddenly Luján stopped his questioning. Madam Verdugo was to be his star witness adding the crowning blow to his case. For some reason she was now elusive and softening her words.

"No more questions, Your Honor," Luján told the judge abruptly. As he turned to his desk, the lawyer exchanged a confused look with the de la Torre's family and *don* Pedro. He wondered why the woman changed her story. She had been adamant, saying the defendant had come to her cantina looking for Diego wanting to kill him and carrying a sword.

The courtroom was hushed as Ron Iverson rose to question Virginia. Billy was sitting next to Celiá, who grabbed his hand and squeezed it hard. He looked down at her tiny hand over his big bear paw. Carlos and Bibiana held hands and Ana Teresa folded her hands in prayer.

Ron Iverson got up and approached the stand. "Good morning Madam Verdugo."

She nodded.

"Madam was the defendant angry? Was he belligerent? Yelling? What was his demeanor the day he came to your establishment?"

"He was polite," she replied.

"Madam on the same day you met my client, Mr. Ortega, did Diego de la Torre come to the cantina?"

"Yes, he came in shortly after Mr. Ortega left."

"Did you speak with Diego?"

"Yes, I told him the Americano was looking for him," Virginia testified.

"What did Diego do when you told him the American man was looking for him?"

"He cursed him as a *desgraciado mestizo* and swore to take care of him."

"For the court's records Your Honor, Madam Verdugo is using a Spanish term for a wretched person of mixed blood."

The judge nodded his head.

"Madam, was Diego angry? Was he belligerent? Yelling? What was his demeanor the day he came to your establishment?"

"He was angry. He and his friends quickly left to find the *mestizo.*"

I have one last question Madam. "Was Diego armed? Did he have his rapier with him?"

"Yes. He always carried his sword."

"Thank you Madam. No more questions, Your Honor," Ron Iverson said and went to sit next to Rafe.

"I have no more witnesses, Your Honor," Luján stood up and stated.

"Mr. Iverson, please call your first witness," the judge ordered.

"I would like to recall Elias Sandoval," Iverson stated.

When Elias Sandoval was seated, Rafe thought he looked nervous.

"Mr. Sandoval, you own a leather shop in town. I assume you make leather saddles and riggings for horses and carriages?"

"Yes sir. I do."

"You consider yourself knowledgeable about horses,

carriages, and the such?"

"Yes sir."

"You testified the defendant's horse was an Appaloosa, black with white markings," the lawyer recounted Sandoval's testimony.

"Yes. It was black with black spots on white on its rear," Sandoval repeated.

"Your Honor, might I ask the bailiff to walk outside and view the Appaloosa which is tethered in front of the courthouse and return to tell us the color of the horse."

The judge signaled the bailiff. When he returned the bailiff said, "The horse is brown with brown spots on a white rump."

"Bailiff, could the horse be mistaken for a black horse?" the judge asked.

"I doubt it, cepting if it was nighttime."

"Now Mr. Sandoval I ask you. Did you actually see the defendant riding the Appaloosa that day? Did you see him riding the Appaloosa and waving a sword above his head as you testified?"

"No," the scared witness said meekly. "I did not see him."

The courtroom erupted in gasps and shouts from both sides. Iverson was surprised the judge allowed the people to vent before banging his gavel to quiet the room.

Benjamin Pacheco walked into the courtroom during Virginia's testimony. He was surprised with what she said. He was sure she would lie on Diego's behalf.

As Virginia walked back to her seat, Benjamin squeezed into the end seat behind Carlos. He tapped Carlos on the shoulder and nodded his head. Carlos took out a small notebook and quickly wrote a note and passed it to Rafe's lawyer. When the lawyer got the message, he looked back at Carlos who nodded toward Benjamin.

"Mr. Iverson, please call your next witness," the judge called out again after he pounded the gavel quieting the crowd.

"Your Honor, may we approach the bench?" Iverson nodded to the prosecutor.

"You may."

"Your Honor, a reluctant witness has come forth. I do not have the person on my witness list," Iverson informed the judge.

"Do you have any objections, Mr. Luján?"

"No Your Honor." Luján was satisfied with the testimony his witnesses gave would find the defendant guilty as charged, even without Madam Verdugo. He thought the color of the horse was a ridiculous point.

"Your Honor, I call Benjamin Pacheco to the stand."

There was a loud murmur from the Spaniards in the room. Alvaro and the other young *caballeros* turned and glared at their friend Benjamin, as he approached the stand. Benjamin did not acknowledge them as he walked to the witness seat.

"Please state your name." Ron Iverson said as he walked to face the jury.

Rafe's lawyer talked to Benjamin during his investigation of the facts and Benjamin told him Rafe had attacked Diego. Ron was unsure how to question the man and wondered why he asked to testify. However, Carlos told him he hoped to sway Benjamin to tell the truth and Ron hoped it was true.

"My name is Benjamin Pacheco."

"Mr. Pacheco did you know Diego de la Torre?"

"Yes, I knew Diego since we were boys."

"Was Diego your friend?"

"Yes, you could say that."

"Were you with Diego the day he died?"

"Yes, we were at his *hacienda* before we went to the Palacio Cantina."

"What happened when you got there?"

"Virginia told Diego the Americano was there wanting to talk to him. Diego told us to follow him to the plaza to find the *mestizo.*"

"You went to the plaza with him?"

"Yes."

"What did Diego do when he saw the defendant?"

"Diego pulled his sword and rushed toward him."

"In your opinion, did Diego intend to kill the defendant?"

"Yes, Diego hated him."

Luján jumped to his feet with an objection. "Overruled," responded the judge.

"Why did Diego hate the defendant?"

"Diego was a true believer in the Spanish caste system. He believed Rafael was inferior because he was born in Mexico of mixed blood, a *mestizo.*"

"Was that the only reason Diego hated the defendant?"

"No. He wanted to keep Rafael away from Ana Teresa de Soto." Benjamin pointed to Ana Teresa sitting behind Rafe.

"Keep him away from her? I do not understand," Iverson asked.

"Diego wanted Ana Teresa for himself and was jealous she wanted Rafael and not him. It really grated on him and he ordered us to kill him."

"He ordered you to kill him?"

"Yes."

"And who is the 'us' you refer to?"

"Oscar Peralta, Vicente Vargas, Alvaro Gutierrez and myself."

"And did you try to kill Rafael?"

"Yes, but we failed."

Again, a murmur filled the courtroom.

"I have one more question Mr. Pacheco. Was Diego engaged to Ana Teresa de Soto?"

"No. He intended to spoil her and publically defame her because she preferred Rafael to him. He did not intend to marry her."

"Thank you. No more questions, Your Honor."

Virginia Verdugo rushed from the courtroom as Benjamin finished his testimony. Alvaro, Oscar, and Vicente quickly followed the madame out the door after being implicated in Diego's plan to kill Rafael.

CHAPTER 51

Later that evening, everyone gathered at the Summers' home to celebrate Rafe's acquittal. He was found not guilty after the testimony by Virginia Verdugo and Benjamin Pacheco and was immediately released. His mother was the first to run to him wrapping him in a sobbing *abrazo*. Ana Teresa was next, hugging and kissing him, no longer afraid to kiss him in public. Now, everyone was seated at the large dining table talking at once.

Carlos and Bibiana sat across from Rafe. Rafe sat to George's right with Ana Teresa by his side. Billy sat next to Celiá. Even the two children were included around the table instead of being fed in the kitchen.

George quieted the family and said a special prayer of thanks.

"Oh Rafe, it is so wonderful!" Lolo exclaimed. "We were so scared."

"I was afraid they were gonna dangle you on a rope, after I heard all those witnesses testify against you," Billy spoke out teasing Rafe. "I'm glad I didn't have to start shooting people to save you." Everyone laughed, not realizing Billy was dead serious.

"Your mother told me she prayed to Saint Vincent de Paul, the protector of the innocent. He answered her prayers," Josefina told him.

"Gracias a Dios," Celiá thanked God in Spanish and made the sign of the cross with her thumb and index finger and kissed it. Celiá was learning English since she arrived in Santa Fe, but could not yet formulate long sentences. She was beginning to understand some words and conversations. She certainly understood her son was free. After thanking God, Celiá looked at Billy, laying her hand on his for a short moment, then pulled it away.

"Gracias mamá, I am sure Saint Paul heard your prayers." Rafe said lovingly to his mother who was seated down the long table.

"Carlos, how did you get Benjamin Pacheco to testify on Rafe's behalf?" George asked.

"I went to his house and asked him, but though he knew Rafe was innocent he was afraid of reprisal against him and his family from the *dons* who wanted Rafael found guilty. He told me they paid off the witnesses, but I knew we could not prove it. I don't know what changed his mind."

"It was a very brave thing to do. He is a good man," George replied.

"I'll go tomorrow and thank him personally and I want to give him a new double-action pistol for protection. Is that all right with you father?" Rafe asked.

George nodded. "I believe it is a good idea son. I have several on my desk. Go ahead and take one."

"I will go with you," Carlos agreed.

"What about Virginia Verdugo? Her testimony was very surprising. I could tell the prosecution was as surprised as we were," George said.

"I don't know why she changed. I heard she and Diego were lovers. I cannot understand what made her testify as she did," Carlos said.

"No matter, we should all be thankful she did," Josefina responded with a huge smile. Her adopted son was safe and finally her family could look forward to a wonderful year. Rafael was married, Bibiana and Carlos were expecting a child, and Lolo was graduating from school and becoming a woman.

The family feast continued into the late evening. The men retired to the parlor, while the women helped in the kitchen. George poured brandies. His heart was joyous. Rafe was free and the past was not hanging over his head.

George looked at his adopted son and then at Carlos. He now accepted Carlos as much more than just Rafe's friend. He and Rafe were more like brothers, and Carlos a part of this family. George toasted with his brandy thanking God for his help.

"I can't wait to get my house finished now. Ana Teresa and I want to start a family," Rafe said.

"Our children could play together," Carlos said smiling. His child with Bibiana was expected in the late spring.

"You have a head start. I better get busy," Rafe bantered.

The men were on their second brandy when horse hooves clattered in the courtyard. Several moments later Benjamin Pacheco was ushered into the parlor.

"Benjamin! Thank you for coming. I was going to see you tomorrow," Rafe stepped up and offered Benjamin his hand. "I can never repay you," Rafe told him.

"I had to tell the truth. I knew you were innocent and I'm sorry we attacked you that day at the abandoned *hacienda*. You and Ana Teresa have every right to be married. Diego only had dishonorable intentions for her," Benjamin admitted.

"It was very brave," Carlos added.

"Brave or perhaps foolhardy. I've come with news. Alvaro has sworn to kill you. Oscar Peralta came tonight and told me to watch my back. Alvaro wants revenge on both of us," Benjamin warned him.

CHAPTER 52

"El pinche mestizo escapó el mecate," Alvaro complained how the fucking *mestizo* escaped the rope. Slumped on an over-stuffed chair, it was Alvaro's first time back at the Palacio Cantina since he promised Virginia the *mestizo's* head.

Vicente sat near him and they were well into drinking their fill of tequila. The strong alcohol was only fueling the anger and disappointment about the outcome of the trial. The trial was the only talk in the cantina and the normally boisterous conversations were subdued.

"Pinche Americanos. Their law is worthless," Vicente said.

Alvaro said nothing in return. It was not the law, it was the *culón,* Benjamin. He told the truth and now the *mestizo* dog was free. Alvaro's mind flicked to Virginia's testimony. She too did not help. She testified the *mestizo* was polite and Diego was angry.

"What do we do now?" Vicente asked.

"We kill the *desgraciado!* First we will go and pay a visit to Benjamin and deal with the traitor," Alvaro growled.

"The *dons* will not allow us to go after one of our own," Vicente said.

"Fuck the *dons.* They did not fight when the Americans came. It is the *dons* who lost our birthright. Now we have to show them we are not afraid to correct the wrongs perpetrated against us, even if it is one of our own," Alvaro avowed.

Oscar Peralta walked into the cantina and greeted Alvaro and Vicente. He tried to act nonchalant after visiting his friend Benjamin Pacheco. If Alvaro knew he warned Benjamin, he too would become a target of Alvaro's revenge.

"Where have you been?" Alvaro grumbled.

"I went home to tell my parents the news. They were not at the trial today," Oscar replied. It was partly the truth and partly a lie. He also stopped on his way to warn Benjamin.

"I think it is a bad idea to go after Benjamin," Vicente said resuming their conversation.

"Yes, forget Benjamin. It is the *mestizo* who has wronged us, not Benjamin," Oscar said.

"Do not be a *culón* like him, Oscar. We must teach Benjamin a lesson. He is the reason the *mestizo* escaped the rope. We cannot let it stand," Alvaro retorted.

"Benjamin should be taught a lesson, but I want to go after the *mestizo* and the *señorita* from California who married him. We must teach her a lesson too," Vicente spouted out.

Alvaro thought about the beautiful *señorita* from California. He wanted to deal with her personally. She was nothing more than a *puta*, a whore, for her marriage to the *mestizo*. Alvaro relished thinking how he would rape her repeatedly and then make her watch him kill her *mestizo* husband.

"I agree with you Vicente. We will kill the *mestizo* and deal with Ana Teresa, but first we will deal with Benjamin," Alvaro asserted.

Alvaro ordered more tequila wondering why Virginia had not come down yet. She too was responsible for letting the *mestizo* escape the rope.

"I wonder what is keeping Virginia from coming down. She better have a good explanation for what she did or perhaps we should shut this place down and run her out of town," Alvaro muttered a threat. He knew it was not possible. The Palacio was the only purely Spanish bastion left here in Santa Fe. The only place where Americanos were not allowed. His eyes glared up to the balcony were he could see the door to her room.

Upstairs, Virginia took extra time preparing her makeup and picking her dress. She left the courtroom immediately following her testimony. It was only when her patrons came to the cantina shouting the verdict, she learned what happened. Her maid told her the talk was how Benjamin's testimony freed the *mestizo*. Benjamin said

292 Robert J. Alvarado

Diego hated the *mestizo* and wanted him dead.

Regardless, she might have to answer to the *dons* and to Alvaro and the other young *caballeros* for what she testified. No doubt, Alvaro would ask her directly why she changed her testimony. She waited until the flow of alcohol diminished the *dons'* anger. More than an hour later, Virginia sauntered down to the main floor of the cantina.

"Buenas noches caballeros," her sweet voiced wished them a good evening.

She could see Alvaro was drunk. "Virginia, why did you change your testimony?" Alvaro slurred his words, but his voice was angry.

"I told the truth. It is all of you who lied to me. It is your fault," she said glaring at them.

"Our fault? You are crazy," Vicente spoke out.

"Yes, why did none of you tell me Diego was engaged to the woman named Ana Teresa?"

"Diego ordered us not to say anything, besides he only wanted to have his way with her," Alvaro told her.

"He vowed to *don* Pedro to marry her. The fact is he wanted her, when he was mine. No man does that to me, not him, and not any of you. You and your friends helped Diego betray me and I will not forget it," she said looking directly at Alvaro. Virginia felt herself shaking as she tried to keep her feelings under control.

"I will kill the *mestizo,* just like we planned," Alvaro reminded her and grabbed her arm tightly. If the cantina was not full of the older *dons,* he pictured himself dragging her upstairs now and taking her to appease his anger.

Virginia shook off Alvaro's grip and it tore her dress sleeve. She looked at the torn dress thinking Alvaro a pompous asshole. She would never take him to her bed, never.

"I do not care what you do. You are nothing to me," she said and walked away to where the old *caballeros* were playing cards.

Alvaro knew he had lost his prize. He looked at his friends. Oscar's face was blank, but Vicente had a sly smirk on his face and it infuriated Alvaro even more.

"We must kill the *mestizo*. We cannot fail this time. He must die," Alvaro snarled in a rage which turned his soul dark.

CHAPTER 53

Two days after the trial, Rafe and Carlos went to visit Benjamin Pacheco after a quick trip into Santa Fe to collect mail and several sets of new horseshoes for the young colts. Carlos was insistent Rafe did not travel alone, especially into town. Though all was quiet, Carlos worried about Benjamin's warning the night after the trial. He thought Alvaro's threats might be put into action.

On the way home, they rode to the Pacheco *hacienda*. Benjamin was out in the barn with several of the Pacheco cowboys unsaddling their horses.

"Carlos, Rafael, bienvenidos," Benjamin welcomed them. The *vaqueros* stood in the barn watching their young boss greet the Spaniard and the *mestizo*. Several of the *vaqueros* attended the trial and wondered why Benjamin supported the *mestizo*, though they remained loyal to the Pacheco family, sworn to ensure their safety.

"Benjamin, I want to thank you again for what you did for me. It must have been difficult. I have a gift for you," Rafe said and handed him a GSW double-action pistol.

Benjamin took it and turned it in his hands feeling the weapon. *"Gracias.* It is much better than this old *pistola* I carry," he said and pulled an old single-action pistol from his holster.

"This is a double-action pistol. All you have to do is squeeze the trigger and it fires. Let's go outside and I will show you," Rafe told him. They walked out to the side of the barn.

Rafe pulled out his pistol, aimed it at an old stump about ten feet away, and fired three shots in rapid succession. Benjamin's eyes lit up in amazement. Rafe shot the pistol without thumbing the hammer.

"Aim at the stump and squeeze the trigger as many times as you want it to shoot," Rafe told him.

Benjamin aimed at the stump and fired twice. The

pistol bucked in his hand making it hard for him to control. He shot three more bullets and a huge grin spread across his face.

"You will need to practice until you get a feel on how it reacts. It will take a little time," Rafe told him.

"Muchas gracias," he thanked Rafe. "I want you to know, I did not approve of what Diego and Alvaro wanted to do to you. It is why I came to warn you about Alvaro. He will come after you, him and his two friends, Vicente and Oscar. Alvaro has control over them and they will do his bidding. You are not safe in this town. They may come after me for what I did to help you, but now I have this," Benjamin warned Rafe and motioned with the new pistol.

"I hope they don't harass you. Call on us if they do. We will stand with you," Rafe told him indicating he and Carlos would be ready to help defend him.

"Yes we will be neighbors in good standing, I hope," Benjamin replied.

"Again, I thank you Benjamin for what you did for me. If you need horses, please come to me and I will sell them to you at a good price," Rafe offered.

Before they departed, Benjamin shook each of their hands. As they walked away, he thought it odd he had never shaken a *mestizo's* hand in friendship. He could see in Rafael's eyes; he was a good man. He heard how he saved Carlos' life forging their friendship. Now, he had saved Rafael's. Benjamin walked toward his house with the new pistol in his hand.

When Rafe and Carlos returned to the Summers' house, Ana Teresa told them she received a note from her uncle Pedro inviting them to his house for dinner on Friday evening. "Carlos, the note says you and Bibiana will be there too."

"Rafe, what do you think about this invitation?" Carlos asked. "I hope it's not a trick to hurt you." The invitation seemed out of character for Bibiana's father. *Don* Pedro was instrumental in orchestrating the murder charges and paying off the witnesses.

"Why would he ask us to come to his house after all

the problems he caused us, especially you," Rafe said looking at his wife.

"I'm not sure, but I'm afraid to go because he might hurt you. Perhaps it is a trick," Ana Teresa said.

"It is a matter of honor," Carlos replied. "If you refuse him, it would be an affront."

"Yes I agree. We have to go and see what happens. I don't think he would do anything drastic with you and Bibiana there."

"Where is my mother?" Rafe asked remembering a letter in his pocket.

"I have not seen her since the noon meal. I think I saw Billy helping her carry some things from the storehouse," she said.

"When you see her, give her this letter from María. I will be at the shop helping George finish setting up for the next order." Rafe pulled the letter from his coat pocket and handed it to Ana Teresa. He read it already and María and Rodolfo asked his mother to bring the children for a visit to Torreón. María wrote she hoped their mother would be there when her child with Rodolfo was born.

Alvaro and Vicente rode to the Pacheco *hacienda* shortly after Carlos and Rafe left. Alvaro was full of spite toward Benjamin, though tempered his anger over the last few days. He preferred to humiliate him, instead of killing him. Oscar was correct. To kill him would be frowned upon in the eyes of the *dons* and get them hanged.

They heard gunshots from behind the barn. Jumping from their horses, they found Benjamin shooting a pistol at an old tree stump.

"You betrayed us. You betrayed all the Spaniards here in Santa Fe and tarnished our reputation. I have been telling all the *dons* of your betrayal," Alvaro spoke full of malice and without any greeting. Seeing the traitor rekindled Alvaro's fury and he glared at Benjamin.

"Go away Alvaro. Go spread your venom elsewhere. I do not have time for your nonsense," Benjamin retorted. He looked at the man he used to call a friend and wondered why he ever followed him or Diego. All he saw in front of him was a weak man filled with hate.

Alvaro saw his words were not scaring Benjamin, in fact, he was surprised at his old friend's proud attitude. Benjamin was not buckling as he expected.

"Show him Vicente. Show him what we do to traitors," Alvaro growled. In his arrogant superior manner, he expected Vicente to do his bidding.

"I would not move Vicente," Benjamin said pointing the GSW pistol at him.

"You are a chickenshit; you will not shoot me," Vicente told him.

When Vicente made a slight move, Benjamin squeezed off two quick shots at Vicente's feet stopping him in his tracks. The shots came in rapid succession shocking Vicente.

Benjamin then pointed the pistol at Alvaro and warned him, "It is time to stop this. I do not want to kill you, but I will, now leave my place and leave me alone."

Alvaro saw something in Benjamin's eyes – a determined man. It was something he had never paid attention to before, always believing Benjamin a *culón*. Benjamin stood defiantly with the pistol in his hand.

"*¡Vámonos!*" Alvaro said, let's go, and jumped to his saddle. They left with Benjamin holding the GSW pistol and glaring at their backs.

CHAPTER 54

Billy was on his way home driving the wagon back from purchasing supplies in town for Juanita. Since completing the large order for Fort Bliss, Billy started helping in other ways. He often chopped wood or carried heavy supplies for the cook. He was tremendously relieved, as was the family, with Rafe's acquittal.

Outwardly life here at the Summers' ranch returned to normal. Smiles and relief could be seen everywhere. The morning after the trial's end and Benjamin's visit, George pulled Billy aside in the foundry. "Keep a watch on Rafe's back for me," George asked him. George was taking the news from Benjamin seriously. He thought the Spaniards might still try to enact their revenge after losing in the courtroom.

George did not have to ask. Billy owed Rafe his allegiance, though George and the family did not know the story about Desperate Billy.

Something else happened over the last several weeks, though Billy doubted anyone took notice with the trial hanging over Rafe's head. Billy found Rafe's mother, Celiá, enchanting. Her long black hair and dark eyes flashed when she smiled. He saw her beauty soon after he arrived at the Summers' ranch. Lolo told him Celiá was only sixteen when she had Rafe. She was just a few years older than he was, but he thought she looked younger. She was almost a foot shorter and tiny by comparison to him. Her olive tan complexion was smooth and supple.

Often during the trial, Celiá held his hand for support. Her small delicate hand looked dwarfed by his large one. When Rafe was acquitted, Celiá stood and hugged Billy tightly. He could still feel her slender body as it pressed into him.

Yesterday she asked him to help her carry some heavy supplies from the storeroom to the kitchen. As they worked in the storeroom, Billy turned her by her shoulders and held her gaze. Bending down he kissed her cheek tenderly. She seemed to understand and wrapped her arms around his waist.

Billy's thoughts were consumed with Celiá as two dandies rode up behind him south of the Summers' ranch. He knew they were Spanish dandies by the style of their suits and the elaborate swords hanging by their sides.

"Hey gringo," they called to him.

Billy slowed the wagon wondering what they wanted.

"Where are you going?" the more animated of the two demanded to know.

"What business is it of yours?" Billy replied. The arrogance of the young dandy was insulting.

"Do you work at the Summers' ranch?" Alvaro asked.

"Yes," was all Billy replied.

"Is he the gringo who hides the *mestizo?*" Vicente asked Alvaro.

"No. *Señor* Summers is older," Alvaro replied.

Suddenly Billy wished he had brought a pistol with him. He did not think one was necessary for a trip to town for supplies. Besides any hostility by the Spaniards, such as these two, would not be aimed at him.

"Is the *mestizo* at the foundry?" Alvaro continued pressing Billy for answers.

"*Mestizo?* Why don't you speak English," Billy grumbled. He knew exactly what the word *mestizo* meant. He heard it many times at the trial. To them it meant Rafe was not good enough, not worthy of respect or of justice. These two were part of the conspiracy trying to frame an innocent man.

Alvaro fumed at the Americano. They all hated the Spaniards for not speaking English. Alvaro pulled his sword, pointing it at Billy.

"You tell the Mexican dog we are coming after him. You tell him his head will be severed by this sword. You tell him that," Alvaro threatened and quickly whirled his horse. Billy turned, and watched the two as they rode away. He would never forget their faces.

Celiá was standing at the counter peeling vegetables when Billy arrived to the kitchen.

"Buenas tardes," she greeted him.

"Buenas tardes," he replied.

She flashed Billy a smile and Billy's heart sang.

He unloaded the boxes and sacks into the pantry for Juanita. Each time Celiá caught his eye, she smiled at him. When he told Juanita he was finished and turned to take the wagon to the barn, Celiá said something to Juanita in Spanish and walked out the kitchen door into the sunshine.

The sun's rays caught her jet black hair and sparkled it like diamonds. Without a word, Celiá jumped to the wagon seat. Billy jumped up next to her and snapped the reins. Instead of driving the wagon to the barn, Billy steered it to the north road leading toward the bigger barn where Rafe kept his horses. From there Billy continued on the northern road toward the foothills.

After supper that evening, Billy told Rafe and George about the encounter with the dandies on his way back from town. George and Carlos looked concerned, but Rafe seemed to accept the threat as bluster.

"My guns can answer their swords," Rafe said when Billy told him Alvaro ranted his sword would take Rafe's head.

"You should not take this threat lightly," George responded. "I'm afraid Alvaro will never let you live in peace." George sighed knowing what he said was true. Regardless of the trial's outcome, the Spaniards still harbored revenge in their hearts. If Rafe and Ana Teresa resumed a normal life here in Santa Fe, the dandies could catch either of them at any time. Any innocent moment could be their last. The thoughts made his heart ache.

"Perhaps you should think about restarting your horse ranch in California. You told me how green and mild you found the terrain in Rancho Simi. You said it would be perfect for breeding horses," George told Rafe.

"Yes, I agree with George. It may never be safe for you here in Santa Fe," Carlos added. He hated the thought his best friend might have to leave, but nothing was more important than Rafe's safety.

"I went through the trial to clear my name. I am not going to run away now. This is my home and this is where I will raise my children," Rafe asserted. He did not hear the threats as hollow. Diego's friends might be a force here in Santa Fe, though he hoped after the trial for change. Benjamin and Madam Verdugo had told the truth, despite any repercussions.

"If you hear any more threats, come tell me immediately," George told Billy. "In the meantime Rafe, you need to be very careful. Do not go riding alone," George warned him.

Later that night as George tried to sleep, Billy's description of Alvaro's threats filled his brain. He thought Rafe's life here in Santa Fe was perilous. The Spaniards would not let go of the outcome of the trial nor Diego's death easily. As he tried to relax into sleep, George thought about ways to make his son safe.

Josefina felt him tossing and turning. "What is the matter George?" she asked. "Are you having heartburn again?" Over the last year, George had bouts of indigestion. He promised her to see the doctor, but Josefina knew he had not gone.

"It is nothing. Go back to sleep," George told her.

It was late when Alvaro, Vicente, and another *caballero* came out of the Palacio Cantina. The three dandies wore tailored suits with short suit jackets trimmed in silver buttons. Alvaro's spurs jingled with his drunken, uneven gait.

"Virginia would not have you again tonight Alvaro. Perhaps she will never have you. Perhaps she will have me instead," Oscar goaded him.

"*Cállate,*" Alvaro growled at Oscar to shut up and pulled his sword. Virginia remained cool and aloof to him since the trial. It was several days since the end of the trial and the *dons* lost their distress over the outcome. The Americano laws ruled and life was returning to normal in Santa Fe.

Alvaro was not sure whether Virginia's detachment to him was because he had not produced the *mestizo's* head or from protecting Diego's interest in Ana Teresa.

Oscar and the other man laughed and rode away leaving Alvaro turning his horse in circles and cursing.

CHAPTER 55

Early Friday afternoon, Rafe told Billy to clean up the machine shop and close the furnace at the end of the workday. Usually Rafe helped in the process, but Rafe explained to Billy he and Ana Teresa were invited to *don* Pedro de Soto's *hacienda* for supper.

"Ain't he one of them aristocrats who wanted you to hang?" Billy asked.

"Yes, but he is Ana Teresa's uncle and we have to attend," Rafe responded. Billy could hear anxiety in Rafe's voice.

"Do you need me to go along?"

"No Billy, but thanks. I'm sure everything will be all right."

Rafe left the foundry around four in the afternoon. On the way to the house, he told Esteban to ready the buggy as he saddled Rayo.

"Where are you going?" Esteban asked.

"I'm taking Rayo for a run," he replied.

"You should not go alone. I will saddle the mare and go with you," Esteban told him.

"No. I have these." Rafe patted the two GSW pistols, which he wore at all times. "I will return in a couple hours. Don't tell George I have gone or he will worry."

Jumping to Rayo's saddle, Rafe spurred the horse to a lope as soon as he cleared the barn doors. He took the path around and behind the barn, which was not easily visible from the house or foundry. He turned south toward Santa Fe and let Rayo pick a path through the pines.

His stomach churned from frayed nervousness. *Don* Pedro invited him and Ana Teresa for supper. She hoped he had changed his attitude, though Rafe doubted it could ever happen. The Spanish caste system was ingrained in the Spaniards souls.

Though Benjamin Pacheco seemed to have a change of heart, Rafe knew it was not so with Alvaro and his other friends. Billy told him of Alvaro's continuing threats. Like Diego, Alvaro carried only hate in his heart for *mestizos*. He and Spaniards like him would carry that hate until someone stopped them. Reaching the edge of the Summers' property, Rafe spurred Rayo to a full gallop as he rode off down the lane toward Santa Fe.

Ana Teresa spent the afternoon taking a leisurely bath and choosing her gown for the evening. Butterflies intermittently wiggled in her stomach when she thought about seeing her uncle this evening. Their last encounter ended when he called her a whore and dismissed her and George. Now he invited her and Rafael to supper.

The sun was cutting a long shaft of light through the bedroom window as it dropped low in the afternoon sky. It was mid March and darkness still fell early. Ana Teresa wondered why Rafe was late. He needed to bathe and dress for their dinner appointment.

She was already dressed and finishing her hair when Rafe entered their bedroom in a hurry. Ana Teresa thought he seemed breathless and agitated.

"You're late. We need to be leaving soon," she said to him.

"I'm sorry. I had something to take care of," he answered her vaguely.

A half hour later, Rafe and Ana Teresa strode down the stairs. George was in the parlor and met them in the foyer. Ana Teresa looked lovely in a red and tan gown. Her hair was twisted and clipped high on her head. Rafe was wearing his best business suit, but was not wearing his pistols.

"Perhaps you should have Billy ride along. At least he could protect you on the buggy ride to *don* Pedro's," George suggested feeling they could be vulnerable.

"I saw him ride off a little while ago," Ana Teresa replied.

"Then at least take this," George handed him his pistol.

"No father. This is a social call. I do not want to show up armed. *Don* Pedro will think I am looking for trouble. We're already late and need to be leaving," Rafe responded. Leaving his guns upstairs bothered Rafe and he felt naked and exposed, but gentlemen did not go to dinner armed.

In the courtyard Rafe helped Ana Teresa up to the buggy seat and wrapped a warm blanket around her, then jumped into the seat beside her and snapped the reins.

George shook his head as they left. Rafe's hardheadedness could lead to his demise. Turning, George walked to the parlor holding his pistol in his hand. He watched the buggy as Rafe drove it down the lane and out of sight. After a few minutes he walked to the kitchen and told Josefina he had to do an errand. Grabbing his heavy coat and scarf from the hook near the door, George strode out the kitchen door and headed to the barn.

Ana Teresa could tell Rafe was preoccupied. He stared intently forward and said nothing to her about her hair or new dress. It was not his way to ignore her. Assuming he was upset over the upcoming dinner, she broke the silence.

"Stop fretting," Ana Teresa said. "I believe my uncle only has honorable intentions."

"How can you say that after all he has done to you and me?" Rafe said turning his face to her. The line of his jaw was tight.

"He is not a bad man, Rafael. He only believes what the old traditions taught him."

"He was throwing you to Diego, the wolf, and wanted me to hang."

"Perhaps he wants to make amends," she said quietly putting her hand on his.

Rafe respected the fact his wife forgave past sins so easily. Her kindly nature forced him to excuse Billy's behavior and now the man who once called himself Desperate Billy was his friend. Perhaps her intuition was correct and *don* Pedro did not have evil intentions.

"Carlos and Bibiana will be there. I doubt my uncle would try to kill you in front of his beloved daughter. After all she is pregnant with his first grandchild," Ana Teresa continued.

She was convinced her uncle would not try to hurt them. He might scold them and disown them, at worst. He had done it already, so it did not matter to her. She hoped his invitation was more pure of heart and he wanted to make amends.

Several minutes behind the buggy, George followed keeping out of sight. The twilight of the evening created shadows everywhere and George twitched at every unseen movement. As he rode as a silent guard, his thoughts were only on the Spaniards who wanted to kill Rafe. Someday, somewhere they would find him defenseless, like he was tonight.

As Rafe and Ana Teresa pulled the buggy into the de Soto *hacienda's* courtyard, George veered off. He watched as the footman took the buggy and Rafe and Ana Teresa walked to the house.

He breathed a sigh of relief their trip tonight was uneventful. Night had fallen completely in Santa Fe and George wondered if he should remain at his vigil until Rafe and Ana Teresa were safely back home. In his heart he knew it was a ridiculous idea. He could not follow Rafe everywhere to protect him from Diego's friends. Only their change of heart or death could give Rafe the peace he deserved.

It seemed odd and George wondered why *don* Pedro invited them for supper. George watched as Rafe and Ana Teresa were welcomed into the house and the maid shut the front door. Turning his horse around, George spurred the horse into the darkness toward Santa Fe.

A few minutes after the appointed hour, Rafe and Ana Teresa arrived and were escorted to the living room by the maid. They were seated when *don* Pedro and his wife *doña* Agustina walked in. Rafe and Ana Teresa stood up to greet them.

"Bienvenidos a mi casa," *don* Pedro welcomed them in a pleasant voice. Agustina acknowledged Rafe, then walked to Ana Teresa and hugged her tightly. Ana Teresa loved her aunt and happily accepted the warm embrace. Within a few

minutes, the maid showed Bibiana and Carlos into the room. Greetings were exchanged.

Doña Agustina led the girls to the dining room while the men stayed behind. *Don* Pedro offered brandy.

"Rafael, I wish to apologize to you for treating you as I did. I know now Diego de la Torre deceived me about his intentions with my niece. I did not know until Benjamin testified, Diego had tried to violate Ana Teresa." *Don* Pedro's words amazed Rafe. He thought Ana Teresa's uncle wanted to kill him, not apologize.

"Carlos told me how you saved his life. He told me you were an honorable man, but my many years of intolerance blinded me. I was told you attacked Diego. I know now it was a lie. Please accept my apology," *don* Pedro said and held out his hand to Rafe.

Rafe shook the *don's* hand and said, "No apology needed *señor,* but I accept it and I hope we can be friends. I still want to train a colt for you."

The old *don's* eyes lit up. "Yes, I would like that. Perhaps I could come to your barn and we could talk about horses on Sunday afternoon," *don* Pedro said.

Rafe was amazed at the old man's change of attitude. His apology seemed genuine. Carlos grabbed his father-in-law in a hearty *abrazo.* A short time later, the maid announced dinner was served in the dining room.

The maid led them to the dinner table. Everyone was seated according to Bibiana's plan. She seated Rafe right and Carlos left of her father. Ana Teresa sat across from her and *doña* Agustina sat at the other end of the table from her husband. Emilio, Bibiana's brother and her sister sat on either side of her mother.

Don Pedro said a prayer. If was not very different from the ritual performed every evening in the Summers' dining room.

CHAPTER 56

True to their habit, three *caballeros,* Alvaro, Vicente, and Oscar rode up near the small corral adjoining the Palacio Cantina. A small gas lamp gave the corral an eerie shadowed glow. Vicente was ribbing Alvaro as they stepped off their horses.

"Perhaps Virginia will offer you a *puta* again tonight, Alvaro."

"Cállate," Alvaro growled at him to shut up as he jumped from his horse.

"Your money pouches, *señores."* A masked man stepped from the shadow of the alleyway into the dim light of the corral.

"Fuck you gringo. Go away or we will kill you," Alvaro growled at the intruder.

"I said your money or I will fill you full of lead you wretched swine."

Alvaro went for his gun and tried for the hammer, but the masked thief shot him through the heart. Vicente pulled his gun, and a second shot went through his neck. Vicente stumbled back, then knelt on the ground holding his hands over the wound. Oscar threw down his weapon and ran into the cantina. The thief stepped up, kicked Vicente's gun out of range, rifled through their pockets and found money pouches tucked in their sashes. Jumping to a horse, the darkness of the night swallowed the thief as he galloped off.

The traditional Spanish dinner at the de Soto's started with a small bowl of hot soup. Spaniards enjoyed a late meal in the evening with many small *tapas* before the main dish. Three rounds of small appetizers were served. Rafe thought the stuffed red peppers exceptionally delightful.

At first the conversation was somewhat awkward and Rafe sensed Emilio was nervous, but as his father extended a gracious attitude, Bibiana's brother began to smile and laugh. *Don* Pedro poured several rounds of a rich red wine.

The conversation at *don* Pedro's house over the supper table turned lively. *Doña* Agustina asked him about Mexico City and was enthralled at Rafe's description of the huge city surrounded by a lake. He described the beautiful Spanish colonial houses, like the one *don* David lived in. The temperate climate allowed the houses to have flowers hanging from the iron railings all throughout the year.

"Wouldn't that be wonderful to have flowers all year long," she marveled. "And there is never any snow?"

"There may be snow in the high mountains, but not in the city," Rafe respectfully told her.

Don Pedro was fascinated with Rafe's talk of the Zócalo Plaza. He had read a book about the Aztecs and told Agustina they should travel to Mexico City to see it for themselves.

"I am sure I can arrange for introductions, *don* Pedro. My uncle, *don* David, knows many people in the city," Carlos told his father-in-law.

The *don* listened intently when Rafe spoke about breeding horses. He was shocked Rafe learned so much about horses on the *hacienda* in Torreón when he was a young boy.

"The horse master was kind, *don* Pedro. He taught me everything he could about horses."

The women talked about Bibiana's expected baby. Though still three or four months from the birth time, the women were already talking about names and baby blankets.

Don Pedro offered tequila after the meal. Rafe explained the harvesting process and *don* Pedro was intrigued by his description of the agave fields in Jalisco and how the root ball was harvested. Suddenly they heard noises outside and yelling.

"Don Pedro, don Pedro, ¡dos caballeros han sido asesinados!" the stableman yelled as he ran into the dining room, saying two Spaniards were murdered in Santa Fe.

"Who was murdered?" *don* Pedro asked pushing up and away from the table.

"The messenger said Alvaro Gutierrez and Vicente Vargas were robbed and killed outside the Palacio Cantina."

"Did they catch the murderer?" *don* Pedro asked.

"No, the *dons* have been called to the sheriff's office to form a posse."

"I must go to town and help the sheriff look for the outlaw," *don* Pedro said to his guests.

"We will go with you, *don* Pedro. Carlos and I will meet you at the sheriff's office as soon as we saddle our horses and get our weapons," Rafe spoke out.

"You will do this, after what they have done to you?" *don* Pedro asked looking into Rafe's eyes.

"Por supuesto," Rafe replied of course he would go.

Rafe and Ana Teresa quickly left the de Soto *hacienda* and drove the buggy into the barn at the Summers' house just before ten. Rafe asked Esteban to saddle Rayo while he hurried to change out of his dinner clothes.

Upon hearing the front door slam, Josefina looked at the clock. It was almost ten, still early by Spanish tradition. Supper was often not served until after nine. She wondered if the visit had gone poorly with *don* Pedro, but had other worries on her mind.

She met Rafe and Ana Teresa as they came into the house.

"Alvaro Gutierrez and Vicente Vargas were robbed and murdered tonight at the Palacio Cantina. Carlos and I are going with *don* Pedro and some other *dons* to help the sheriff look for the murderer," Rafe told her.

"Murdered?" Josefina clutched at her chest and took a step back.

"Yes, where is George?"

"He is not here. He left shortly after you did earlier tonight and has not returned. I'm worried. It is not like George to stay out late at night. Perhaps in his younger years he might have joined a poker game at the saloon, but now he enjoys a brandy and cigar in the evening here at home," she said.

Rafe took Josefina by the shoulders. "Don't fret. He's

probably in town talking politics with the mayor. If I see him, I'll send him home."

As he turned to climb the stairs, she touched his arm. "Ask Billy to go with you."

Taking the steps by twos, he quickly reached the upstairs bedrooms. Knocking on Billy's door, no one answered. Rafe pushed the door open, but Billy was not there and his bed was made up. He thought it odd for a moment, then quickly went to his room and changed. He pulled on a warm coat and hat and strapped his holster around his waist.

When he arrived back downstairs, Josefina and Ana Teresa were waiting in the parlor. "Be careful Rafael. I fear you could still be a target of the Spaniards," Josefina said.

"I will be careful. Have you seen Billy?"

"No, not since lunch. He said he was helping your mother with something, then had some errands in town and would not be home for supper." Rafe shrugged at the news. Billy was a grown man and certainly entitled to a night in town.

Rafe jumped on Rayo and reached the sheriff's office about forty minutes later. A dozen or more Spaniards were talking in the small room when Rafe walked inside. Rafe recognized most of the older *dons,* though not all. Benjamin and his father acknowledged him. *Don* Pedro stood near them.

Don Ramon gruffed at him, "Why is the *mestizo* here? He is probably the one who shot Alvaro."

"He was at supper at my home when Alvaro was shot, besides *don* Ramon, Oscar reported it was a gringo with a masked face," *don* Pedro said sternly. Several of the *dons* huffed, but no one else questioned Rafe's presence.

The sheriff organized the search parties, sending them in different directions. Oscar Peralta reported the gringo was a big man, but he had not really seen his face in the shadow of the gaslight. He demanded their money when they arrived at the Palacio. Apparently Vicente lived a short while though was not able to speak before he died. Alvaro was dead from a bullet in his chest.

"We only know he was a big man. Oscar could not give us any other description. I presume he is on horseback. Check all the saloons and cantinas. Ask if anyone fitting that description has been seen. Also, roust all the liverymen and ask about a big man on a horse. Someone must have seen something," the sheriff instructed before the groups left his office.

Chapter 57

Rafe rode with *don* Pedro and Carlos. Starting at the sheriff's office, they worked east. It was dark and clouds covered the moon, which might have given them a little light. Rafe kept his hat low and his collar pulled up against the biting wind. The town was completely still, most of the houses were dark, and the residents sleeping. An occasional dog barked as they rode by on their search.

His stepmother's worry about George nagged in his brain. It was not like George to stay out late or to worry Josefina. Unfortunately, the sheriff sent them east and away from the central plaza in town. Rafe had no way to search for George in any of the saloons he sometimes frequented. He thought about letting Carlos and *don* Pedro continue the search for the murderer without him, but thought the idea foolheaded. George was probably already home asleep by Josefina's side.

The masked thief and murderer headed on the trail south of Santa Fe in a gallop. He rode hard for about an hour, stopping only briefly to see if anyone was after him. The attack at the Palacio Cantina worked mostly as planned. The leader, Alvaro, was dead. The other man probably mortally wounded. They were the two who threatened to kill Rafe. The other Spaniard with them ran off into the cantina. He doubted the scared young dandy would be any threat to Rafe in the future.

Finally, he saw it. The small covered wagon was waiting by the side of the road. He rode up and jumping off his horse, he tied it to the back of the wagon.

"It is done?" Celiá asked him in her newfound English.

"Yes my love. It is done. Alvaro and his friends will not hurt Rafael anymore."

Celiá fell into his arms and he held her tightly.

"Come, we must be going," Billy said. He helped

Celiá up onto the seat. The children were asleep in the back. Billy snapped the reins and the wagon started to roll slowly.

Everything worked out as he and Celiá planned. Rafe's enemies were dead and he and Celiá were headed to Torreón. Mexico sounded like a good solution. The Army could not arrest him for escaping from the Fort Yuma stockade and no one would ever know the identity of the masked gringo who robbed and killed two *caballeros* in Santa Fe. Best of all, the woman he truly loved was sitting by his side.

Celiá covered her head with her shawl to ward off the chilly night air. She linked her arm through Billy's as he drove the wagon south toward Mexico.

As the sun started to lighten the eastern sky, Rafe thought the night a futile waste of time. The robber and murderer would be long gone, probably riding a fast horse. Rafe was cold to the bone.

By late the next morning, the sheriff called off the search. Alvaro and Vicente's money pouches were gone. Whoever committed the murder was long gone. "Probably some drifter. Alvaro and his friends were just easy targets," the sheriff told the searchers. "Go home. If we learn anything new, I will let you know."

Carlos rode home and Rafe headed back to the Summers' ranch. He was tired, cold, and hungry. He tried to feel bad about Alvaro, but found it hard. Alvaro threatened him many times and was one of the *caballeros* who wanted to see him hang for Diego's death.

Weary to the bone, Rafe slid from Rayo's back. Esteban walked from the back of the barn to meet him.

"Did George arrive home safely last night?" Rafe asked.

"*Sí.* I think he had a little too much brandy," Esteban said with a grin. Rafe sighed with relief.

"Brush him good and give him extra oats," Rafe said patting Rayo's rump.

"Have you seen the small wagon? I do not know where it went," Esteban asked as he took Rayo's reins.

Rafe looked around and agreed the small wagon was missing. "I don't know. Perhaps George asked Billy to take it to town to be fixed."

Rafe walked into the warm kitchen and sat down. Juanita placed a cup of hot coffee in front of him. She turned to the stove and cracked several eggs in a hot pan and pulled four pieces of cooked bacon into another. Rafe sat quietly sipping his coffee letting it warm him.

In short order, Juanita placed a plate heaped with bacon and eggs and a tortilla on the table in front of him. She refilled his coffee cup.

"Where is my mother?" he asked her between bites. Usually Celiá was in the kitchen working with Juanita. Often Alicia was playing nearby. She always said she enjoyed helping and it was not like working at *don* Bernardo's *hacienda*.

"I have not seen her today. Perhaps she is not feeling well," Juanita said.

Rafe thought is odd, but was too tired to be overly concerned. The long night riding Rayo in circles around the city in the cold was exhausting. When he finally finished his breakfast, he asked Juanita to tell George he would need a few hours of sleep before going to the foundry.

Walking up the stairs to his bedroom, he decided to check on his mother. Knocking on her door, no one answered. He turned the unlocked handle and pushed at the door.

Light from the half-open curtain illuminated the room. It was neat and tidy and both of the children's beds were made, as well as hers. Nothing really looked amiss. Perhaps she took the children somewhere this morning. Perhaps she took them in the wagon to see the new house on the hill he was building for them. He looked around and was about to leave when he saw an envelope on her dresser. It was simply addressed 'Rafael.' He opened it and read:

Rafael,

Billy is taking me and the children to Torreón. It is time for me to take the children to join María and I want to be there when the new baby comes. You must be free to give your love to Ana Teresa and not divide it between her and me. She deserves all of your love. You can come visit us in Mexico when the time comes.

One other thing, I am very happy now. Billy and I are in love and plan to marry when we get to Torreón. He is a good man. You know that or you would not have brought him here. Please do not worry about us.

My love always,
Mamá

Rafe sat on the bed, shocked. How had he missed realizing his mother fell in love with Desperate Billy? He bowed his head and said a prayer for their safe journey to Torreón. Then he stood and stuffed the note into his pocket and shut the door on his way out.

FIN

Please continue reading a preview of the next Young Pistolero Series adventure by Robert J. Alvarado, *Dangerous Venture* (Book 6) 2019 Sierra Press.

CHAPTER 1

Jed Clements sat at a two-chair table near the rear of the Golden Horseshoe Saloon nursing a beer and watching Bonnie Brunel work the room. Wearing a red velvet ruffled dress, which was cut high showing her stocking covered legs, helped to make the cowboys buy the watered-down whiskey. Watching her swing her hips, Jed sure was glad to be back in Texas.

"Yew doin all right, Jed," Bonnie purred at him as she walked by his table.

"Shur nuff. Kinda slow tonight," he responded.

"I got a cuple high rollers over at the roulette wheel. They say I'm bringin em luck."

Jed had come back to Round Rock, Texas, and back to Bonnie after the trip last summer to the New Mexico Territory with Luke Payton. Luke forced Jed to go back to New Mexico with him to find and kill the greaser who killed Luke's brother, Butcherknife Bill. Bill had been Jed's foreman at the Sutton Circle B Ranch just south of San Marcial, New Mexico.

Jed was at Big Ed's Saloon the day when Butcherknife and another cowboy, Ponyboy George, tried to dry gulch a greaser for some blooded horses they thought John B. Sutton wanted. The greaser should have been an easy mark. None of the Circle B cowboys could believe it when the greaser came back into town with Butcherknife and Ponyboy's bodies draped over their horses. No Texas cowboy would believe a greaser could ever be that fast.

Jed left New Mexico after Butcherknife and Ponyboy

were killed and went back to Austin where he should have
stayed. For some stupid reason he came to Round Rock
and found Bill's brother Luke and told him the bad news
about his brother. He thought Luke might be obliging and
would maybe help him find a new outfit needing a drover
or just give him some money for his trouble. Instead Luke
forced Jed to go with him back to New Mexico, back to the
shitheel greaser town of San Marcial.

Jed left San Marcial the second time shortly after
Luke was killed by Big Ed Seeley. Big Ed caught Luke
trying to rape old man Sutton's widow. Luke swore she was
just a high-priced whore from Austin who used to call
herself, Cinnamon Baker. Luke told Jed he knew Cinnamon
when she worked at the Chrystal Palace before she got
married. Jed thought Luke should have stuck to the mission
of finding and killing the Mex who killed his brother
instead of going after some whore. Now both Luke and his
brother Bill were buried in the shitheel town of San Marcial
in the New Mexico Territory.

By the time he got himself back to Round Rock,
droving season was over and he was spending the winter
doing odd jobs and living with Bonnie Brunel. She was the
only good thing that came out of the whole mess with Luke
Payton. Though a whore by trade, Bonnie was the first
woman who ever made Jed feel good about himself. He
used to wonder why John B. Sutton ever married a whore,
but he found himself having the same ideas about Bonnie.

Bonnie helped him find the only jobs he could get
here in Round Rock, tending bar or cleaning up saloons
after closing. After a few months, Jed wanted no part of
either one of those lousy jobs, but he also did not feel good
about living off Bonnie's meager earnings. Most of all he
hated seeing Bonnie in the arms of other men. She hustled
cowboys so she could pay the rent and buy food.

The long winter months allowed Jed to do some
reflecting. He was tired of working as a cowboy. Living on
the hot prairie chasing stinking cows was getting old real
fast. It was a life for drifters and ex-outlaws and he knew
plenty of the hardened men who made their beds on the

hard ground. Jed wanted more from life, a soft bed and a warm woman next to him. An idea percolated in his brain since he left San Marcial. It was an idea which could make him rich. It was also an idea which could get him hanged.

Jed took Luke's money after paying the undertaker in San Marcial and used it to get back to Round Rock to find Bonnie. He still had a sizable amount, which he stashed in a safe place. It bothered him some he never told Bonnie about the money and felt some guilt living off of her, though convinced himself if his idea worked, he could take her away from all of this and make her an honest woman.

Several weeks later Pete Carter and Jake McNab rode into Round Rock after being fired from the Bar S Ranch in Fort Worth. Jake suggested passing through Round Rock on the way back to Austin. The town of Round Rock, where the Chisholm Trail crossed Brushy Creek, had a wild reputation and a town where the law looked the other way. After their foolishness on the way out of Fort Worth, Jake thought Round Rock might be a safe place to hide until spring. Once the cattle drives started hiring, they hoped to get hired onto one of the large outfits and get out of Texas.

Riding in from the north, Pete pulled up to the rail in front of the Golden Horseshoe Saloon. It was about sundown and he and Jake were cold, dirty, and plenty thirsty. Trail travel in Texas during the winter was no easy time. Walking into the Golden Horseshoe, Jake was surprised the saloon was quiet and there were lots of open spots at the tables and along the bar. It was not the rowdy place they expected.

Jake placed a nickel on the bar and ordered two beers. It was Pete who spotted Jed Clements sitting at the back of the saloon and they yelled out to him.

"What the hell r yew'll doin here? Jed asked after they shook hands. Pete and Jake had worked with Jed at the Circle B in New Mexico and had been part of a group of cowboys who left after Sutton was killed. Sutton's widow took over and hired local Mexican cowboys to work on the ranch. Over half of the Texas cowboys left and came home to Texas. Jake and Pete had gone to Fort Worth when Jed had gone back to Austin.

"We're headed backta Austin ta see my folks," Jake told him.

"I thought yew was in Fort Worth at the Bar S?" Jed asked.

"Yeah we was. Got fired by the butthole ramrod cause we didin like how he was runnin things. We was tired of takin his crap," Pete grumbled.

"Yeah, that jasper had no clue how ta run cattle," Jake added.

"What the hell yew doin here in Round Rock?" Pete asked.

"Well, yew ain't gonna believe what I bin through since we got back to Texas. When yew boys left me to go to Fort Worth, I came to Round Rock to find Butcherknife's brother, Luke Payton. I wanted to tell im bout Bill being killed by that curlywolf greaser over ta the New Mexico Territory. Luke made me go back with him to that shitheel town to find and kill the Mex. Only in the end Luke got himself kilt. I came back here to be with my gal, Bonnie. That's her over there," Jed said and pointed over to where Bonnie was hustling a young cowboy.

"Shur is mighty purdy," Jake said.

"So, did the Mex kill Luke?" Pete asked. Pete remembered the young Mexican *pistolero* who gunned Butcherknife and Ponyboy and shot Sutton in Big Ed's bar. Sutton drew first, but the greaser was lighting fast. Shot Sutton in the chest and killed him dead with one shot.

"Naw, yew member Big Ed? He killed im," Jed said.

"What? Why would Big Ed do that? He seemed like a good ole boy," Pete asked.

"Well, I tell yew. Yew member the whore old man Sutton married and brought to the territory? Luke knew her as a high priced whore from the Crystal Palace in Austin. Luke went over ta the ranch house and tried to rape her and Big Ed caught im and kilt im."

"I'll be damned," Jake said.

Jed signaled Bonnie to bring three more beers. It sure

was good to see Pete and Jake. Jed could not say he had many friends here in Round Rock, except Bonnie. When Bonnie brought the beers, Jed introduced her.

"Just let me know if you need another. A friend of Jed is a friend of the house," she said as she walked off. Pete watched Bonnie walk away and thought Jed was pretty lucky.

"Say Jed, we r in sum trouble. Yew see, Jake and I robbed a Wells Fargo stagecoach on our way outta Fort Worth. We winged the shotgun man, but don't think we kilt im. We got away with a thousand dollars. Me an Jake need to get outta Texas fer a while," Pete admitted.

"Yew boys ain't crooks, why the hell did yew do a fool thing like that?" Jed asked.

"We was desperate fer money, cause that ramrod stiffed us. I's sorry we did the dang fool thing and now we gotta get outta Texas. We thought maybe we could hole up here in Round Rock fer a little while. We heard they don't like law dogs much here," Jake added.

Jed pondered Pete and Jake's dilemma. He was not too keen on getting himself tangled up with wanted outlaws, but wondered if it would help him with the idea he was pondering since he left San Marcial.

"Yew boys just make yerselves comfortable," Jed told them. He walked to the bar and ordered a bottle of good whiskey and three glasses. When he returned to the table and poured the shots, Pete and Jake tossed them back quickly.

"Boy, that shur is good stuff," Pete said. He pushed out his glass for another shot.

"I shur am glad yewr here. I got me an idea that will make us all rich. Cain't say it's legal and cain't say it ain't dangerous," Jed said after finishing his first shot.

"What yew talkin bout, Jed? We's already in trouble here in Texas and we gotta git outta here, maybe go down to Mexico fer a while," Jake spoke out.

"Let im say his peace," Pete retorted.

"Yew member the cattle ranch we helped Sutton start in San Marcial. Well, when I's there with Luke, his widder's runnin it with a bunch of greasers. A few of the boys stayed on, but not many. Well I's been thinkin, someone cud go down thar and rustle mostta the herd and take it up to Wyoming and sell it to the Army. It be easy pickins," Jed revealed his plan.

"We git caught fer that and we be hanged fer shur," Jake said.

"What makes yew think it be easy pickins?" Pete asked.

"Sutton's widder hired a bunch of local greasers. They wouldn't be no match fer us."

Jed poured another round of whiskey. He knew it was a bit dangerous to let Pete and Jake in on his plan, but he also needed help to pull it off. He knew a few cowpokes here in Round Rock who might be willing, but he trusted Pete and Jake.

"What do yew say? Yew boys want in on this?" Jed asked.

"I ain't so shur bout yer plan. I wanna go see my folks in Austin," Jake whined.

"Hell, it would git us outta Texas. They didn't have no law in that shitheel town. Just a mayor," Pete replied. "I think Jed's right. It be easy pickins."

"Yew know, I bet some of the boys who stayed there at Sutton's, like Rusty and Jimmy, would jump in and hep us. They's probly tired of workin with greasers anyways," Jake replied.

SPANISH GLOSSARY

Italicized Spanish words used repeatedly throughout the series which do not have an English counterpart, such as important = *importante* or Mama = *Mamá*. Other infrequently used words, phrases, and sentences written in Spanish are immediately explained within the text itself.

abogado: a lawyer, attorney at law

abrazo: a hug

abuelo; abuela: grandfather; grandmother (m;f)

adios: goodbye

alcalde: the mayor of a town or city

amigo(s); amiga(s): friend (m;f)

anglo(s): a word to mean a white man, an American

ayúdame: help, asking for help

baboso(s): drooling idiot (a slang or curse word)

bandido(s): a bandit or outlaw

bueno: good

buenos días; tardes; noches: good day; evening; night

bienvenido(s): welcome

cabrón: asshole or bastard (a curse word)

caballo(s); caballero(s): horse; horseman or gentleman

cállate: shutup or be quiet

cálmate; cálmese: be calm or calm down

camisa: a blouse or top

casita; casa: small home, home

chaqueta(s): jacket or suit coat

chico(s); chica(s); chiquita: young boy or young girl (m;f)

chingado: shit or fuck (a curse word)

cojones: slang for a man's testicles

compañero(s): companion, friends

criollo(s): pure-blooded Spaniard born in the New World

ciudad: a town or city

culón: a chickenshit (a curse word)

desgraciado(s): a miserable wretch or terrible person

Dios: God

don; doña: title for nobleman/woman

gachupín(s); peninsulares: pure-blooded Spaniards born in Spain

garrancha: means sword, slang for penis

gracias; muchas gracias: thank you; many thanks

grandee: Spanish nobleman, aristocrat (i.e. dandy)

hermano; hermana: brother; sister (m;f)

hacienda: a large plantation or estate

haciendero(s): the nobleman owning the hacienda

hola: hello greeting

Indio(s); India(s): means Indian (m;f)

jacal(s): small ramshakle house of mud and sticks

jefe: the boss man

mañana: tomorrow or the sometime later

mestizo(s); person of mixed Spanish and Indian (m)

mestiza(s): person of mixed Spanish and Indian (f)

mierda: same as shit (a curse word)

mi hijito; hijo; mijo; hijita; hija; mija: my son; daughter

muchacho(s); muchacha(s): like saying 'the guys' (m;f)

nada: no or nothing

Nana; Tata: nickname for grandmother; grandfather

padre: head friar, monk, minister, priest

pantalones: pants

paseo: the road, boulevard; place to stroll or ride

patrón; patróna: formal for a boss; a mistress (m;f)

pendejo(s); pendeja(s): slang for asshole (a curse)

pene(s): slang for a penis

peón(s): a peasant

peso(s): Mexican money

picaro: a womanizer

pinche: fucking (a curse word)

plata: silver

primo(s); prima(s): cousin (m;f)

pulque; pulqueria: a poor man's drink in Mexico

puta(s): a whore (a slang or curse word)

que?: what or why

querido; querida: affectionate meaning my dear (m;f)

rayo: thunderbolt

sarape: cape, loose coat or blanket

señor(es); señora(s): like saying Mr. or Mrs.

señorita(s): like saying Miss (young woman or girl)

sí: yes

tío; tía: uncle; aunt (m;f)

traje(s): ornate Spanish aristocrat's style of suit

vaquero(s): livestock herder or cowboy

vámonos or vamos: let's go, get out of here